LEGEND OF THE EAGLEMAN

Wayne Parrish

Morro Press
Morro Bay, CA

Other Books by Wayne Parrish:

Legend of the Blue Owl

Sons of the Tropics

ACKNOWLEDGEMENTS

I want to thank and acknowledge the valued contributions of many people to the final draft of *Legend of Eagleman*. Creating a meaningful contemporary cautionary tale from the legendary warning of gambling and greed entailed hours of research and discussion with people from diverse backgrounds and expertise.

To the Gallery in the Sun, I wish to express my gratitude for their permission to use Ted De Grazia's painting, the Eagleman, for the cover, and for their enthusiastic support.

To Rocky De Llamas of De Llamas Design and Graphics, I'm thrilled with the attractive and colorful cover design.

To Phil Garn, I'm appreciative once again, for his research, support, and editorial wit and wisdom.

To Ty Headman, a Native American sculptor, thanks for lending his mind, body, and spirit to this project.

I'm in debt to Frank Russell and to Anna Moore Shaw for their memorable interpretations of the legend of the Eagleman.

To the volunteers who serve in the Maricopa and Yavapai County Sheriff Posses, I thank and applaud. They cannot be praised enough for the time, energy, and assistance they render, often at great risk, to the people of Arizona.

I'm especially indebted to and appreciative of my wife Berta for her computer skills, patience, and perseverance as well as sharing her passion for sunshine days and foggy nights with me.

LEGEND OF THE EAGLEMAN

Avoid the reeking herd
Shun the polluted flock,
Live like that stoic bird,
The eagle on the rock

--- Elinor Wylie

PROLOGUE

It was dawn on a summer morning in the days before I'itoi lost the love of the Green River People. The women were humming as they ground roasted corn on their metates. The men were talking excitedly as they prepared to go hunting.

Ha-vik, a young brave, suddenly cried, "I have no arrows! I left them in the village."

"Go home and get them," ordered the chief. "We will wait for you in the Canyon-That-Speaks."

Instead of returning to the village, Ha-vik ran to the old witch's hut near the Spring-That-Stinks. The witch was squatting by the black rock which had fallen from the sky. "You must help me. I lost my arrows playing the cane game with the feather-pleated evil one. I lied to the chief. He will send me away."

The old witch cackled. "And so he should. You did not speak truth. You used the canes that I marked with the magic that comes from this moon rock." Ha-vik hung his head in shame. The witch shook her gourd rattle. "I warned you, if you were beaten, not to play again, and, if you won twice, you must desist from playing again. You were not to play at night or do anything with women without my permission. You disobeyed. You are not worthy of the people's trust." Ha-vik could not raise his eyes. She shook her rattle again. "Come I will help you just this once. I have some good pinole. Drink it. You look thirsty. It is cool."

Ha-vik drank it eagerly. At the first draft, he began to tremble, a second caused him to shake violently, and, after the third, feathers began to form all over his body and shortly thereafter, he took the form of a bird resembling an eagle. "What has happened to me? I feel so strange."

"Ha ha ha," the witch cackled. "I mixed ground eagle feathers in the pinole. Hereafter you will be an Eagleman."

1

In the meantime, the chief grew impatient. He sent a runner to find Ha-vik. When he reached the Spring-That-Stinks, he saw a large bird perching by the spring. The bird had the head of Ha-vik, but his body, wings, and talons were those of a large eagle. The runner returned to the chief and told him what had happened to Ha-vik.

The chief and the hunters ran to the spring where they found Eagleman perched in a palo verde tree. "This is an evil thing. We must destroy it before harm comes to our people."

The hunters aimed their arrows at the birdman, but he deftly caught the arrows with his talons. Then he flew away, up over the Black Mesa until he found a big cave near the top. "There is nothing to do but go home and warn the people," the chief said.

In the following days and weeks, Eagleman hunted all the game in the Green River valley. Then he began killing the people. The villagers were terrified. One day Eagleman swooped down on Corn Flowers, a young maiden, who was washing gourds in the stream, and carried her away.

After this, the chief sat with his counselors, who urged him to seek the help of I'itoi, Elder Brother. A runner was sent to I'itoi's home on the Greasy Mountain by the great river. The runner returned with the news that I'itoi would come in four days to help them. Meanwhile, Eagleman continued his raids on the village.

When Elder Brother arrived, they showed him the high cliff where Eagleman lived. I'itoi procured charcoal from cactus fruits, rocks from the Spring-That-Stinks, and pebbles from his pouch and ground them into powder. Next he made some sharp-pointed sticks from the trees that grow in the White Mountains and he shaped some of them into pointed awls. He told the warriors "Keep a watch. If you see white clouds floating over the Black Mesa, it will mean that I have killed Eagleman. But if black clouds appear, you will know I have been killed."

I'itoi slowly ascended the high cliff, driving the pointed awls into the canyon wall and using them as a ladder. It was a slow climb, but he eventually reached the top and crawled into the cave. He found Corn Flowers there.

2

"Where is the Eagleman?" he asked.

"He has gone, but he will return soon," Corn Flowers said.

I'itoi changed himself into a fly and crawled into a crevice to hide. When Eagleman returned, he demanded food. After he ate his meal, he fell asleep. Corn Flowers whistled three times. Hearing the prearranged signal, I'itoi crept out quietly and hit the Eagleman hard on the head with his stone ax. But even with his head chopped off, the Eagleman's body flopped around so violently that the cave shook and trembled like an earthquake. Then the eagle's down feathers floated out of the cave and skyward, looking like white clouds.

Corn Flowers heated some water and poured it over the dead bodies on the cave floor and they came back to life. Some were noisy, jumping up and down. They were Apaches. I'itoi told them to go into the mountains. Others were peaceful and quiet; they were Papagos. He told them to stay close by the rivers, Gila and Salt. The next were slow and didn't talk much. They were the Yavapai and he told them to go live in the hills near the mountains. The bodies at the bottom were pale and white. No one knows who they were. I'itoi told them to go live on the other side of the ocean.

Then he threw powder from his pouch onto the fire, and quickly led Corn Flowers down the ladder of stakes. As they climbed down, there was a noise, like thunder. The earth shook violently. Because the earthquake had shaken the mountain so hard, the boulders made it easy to go down. When they reached the canyon floor, I'itoi lit his pipe and inscribed the story on the rocks above the Spring-That-Stinks. The people saw the white clouds flouting over the Black Mesa and they raced to the springs to rejoice.

But I'itoi raised his hand and told the people. "It is not done. There will always be evil ones who cast their spells. There will always be evil men. One day there will be many Eaglemen. Some will help the people. One day they will battle each other. If there are Eaglemen with pure hearts, they will prevail. If not, I will not be able to help you," he said sadly. "I will have been forgotten by the Green River People when this time comes."

"What must we do, I'itoi?" asked the people.

"Keep your hearts pure," I'itoi said, and he disappeared into the smoky haze that drifted down from the mesa.

"Come back, I'itoi," the people cried, but it was too late. I'itoi was gone.

CHAPTER ONE

The red-and-white Volkswagen Kombi crawled up the grade, dusty mile after dusty mile, into the high desert. The outstretched arms of the giant saguaros gave way to prickly pear and cholla cactus. Matt pulled into a scenic overlook and stepped out of the van to stretch his legs. Below him the desert floor, a vast tranquil sea of yellow ocher and umber waves of caliche and sand, undulated in the grayish haze. To the north, the green-blue escarpment of the Mogollon Rim stretched across the cloudless horizon.

Even at this altitude, he could see, smell, and taste the noxious brown cloud of toxic soup that covered the greater-Phoenix metropolitan area 40 miles to the south. Back on the I-17, he tailgated an obliging 18-wheeler and let its draft help the van across the Black Mesa. Twenty-five miles later, he honked a "thank-you" as he exited at Cordes Junction. A bright orange arrow on a blue triangle, an invitation to the curious traveler, pointed the way to Arcosanti.

Two miles down a dusty, unpaved road, Matt turned into a lane. A tall construction crane hulked over Arcosanti's array of towers and roofs. A dozen concrete buildings ringed the edge of a dry river gorge. Matt drove to the opposite side to get a better view of the sci-fi structures and domes which oddly resembled a string of wind bells. The construction equipment reminded Matt that Paolo Soleri's 25-year prototype, showing how a crowded society exists in harmony with its environment, seemed stuck in time, incomplete for lack of long-term funding.

The terraced workshops, green houses, residential complex, and amphitheatre were designed for food production and solar heat collection. Matt recalled hearing Solari's vision at a lecture series at Arizona State University. "Arcology is the blending of architecture and ecology. Arcosanti demonstrates that integrated and compact living space is a rational alternative to urban sprawl with its wasteful consumption of land, energy and time," the tall Italian in a crumpled khaki suit had told the audience. "An arcology's direct proximity to uninhabited wilderness would provide the arco-dwellers direct access to their food base, the lean alternative." To Solari the choice was clear: "Either the single-family homes go and suburbia with it – or we humans go."

Matt took his binoculars from the glove compartment and focused them on the foundry where the Solari ceramic and bronze bells, the principal source of income for the Arcosanti project, were cast. The constant, soft clanging of the wind bells gave Arcosanti the dreamlike ambiance of a monastery. I could live here, he thought. The Old People lived high up in their solar cliff houses, just like this one.

Back on the I-17, the heat intensified as the sun moved directly overhead. Nothing but sun, sand, semis, and road kill, he thought as he slowly passed another semi-truck. Gratefully, he turned off the freeway at the Black Hills casino exit, edged his Kombi gently off the frontage road, and parked near a shack which was patched together from saguaro cactus ribs, plywood scraps, and adobe bricks. It was surrounded by a ratty-looking fence made from Ocotillo branches and adorned with brightly shining hubcaps. A hand-lettered sign attached to the fence with rusted barbwire read:

CACTUS WALLY'S
Skulls for Sale
Turquoise
Mormon Tea
Free Advice

Matt turned off the engine and slowly surveyed the strip of weathered false-fronted stores on the opposite side of the road. A pair of white cubes, five black dots on one and two dots on the other against a faded flamingo pink background, caught his attention. "The Pair-a-Dice Inn. Lucky seven. Lucky me," Matt grunted as an 18-wheeler pulled away from the front of the motel revealing a single row of circa 1950s kitchenettes and carports tacked together by a common red-tiled roof. A newly painted green block wall and multi-tiered Mexican fountain filled with freshly planted pansies failed to offset the shabby, but not so chic, appearance of the Pair-a-Dice Inn.

Two pickups were parked in front of Jardeen's Laundromat. Canyon Video had a "For Sale" sign in the window. Next door at Black Hills Realty, a balding man, his feet on the desk and a flyswatter in his hand, was staring intently at the ceiling. A waitress was clearing a table by the window at Ruth's Home Cooking & Fresh Pies. She wiped her hands on her apron, stared out at the street for a moment, and reset the table.

A dozen Harleys and Yamahas were lined up like horses at a hitching rail. The riders, beer cans in hand, stood in a semi-circle. A yellow-haired biker in a black jacket dropped his empty can into the dirt and crushed it with the heel of his boot. A heavy-set biker with faded tattoos on his arms laughed loudly and the other bikers snickered at the private joke. An empty lot separated the storefronts and the Black Mesa Saloon and Packaged Goods, where a short, pear-shaped man with a black cowboy hat pushed through the swinging doors and disappeared into the dark interior.

Two tourists stood next to a white Lincoln parked in front of a brightly painted roadside stand. A young woman with a single strand of dark braided hair set some trays on the counter. The woman in a tank top and shorts fingered the beaded necklaces, and then shifted her attention to the rings. She tried one on and held up her hand for her companion to see, but he ignored her. He put his hands in his pockets, walked behind the stand and stared at the brown hills.

Just beyond the roadside stand, a large billboard supported by peeler poles read *Black Mesa Indian Reservation*. A dark complexioned man wearing a tan Stetson slouched on a black-and-white pinto in the shade beneath the billboard, coiling and re-coiling a riata. A silver badge flashed on his vest.

The pear-shaped man with the black cowboy hat staggered out of the saloon clutching a brown bag, reeled down the side of the Saloon, shoved the bag inside his shirt, and peered around. He put one hand on the side of the building, fumbled with his fly, and began to pee on the Saloon wall. The rider broke from behind the billboard and galloped his pinto towards the miscreant, who jerked at his fly and tried to escape down the alley. The rider raised the riata over his head and sent a loop sailing forward, dropping it neatly over the man's shoulders. The rider pulled up, jerked the man off his feet and backed his horse away from the building, dragging his captive, half staggering and half running into a small wash behind the billboard. Moments later the lassoer returned behind the billboard, spit into the dirt and re-coiled his riata.

"It don't pay to be a Rez Indian when the eagle flies." A loud rasping voice, somewhere between a screech and a cackle, startled Matt. "Sure is that buck's unlucky day. Over here, on the porch. Come and sit a spell. It's too hot to sit out there in the sun."

Matt got out of the van, stood, stretched and pretended not to notice that the dark-haired woman, in the bright blue squaw-dress, was watching. She turned back to her customer, who laughed as she slipped a necklace over her head.

"Corn Flowers. Pretty thing, isn't she?" The voice cackled as Matt stepped through a gap in the Ocotillo fence. An old refrigerator wrapped with a chain leaned against the wall of a shed. Odd-shaped bottles, purpling in the sun, were laid out in rows. Mounds of mineral and rock specimens were scattered around the yard. Some rough hewn tables filled with bleached white animal skulls and spiny cacti in clay pots added to the clutter.

"Any kind of skull you want. Rattle snake. Javalina. Jack rabbit. Coyote. Mountain goat. They're expensive. Well, they ain't cheap." A slightly stooped grizzled and weathered man with a big triangular nose that jutted out of his face like an eagle's beak and piercing gray eyes greeted Matt. "My name's Wally Ervin."

"Matt Dillon." They shook hands.

"Indian herbs," Wally pointed at fuzzy leafed, brown and green plants spilling lazily over the sides of dirt-filled rubber tires.

8

"They'll cure anything -- sore throats, colic, skin diseases, arthritis, and snake bite. Want some Mormon tea? Some call it Witches Brew. The Pai say it turns you into an Eagleman; that is, if you're a card cheat. If you're honest, it's refreshing. And if you're like me, well, it beats Kool-Aid." The old man offered Matt a clean paper cup and poured a brown fluid out of a large stone jug. "Drink it slow; better yet just sip it. Have a seat."

Matt sat down in a surprising comfortable chair made from saguaro cactus ribs, stretched out his legs and sipped the bitter sweet tea. "Cuts the dust," the old man cackled. Matt's lips, gums, and cheeks tingled and then, strangely, he felt his facial muscles relax.

"You're a tall one, Matt Dillon. You could have played Matt Dillon on *Gunsmoke*. But he was white and you're an Indian, Apache or Comanche, I'd guess."

"My father was Cherokee. His mother was part Comanche, and my mother was mostly Paiute."

"That's a mix. What brings you here? You lookin' for work at the casino?"

"Already have a job. I've a commission to sculpt a piece for the Black Mesa tribe."

"Oh, I know who you are! You're the fella I read about in *The Village Voice*. They did quite a piece on you. You do bears, porcupines, coyotes, and eagles -- all kinds of critters. You must make a pile."

Matt chuckled. "My tools and bedroll are in the van. Most of what I make goes back into materials and pays my foundry costs. Sometimes it's a living; sometimes, it's not." He took another sip of Mormon tea and looked around as his eyes adjusted to the sunlight filtering through the Ocotillo branches that covered the porch. A haphazard jumble of cardboard boxes and wooded crates was stacked against the side of the shed. Tattered burlap sacking covered the single window and a plastic shower curtain with faded tropical fish and sea horses covered the doorway. A dusty glass-eyed barn owl peered down from the top of a crate. A

beaded Gila monster, frozen in time, glared ominously at Matt
from its hiding place under a broken chair.

"They look real, don't they? Got one or two specimens of
nearly every desert critter -- lizards, snakes, owls, frogs,
jackrabbits, and coyotes. Even got a sailfish." Wally pointed at a
bluish silvered sailfish with a speckled dorsal fin and an elegant
black bill mounted on a crossbeam.

"Old man Arnold gave that to me. First thing he made
when he got here from the east and set himself up as a taxidermist.
He came to recover his health over forty years ago. He had T.B. or
so they said, but he's still alive. He claims it was the clean air and
good living. He built that adobe over on Black Mesa and strung
those crosses up on the boulders. Built it over a cave. Cool in the
summer and warm in the winter. Just about the opposite of this
shack. But I make do." Wally picked up a long-eared jackrabbit
and handed it to Matt.

"You and Arnold have something in common. He says if
you want to be taxer, you've got to be a sculptor. He builds
models out of wood and wire and stretches the hide, skin or
feathers over the frames. Course, he uses chemicals and glue.
Looks like the real McCoy, doesn't it? At night sometimes, I sit
out here and they come alive, kind of spooky. Do your pieces look
like the real thing or are you one of those abstract artists?"

Matt set the jackrabbit on the table and picked up a barn
owl. "Your man knows his craft. But to me, they lack energy, like
a still life painting. I want movement and emotion, not just form.
If I get it right, you don't see the owl in flight or the jack rabbit on
the run. You become the owl; you are the rabbit. You sense the
drama."

"I take your point. There's no way I'd want to be a
jackrabbit. I could sell Arnold's pieces and my rock specimens if I
had a better location, somewhere in town. Course, I would have to
clean up my act, get some lapidary tools, and that takes cash. If I
had a partner to stake me." Wally eyed Matt owlishly.

Matt put the owl back on the shelf. "That's so? Well, I'm looking for Sam Cook, the tribal chairman for the Black Mesa tribe. I was told he lives near here."

"Old Sam and his granddaughter have a place on the top of the hill just behind us. He lets me squat here. Can't say he could have stopped me, though. I've been squatting here for nearly twenty years. That's his granddaughter Jennifer over there in that jewelry stand. She takes care of old Sam. She's sweet on me, but she's got a temper. Sam was the tribal chairman, all right, was for years. But he ain't any more. Tribal politics. Lately they seem to change chiefs every two or three years. Russell's the big man now. He convinced the young bucks he could do a better job. He's got the tribe in his fist now that they have a casino. He's run off the smart ones. Well, enough gossip. Let's go see Jennifer. She'll know where Sam is."

Matt raised himself out of the saguaro chair, set his cup on the porch rail, took off his Good Year cap, ran his fingers through his hair, adjusted the cap, and followed Wally across the street. Jen smiled shyly at Wally and Matt as she wrapped a string of beads in tissue paper and put them carefully into a thin box. The man counted out several small bills.

"Where can we get something fit to eat?" he asked.

"Try Ruth's. She has great homemade pies." They watched the couple get into their Lincoln. The woman waved at Jen as they drove off.

"This man says he's a sculpture. Says he wants to meet your grandfather, Jen."

"You mean he's a sculptor, Wally."

"No. I mean he's a sculpture. You can see that can't you?"

"Okay, Wally, have it your way," she said gently, touching his arm affectionately.

"Hi, Jen, I'm Matt Dillon. Your grandfather asked me to drop by."

Wally interrupted, "Uh, oh. Big Nose and Annie are going at it again."

In front of the saloon, a heavy-set man with a barrel chest and gut that spilled over his belt was trying to drag a woman out from behind the wheel of a red pickup truck. . She screamed and hit him with her purse. His Stetson fell to the ground, revealing a mane of black hair tied into a que at the nape of his thick neck. He swore loudly, and began punching her. Annie covered her face with her arms. When the man landed a heavy punch on her shoulders, she screamed again and tried to crawl out of the nearside door.

Matt sprinted to the truck, grabbed Big Nose from behind and spun him away. Surprised, Big Nose swore and swung wildly. Matt ducked and stepped forward, driving a fist into his gut. Big Nose's breath went out with a whish. He fell to his knees and tried to grab Matt's legs.

"Look out!" Jen warned.

A lasso looped over Matt's shoulders. He instinctively slipped a hand inside the loop as he was jerked backwards and landed on his back. He rolled, grasped the rope, pulled himself to his feet and scrambled after the horseman, loosening the tension on the loop as he ran. Freeing his shoulders and arms, Matt grasped the rope with both hands, dug in his heels, forcing the pinto to half turn. He closed with the horse and pulled the startled rider out of the saddle. As Matt pulled him to his feet, the rider reached for the revolver strapped to his hip. Matt grasped the rider's wrist and pinned it behind his back as he grabbed an ear and raised him onto his toes.

"Take your hands off me," he yelled. As his hand clawed for his pistol, he struggled to free himself from Matt's grasp.

Matt turned the man on his hip, reached with his free hand, pulled the revolver out of the holster and flipped him onto the ground in one motion. The stunned rider lay motionless as Matt opened the revolver, dumped the shells, threw them into the brush and tossed the pistol on the ground. Struggling to his feet, the rider picked up his pistol, and shoved it into its holster.

"You shouldn't have done that. You're in trouble, Sonny."

"If you throw a rope on me again, you'll find out what trouble is," Matt said, and walked back to the pickup. "Are you okay?" he asked Annie, who was covering her face with her hands.

"Big Nose hit me. I didn't do anything." She opened her hands and glanced at the man on the ground. "I'm okay. I'm okay."

"She's scared. Her face is bruised." Jen put her arms around her. "You need to go to the clinic, Annie. You're hurt."

A black-and-white Arizona Highway Patrol car pulled off the road and parked behind the truck. A patrolman stepped out of the car, set a trooper's cap on his closely cropped, bullet-shaped head and walked slowly towards them. Stepping cautiously around Big Nose, he studied Annie's face carefully, and looked squarely at Matt.

"What seems to be the trouble here?" he asked without taking his eyes off Matt.

"Big Nose was beating up on Annie," Jen said. "Matt was trying to help her when Carbahol roped him."

"I rope all the drunks, Jenny. These guys were drunk, Hubbard," Carbahol said loudly and moved alongside the trooper. "They were fighting over the woman. So I lassoed him and was dragging him back to the Rez when he pulled me off my horse, took my gun. That's a Federal offense."

"That's not true," Matt said. "I was just trying to help when he tried to drag me onto the Rez, if that is the Rez. I thought he was going to use that pistol, so I took it away and tossed the shells."

"You heard him, Hubbard. If you don't charge him, I will," Carbahol said.

"Carbahol, you're not on the Rez," the trooper replied.

"Well, it started on the Rez," Carbahol said.

"That's not the way I saw it, Hubbard. What Matt here is telling you is absolutely true. I'm a witness," Wally said.

"Big Nose was beating the hell out of me," Annie interrupted. "He stopped him."

Big Nose groaned and started to get up. "Stay put, Big Nose. You're in enough trouble all ready." Hubbard used the tip of his baton and pushed Big Nose back down to the ground, kneeled and cuffed him.

"Annie needs help," Jen said. "She needs an ambulance."

"Okay, Jennifer. I know my job. Why don't you all wait for me over by the stand?" he asked as he reached inside the truck for the keys.

"Do as the man says. Come on, Matt," Wally said.

"Carbahol, take your horse and wait behind the billboard." Carbahol scowled, shrugged his shoulders and led the pinto away. Officer Hubbard went to his patrol car and picked up a handset.

"That was slick, Matt," Wally said as they crossed the road. "I thought Carbahol had you."

"He would have if I hadn't seen him rope that drunk earlier."

"Let me see your hands," Wally said.

Matt turned over his hands, palm up. "No harm done."

"Your hands must be made of steel," Wally said, "not to get a rope burn. Hell, they look more like talons. Carbahol didn't have a chance. You took him like a hawk takes a chicken."

"Matt didn't do anything wrong. Will Hubbard arrest him?" Jen asked Wally.

"No worries, Jen," Wally said. "Big Nose is going to the county jail and Hubbard will send for an ambulance. He'll hear Carbahol out and tell him that he was out of line. They both know the frontage road is off the Rez. Hubbard lets Carbahol drag the drunks off so they won't wander onto the highway and get themselves or somebody else killed. But Carbahol knows he can't hassle 'civilians.' There's a thin line over who has jurisdiction here, Matt. They'll decide they don't want the hassle. Anyways, Hubbard won't arrest Matt. He knows an honest Injun when he sees one."

"That's not funny, Wally!" Jen said.

Wally ignored Jen. "Big Nose will do thirty days. He'll pick up Annie on payday and it will start all over again. Same time, same place."

A Yavapai County Sheriff's van pulled in behind Hubbard's car. A burley officer got out, cuffed Big Nose and placed him in the rear seat. An ERV showed up, sirens blaring. The medics put Annie in the back and headed south to Black Canyon City. A tow truck from Camp Verde backed up to the red pickup truck, chained it and drove off.

Turning to the spectators, Hubbard said, "Show's over folks." Then he drove down the frontage road, parked beside the billboard, and exchanged words with Carbahol. He didn't even bother to get out of his vehicle. After a few minutes, he flipped Carbahol a wave, checked the frontage road, made a U-turn, and drove back to the roadside stand. He stepped out of the patrol car and pulled a small pad out of his shirt pocket.

"Your name," he asked Matt.

"Matt Dillon."

"Address?"

"112 Pinion Lane, Santa Fe, New Mexico."

"May I see your driver's license?" Matt handed him his license. "Is that your van?"

"Yes." Matt offered his insurance and registration cards.

"I didn't ask for these."

"But you were about to."

"Don't need them. I ran your plates. But I'm curious. You have a New Mexico driver's license, Oregon plates, Texas insurance, a recently purchased van from an Oklahoma auction, and now you are in Arizona."

"So what's the question?" Matt asked.

"Uh. Do you have business here, Mr. Dillon?"

"I do, but it's none of your business, officer."

Hubbard's face tightened and then he forced a smile. "Well, your scrap occurred on a public roadway. Carbahol wants you arrested for creating a disturbance. But since you have witnesses that you were just trying to help, I won't. For your

15

information, Carbahol is a tribal policeman with no jurisdiction on the frontage road. But I would stay off the Rez if I were you. Next time, I wouldn't try to be a Good Samaritan, just call 911." Hubbard smiled and got back into his vehicle.

He looked at Wally. "Wally, if your friend here ever tangles with Carbahol again, give me a call, especially if he's going to drag him off his horse onto his ass." Hubbard checked the traffic flow, eased the patrol car into a U-turn, tipped his hat, and headed south towards Black Canyon City.

Several bikers revved their engines and eased onto the highway behind the patrol car. A yellow-haired biker flipped the patrol car a bird, but Hubbard apparently didn't see the gesture or chose to ignore it. He slowed his bike in front of the stand. "Nice going dude. That was cool!" he said to Matt. The other bikers flashed a thumbs up and the pack headed north toward Camp Verde.

"Halloo!" Jen shielded her eyes with her hands and looked upwards. A slightly stooped, white-haired man was looking down from the top of a granite boulder. "Show Matt the steps, Jen."

"I'd best get back to work," Wally said. "I'll keep an eye on your van."

A motor home slowed and came to a stop in front of the stand. "There are some steps behind the stand, Matt. Just follow them to the top," Jen said. "I've got customers; tell him I'll be up in a little while."

Matt began climbing, and counting, the narrow flagstone steps. "Ninety-One, ninety-two, ninety-three."

"There's ninety-nine. It's the Apache Trail to the stars, to paradise. Welcome to paradise, Matt. Good to see you again," Sam Cook said and extended his hand.

Matt looked around while he caught his breath. A small pool of water reflected the blue sky, horsetail reeds rimmed its edges and a pair of orange dragonflies hovered overhead, eyeing several Koi near the surface.

"Jay built the steps and the ponds. Jen planted the flowers. There used to be a dozen Koi, but only five are left. Coons got them. I was going to trap them, but I decided they were here first."

An ancient pine tree provided shade for a small round dwelling partly hidden among the boulders. Nylon strings and netting filled with herbs, chilis, and squash hung from the eaves. Colorful Navajo rugs were scattered across the rough-hewn pine floors and stacks of cushions were piled to one side.

"Jay built the hogan," Sam said. "He got the idea for the canvas walls and screens from a Mongolian yurt that he read about. In a way it's like a tepee. But I never lived in one. Didn't think it would work, but it does. It's real comfortable. When the sun comes out, you raise the sides and you close them when it gets windy. Jay put solar panels on the roof for the generator and ran tubing under the floor; they cool in the summer and heat in the winter. We sleep on the floor, or at least Jen does. I get too stiff; I sleep on the cot," Sam said over his shoulder as Matt followed him down a flagstone path to a bench under a pinion tree.

Matt whistled. "You can see the whole valley from here."

"That brown cloud to the south covers Phoenix. Some days it blows all the way to Palm Springs," Sam said. "That's the Mogollon Rim to the east and that's the Red Rock country off to the west. Below you is the Verde Valley, most of it." Dense groves of cottonwood trees lined both sides of the watery ribbon that weaved through the wide valley below the mesa. "That's Camp Verde on the edge of those trees and Cottonwood beyond that. Cornville is on the right; beyond that is Clarkdale. You can't see Sedona; it's behind that ridge of red rocks. That clump of buildings hanging on the side of Mingus Mountain is Jerome."

"You've got quite a view," Matt said.

"Yep. I can keep an eye on everything. The locals call it the Eagle Nest. But it doesn't set well with me."

"Why not?"

A frown creased Sam's face. "Apaches have mixed feelings about eagles. On one hand, eagles are sacred and, on the

17

other hand, they are evil, associated with Eaglemen. You know the legend?"

"Not really."

"Apaches fear that some witch will cast a spell turning them into an Eagleman. It's usually gossips, gamblers or liars that grew the feathers, but it can happen to good men, too, especially if they oppose the greedy ones. It depends on who casts the spell. Get Jen to tell you. She knows more about the legend than I do." Sam looked directly at Matt. "You dusted off Carbahol pretty quick."

"Sorry, Sam, not exactly a good start."

"I was watching. You didn't have a choice. Carbahol's problem is that he's a metal-chest Indian. He handles drunks, dopers, domestic disputes, but he pushes too hard and people don't like being pushed around by any policeman. It's too bad. Down deep he means well."

"I'll try to stay out of his way."

"That may not be easy, especially when you're on the Rez." Sam cleared his throat. "We better talk business before Jen shows up. I don't want her to know why you are here."

"She doesn't know?"

"Nobody here knows except Tom Fallon and we have to keep it that way. The tribal counsel can never know. If they found out that I asked the Gaming Commission to send an investigator, I'll never be elected anything again. No one here trusts the government, Matt, especially the FBI. If there is a leak, you could be in danger and no one would talk to you. But Fallon did a good job setting you up as a sculptor. You're big news in the Verde, write-ups in the papers -- the local ones anyway, and that's all that counts." Sam handed Matt a newspaper clipping. "*The Village Voice* article says it all."

Matt studied the article:

> "*Matt Dillon, a well known Native American*
> *sculptor, has been commissioned by the local*
> *Black Mesa tribe to design and cast a sculpture*
> *for the entrance of the Cultural Center which is*

18

*under construction. It is scheduled to open during
Camp Verde Days."*

"On the surface, it looks like a good cover, but I'm not sure it's going to play," Matt said after reading the article.

"It will play. Being in the spotlight is the best way to hide. The Arts and Crafts Associations and the Chamber of Commerce will welcome you. You can go anywhere, meet with anyone. They'll expect you to. Your commission is to design something appropriate for the community, not just for the tribe. It's the tribe's peace offering to the Verde Valley."

"What does the Council think about my being here?"

"Tom and I set aside three million dollars for the Center before Russell became Chairman. The Arts Council oversees it, and I'm chairman, so there's not much they can say. I still have three years to serve on the Tribal Gaming Commission. Russell can't move me out of that either. The Commission wants you to investigate any possibility of illegal activities connected with gaming on the Rez and to survey the impact that gaming is having on the tribe and the community. And the Council won't be happy if they hear about it." Sam took a deep breath.

"Matt, there's something wrong at the casino. I can't prove anything, but I can smell it. The gaming syndicate that's running the operation keeps a good set of books. But, as Tom says, they've probably got more than one set. The operations manager is from the East coast and he brought his own crew. He hired just a few locals, but we don't have anyone inside to keep an eye on him."

"Sounds like you need a fly on the wall."

"You're going to be that fly," Sam said. "Tom has an idea. He'll fill you in tomorrow. If you get inside and if you learn anything, let me know. I'll decide what to pass on to the Commission. Tom's okay, but I want to hear about it first."

"Can you trust the Commission members?"

"Individually yes, but there are too many chances for leaks. You've got members from all the tribes and representatives from the FBI, the DPS, the Governors' office, the State Department, the Tourism Commission, and three citizens at large. Another problem is that most of us were appointed by the last Governor. The new Governor can't change the Commission membership, but she is watching the casinos like a hawk. She flipflops on the sovereignty issue. What she really wants is a piece of the gaming pie. Like all the new Governors, she can't grasp the fact that we are a sovereign nation inside the State of Arizona. I'm not sure that anyone knows what that means, including us, but we won't be sovereign if we sign gaming contracts with the State."

"Will the sovereignty issue ever get resolved, Sam?"

"Yes. It gets resolved by our surviving. We have survived being conquered by war, destroyed by diseases, assimilated by boarding schools, and proselytized by religion. But I'm not sure we're going to survive the impact of the casino culture."

"Casino culture?"

"It's the return of the White Buffalo. It's the belief that money changes everything. It does, and it's changing us. We're turning into apples, red on the outside and white on the inside. There is an upside and a downside, as the jargon goes. The upside is that the casino money provides employment, housing, welfare, medical services, education and all kinds of economic development. The downside is that the con men and the drifters move in. The crime rate is up and the locals blame us. Worse, our people are being paid to sit and breathe air. They think the money from the casino is an endless flowing faucet. But it's not true. We're spending money faster than we're bringing it in."

"On what?"

"Low income housing developments, for one thing. They're a bust. Russell opened a gravel operation on the Verde and that's got the locals riled up. We're not making any money; everything goes for trucks, equipment, and handouts. Every time you turn around, Russell raises the subsidies and that gets him votes. The kids use the money for trucks, drugs, and alcohol. They drop out of school and have no respect for our customs."

"That's happening everywhere, Sam."

"It is, everywhere a tribe has a casino." Sam stared at the sky and then looked into Matt's eyes. "I guess that I'm responsible."

"How are you responsible, Sam?"

"Huh, I got bit by the gambling bug. I got a government grant to build a Community Center for a Bingo Hall. It's that big tin shed on the Cottonwood side of the Rez. When it was finished, we used the Center for community services in the daytime. On the weekends, we turned it into a Bingo Hall. We didn't make a lot of money, but we spent the dollars wisely. Then the Indian gaming craze took off. The Yavapai/Apaches and many other tribes added slot machines to their Bingo Halls. Then some tribes back East built casinos, and the idea spread like wild fire. We have casinos everywhere, and the tribes are building more. The Prescott Yavapai have two casinos and the big hotel in Prescott, and now there are two here in the Verde Valley. Only the Hopis and Navajos have resisted jumping on the bandwagon. I tried my best to keep the casino off our reservation, but Russell and his crowd won out."

"You can put your fingers in the dike, Sam, but it wouldn't do much good if the water is coming over the top," Matt said.

"That's true. Gambling fever is a disease, a national disease. We're all caught up in it, red and white. Our people have always been gamblers. Our stories tell of men who would gamble away their horses, their wives, the children, even sell themselves into slavery on a single cast of the dice or a footrace. But this casino business is worse. We are becoming Eaglemen."

"The money has helped the tribes. It may work out."

"It's too late. We're caught in a cycle of greed. There was an election. Yes, I spoke to the tribe first. I told them that I did not like to see us living in poverty, in sadness. But we should not open a casino. I urged them to think about the impact on our land, our culture. I told them that it is hard enough to hold on to our traditions, but a casino is against our beliefs. There are things more important than money. I told them if we do this, we would become just like the whites, and that we must consider what our

21

ancestors would say. But my message was for the 'old ears.'
Russell said it is time to take action and make money of our own.
It is time to get off the white man's dole. 'Yes,' he said, 'I agree
with Sam. I, too, am tired of seeing poverty and a casino will
bring the white man to our land. But for the first time, they will
leave something…money, instead of taking it.' It was a good joke.
Everyone laughed. The money will be for the children and our
futures, he promised. Our people are often like mice and can only
see what is in front of them. They don't see what white men
Russell and his stooges have become.

    "Anyway, they elected Russell and things went downhill in
a heartbeat. Jay was out, and they wouldn't listen to Tom, who
threatened to resign, but I talked him into staying. Russell passed
out jobs to his friends and relatives. Most of them were
incompetent. He paid his cousin Charlie $18,000 to draw up a
sewer plan. Charlie drew some lines on a yellow pad. There was
no survey, no drawings, nothing. He might as well have drawn
lines in the sand. That stuff goes on all the time. There's no end to
it."

    "When is the next election?"

    "Next September, but it won't matter. It's all big casino
talk now. Everyone's got their hand out, and as long as the money
keeps rolling in, Russell will stay. People don't care. Oh, some
do, but there's not enough to vote him out. My only hope is the
people will see the white man's way is not working. And they'll
see Russell for what he is."

    "Have you heard from Jay?"

    "Not for some time; same as I told you. The last time we
talked, he said he was onto something."

    "Where was he?"

    "He wouldn't say, but it sounded like he was calling from a
phone booth in Phoenix. I heard a lot of traffic noise that drowned
him out at times. I heard planes in the background, too, so he
could have been near Sky Harbor."

    "Did he say anything about the robbery?"

22

"No. When I told him about it, he seemed surprised and wanted all the details. But there wasn't much to tell except they took Carbahol and the two guards, Billy Frail and Chester Fields, by surprise."

"Chester Fields?"

"Chester's dad had a sense of humor. Anyway they were moving the cash out the side door of the casino, through the breezeway, and into the counting room in the basement of the Center. A limo pulled up alongside the breezeway. They thought it was just another high roller, that's where they drop them off. Three men got out. They all had shotguns. The driver stayed in the limo."

"The guards didn't do anything?"

"The tribal police aren't armed. The casino manager doesn't allow them to carry side arms. He says it doesn't look good and he doesn't want anybody hurt. They keep weapons locked up in the cash room. Carbahol had his pistol, but they took it away. He may be stupid, but he isn't crazy. They made the police load the cash into the limo and then took the police with them. They taped their hands, eyes, and feet and dumped them off at an old campground and the limo vanished into thin air. Later Chester remembered that the limo had Nevada plates, but he didn't get a number. Didn't have any reason to, until he realized they were being robbed."

"So where do you think Jay is?"

Sam studied his hands and sighed. "I honestly don't know. He was supposed to hand deliver a report to Washington. We found lead and arsenic and other pollutants on the Rez and in the Lower Verde. Tom and I left him at the airport. Jay must have taken off on a binge. I was hoping he would go the Rehab Center, but he didn't." Sam sighed.

"I'm sorry, Sam."

"Nothing to be sorry for. Jay can't help himself. Alcohol is our curse." Sam stood up. "I have to get ready for a meeting."

Matt made his way down the steps and stopped at Wally's. "I need a shower and a place to stay. How about the Pair-a-Dice?"

"I wouldn't recommend it to man or beast. It's a roach trap. You're better going up the I-17 to Camp Verde or Cottonwood. There're a lot of motels there, a real nice one at the Yavapai-Apache Cliff House casino. You'll need a reservation though. It's always tourist time in the Verde Valley. If you want, you can shower here and you can bunk on the porch." Wally pointed to a fifty-gallon drum on the roof of the shack. "Solar heated. The water comes from the spring on the hill. It's good drinking water, stinks a little though. Got some sulfur in it, but keeps you loose."

"Thanks, Wally, but I think I'll pass. Next time, maybe."

"You take care, Matt."

"You, too, Wally."

Matt walked over to Jen's stand. Strings of coral, cobalt, and glass beads hung from hooks on the walls. Elegant turquoise and silver pieces, squash blossom necklaces, and bolo ties were displayed on the back wall. Some worn cardboard jewelry cases were neatly arranged on counters along the sides of the booth and a card table in the center, covered with a Navajo rug contained several finely-crafted rings, earrings, and bracelets. Matt picked up a piece and said, "Zuni? It's beautiful."

"Yes, it is," Jennifer said. "The Zuni jewelry and some of the Navajo pawn pieces are on consignment. The other stuff is mostly for tourists, but it's all authentic. No Japaho here!"

"Do you sell much here?"

"Weekends are so so. Weekdays it's mostly wind, sand and dust. Sometimes I sell at the flea market. The tourists don't stop here much any more. They get off the I-17 at Camp Verde or Cottonwood. The pie shop draws mostly locals, and a few regulars take a pit-stop on their way to Flagstaff."

Matt examined some exquisite earrings and a matching bracelet. "These are different. They aren't Zuni. They look traditional, yet they are very contemporary."

"My brother Jay made the bracelet. Traditional is out he says. Too many Asian imitations on the market. I made the earrings. Jay has sold a lot of these sets to the casino. The manager gives them as gifts to the high rollers."

"That must be expensive."

"Jay gets $2000 to $3000 for each set."

"Some gift." he picked up a necklace. "I haven't seen pipe stone like this. It has texture, and this turquoise is an unusual light green. Where did you find them?"

"The pipe stone comes from Lynx Lake, and the jade turquoise comes from the old Jerome Copper mine tailings, or so Wally says. He brings me stuff from his field trips, but I think that turquoise is from the Black Mesa above Page Springs. Wally doesn't tell anyone where he prospects. He's afraid people will follow him."

"Gold Mine? Really?"

Jennifer laughed. "Wally didn't tell you about his mine. He didn't show you his nugget?"

"No."

"Well, you're the first one he hasn't tried his scam on. He must like you."

"Meaning?"

"Wally cruises the highway from Black Canyon City to Camp Verde and Cottonwood. They ran him out of Sedona. He ties his pack burros outside a saloon or restaurant. When he spots a 'prospect,' he follows them inside and goes into his local character bit."

"What's the local character bit?"

"He slams a big nugget on the bar and orders a beer. He'll ask the bartender what they'll give him for his nugget. It's all an act that the bartenders usually go along with. Whatever they offer, Wally treats it like a big joke. Nine times out of ten someone buys him a beer and he'll spin a yarn about how he found the nugget in a dry wash. 'Plenty more where that one comes from,' he cackles. 'Why don't you open a mine?' They ask. They set their own hook, Wally says. 'I can't. It came from a dry wash and I need a dry dredger that takes cash I don't have.' 'How much cash?' they always ask. 'At least two thousand. Have to haul water in.' By now he's had more than one beer.

"Sooner or later they ask him the location. Then Wally pulls a long sly look, 'Could be here, could be Four Points, the Bradshaws, or Four Peaks, where the Dutchman's gold mine was.' That earns him a few more beers. Once in a while Wally finds an 'investor' who actually stakes him to a dredger and supplies. Then Wally parks it behind his shack for a few weeks and stalls the poor fool. It's always too wet or too cold or too dry or too hot to work the dirt. One guy even staked him a jeep. Eventually, the partner gives up and Wally sells whatever he's picked up. Don't get me wrong, I like Wally and he brings me some fine stones."

"So where did he get the nugget?"

"I don't know." Jen smiled at Matt. "Why don't you buy him a beer, maybe he'll tell you?"

Matt groaned. "Thanks for the warning."

CHAPTER TWO

Matt chose a small table by the window and Ruth, the attractive owner of the café, set a heavy white mug in front of him."Coffee?"

"Please," Matt said.

"Breakfast?"

"Yes, thanks."

Ruth handed Matt a menu and filled his mug. "I'll be right with you." After circling the other tables and offering refills, Ruth put the coffee pot on a hot plate behind the counter and came back to Matt. She pulled a pencil from underneath the VFW cap which concealed most of her strawberry hair and a pad from the spotless apron which covered tee-shirt and jeans. "Are we ready?"

"I'll have a short stack and some fresh fruit, if you have any."

"We've got strawberries. They came in this morning. The eggs are fresh, too."

"I'd like a side of both."

"I'll take a refill, Ruth, whenever you're ready." Matt recognized Carbahol's voice and caught the spark that flashed in Ruth's eyes.

"Help yourself. You know where it's at," Ruth said. Her scuffed boots pounded on the wooden floor as she headed for the kitchen.

Carbahol went behind the counter, picked up the coffee pot, filled his mug and returned to his stool. He put two spoonfuls of sugar into his cup and stirred it furiously. "Some kind of service," he grumbled, spinning around on the stool. The other customers, mostly truckers, ignored him and continued attacking their super-sized breakfasts.

Matt picked up a copy of *The Verde Voice* from a nearby table and skimmed through it. The headlines announced the fire danger potential, a water shortage, higher water rates, a dispute regarding incorporation, and a warning that Highway 238 had become a deathtrap. He read about the Apache tribe wanting to declare a recently purchased eighty acre parcel as Indian Trust Land. According to the article written by Renee Royer, the tribe was entering discussions to attract Home Depot, Wal-Mart and other mall stores. The Tri-villages Jaycee President was lodging a vehement protest against the proposal, claiming that unfair trade practices and insufficient tax revenue would hurt the local economies. According to Mayor Strickland, the article stated, it would undermine the years of effort to attract the mall developers. Some local residents were pleased. One correspondent responded: "Who will get hurt? The gift shops, the tourist traps? It's too far to travel to Phoenix for major ticket items."

Carbahol laid some change on the counter and stomped out the front door, banging it behind him. Matt watched as he got into the tribal police car, backed up, spun his wheels in the gravel, and headed down the highway towards the Reservation. Carbahol hadn't even looked his way as far as Matt could tell.

Ruth placed a plate of eggs and fruit in front of him. "Enjoy." He laid the paper aside and dug in. Across the street, he could see Wally packing gear onto a pair of burros. Jen was lending a hand. One of the burros nipped Wally's butt; he jumped and slapped his hat across the burro's nose. Jen started to laugh, and then she covered her mouth, trying to hide it. Wally muttered something, went back into his yard, returned with some canteens and strung them over the pommel of the larger burro. Wally and Jen began packing the smaller burro with some canned goods.

Matt got up and walked over to the cash register, opened his wallet and handed Ruth a five dollar bill. "I haven't had fresh eggs in years. I forgot what they tasted like. The strawberries were terrific."

Ruth grinned, "Thanks, Matt."

"How do you know my name?"

28

"Since yesterday, everyone knows your name, except maybe Carbahol. He sure started muttering in his coffee when you pulled up. What did he call him, boys?" Ruth turned to the truckers.

"Carbahol called him Chief Sitting Bull, Ruth, but we told him that figures since you sat down on him. What's your real name, fella?" a trucker with a large belly and a full beard asked.

"Matt. Matt Dillon."

"Well, keep your eyes open, Matt. That Carbahol is a real mean weasel. He ain't likely to forget," the trucker suggested.

"We call him Wailing Eagle," another trucker spoke out. "That's Injun for an eagle that's too full of shit to fly."

Matt smiled and stepped onto the porch, checked under the billboard for Carbahol, and then crossed the frontage road.

"Good to see you, Matt," Wally said.

"Good morning, Wally. Morning, Jen."

"Good morning, Matt. It's going to be great day. Look at the clouds," Jen said. "They look like a fleet of white sailing ships." Matt said.

"Or a flock of white doves," Jen replied. "Las palomas blancos. That's Spanish for 'the white doves.'"

"I knew that," Matt grinned.

"Did you now?" Jen asked.

Matt turned to Wally. "Where are you headed?"

"Going on a walk-about. Horsethief Basin, maybe up the Big Bug. Won't know 'til I get there."

Matt inspected the rigs on the burros. "Looks like you'll be out for awhile."

"Maybe yes, maybe no. Maybe a week, more or less," Wally grinned. "I just follow the burros. They let me know when it's time to come home." The small burro tried to nip Wally again. "Shoo!" he waved his hat. "That's Jen for you. She's stubborn and ornery. Aren't you, Jen?"

"Cut that out, Wally!"

"See what I mean, Matt? I named this burro after Jen, or was it the other way around? I forget. I tried to get Jen to go with

29

me, but little Jen doesn't want any part of it. Two Jens on the trail would be more than I can handle."

"You couldn't handle one Jen on the trail, Wally." Jen added.

"Be careful what you say; you might hurt Jen's feelings," Wally said. "She's kind of sensitive. Well, I gotta get going. Tempest fidgets. You're welcome to use my place, Matt. Better than that flea bag you were in last night."

"You got that right. I didn't sleep much. Thanks anyhow."

Matt got in the van and fastened his seatbelt. He mentally ticked off his check sheet -- Contact Sam Cook: Done. Contact Tom Fallon.

"Fallon is one of the good guys," Al Johnson, the Gaming Commissioner, had told Matt when he gave him this assignment. "Tom's on our side. He's sharp. You'll have to play it by ear on the Rez. We can't help you much there. If you have a problem, use your beeper. Someone will answer, 24 hours a day, and transfer you to me. It would be nice if we could find Jay Cook; he knows something, but your prime responsibility is to find evidence of any illegal operations at the casino. So far, the gaming syndicate is operating within our guidelines, but Vince Salvatori is the joker. He has connections with the Nevada and Toronto bunch and he worked as a stringer in New Jersey. We'll need solid evidence. If you can establish a link, that'll help, but it's possible that Salvatori is running his own scam. If the syndicate is bribing Russell or the Council, we need to know. And we need to know if they are straight arrows or possibly, just dupes. Anything's possible."

Matt slowly drove down the frontage road, and then turned west on the double lane highway that led to the casino. He pulled off the road at the flagstone archway that marked the entrance to the Black Mesa Casino grounds and surveyed the hillside. The casino and the Cultural Center were linked by a covered breezeway scraped out of the side of the mesa. The two hand-laid flagstone buildings, bathed in lavenders, pinks, and yellows, were dwarfed by the towering red-earthed mesas that stretched north and south.

Small doorways and windows gave the illusion of a Sinagua cliff dwelling. In front, acres of newly planted desert shrubs and trees covered the hillsides below and lined the roadway leading up to the entrance.

Solar panels lined the roofs of the shaded parking lot stalls on the south end of the buildings. "We generate enough power to run the casino, the administrative center, and the housing projects," Sam had told Matt. "Jay drew it up and Dennis Lipitano did the engineering. It's a wonder. Indians using the cutting edge of technology. We're ahead of the white man in Arizona. People come from all over to see how it works. Not just engineers and energy nuts, but all kinds of people."

Matt lifted his binoculars and studied a cluster of buildings a mile north of the casino. A bridge spanned an arroyo and led to a gated compound. A white-paneled two storied steel building with a painted blue roof housed the police and fire departments. Several white fire trucks and emergency vehicles were parked in the open bays. Across the street, a series of sand-colored, stucco buildings ringed a cul-de-sac, a senior citizen center, a daycare center, and an economic development unit. He focused on a gazebo in the middle of a small park in front of the tribal development building. A man with curly salt-and-pepper hair was studying papers. An open briefcase lay at his feet.

Matt put down the binoculars, started the engine, drove up the service road, and crossed the bridge. Checking his watch, he realized that he was a few minutes early. The parking lot behind the casino was nearly empty; a few vendor vans were parked at the service entrance. Beyond the parking lot, a narrow road led to the tribal offices. He turned onto it and followed it over a hill. On the other side, the road dropped through a cut between two banks lined with trees which filtered the sunlight.

As he glanced into his rearview mirror, Matt saw a white patrol car following him closely, too close for comfort. The rough planks rattled the van as he crossed a narrow wooden bridge. The descent from the bridge was steep and the road dropped sharply away on his right. Red and white flashing lights blinked in his side mirror. He braked as the patrol car cut in front of him, forcing him to the side of the road.

Carbahol and a uniformed policeman got out of the patrol car and walked towards Matt. "Well, look who we have here. This is the joker that noodled me yesterday, Ned," Carbahol said. Ned started to snicker, but scowled instead.

"Officer Carbahol. Why am I not surprised?" Matt said.

"Well, mister, you were the big man yesterday, but today for sure you're on the Rez and you'd better have a good reason for being here, Chief." Ned snickered again.

"I'm just visiting."

"He says he's just visiting, Ned, just another Indian looking for a handout. Or maybe you're pushing drugs. Better search the van, Ned. You don't mind, do you Chief?"

Matt squared his shoulders. "Yes, I do mind. Unless you have a warrant, I don't want you searching my van."

"Don't need a warrant on the Rez. Got something you're hiding, Chief?"

"Don't call me Chief. And before you do something stupid, I think you better call the tribal office. I have an 8 o'clock appointment with the tribal manager."

"Make the call, Ned." Ned went back to the police car and picked up his handset. Carbahol tried to stare Matt down and then gave it up.

"They're expecting him," Ned yelled. "They want us to escort him. He works here. He's on the payroll."

"Shit," Carbahol said and spit in the dirt. "The tribal office is straight ahead. Just follow your nose."

"Carbahol, I'm sorry that we got off to a bad start." Matt offered his hand. "I'm going to be around for a while. Let's shake and forget it."

"You should be so lucky." Carbahol spit in the dirt again and walked back to the patrol car. He climbed in, turned off the flasher, and spun the wheels, showering Matt with gravel.

"Bad choice," Matt said, dusting himself off. He parked the Kombi on the edge of the cul-de-sac. Tom waved as he got out of the van and walked down a graveled path lined with small, odd-shaped rocks covered with Indian rock writing.

"It's good to see you, Matt," Tom said as they shook hands. "I brought coffee." He offered Matt a Styrofoam cup. "It's black and strong."

"That's fine." Matt took the cup, put it to his lips, took a large swallow and grimaced.

Tom laughed. "Injun Joe."

"What's in it? Or maybe I don't want to know."

"Chicory, roasted corn and day-old re-boiled coffee."

"No refried beans or snake rattles?"

"No, but it'll keep you going all day and all night," Tom said. Matt tentatively sipped his coffee. "I understand that you've met Officer Carbahol."

"We sort of ran into each other yesterday and he pulled me over on the way here. I'm afraid I didn't make a very good impression."

"Oh, I think you impressed him all right and the Council. They're looking forward to meeting you. Everyone got a good laugh, but it's not exactly a laughing matter. Carbahol looked foolish yesterday, and that's not good if you're a reservation cop. He has a tough job, Matt, and he's been real uptight since the casino robbery. He and the other tribal police lost a lot of respect that night, and it's worse since the FBI stepped in."

"Any word from the FBI?"

"Not a thing or at least nothing that they care to share."

Matt cautiously took another sip. "The coffee's not bad once you get used to it. Where is everybody? It looks like a ghost town."

"Most of the employees are in the gym. Russell is having a powwow with them. The rest are on Indian time." Tom glanced at his watch. "There's a Tribal Council meeting scheduled at nine, so we have a few minutes to talk and I can show you around the Arts Center." Fallon looked at his watch again. "Let's walk and talk."

"We have a full schedule today, so I don't have a lot of time this morning. The Tribal Council meeting will probably last all day. We can talk again tonight, unless the Council decides to start the voting process, which could go on all night. It's a hellava way to run a business."

"What's on the agenda?"

"Water, sewers, fire station plumbing, complaints, disputes, and the Governor's visit. She wants to do a dog-and-pony show to demonstrate affinity and friendship with the tribe. It's all show. What she really wants is a piece of the action – tax dollars." Tom's eyes twinkled. He was waving his arms as he talked. "Everyone wants a piece of the action. We're meeting with the Cottonwood and Camp Verde city councils this week. They don't like our gravel pit operation and they're worried that we're going to lease land to the big chain stores. And, of course, they're afraid they'll lose those tax dollars. Diversity is the game today, putting the gaming operation profits to work. But we're moving too fast. We hear about something that some other tribe is doing and we jump on the bandwagon. We don't take the time to test the waters. And there's a lot of concern about the management group. Personally, I have a lot of questions about them. But we can talk about that tonight. Why don't we meet at the casino? You could grab a bite to eat and look around."

"That's fine."

"Here we are." Tom took out his keys, opened a heavy door, stepped inside and flipped some switches. They entered a large high-ceiled space with enormous north-facing windows. The other three walls were windowless. A bathtub-sized sink was mounted on one wall. Benches and worktables lined the other two walls. A larger worktable filled the center space.

"Will this work?" Tom asked.

"It's a good space. I like it."

"Jay did a great job. We've had a lot of guest artists here and they've done some good work. They all like the place." Tom raised a metal panel. Matt ducked and looked inside. "It's a full kitchen, Matt. It's got everything – fridge, ovens, and micro – the works. We can cater a small crowd. Let's look upstairs."

34

Matt followed Tom up two flights of stairs. "It's supposed to be a storage loft, but right now it doubles as a sleeping space." Several cots were stacked on one side of the loft. Tom opened a closet. "There are sleeping bags, blankets, pillows. Everything you need. People are used to seeing artists work here and staying over. The best part about it is that you'll have access to the casino and you can keep an eye on the Rez from here." Tom opened a side door and turned on a light. "This is the old camera room. Jay was going to turn it into an audio-visual education center. All the cables for the televisions and satellites come in through here." Tom turned on several TV monitors. "This was the original surveillance room. They run everything now from the casino side through that door. The only reason they come over here is to store the tapes or if they have a problem they use this studio as a back-up."

"It's interesting, Tom, very interesting. But I'll have to think about it."

"You have a problem?" Tom frowned.

"It just crossed my mind that, if I'm here all the time, people can keep an eye on me, too."

"Well, think it over. Let's go see the Queen Bee. She's dying to meet you. Be careful; she listens with her eyes, not just her ears. I've scheduled you to meet the Tribal Council for Big Lunch. They want to size you up. Russell will do most of the talking. The Council probably won't ask many questions. Take my advice and keep your answers short."

"Big Lunch?"

Tom laughed. "We eat from 11:30 to 12:30. After that the Council takes a siesta while I do their work."

"Is the Queen Bee on the Council?"

"No. At the moment, she's in charge of social welfare and is serving as temporary director of the Cultural Center. She also supervises the senior and daycare centers. She wears a lot of hats. She runs around like her hair is full of bees. She has a say in everything that happens here. Some say she's an arrow short of a full quiver, but as far as I'm concerned, she's a sharp lady. I think you'll like her."

Tom led Matt down a wide hallway past a series of mostly vacant cubicles, although the computers monitors were lit. A black woman glanced at them as they walked by and resumed typing. A heavy-set blond smiled and waved at Tom. A brunette arched her eyebrows, pursed her lips, and went back to work. A Latino woman was explaining something to two Native American women who were looking over her shoulder. The hallway opened into a large space where rows of computer stations were boxed in with gray steel bookcases.

"Computer Training Center," Tom said. "The computers are available to tribal members and employees during nonscheduled times, but it isn't used very much. Most of the money would have been better spent elsewhere." Beyond the Training Center was an open workspace with stacks of manila folders piled on two circular tables.

"Good morning, Betty," Tom said to a moon-faced woman with black braids, her face creased with a perpetual smile. She had extraordinarily attractive laughing eyes that drew Matt like a magnet. She rose from her chair and extended a stubby plump hand covered with rings. Her large round breasts and an even larger rump which sat on stubby legs gave the illusion that she was shorter than she really was.

"Who did you bring me, Tom?" she asked.

"Matt Dillon, your sculptor, and right on time as I promised."

"And what did you tell him about me?" Betty asked. Her bracelets jingled and flashed as she rested her hands on her broad hips while her face registered indignation. "Did you tell him I was the spider woman?"

"No. I told him that he was going to meet the Queen Bee."

"You told him, then, that I have my hands in every pie?" Her face took on a hurtful expression. Then she smiled broadly. "Did you also tell him that I am a gossipy woman who is an arrow short of a full quiver?"

"Everyone already knows that, Betty. Matt would have heard it sooner or later."

"Show me your hands, young man," Betty said.

Matt was surprised but extended his hands. Betty grasped his wrists and turned his hands palm side up. "Strong fingers, powerful, yet sensitive hands. You have callused, working hands. I have always wanted to touch a sculptor's hands." Betty traced her fingers across his palms. "You could have been a surgeon or a pianist. Your hands tell me that you can be anything you want to be." Her eyes took on the appearance of the wise old woman. "You are a sculptor. Or are you more than that?"

Tom laughed nervously. "You not only have good hands, Matt, but you are in good hands. I'll leave you two. Maybe you can get Betty to tell your fortune. Matt's having Big Lunch with the Tribal Council, Betty. Be sure you turn him loose by then." Tom left Matt standing there holding hands with Betty in the middle of the room. "Bye," he said as he closed the door.

Betty dropped Matt's hands and pointed at the director's chair next to her desk. "Sit down, Matt." Betty sat down in her swivel chair and opened a file folder that was lying on her desk. Matt noticed it had a yellow tag and that there were a few pages of handwritten notes inside the folder as Betty spun her chair around and faced him, their knees almost touching.

"I keep a record of everything. Visitors, powwows, conferences, disputes, blanket parties. I have a file on every tribal member, on and off the reservation. Newspaper clippings, events, birth notices, deaths, marriages, ceremonies, illnesses, arrests, employment, grants, federal, state, and local rulings --- everything and anything that affects us: compliance requests, GED degrees, military service, drugs, training sessions, tribal surveys, food stamp applications, housing permits, child abuse, dead animals, requisitions for paint." Her bracelets glittered and tinkled as she waved her arms and pointed at the files cases. "I record everything. If people tell me about their dreams, I write them down."

"Wouldn't it be easier to store this stuff on the computers?"

Betty giggled. "I am a computer and the tribal historian and storyteller. I put all this stuff in my head and decide when and where to use it." She tugged at her hair. "We have a room full of computers. They don't think like Indians; they can crash. Computers gossip. My records are safe. I use my own version of Cherokee shorthand. It would drive a snooper crazy."

"Do you have snoopers here?" Matt asked.

"Sure we have snoopers. We have BIA snoopers, FBI snoopers, Arizona Government snoopers, EPA snoopers, Gaming Commission snoopers. We have snooper snoopers and we even have pooper snoopers." She laughed gaily. "I'm serious. There are people who inspect the effluent that pours into the river. They want to be sure that it's grey enough."

"Interesting. Can I ask you a couple of questions?"

"Sure. Go ahead."

"What's a blanket party?"

"When you need to raise money for an initiation ceremony or any special occasion, you throw a blanket on the ground. Male relatives sit outside the blanket and beat their drums and the women dress up in their costumes and dance. Everyone comes out to see what's going and they're obligated to throw money on the blanket."

"Why are you keeping all this information?"

Betty's dark eyes clouded and then cleared as she gazed intently into Matt's eyes before she answered. "Let me tell you a story. Once upon a time, before the white men came to the Verde Valley, we were a proud people. Our warriors protected us from our enemies. We spoke with one voice. Game was plentiful and we grew maize and beans by the river. The white men came and murdered our people with their guns and diseases. They stole our lands and our culture. In 1871 the treaty gave us 800 square miles of land here in the valley. But the white men said that was too much land. So they drew up a new treaty and gave us 8000 acres. And then they said that was too much. So they forced us onto a reservation by the springs that was 650 acres. We couldn't raise enough food for ourselves or feed for our animals. So the whites gave us the dole and it kept us in chains, in poverty, and our children were forced to attend their schools. But you know the stories of the bad times, Matt. Every tribe has a "trail of tears". We were forced to live in concentration camps. That's what rezs really are. It makes no difference if it's a little rez or a big one; they are little boxes and big boxes. If you can't go outside the box, you're in a ghetto. These things were not written down, Matt, but they are part of our oral tradition. Someone has to instruct our young people or we will no longer be a people. " Betty flounced her skirts, revealing silver rings on her toes. The silver coins that dangled from loops in her ears jangled as she shook her head.

"Things are changing. Tom got us this land on Black Mesa. With the money from the casino, we're buying more land, some of our old land. We need more, because the people are coming back home to live. The money draws them, so we need housing. But the people who come back are different than when they went away."

"In what way?"

"They went to the city to make money and tried to become like white people. Some are fast talkers; they influence the old people and the young, too. Some married whites, Blacks, and Latinos; many married into other tribes. Many act like they are victims and they bring their anger, illnesses, alcohol and drugs with them. Those who stayed behind resent them. They think the assimilated ones only come back for the money. And now we have new enemies, those who looked down on us despise us even more now that we are wealthy."

"Who are the new enemies?"

"I could say the rednecks, the old-time ranchers, the newcomers, the retirees, the developers, the government, but that would be unfair. Mostly, we are our own worst enemies." Betty sighed.

"We have money now. But we have no substance; no real culture. We have no warriors, just drunken brawlers. We have no chiefs, just fast-talking men who get elected by making promises. We are shells of what we used to be. We have our stories, but no one has lived the stories. How can we go back to the way we were if we take the money? And if we don't, we all can't live on a small reservation. The young will be forced to the cities and be

39

assimilated. The whites can't massacre us anymore; it's against the law. We now have sovereignty which means we are a small nation living inside and protected by a larger nation. The federal government still controls the water we drink and the land we live on. Do not misunderstand me. A few years ago we lived in abject poverty. I celebrated when we opened our clinic, the daycare center, and a senior center. I celebrated each morning when a person or a family came back to the Rez and when we built a new home. But now I fear what will happen if all of this money corrupts us. So I keep my records. We need strong leaders; people like you to be our role models."

"What do I have to offer?"

"Your vision." Betty tapped the file folder with her fingers. "Your creativity. We need you to be God's flashlight, to cut holes in the clouds so the people can find their path. My file tells me that you think of yourself as a white person. It says you grew up in the city, that your mother was a lawyer and that your father was a preacher. But it also says that your students thought you were a good teacher. The government says," and she looked inside the file, "that you were a brave soldier." She pulled out some photos and laid them in Matt's lap. "These photos of your work tell me that you can create and that your eyes see the truth."

Betty leaned forward and placed her hand on Matt's chest. He felt a surge of warmth and energy. "Your heart tells me you are Indian. You're like Jay. You both went to the white man's schools and lived in the city, but you have kept your vision. And now I ask again, why are you here?"

He hesitated. "This project gives me a chance to create something. But I really came because Sam Cook needs me and I want to find out what happened to Jay."

Betty's bracelets jingled as she tugged at her skirt and folded her hands in her lap. "I think what you say is true. But I feel that that you have not told me everything." Betty pursed her lips and whistled softly through her teeth, a sound that was almost a hiss. "It would not be wise to look for Jay, or ask questions, at least not here."

"You think that something has happened to Jay?"

Betty nodded. "He's been missing since the night of the robbery. There has been a lot of gossip. The young men say the policemen robbed the casino and Jay saw them. Others say that it was druggers."

"What do you think?"

"I think it was someone outside of the tribe."

"Like who?"

"Whoever is making trouble for us."

"The gambling syndicate?"

"Maybe. Somebody who doesn't want us to succeed or someone with a grudge. Perhaps the Eagleman did it."

"Who's the Eagleman?"

Betty smiled, "A good question. Why don't you ask Sam's granddaughter."

"Jen?"

"I call her Corn Flowers." Betty rose from her chair and waited until Matt stood up, touched him on the arm and pushed him gently toward the door. "Matt, we will talk about your vision for the Cultural Center next time. Now you have just enough time to look around before Big Lunch. Be careful. It's not wise to ask too many questions. People might get the idea that you are, maybe, a fly on the wall."

Matt joined the council members at a long table in the corner of the restaurant. They were mostly Tom's age with gray or black-turning-gray the predominant hair color. Two of the men wore their hair in queues. All were wearing western shirts and bolo ties with large turquoise clasps. "Bill Russell, our Chairman. Don Price, our treasurer. John Peaks, Ron Howard, Vice Chairmen, Glen Price, George Eliot, and Charlie Parker," Tom said. They shook Matt's hand and sat down.

"The Council wants you to know you are welcome, Matt. In fact, they want you to know that the welcome mat will always be out for you. But I'm sure you've heard that one before."

41

Matt smiled, "More than once, but it's always good to know I'm welcome." The waitress brought him a menu. He handed it back to her. "I'd like an iced tea, please, and the house salad with vinegar and oil dressing."

"That's it?" the waitress asked.

"That's it. I'm a light eater," he said, nodding at the men at the table.

"For a big man, you eat like a bird," Glen Price commented. "You need to put fuel into your furnace," he said, patting his stomach.

"You have enough fuel in your belly to lift a horse, Price," Parker said. They all laughed, "But not enough to pull a man off his horse." Parker's eyes challenged Matt. The Council members looked at each other and smiled knowingly.

"Matt here looks strong enough to lift you, Carbahol, and his horse." Russell said. "Matt, Tom tells us there was a misunderstanding."

"I was trying to help a woman in trouble," Matt said quickly. "I just reacted."

"Well, we would have liked to have been there to see your reaction," Don Price said. "If it ever happens again, the whole tribe would like to be there. We could sell tickets."

"I don't think it will happen again. Carbahol may be many things, but he isn't crazy," Russell said.

The waitress set Matt's salad and tea in front of him and refilled the coffee cups. "Anyone want anything else?"

"We're fine," Tom said, "we'll let you know."

"I'm not fine," George said. "I could use another steak. We all could. We're big eaters. We need fire in the belly."

"I'm not going there," Tom said.

"Are your people all big like you?" Don asked.

"Not really; there are few big men. I guess I started out pretty big."

"Why did you become a sculptor, Matt?" Russell asked.

"I had a job in a marble orchard." Matt paused. "Well, not exactly. A marble orchard is a cemetery, but I worked in a factory

42

where they made headstones. Basically, I turned the marble and granite slabs for the grinders and the shapers. Later, the foreman taught me to make roses, birds, leaves, and trim for the headstones. It was on-the-job training for a sculptor. Then I went into the Navy and afterwards studied art at ASU." Matt nibbled at his salad.

"What do you have in mind for the Cultural Center?" Russell asked.

Matt shrugged. "I need some time to come up with something appropriate. I really need to get a feeling of who you are and what you want by talking to a lot of people."

"You need a vision," the Price brothers said in unison and stared at each other.

"Something like that. Maybe a first impression, a perspective, but it's hard to explain that I need a feeling; something has to happen inside me. It's something that comes through me, and then my hands do the work."

"We were right, then." Glen said, and stared at his brother as if daring him to chime in. "You do need a vision. Do you go off by yourself?"

"Some times. Usually, I just sit and look out the window."

"Have you ever tried a sweat lodge?

"No, but I've used saunas."

"It's not the same thing; you need to go to a sweat lodge. It has to be dark inside, and you throw herbs on the stones. That's what I do when I need a vision."

"Don't listen to Glen," Don said. "He only goes to a sweat lodge when he wants to get over a hangover. When he pours ice cold water over his body, he gets a new vision. Like he needs something to drink." The council members laughed loudly.

"I need a drink now," Charlie said. "But I don't have to go to a sweat lodge to find that out. When I go to a sweat lodge, I don't visualize a drink."

"We all know what you visualize, Charlie. But a vision won't do you any good. It's all in your head. Right now, you're probably visualizing that waitress." The men laughed again.

43

"When you do a sculpture, Matt, do you do it for yourself or for you clients?" Russell asked loudly, drowning out the laughter.

"Well, honestly, mostly for myself, but I try to give the client what he wants. If I can't, I don't accept the commission. But the bottom line is that, if I had the materials, I would do my own work, whether I get paid for it or not."

"So, if we don't like your work, do we still have to pay you?" Russell persisted.

Tom interjected, "Matt will make some sketches and maybe a clay model or plaster mold for the Arts Council's approval. If they give the OK, then he will cost up the project. If that's agreeable to the Council, he'll cast and assemble the pieces. That's the way it works. His fees and expenses are paid out of the grant money. No skin off our noses."

Russell spoke loudly, "We know that. We've gone over that often enough. But somebody always has to sign off on a grant and that always falls into my lap. What I want to know is, when it's finished, who decides if we want it -- us, the tribe, the Arts Council, or the casino people? And what happens if we don't like it, and they do?"

"What you mean is, are we or the Arts Council going to decide?" Don said flatly.

"As far as I'm concerned, they can put anything in there they want. But let's make it easy, we'll put it to a vote at the tribal assembly," Glen added.

Matt finished his salad, sipped his iced tea, and made eye contact with Russell and then the tribal members. "If I can make a suggestion? When I'm finished with the project, why not put it in the atrium for a few weeks? Let everyone have a chance to see it, get used to it, and then vote."

"And if we don't like it, we can store it out of sight in the property room with the rest of the crap that we don't like, including all those bones and mummies Jay Cook had the Smithsonian ship to us," Don said.

"If you don't like my work, I would be happy to buy it back from you."

"You'd buy back?" Don asked.

"It wouldn't be the first time!"

"I like this man, Tom," Russell said. "He's sure not a fast talker. You don't have to worry about not being paid, Matt. We are not blanket Indians anymore, although sometimes I wish we were. We just wanted to be sure about you. We are paying people nowadays to sit here and breathe air. They do nothing but complain and hold up their hands for more."

"Why not give them something to do?" Matt asked.

"We've been there and done that. We've had a dozen training projects. There are no jobs in the local towns and the casino can't use our people, except as domestics and laborers. The social workers and the casino managers are all well-educated and skillful. In fact, we have more white people on the Rez than we do Indians. We are the biggest employer in the valley," Russell pointed out. "The local governments and the state all have their hands out for our money, but they don't offer us jobs. We are making deals and signing contracts with everyone. We are negotiating to convert our trust lands into lease lands so the developers can open a Home Depot and all the mall stores that will serve the whole valley. But we still won't get much employment for our people. I don't know what it is, but they just don't want us. Tom keeps urging us to diversify so that when this gaming craze ends, we have a solid economic base, but that way we keep the handouts going on forever. Our people will still be idle."

Tom spoke up. "All the tribes with have casinos have the same problems and the same opportunities. The non-casino tribes are afraid they will lose sovereignty if the casino tribes sign contracts to pay taxes, and to share infrastructure costs."

"To hell with the Navajos." Glen interrupted. "What do they know? They give away their coal and water, and they let their land be a dumping ground for atomic waste. They're jealous that they are too far away to draw the gamblers."

"And we are jealous that they have so much damn land so damn far away from the white man," Charlie said. "They're not a nation or a tribe really, just a bunch of clans who live in isolation and chase sheep. Who wants to live like that?" Glen said.

The waitress picked up Matt's plate. "More tea?" she asked. "No thanks."

"Matt, now you know why we call it Big Lunch. We eat and talk and talk and eat. We don't solve anything; we just get fatter," Charlie said.

"And all this talk is giving me indigestion. I think it's time to go home and take a siesta. Maybe I will have a vision," John said hopefully.

"Before you go, Matt," Glen said. "I want to tell you a little hunting story. Last fall, Carbahol and Ned, that deputy of his, went hunting on Black Mesa. They went up and down the canyon and got turned around, couldn't find their way back. So Carbahol says, 'We're lost, Ned. You better fire three shots in the air. Maybe someone will come looking for us.' So Ned fires three times. They wait a couple of hours, but no one shows up. So Carbahol tells him to try again. They wait some more. It is moving on towards dark and Carbahol is getting nervous. 'You better try again. It's getting late.' Then Ned says, 'I don't know about you, but I'm all out of arrows!' The moral to the story, Matt, is, if you go hunting on Black Mesa, be sure you take plenty of arrows." The men laughed.

"Let's go," Tom said. "I've got work to do." Matt shook the Council members' hands; Don patted him on the shoulder. They left the casino and walked to the parking lot together.

"You can see what I'm up against. It's like being in a room full of hot air balloons. Yak, yak, yak. It's all a smoke screen. They welcome the deadbeats. They don't want change; they just want votes. But it went well. You won't have any problems with the Council. They really wanted a Native American, even though there are a few sculptors in the valley; Waddell and Sorenson are first-rate. Sedona has a couple, and there's a talented woman working at Arcosanti. But it's pride, one of their own. They want you to succeed, and so do I. I'll meet you back here around eight."

"That suits me. Think I'll drive down to Camp Verde and Cottonwood and look around."

"Well, if you get lost, fire some arrows."

"Thanks, Tom, I'll remember to do that."

CHAPTER THREE

Matt turned off the frontage road onto the freeway. He pointed the Kombi north and climbed to the top of the mesa. In front of him, the I-17 plunged downward for several miles before it leveled off on the valley floor and crawled up the mesa on the other side. He pushed the accelerator to the floor and enjoyed the rush of wind through the windows as brown, gray, and red hills dotted with cactus and a sprinkling of desert flowers flashed by. On the horizon, the striated mesas of the red rock country glimmered in the sun. The ribbon of water, the Verde River, weaved its way across the valley from Cottonwood to Camp Verde. The dot that was Camp Verde, interlaced by miles of blacktop and dirt roads, grew into a cluster of buildings that marked the village.

Matt took his foot off the accelerator. He was tempted to race across the valley and climb the mesa on the other side; instead, he turned off at the Camp Verde exit and coasted for a mile until he reached the first stop sign. He turned at the Mobil station, passed a second-hand furniture store, an antique barn, a video store, a small grocery, and an income tax service, and pulled into a parking lot beside the visitor center.

He got out of the van, walked over to a large rack and picked up a Verde scenic map and brochures from Sedona, Jerome, Prescott, and the Central Valley Railroad. "All aboard," he said, and added brochures for a pink jeep and kayak excursion company and the Montezuma Castle to his stack.

"You've got everything there except the balloon ride," a portly, blue-eyed man with an ingenuous smile said as he stepped out of the darkened doorway and onto to the sunlit porch. "Verde Days are next week. Then it's the birders; then it's the rodeo and Indian powwow. Not much happening this week. I'm Sonny

Strickland, official greeter, chamber of commerce prez, and village mayor. I'd be the village drunk and the village idiot, too, but those jobs are taken. If I can't answer your questions, nobody can. Are you staying or just visiting?"

Matt instinctively knew that Strickland habitually used inane small talk as a distraction, like a matador wielding a red cape. He was tempted to say, "I don't need insurance and I'm not in the market for real estate." Instead he said, "I really stopped for directions to the Iron Works."

"The foundry? Stay on the Crook Trail, turn east on the first dirt street, follow it across the wooden bridge. You can't miss it. Dan Carpenter's place. It's a going concern. He brings a lot of business to town."

"Thanks."

"You wouldn't be the sculptor the tribe hired, would you?"

Matt was surprised by the question. He thought he detected a glint of hostility in Strickland's otherwise limpid eyes. "You got me. I'm Matt Dillon."

"The Arts Council was wondering when you'd show up."

"I'd like to meet them."

"First Tuesday of every month we meet at the Community Center." Strickland pulled a handful of cards from his pocket, fished through them, and handed one to Matt.

"You're president of the Arts Council, too?"

"Yep, I'm president of just about everything here that no one else wants to do. We're doing some planning for Camp Verde Days, but come down and say hello. You can get acquainted, and we could use another volunteer."

"Thanks, Mr. Strickland, I'll do that."

"Call me Sonny. Gotta run. Take care, Matt." Strickland touched his hat, locked the Visitors Center door, and walked off.

Matt got into his Kombi, drove past several false-fronted buildings with high wooden sidewalks, turned east on the dirt road, followed it for two blocks, and crossed over the Verde River on a narrow wooden bridge. The Iron Works was housed in a long adobe building surrounded by an adobe wall. Matt parked and entered the foundry through a small gate.

Hands on his hips, Dan Carpenter was directing two men who were gripping long wooden handles of a yoke that was attached to a small crucible of molten metal. They tilted the handles and directed the flow into a large funnel that protruded from a ceramic mold. "Steady, steady, boys," Dan said. The men were pouring molten metal with the precision that comes from long experience. "That's it. Cover. Now step back." The men eased the bucket onto the sand-covered floor and crab-stepped away from the casting. They removed their goggles and wiped the sweat off their foreheads with their shirt sleeves. "Ta da! Good job! Take a break. We'll let it cool and then break it down."

Dan turned towards door. "Matt!" he exclaimed, wiping his hands on his leather apron. "You're a sight for sore eyes." The grinders and the chippers looked at each other as the two men embraced, separated, and shook hands. "Come on over, boys, and meet a friend of mine."

The workmen shut down their machines and drifted over. "This is my friend, Matt Dillon, the sculptor I told you about. You're in for a treat. Matt knows what this business is all about. He's an iron monkey; he can outlift, outpour, outgrind, and outchip any of you. And if I'm right, we're in for something big. Matt's motto is "If you're not good, make it big and nobody will know the difference." The men laughed.

"That's not exactly my motto, Dan. My motto is…"

Dan cut him off. "Matt made a needle for his thesis project at ASU. The eye was so big that he could sit in it. The damn thing is still in the art room because only he could lift it. He melted down scrap metal he borrowed from junk yards. Matt couldn't afford quality metal, none of us could, but he won the Scully Award anyway. Let's see, that was for the cheapest and most aesthetically disgusting casting. In any case, he won and I lost."

"What did you make, boss? A thimble?"

"Dan cast a bronze mermaid. Great lines and movement. The patina was exquisite," Matt answered.

50

Dan's face reddened as he shed his apron. "Take a break, boys. Come on, let's get some fresh air. It's too damn hot in here." Dan led Matt to a shaded bench under a palo verde tree.

"Quite an impressive set up, Dan."

"Four acres of rust. Business is good, but everything I make goes back into it. We're the biggest foundry east of the Colorado and west of the Verde."

"Meaning you're the only foundry?"

"No, just the biggest. There's Arcosanti and a few good mills in Prescott. There aren't enough sculptors doing big pieces anymore. No money out there. I keep going with the welding work and the cut-out junk. But even so, we'll need to schedule you in. A couple of big pieces are coming in July."

"That's why I'm here. But I'm just getting started, Dan. I haven't got a clue as to what I'll design or need. It's got to work for the tribe."

"Do an Indian on a horse. Have a large tear rolling down his face. How about a broken lance?"

"It's been done, Dan."

"So has everything else. The Native American theme is over-worked."

"I'm going to study the tribe's history and legends and talk to the elders. Something will come to me."

"The Trail of Tears is important with the Yavapai and Apaches, Matt. They were forced to march from Fort Verde to San Carlos. A lot of people died on the way."

"I know. All the tribes have a trail of tears story."

"Well, there were no Geronimos here, or least I don't think so," Dan said. "Did you get an advance?"

"No, and I don't think I need one, at least not until I begin casting. They've given me a studio and a place to stay, but I don't want to do all my work there. I need to get away from the distractions. Too many gawkers are a hassle. Can you spare me some space here?"

"I could, but I've got a better idea. Al Killinger's old studio. He hit it big time and moved to New York City. He gave it to the Birdlady and she leases it out from time to time."

"The Birdlady?"

"Paloma Patterson. I'm not sure if that's her real name, but she's no dove. She runs a bird rescue station on the Verde. It's at the end of Wood Street, about a mile upriver. Really quiet if that's what you want. If you're interested, I'll call her."

"I'm definitely interested."

"Be right back."

Matt wandered around the yard. He picked up a bronze mouse off a table and held it in the palm of his hands, rubbing the smooth and pleasant-feeling patina.

"Screaming mouse," Dan said behind him. "I made a mold from an artifact I picked up from a pothunter, probably a Sinagua figure. It was carved in lava rock, probably from the San Francisco Peaks. Sacred land to the Navajo and Hopi. The guy I got it from owns a ranch just below the Black Hills. He uses a bulldozer to cut out the side of the mesa. All sorts of weirdoes show up at his place to dig. Executives fly in from New York City. He calls it a stress management camp. They pay him $2000 a week for rice, beans and a chance to dig. They have a blow-out on Saturday night at the casino and a balloon ride on Sunday."

"That's it?"

"Yep. We're in the wrong business, Matt. Anyway, I think the artifact is based on an Indian legend. The story is that when you are too close to something, like the mouse, you see only what's in front of you." Dan smiled. "The Birdlady says come on over for a chat. Take the mouse with you. Tell her I said that it's a decoy. She can try her claws on it instead of you."

"Are you setting me up?"

"No worries. She's a handful, but you'll be alright. I need to get back to work. The boys always know how to get more time to do less. Get settled in if you like the place and come back later for a beer."

"Not tonight. I've got a meeting with the tribal manager at the casino."

"Listen, if it doesn't work out, you can use my drafting room. I've got plenty of clay and plaster. Anything you want."

"Thanks, Dan."

"Come see me Monday. We're closed, but I'll be here."

"Sure."

"Back to work, boys," Dan shouted and waved the men back into the foundry.

Matt took a side road to Wood Street and turned off onto a lane that led into a grove of cottonwood trees. He parked beside a small adobe. A flagstone patio separated the house from a flat-roofed studio. He followed the path to the front of the building. A high bank overlooked the Verde River where a gravel shoal separated a sand beach from the main channel. Massive cottonwoods arched over the shallow stream, their roots searching through the boulders to reach the cool water. It was quiet except for a yellow bird warbling high overhead. The main channel swept around a bend and disappeared on his left. Brown trout were feeding near the shoals.

He walked back to the adobe and looked through the open door. A corner of the room was filled by a curved adobe fireplace faced by a worn but comfortable-looking sofa. Navajo rugs on the tile floors gave the room a homey feeling and a pair of Mexican leather chairs and a large leather table added to the sense of comfort. Matt stepped inside. A pueblo-styled pole ladder leaning against the wall led to a large loft. Open cupboards held a variety of pots, pans, and dishes, and mugs hung from hooks on the wall. He opened a drawer filled with knives, forks, and spoons that didn't match.

"You'll find everything you need." Startled, Matt turned. A willowy woman with dark red hair, sparkling cerulean eyes, a slightly upturned nose, and a wide smile showing perfect white teeth stood in the doorway. She wore a brocaded Mexican peasant blouse over a white skirt that extended over the tops of her soft tan leather moccasins.

"Sorry," he said. "The door was open."

"I left it open. You're Matt, I take it."

"Yes." He struggled to add something, but gave up.

"I'm Paloma Patterson. But everyone calls me the Birdlady." She smiled. "I scrubbed everything yesterday and chased out the bats."

"Bats?"

"There're no bats, but squirrels nest under the eaves. We have skunks and the occasional porcupine and sometimes coyotes come into the yard at night. Come on. I'll show you the studio."

Matt followed Paloma across the patio and into the studio. Two open windows faced north and the south wall had racks to store canvases. An old easel leaned in one corner, a large workbench filled another, and a serviceable drafting table was against the back wall.

"Will this do?" Paloma asked.

"It's awesome. In my dreams I've wanted a place like this."

"Well, there're a couple of problems. No hot water, but there's a solar shower outside on the patio. It's protected, but it can get cold and, uh, the, uh, john is down the lane. You'll need a flashlight on a dark night. It's a bit primitive."

"Perfect. I like it that way. I'll take it."

"We haven't discussed the price. Since it is perfect, how about a $100 a week or $350 a month?"

Matt reached for his wallet. "How about a thousand, cash, for three months?"

"You've got a deal."

He counted out ten one-hundred dollar bills. Paloma folded the money and tucked it inside her blouse. "Thanks. You don't know what a relief this is. The sanctuary depends on donations and right now we're a little short. You made a lot of birds happy. I'll show you around."

They entered the sanctuary through a small gate with the hand-lettered sign: "*Verde Valley Bird Sanctuary, donations*

welcomed. Ring bell for assistance." A large liberty bell was
anchored on top of an eight-foot post. "You can hear it for miles.
Sometimes I ring it just for fun. Go ahead; give it a try!"

Matt yanked the rope hard. The bell swung on its cradle,
creating a loud clang which was followed by barking dogs and by a
shrill shriek. "That's Igor. He's my eagle." They walked along a
gravel path to another gate. A chain-link fence surrounded a large
compound ringed with cages. A pair of Australian Shepherds
raced towards them, followed by a pack of squealing puppies that
danced around Paloma, yipping and nipping at her legs.

"Down boys. Down girls." Paloma kneeled on the ground
and greeted the puppies as they tried to climb into her lap. "I get
this treatment every time I leave the yard."

Matt picked up a red tri-colored pup that squirmed in his
hands and gave a delighted yelp. She was a female, he decided.
He held her close to his face, and she gave him a kiss. "Nothing is
as sweet as puppy breath."

"That's Cassie. She's my sassy, classy lassie." Matt set
the pup down gently and picked up a tri-color pup with a large
white patch on the top of his head who was chewing his pant leg.

"That's Jolly Roger; he's a pirate. That one's Digger."
Matt squatted and Digger ran over, barked and playfully backed
away. "He's looking for a treat. And that's Roo, the mamma, over
there. I wasn't going to let them breed this year, but it happened.
Mark," Paloma pointed at a tri-colored male, "is a sly rogue.
Come on, gang, dinner time." She herded the pups and their
mother into a side yard and closed the gate. "That'll keep them
busy for awhile."

Matt followed Paloma past a large aviary. Inside an eagle
spread his wings, stood on his perch, croaked, and then settled
down. "That's Igor. Someone took a pot shot at him. JR said they
were after his feathers. It's possible, but I doubt it. Some jerks just
like to shoot birds. JR brought him here. We're hoping to release
him next week."

"I wouldn't want to be inside that cage with him," Matt said. "Those are powerful wings. I've made casts of eagles, but I've never been this close to one before."

"You'd be no match for him if you did go into his cage. Those talons can be murderous." The next cage held a red-tailed hawk that tilted its head and jumped to the ground and wobbled its way across the floor of the cage. "That's Gamey. I'm trying to train him. They say that you can learn more about a raptor by training one than you can by watching them in the wild.

"You mean to come to a lure, like a falcon?"

"Sort of, but he's a ground hunter. Sometimes they drive their prey like a pack of dogs."

"What happened to Gamey?"

"I think he found some poisoned bait. The ranchers spread it around to kill the gophers. There wouldn't be so many gophers if the poisoned bait didn't kill the foxes and coyotes. And, imagine, the government pays for all of it! Anyway, the poison works its way up the food chain."

Paloma opened the door to a small rectangular building. "This is my surgery."

"You do surgery? Are you a vet?"

"I have some meager skills," Paloma smiled. "I basically patch up the birds and feed them. But if I get into a mess, a local vet helps pro bono. Volunteers help with the smaller birds. You have to feed the young birds fifteen to twenty times a day. I do the night shift. The bats and owls are nocturnal and eat at night."

Paloma led Matt through the kitchen door of a large building that had been constructed from river rock. A delightful aroma of fresh baked bread and simmering herbs permeated the kitchen. "God, that smells delicious. What is it?" Matt asked.

"Apricot bread." Paloma pulled a towel off two loaves that were resting on a wooden board. "Cool enough to eat. Are you hungry?"

"I'm salivating."

She sliced two thick slices, spread them with butter, put them on a platter and handed one to Matt. She got two glasses

56

from the cupboard, opened the top of a large crock jar, and poured the glasses full of an amber liquid. "Mormon tea. Have you ever had any before, Matt?"

"Can't say that I have," he lied and took a swallow. "It's delicious." He took a bite of the bread and savored it as it dissolved in his mouth. "This is wonderful, Paloma. Are you married?"

"You're easy to please. But you'd better wait until you taste my cherry pie."

The liberty bell clanged and clanged again. "I'm coming, Darlene. Keep you shirt on. Take the short cut, Matt," Paloma pointed to a path in front of the adobe. "If Darlene sees you, she'll talk your arm and leg off. And I'll have to do the feeding."

"Thanks for the bread. I'm on my way." He skirted the adobe, peered through the studio window and then looked out over the river. "This will do very nicely. All this and cherry pie. God is good, sometimes."

On the way back to the Pair-a-Dice motel, Matt found a back road that led through the mesas and ended up on the frontage road. The room wasn't as bad as he was led to believe, at least it was clean. He showered, lay down across the bed, left a message for his controller, Al Johnson, reviewed his day briefly, and fell asleep. It was nearly dark when he woke up, dressed, and stepped outside where purple shadows were making their way down the garden walls and the stars were beginning to flicker in the still night sky.

A swarthy-looking man with tattooed arms and wearing a trucker's cap, a tank top, and a cheap gold necklace was sitting by the fountain with an attractive woman with pigtails protruding from her Stetson hat. She was wearing a red shirt, Levis, and red boots with a white star. She smiled at Matt as he walked across the patio, and then kissed the trucker. Matt could hear them laughing as he climbed into the Kombi.

CHAPTER FOUR

Sodium vapor lamps cast an orange glow on the scattered vehicles parked near the casino entrance. Splashing over huge slabs of granite rock, ribbons of water cascaded into a clear pool. Parallel ramps circled the waterfall, flanked by copper poles topped with soft milky white globes.

"Good evening," a pale blond valet in a brown uniform said courteously. "Welcome to the Black Hills Casino ." Matt nodded and took the ramp on his left. As he reached the top, a short dark-skinned guard looked away and yawned. When the automatic doors swung open, Matt stepped into a brightly-lit entryway.

"Good evening, sir." Matt looked into a pair of deep eyes, shades darker than his own. "I'm Renee and welcome to the Black Hills Casino." He looked with appreciation at her shoulder-length ebony hair and flattering white, knee-length, backless, fringed gown that set off an exquisite inlaid coral and turquoise neck collar. When she reached for his elbow, something inside him responded to her touch. "Are you right?" she asked.

Matt shrugged. "I guess I'm as right as I'll ever be. I'm looking for Tom Fallon."

"And you're Matt Dillon?" He managed a nod. "Tom's in the Eagles Nest. He asked me to watch for you. I'll take you there."

He couldn't help admiring her smooth café-colored back as she led him up a ramp that ended in a circular lounge ringed with red leather seats which overlooked the entire casino. Tom was the only occupant. "Glad you found Matt, Renee. I told her that she couldn't miss you." Tom put his arm around her. "Renee is the casino's hostess and PR liaison, and pinch hits as a dealer. She's also a reporter for *The Village Voice* newspaper. She's a Jill of all trades. Aren't you, Renee?"

Renee smiled. "I try."

"Did she ask for an interview, Matt? She wants one ASAP, which means probably right now or before you leave tonight. Am I right, Renee?"

"Give me a break, Tom. Tomorrow morning would be fine." She smiled at Matt. "That is, of course, if you're available."

"You are available, aren't you, Matt?" Tom teased.

"I think we can work something out."

"Could you meet me at the *Voice*'s office in Camp Verde, say, before noon?"

"No problem. I have some errands in town."

"Great! See you tomorrow, then. You'll have to excuse me; I need to get back to the lobby."

"Isn't she gorgeous?" Tom asked as she walked off.

"And then some."

"That she is. She's smart and she knows how to ask questions. Reminds me at times of a prosecutor. She can charm and disarm, and she can read between the lines. She's also a first-rate writer. The *Voice* is a rag, but it's improved 100% since she went to work there."

"What's she doing here?"

"Do you mean at the casino or at the newspaper?"

"Both."

"Good question. Actually the answer isn't very complicated. She's working on a graduate degree in journalism at Northern Arizona University in Flagstaff. Doing an internship at the *Voice*. Joe Biddles, the editor, likes her work, so he's using her as a stringer. But he can't pay much, so she hired on here as a dealer. A lot of the NAU students work part-time in the casinos. The cocktail waitresses make pretty good money. Anyway, the lady can deal, but Vince moved her to hostess. She's a quick study with lots of sass and pizzazz. The whales like her and when they drop a bundle, she softens the ego damage. Believe me, Vince doesn't want any unhappy customers. He wants everyone to treat the losers like kings and queens. Says it pays off in the long run."

Matt looked around the casino. "Quite a view from here."

"Three hundred and sixty degrees. You can see everything. It's a family-oriented casino, but it has everything."

"Meaning?"

Tom nodded in the direction of a glass-walled room at the far end of the casino. "A bowling alley. They hire models in bikinis for special events and there's legal off-track betting. So you don't have to go to the dog races anymore. It's killing the Black Canyon City dog track. Next door is a videogame room where the kids can play games while their parents squander their college funds and inheritance. It even has a Johnny Rockets malt shop. Five, count them, international cuisine bistros, two lounges, three bars, and a center stage for weekend comedy acts and live bands, just like Laughlin or Vegas. All together the casino employs around 150 people per shift. I don't know how the casino affords them all. It's nine o'clock and only about forty players are here."

Matt counted the crowd: two full tables in the poker room with ten to twelve black jack players, three people in front of the cashier's cage, twenty or more in the cafes, ten in the open lounge, and another dozen trying their luck at the slots. "Closer to sixty or seventy, I think."

"If you're so good at math, figure this one out, Matt. Fifty percent of any casino's revenue comes from problem gamblers. That's two to three percent of the gambling population. Locals and tourists bring in the rest. I don't see many of what I would call problem gamblers here, except on the weekends. Does that add up to two million a month? I don't think so. But what do I know? What worries me is that it is a cash business – no cards. It's all cash'n carry here. That draws the whales, according to Vince Salvatori."

"So where do the whales come from?"

"The big spenders are not doctors and lawyers, Matt. We get a few compulsive gamblers, realtors, and trust fund managers who are probably embezzling their clients' money. Who else could a whale be? They have to be drug dealers getting rid of their small bills and going home with clean money. But there's no way to prove that. Go figure, huh, Matt?"

"How often do you come here?"

"Weekdays, I do breakfast, lunch and dinner here. Saturday nights I drop in to check the house. It's always the same -- the regulars, the weekenders, the tourists. The traffic gets pretty heavy in the summer. I keep my eyes open, but I never see a thing. Salvatori runs a tight ship, but I smell a rat. Speaking of rats, here comes Mr. Salvatori himself. Don't hold your nose. He's a ruthless SOB, doesn't give a damn about anything except getting what he wants. Likes to play God with the employees and customers."

Matt watched as a heavy-set man, his black hair slicked back from his olive face with its aquiline nose and bushy black brows, twisted his gold chain which glinted against the white Savoy suit and moved along a row of slot machines. Even as he greeted the players with an encouraging touch or smile, his eyes scanned the room like a hawk searching for prey. He paused to speak to a lady playing the slots and gave her a quick, friendly hug. Salvatori spoke to Renee and scurried up the ramp, one hand on the rail, while reading the crowd below. He joined them and drew up a chair that was too small for his large frame.

"Hello. I'm Vince Salvatori." He extended his hand and flashed the insincere smile of a practiced politician. Matt was surprised by the powerful but restrained grip. "My pleasure."

A cocktail waitress set a tall glass in front of Vince and moved away quickly. "Perrier with a twist of lemon. It's my vice. I drink a gallon of the stuff every night. Running a casino is hard work. I must cover ten miles every hour, a regular marathon man. So what do think of Black Hills?" Some kind of kiva, isn't it? We try to play up the Indian motif. We bring in drummers and dancers on weekends. The Native Americans wear their costumes and after they do their thing, they mingle with the crowd. It's corny, but the customers love it."

"It's not corny; it's pathetic," Tom said.

"Customers want to be amused, Tom, but great entertainment is bad for the house. It takes the customers' minds off the gambling and it's too expensive. It's more cost-effective to use tribal members. Anyway, what do you think of our set-up?"

"How can he think, let along talk, Vince, while you're doing your song and dance?" Tom said.

"You're real funny tonight, Tom. Sorry, Matt, stroking folks gets to be a habit. But Tom doesn't take to strokes, do you, Tom?"

"I haven't had a chance to look around, Mr. Salvatori, but the view from here is impressive," Matt said.

"Like there's a whole lot of gambling going on is the atmosphere we're after. But it's not an in-your-face layout. Yet you can feel the action."

"There's not a whole lot of gambling going on tonight, Vince," Tom pointed out.

"Stick around. A ship of fools or limo of fools is on the way. There'll be some action." Vince grinned, but his eyes went past them, scanning the room. "I like being up here, Matt. I can see everything, but I usually work the floor."

A pallid, gaunt man wearing a black suit and string tie approached, cupped his hand and whispered into Vince's ear. "Spit it out. These are friends," Vince said to him.

"Table two," he said. Vince leaned forward and stared at a man in a camel-colored sports jacket sitting alone at a black jack table.

"How much?" Vince asked without taking his eyes off the table.

"Twenty-five hundred."

Vince studied the man carefully. "Put a camera on him."

"We have," the man said. "Nothing."

"So why are you bothering me? Send in Annie. Tell her to get it back. That's easy, isn't it?"

"Yes, sir." He scurried away.

Vince turned to Matt and Tom. "Nobody here can think for themselves. The guy at the table is a loner. I hate loners, especially lucky ones. But no worries; we're sending in the heavy guns. You might find this interesting, Matt." Vince took a sip of his Perrier. "Don't look at the guy, but he's sitting at the table next to the slots. Bad spot for most players. This guy's hoping no one will join him."

"We can see him, Vince," Tom said.

"Right. Just watch and learn." Vince rattled the ice in his glass.

They watched as a pit boss spoke to a stunning, statuesque blond. She nodded, made her way to table two, and took over for the dealer. She smiled at the player, opened a fresh deck of cards with nimble fingers, and began to shuffle.

"If that cracker is honest, he'll be broke in ten minutes, unless he's a faggot. And even if he is, he won't last fifteen," Vince said softly. "They test us up here. Con artists, card counters, pro-teams. They drive in from Vegas and fly in from the east coast. They think we're hicks, a soft touch. But it doesn't matter. The word's out that we're up for anything, so they don't bother us much. The real action, Matt, comes from the big spenders who want a quiet, out-of-the-way place. They brag in Vegas that it all stays there, but here you aren't even seen. The moms and pops and the Phoenix weekenders pay the overhead. The slots do all the work and everything else is gravy. We've added a poker room, but I think it's a fad and waste of floor space. But you have to give the people what they want. See? What did I tell you? He's broke! That sucker bet his whole wad. It's over."

They watched as the man got up smoothly, handed Annie a couple of tokes, and headed for the bar.

"So what are you planning for the atrium, Matt? It can't be too big because we need access to the counting room. There's a lot of foot traffic there. I want to put in a Spanish fountain, something subdued with a soft light, kind of ornamental but not too ostentatious. I've explained that to Tom over and over."

"It's going to be a sculpture, Vince. Something appropriate for the entrance to the Cultural Center."

63

"Cultural Centers don't make money. Casinos do." Vince said testily. "You can't have it both ways. I don't need any problems here, Tom. Sorry, Matt. I know that you have been hired to do a piece, but you need to know up front where I'm coming from."

"Well, you've made your pitch, Vince. What do you say, Matt?"

"Uh. What can I say? I'll make some preliminary sketches. If I come up with something everyone agrees to, fine. If I don't, that's the end of it. But let me tell you where *I'm* coming from, Vince. Anything I design will be my own creation. And it's just possible that the atrium isn't the best location. However, I do appreciate your input."

"Tom, I can tell you right now, I like this man. We're going to get along fine. Uh, listen. I have to check the traps." Vince finished his Perrier and sat the empty glass on the table. "It was really nice meeting you. I've asked Renee to show you the factory." Vince reached into his jacket and pulled out a plastic bag filled with tokens. "It's a comp, Matt. Good luck!" He got up and headed down the ramp.

"What a pompous ass! He acts like he owns the casino. He's just a damn syndicate pimp," Tom glowered.

"Take it easy, Tom, slow down. Where's he from?"

"He's a bat straight out of hell. A Count Dracula, by the way of Britain, New Jersey, lately from Boulder City, where the syndicate picked him up."

"And who's the syndicate? Where are they from?"

"All the usual places and some you've never heard of. We chose the Reno group from a long list of applicants. They checked out A1 with no known mafia or drug connections. Supposedly just legitimate investors backed by experienced housemen. But your people know them better than we do. Is this bunch on the take, Matt?"

"I wouldn't know. The Commissioners don't tell me anything. But I don't sense that they detect a problem."

"And what if they did think there was a problem?"

"Then most certainly they wouldn't tell me anything. Basically I'm here to discover the impact of the casino in a general way on the Verde Valley and specifically on the tribe."

"That's it?"

"As far as I'm concerned, that's it."

"That sounds pretty sketchy to me."

"It is and when you add that, while I'm here, I'm creating a piece for the breezeway, it gets real thin. I'm not sure I'll be able to do either job."

"Why did you sign on then?"

"A couple of reasons. I'm returning a favor. I'm not a trained investigator, but I did some work for the Commissioner and he thinks I have a talent for it. And I came up because it's an opportunity to sculpt. I'm ready for a new challenge."

"So, do you have the talent for investigation?"

"I study people, animals, birds, and critters. You learn a lot when you watch people and animals, especially at play. If you watch carefully, you learn a lot about people. Look out there. What do you see?"

"People, a lot of losers."

"Look again. Look carefully."

"I'm looking."

"Do you see greed, fear, envy, joy, elation, anxiety, and excitement?"

"I see a lot of tired, sad-looking people trying to give away their last quarters."

Matt laughed. "Well, you're looking. But if you study them long enough, you'll see more. But I'm really more into critters than people. At least, they are honest. I need to go, Tom. It's been a long day, a long night, and I still have miles to go."

"Where are you staying?"

"Tonight I'm going back to the Pair-a-Dice Inn. Tomorrow I'm moving into a studio along the Verde, close to the foundry,"

"That studio next to the Birdlady? She let you have it?"

"Yes."

"Well, there's a twist. It's been empty since Killinger moved out. Lucky you. She's a special lady."

"I just need a studio, a place to hang my hat."

"Whatever. You don't think the studio here will work?"

"I'll do my heavy work here when the time comes. But right now, there are way too many distractions."

"You could keep an eye on things here."

"And anyone could keep an eye on me. It works both ways."

"Anything I can do to help?"

"I'll need background on everyone; what you know, Tom, and even what you suspect."

"That's it?"

"That's it for now. I'll give you a pager number when I get set up. This week and next, I'm just going to show the flag. Let people get used to seeing me around and then I want to disappear into the background."

"That won't be easy. This is a small town. You could be here ten years and still be a newcomer. You'll stick out like a sore thumb. Hell, you're already a celebrity."

"You're probably right. I made a mistake tangling with Carbahol."

"Well, you probably made a lot of instant friends; at least the locals will be friendly."

"I'll be in touch," Matt said as they shook hands. He went down the ramp and joined Renee, who was waiting at the entrance.

"I'm supposed to take you on a tour," she said.

"I'll take you up on that, but not tonight. It's been a long day."

"How about tomorrow? Would you be interested in a tour of the valley?"

"After the interview?"

"How about during? We can do both at the same time."

"Sounds good."

"I'll see you around ten o'clock then?"

"For sure. Good night, Renee." Matt passed through the automatic doors, stopped and handed the pale blond attendant the plastic bag of comp tokens.

"Lady Luck must have been with you tonight," the attendant chirped.

"Yes, she was. Enjoy!"

Matt drove down the well-lit highway without bothering to turn on his headlights. He parked the VW between two semis. The patio was empty. Matt looked up at the stars, stretched, opened the door, stepped inside, double locked the latches, and sprawled across the bed without removing his clothes. He fell asleep to the sounds of breaking glass, laughter, a flushed toilet, and loud thumping coming from the next room.

It was early when he unwrapped himself from the bedding, yawned, and got up. After an ice cold shower which turned his skin slightly blue, he shaved off his dark stubble. Then he pulled on his favorite faded maroon tracksuit and a pair of worn sneakers and shoved his dirty clothes into a duffle bag. He left the key on the table, tossed the bag into the VW, closed the door, and walked to Ruth's for breakfast.

Matt finished his meal, swallowed the last of the coffee, and put some bills on the counter. "Thanks," he said, smiling at the waitress.

"How was your breakfast?" Ruth called from the galley.

"Terrific."

The waitress picked up the change "Thank you, kind sir. Have a good day."

He stepped out onto the boardwalk, ran his fingers through his hair, adjusted his baseball cap, and looked around. Jen's stand was empty. A scrap of paper blew across the vacant lot, sailed over the fence and landed behind Wally's shack. Except for the wind, there was no sign of movement there or up on the hill where Sam and Jen lived. Still, Matt had the uneasy feeling that someone was watching.

CHAPTER FIVE

Cumulus clouds looking like cotton balls covered Camp Verde as Matt followed the Verde River into town. He drove down Main Street and parked in front of the general store. Twenty minutes later, he struggled out of the swinging doors with a box of groceries, a Dutch oven, an iron skillet, a can opener, a Swiss Army knife, a camping stove, and bottle of propane gas. A small trash can overflowed with paper goods, plastic ware, a rope, a two-way mirror; garbage bags; a small fishing rod and reel, and mealy worms. He stacked the items beside the Kombi.

A red '64 1/2 Mustang convertible pulled alongside the open door of the van. "Going on a safari?" Renee asked.

"Campers R us."

As Renee got out of the Mustang, she pushed her sunglasses onto the top of her head. "I'll give you a hand." She passed him the gear, and he stacked it under the improvised bed and bench, storing the groceries behind the seats.

"That's about it."

"You've got everything but a gold pan, Matt."

"Already figured that one out." He held up a tin dishpan. "It can do double duty."

She handed him a new fly rod, still wrapped in plastic, and looked at him dubiously. "You're not a fisherman, I take it?"

"Does it show?"

"It shows. You've got a fly rod and you bought mealy worms."

"Whatever works."

Renee glanced at her watch. "You're early."

"I haven't found your office yet. That could take awhile."

"The office is across the street, right in front of your nose. You can't miss it."

"You mean my nose or your office?"

"Either. Look, you said you wanted to see the sights. I know of a couple of spots that might interest you. Park in front of the office. I'll tell the boss I have a feature for him and get my camera. I'll be right with you."

Minutes later she came flying out the door. "Come on before Fiddles changes his mind."

"Fiddles?"

"Joe Biddles as in rhymes with fiddles or go fiddle," Renee giggled. "I told him I needed a break and that you are the scoop of the month."

"What did Joe say?"

"Chocolate or vanilla." Renee laughed as she backed the Mustang out into the street and headed towards the center of Old Town. As they passed several wooden buildings housing mostly gift and antique shops, she provided a running commentary. Two minutes later, they were on a highway. "Cottonwood was a wild place in its heyday. Jerome, Cottonwood, and Clarkdale almost disappeared from the map when the mines closed, but there's still gold in the hills. Now it's tourists and retirees. Housing developments are popping up like mushrooms; urban sprawl will fill the Verde Valley from Black Canyon City to Sedona if we don't run out of water first."

"You've got a river full of water," Matt offered as they crossed the Verde.

"Phoenix and the Salt River Project want the Verde River water. The local groundwater tables are dropping because of the drought. Some of the old timers say there's a 30-year or 50-year drought underway. The snowfall in Flagstaff is way off. This whole valley used to be a garden, every arable acre was used to grow food for the miners and the ranchers provided beef. There was enough water for everyone, but not enough for all of these housing developments." They sped past several rows of faux bubble-gum pink adobe homes and turned down a back lane shaded by the overhanging branches of cottonwood trees.

"Where are we going?"

"Montezuma's Castle. We're here." Renee pulled alongside a kiosk, flashed a pass and a smile at the park ranger as he waved her through. She parked beside a small motor home with Canadian plates. "I think you'll like it here. The cliff houses are a treasure. I love camping here."

They got out of the Mustang and went down a trail bordered by a small creek lined with sycamore trees. The trail ended in a box canyon where a sandstone cliff-dwelling was sculpted in the limestone walls towering above them. A few yards down the trail, a ranger was conducting a guided tour for the Canadian couple. They stopped and listened.

"The castle has nothing to do with Montezuma. The locals back in the 1860s named it and the name stuck. It was really built by the Sinagua people sometime before 1250 AD. It took three centuries to complete. It's five stories high and, at one time, at least 150 people lived here. There are several other similar structures within two or three miles of here."

"What happened to them?" the broad-shouldered Canadian asked.

"We don't really know, but they abandoned the valley somewhere between 1350 – 1400. We know there was at least a 50-year drought then," the ranger said over his shoulder as the Canadians followed him down the trail.

Renee fiddled with her camera and aimed it in his direction. "Try to frown, Matt." He grinned as the shutter clicked. "Good boy." Renee slung the camera over her shoulder. "What are you feeling?"

"Stillness, wonder, mostly admiration."

"Admiration for what?"

"For our ancestors who came from somewhere else, all this way to build condos in the cliffs. My God, how proud they must have felt perched up there like eagles. The winter sun warmed them and, in the summer, when the sun was straight up, the caves stayed cool. They were farmers, engineers, architects, and artists. I studied their artifacts in a kind of abstract way in an anthropology course at ASU. I saw them only as remnants, reminders of a primitive, but artistic people. But, sitting here, you can almost see them molding and shaping the clay, and weaving those reeds into baskets. It's almost as if we can hear them talking."

"What are they saying?"

"I can't really hear them. But I can imagine the end, the fear and the confusion. Imagine what it would have been like seeing their crops wither, seeing the irrigation canals dry out, and realizing they must leave to find a new home. We're lucky that the early settlers didn't destroy this place, that their lost paradise is still here."

"You're a romantic, Matt. I think you would rather have lived back then."

"Maybe. Maybe not. Today is a pretty good day to be here and alive. Back then people didn't live much beyond twenty-five. They venerated the old ones who probably weren't much older than forty-five. Does that sound like a romantic?"

"I think so. Want to see something special?"

"Sure."

"Just in time," Renee said. A horde of noisy jostling floppy-hatted tourists armed with cameras and tote bags was descending onto the tarmac from a pair of Gray Lines tour buses. She turned north at the entrance.

"Where are we going?"

"To Montezuma's Well." She waved at a pickup truck which honked as it passed them heading south. A few minutes later, another pickup truck honked and someone else waved at them.

"Know them?" Matt asked.

"I'm not sure, but they seem to know me. Everyone knows I'm from *The Verde Voice*."

"I'll bet they don't honk at Fiddles."

Renee laughed. "No. They just throw rocks at him."

"I'll bet that, when you're editor, they won't throw rocks."

"If I ever become the editor, they'll probably burn the building and wreck the presses."

"Are you a fiery crusader?"

"More like someone who's indignant over nearly everything. That's SWINE, for short."

"Cowboys don't honk at pigs, even Miss Piggy."

"Moi. That's because they don't know me."

"Well, I'd honk."

"You don't know me either."

"Do you have to know someone to honk?"

"If you don't know what you're honking after, you could get into trouble. But I'll bet you never honk at anyone, Matt. You don't have to."

"No one has ever honked at me."

"You wouldn't notice if someone did. A girl would have to do more than honk to get your attention." Renee turned off the main road onto an unpaved dirt road. The Mustang bounced over a series of ruts and potholes until she pulled over and parked underneath a palo verde tree. "Bring the camera, Matt."

They followed a narrow path way that led to the edge of a large limestone sink. "Montezuma's Well." The cotton candy clouds had changed into strings of marshmallow beads strung across the azure sky, casting their reflection in the blue, almost oval pool below. Banks of reeds surrounded the pool. Clumps of dwarfed oaks clung to the sides of the cliffs. On the far side, a cliff dwelling had been built in a cave. Swallows darted above the pool. They heard a hawk cry, and a black-and-white magpie squawked and landed in the palo verde tree, breaking the silence, and then it was quiet again.

"I call it my Blue Lagoon, Matt."

"It's awesome. I could never have imagined anything quite like this here in the middle of the desert."

"It's magical. Sometimes I ache to go for a swim, especially on hot days. Last year, I crawled down to the bottom. I was sweaty, dirty, and covered with burrs. I stuck my foot into the water, but it was too cold. The springs pump out thousands of gallons a day of pure ice water. My foot ached for half an hour."

"Want to try again?"

"If you strapped cement blocks to me, I wouldn't go in." The camera whirled several times in succession as Renee panned. Then she glanced at her watch. "I hate to say this, but there are a couple of more spots I want to show you, and we have to do the interview. We can come back again if you'd like to."

"I'd like to make some sketches."

"For your sculpture?"

"Background, just to get in the mood. I'm a little rusty."

"What do you do when you're not working on a sculpture?"

"I don't do anything."

"You don't do anything? Fascinating."

"Sorry, people get upset when I say that. What I mean is, I do what I please."

"You do as you please? Go on."

He laughed. "People really get upset when I say that. So I usually stick with 'I don't do anything.' Most people define you by what you do, not by what you are. They get uncomfortable if you say you don't do anything or that you do what you please."

"But you're a sculptor. You *do* do something."

"If I tell people I'm a sculptor, the next thing they want to know is do I make a living at it. If I say no, they figure I'm a struggling artist or I'm some kind of a free spirit, a dabbler. No one ever asks me why I sculpt."

"Okay, why do you?"

"Because I feel alive when I'm creating a piece. When things are going good, it's like I'm a surfer riding a wave – you're in the wave; it surrounds you. You become the wave. You're creating and you're being created. It's not just living; it's being aware. It's like looking at the same thing as everyone else does, but seeing it differently, and giving that new perspective an existence that will make an impact."

"You're saying that it's the process, not the product you're after?"

"What I'm saying is, it's both and more. It's energy. You reach into the collective unconscious where the energy comes from. It transforms us. It goes through us. If you get it right, a

73

piece is never finished. The piece is alive with energy. It may be cast in bronze or carved in marble, but it moves. You are moved, transformed. It's a process of awareness that is not necessarily conscious. It's like I'm not in control, yet I don't feel out of control. Someone, I don't know who, said that sculpting sculpts the sculptor. I don't entirely understand what happens. Mostly what I try to communicate ends up communicating to me. The result is about itself, not the externalized me. And yet, a piece is always in a state of flux because the viewer is free to experience his or her own reality. Puzzling?"

"So, it's a sort of magic?"

"Sort of, or maybe more like alchemy."

"What happens when the wave crashes?"

He grinned. "If you're lucky, you catch another wave."

"But how do you make a living if someone doesn't buy your work?"

"Renee, making a living is the easy part. Anyone can make a living. Anyone can get rich, if you work hard enough. When you are riding a wave, you don't have time to think about making money. In fact, making a buck is the last thing you think about."

"You're putting me on. Aren't you?"

"Maybe a little. Let me ask you something. You're a reporter. Do you write to live, or do you live to write? It's an old question."

"To tell you the truth, I don't do either very well. I don't have a clue as to why I want to write and I'd starve if I tried to make a living as a writer."

"But you are writing. You are a reporter."

"My reporting is just an excuse to meet people. I get caught up in their stories and I forget about my own problems, my own life story. I try to stay detached, like a spectator, an observer. Writing is just a part-time job for me, a hobby."

"How about your job at the casino?"

"It's temporary."

"How did you get started?"

"That's a long story."

"I'm listening."

"Well, my dad was a professional gambler, a wild Irishman from New Orleans. My mother was a full-blooded Choctaw. My grandparents operated -- now don't laugh --a catfish farm, and they hatched crawdads for the restaurant trade. My dad met my mother one night at a Cajun dance. Love at first sight, Matt, something like that. She adored my father; we both did. I was dealing cards when I was five years old. I was 15 when he died." She hesitated. "The loan sharks were after him. He had markers all over Texas and Louisiana. He was broke, but we had a wonderful Irish wake. Hundreds of people came. Even the gamblers he owed money to pitched in. End of story. Say, who's interviewing whom? And speaking of starving artists, I'm hungry. Let's get rolling."

Renee turned northeast, and after couple of miles, she circled through a round about, took a small secondary road that led up the side of a hill, and parked along the edge of the highway. "Tutzigoot. It's not as impressive as Montezuma's Castle, but in time, it grows on you." Terraced rock walls lying in symmetrical rows were crowned by a two-story structure that looked like a medieval fortress. Below the ruins, the Verde River made a sweeping bend in front of a range of low hills and mesas.

Renee pointed. "That's Cleopatra Hill. That cluster of buildings near the top is Jerome. That's Clarkdale down there at the bottom. We can have lunch in Jerome. Fiddles' is buying."

"I'd like to make some sketches."

"We can come back anytime. It's never crowded. The tourists tend to ignore it." Renee aimed her camera out of the car and snapped a couple of shots. She started the Mustang, turned onto the highway, raced down the grade, and started the long climb up Cleopatra Hill, passing a dozen wooden homes before they entered a labyrinth of buildings on stilts hung precariously above the narrow streets. Renee engineered the car into a small angular space between a rock wall and a metal refuse container. Matt squeezed out of the car, walked to the front, and saw that a short retaining wall separated them from a sheer drop.

Far below a dilapidated brick structure had obviously undergone several major repairs over the years. Renee stood close to him. "That's the old city jail. It used to be up here, but it slid down the hillside. Incredibly, they still use it."

They walked up a steep hill, passing several narrow wooden houses that been converted into storefronts, the upper floors mostly residences. On the third story of one of the buildings, a man tended a small garden which was apparently at street level on the winding road above. Further up the street, the foundations of the houses looked down on the roofs of their neighbors. Renee and Matt stepped into a doorway to allow some cars and motorcycles to pass.

The narrow lane opened into a slightly wider street. They walked onto the deck of a small café that cantilevered over a roof of a building below. Renee led the way to the rear of the deck. Matt whistled. "Now, that is a view."

"Those are the San Francisco peaks, the sacred mountains of the Hopis, Navajos, and ski developers." Far below, the Verde River wound its way like a ribbon through Clarkdale, Cottonwood, and Camp Verde. Renee set her bag in an empty chair. "I need to take a hike. Enjoy!"

As Renee made her way across the deck, passing a party of uniformed men seated behind a wooden table with their backs against a rock wall. They all turned and stared as she made her way down a flight of stairs and disappeared into a old, modest, rock building. Then they eyeballed Matt as he found a chair, turned his back on them and faced the river. He traced the Verde River's path through the cottonwoods and into a small valley dotted with ranch houses. He thought he could see the foundry and a small sand-colored building which could be his studio beyond a bend in the river. To the north he could see the red rock country with its isolated domes. The sun was directly overhead. The morning clouds were wisping away, their thin shadows drifting across the valley floor.

"Lunch," Renee said as she sat a tray on the table. "My treat." She handed Matt a taco wrapped in a napkin. "Alfredo's famous fish taco and Sedona Red, the best in the West," she said as she poured a bottle of beer into a Styrofoam cup. "I'm starved. Don't be polite."

"Me, too." As Matt took a large bite of the fish taco, some of the juice gushed out of his napkin and onto the paper plate.

"Alfredo's is God's gift to the Verde Valley. They fly the fish in from Guaymas. Jerome's back in the big leagues." Renee managed to say between bites.

"The beer's not bad, either," Matt replied.

She laughed and touched her cup to his. "Cheers! In its heyday, they brought in wine and oysters from California and brandy from France. Jerome had two railroads, one to haul out the copper ore and one for Clark's private railroad car. That big white monolith of a building over there was Clark's palace. Jerome had 22 saloons and restaurants, and no one knows how many brothels. Just before World War I and into the Roaring Twenties, copper was King. America was entering the electronic age. The mines produced $1 billion worth of wire alone and the Verde Valley supplied all the food."

"Where did you learn all that?"

"It's on the back of the menu."

"Right! So what happened?"

"The crash. Jerome emptied overnight and so did Clarkdale, but it's all coming back. Free spirits, artists, entrepreneurs, and housing developers. They're all cashing in and it's called progress. Anyway, I'm just a city girl, but I don't like Boom Towns. Pretty soon you won't even be able to see the Valley. It will be another haze-colored sea of homes and empty shells filled with hollow people."

"You see. You can write, Renee."

"No. T.S. Elliot can write. I just quote."

"It can't be that bad."

"Do you want to bet? You know it's all over when Wal-Mart comes to town. They have one up at Prescott, one in Flagstaff, and they want to put another in Cottonwood. They do something to people who work and shop there. If I had my way, there would be a law banning Wal-Mart stores within 500 feet of a school or within 30 miles of an unincorporated village."

"How about Bed, Bath and Beyond?"

She laughed. "Beyond what? Beyond the malls? Beyond the blue horizon?"

"Sounds like you've got the NIMBY syndrome; you know, the 'not in my backyard' response."

"Funny, but you're right. I'm sorry for the old timers. They griped because they had to drive to Phoenix to shop. Now Phoenix is moving right up the I-17. They're going to lose everything they came here for: space, peace and quiet. Oh, it's still slow moving here, but the clock is ticking.

Matt noticed that two men in dark suits had joined the town marshals. Renee glanced in their direction. "I'd love to hear what's going on over there at that table. It looks like they are having a pow wow."

"Who are they?"

'The uniforms are town marshals. The big one is the marshal here in Jerome. The one with the pot gut and the wide-brimmed Stetson is the Cottonwood marshal. And the little guy with the ferret face is the Constable in Camp Verde. The suits are probably Feds or from the Department of Public Safety, DPS. The blonde on the right looks familiar, but I can't place him."

Renee pulled a briefcase out of her bag, laid it on the table and popped it open. She toyed with the keyboard and then slid her camera into a mount. She toyed with it some more, and then turned the monitor sideways for Matt to see. "Here you are."

Matt stared. A tall dark looking man with a curious grin surrounded by rock walls stared back at him. "Montezuma Castle. Amazing. How did you do that?"

"Easy," she said. She tapped her keyboard and Matt saw that his image was now standing on the edge of the sink at Montezuma's Well. Renee changed the color and the white clouds turned slightly blue-gray and then pink and were reflected in the dark water below.

Matt reached to pull the computer closer. "I could use one of these."

"Don't touch. Sorry, I don't want to lose the image."

"Are they expensive?"

"Yes and no. You can get something adequate under a thousand. The cameras range from $300 all the way to the thousands. This is a custom job, my portable office and photo shop. I can type an article, fill in a photo, and e-mail the copy to *The Verde Voice* right from here. And speaking of copy, I need to ask you some questions. I need an angle on you, a hook. I have some ideas, but you'll have to fill in the blanks."

"It's your story."

"It's your story that I want. So, what do you think about the Verde Valley? Give me your impressions."

"As an artist?"

"Why not?"

"Sky above, red mesas below. It's a great place for artists. I think I'll enjoy working here."

"Why do you want to do a piece for the tribe?"

"Frankly, I needed the work. I was open to a new experience."

"What are your qualifications for a project like this?"

"I have some experience, at least that's what my résumé states, and they chose me."

"Because you're Native American or because you're good?"

"Nice twist. Is this the hook?"

"Could be."

"Are we talking about my rednicity?"

"What you mean by that, Matt?"

"Let's see, there's a lot of good Anglo American sculptors in this area. If they chose me over them, I must be pretty good. Or they chose me just because I'm a Native American and supposedly as a Native American I'm supposed to have some special insight into nature, the red man's vision of life. But on the other hand, if I were some white guy messing around with bronze or marble, I wouldn't even be noticed."

"Are you white or Indian, Matt?"

"I suppose you want a straight arrow answer. Do you mean Indian with a feather or Indian with a dot? Or do you mean, am I an apple, red on the outside and white on the inside?"

"I don't mean anything. You know where I'm going with this. I'm part Native American too."

"Let me put it this way. I'm an American. I don't have a tribe or clan. My parents were Indian. My father spent some time on a reservation when he was young. He was abandoned and later adopted by a Presbyterian minister who took him back east. My mother grew up in New York City. Her father was an iron worker. He taught me how to weld and how to work metal. He ended up with a job in a foundry where they made girders for bridges. He got me a job running a chip gun, knocking off the slag and filing off the burrs. My mother was a rarity, an Indian lawyer. She was killed by a drunk driver when I was still a kid. After that, I played hooky a lot and hung out in the movie theaters. When I played with the other kids, I was always a gunslinger or Tarzan."

"Did you every play Tonto?"

"Hell no, I was the Lone Ranger. The only Indian hero I ever knew was Jim Thorpe, and in the movie he was played by Burt Lancaster. So I sort of grew up with the idea that I was part gunslinger and part Jim Thorpe. I ran track in high school, made the swimming team, and I got a part-time job in a marble factory in a small town that we moved to after my mother died. So, you could say that I'm the grandson of a minister, a gunslinger, a real son of a gun, I guess. I don't even think about being Indian, unless someone asks me and the only answer I can give is that I'm an original American. So, I guess you could say in politically correct terms, I'm an assimilated Indian."

"I'm sorry, Matt. I don't know what to say. I didn't mean to make you angry."

"What I gave you was straight arrow. That's what you wanted, isn't it? Why be sorry? I'm assimilated, isn't that the right word? I'm not a drunken Indian and I'm not a cigar store Indian. I'm not even a good Indian; they're all dead and I'm still alive. I'm just a human being, Renee, and I'm happy to be me."

"Why did you come here, Matt?"

"To Arizona?"

"Well, Arizona, and here to the Verde Valley."

"I got a scholarship to ASU. Criminal Justice was my major. I thought about being a lawyer, like my mother, but I met Jay Cook. He was working on his masters in fine arts and I switched majors, or added a major. Jay was an interesting guy. He was on the warpath. Somehow he has never forgiven our ancestors for surrendering the land, but he didn't like the tactics of the American Indian Movement. He was studying the Hopi Way and wanted to be a peaceful warrior -- a priest or a medicine man, I'm not sure which. After we graduated, I went to Shidoni and Jay moved back home. Jay's dad was the tribal chairman and he sent Jay to Washington to check out the Smithsonian Museum about the time they passed the new Indian Antiquities Act. Jay came home with a semi-truck full of bones and other artifacts. Apparently there was some sort of confrontation at the burial grounds and the bones were stored in a shed on the old Rez after Russell took over. Nobody seems to know what happened, but Jay disappeared. Anyway, Sam sent me the forms and I applied for the job. I got it. Probably thanks to Sam's help. So I strapped on my guns and came looking for Jay."

"This is kind of heavy, Matt."

"Yeah, you could say that. Yet, I'm serious about doing a piece for the tribe, and right now I'm going to feel my way around and hope that something clicks."

"What about Jay?"

"Same thing. I'll look around and maybe something will click."

"Pow wow's over," Renee said. Matt glanced at the table. The uniforms and the suits had finished their meals and were moving onto the street. Renee removed her camera, closed her case and stuffed them in her carry-all bag. She put her hand on top

81

of Matt's "I read something awhile ago about a protest at the cemetery. I'll look through the morgue at the *Voice* and see what I can find out."

"Thanks. I would appreciate any help you can give me."

. "I have a deadline to meet, so let's get going. Let's take the shortcut." They crossed the deck, went down several flights of stairs, and ended up beside the Mustang. A yellow-haired biker was sitting on the rock wall, his bike parked in a small space next to the steel dumpster.

"Hey, dude!" he waved at Matt and rolled his eyes at Renee. "How ya been?"

Matt stopped. "I'm holding up."

"That's cool. You hanging here in Jerome?"

"No, I found a pad in Camp Verde."

"All right! Camp Verde's cool. My buds hang out at the Q & Brew in Old Town. If you need anything, you come by and see us, hear?"

"I'll do that."

"I'm Billy Burger. You're Matt Dillon, right? Like from *Gunsmoke*."

Matt faked a quick draw, fired a round, put the imaginary pistol to his lips, and blew the smoke away. "Yeah. That's me. I'm the man."

"That's cool, dude! See ya." Billy fired up his bike, checked the traffic, and eased down the street.

"Who was that?" Renee asked after they got into the car.

"Just some guy. He was hanging out with a bunch of bikers at the bar when I had a run in with Carbahol."

"I saw the DPS report. You really are a gunslinger, Matt."

"Nah, just a wannabe. I shoot blanks."

CHAPTER SIX

Renee parked in front of *The Village Voice* office. "We're home."

"Thanks for the tour. I enjoyed it"

"My pleasure, Matt, all in a day's work. Speaking of work, I need to get with the program. If I get some time, I'll see what I can dig up on Jay."

"I'd appreciate that."

"If I find anything, I'll bring it to the town meeting tomorrow night. Maybe we can go for coffee afterwards. You can check out the locals; the squirrels and nuts will be there in force. You can count on it," she said over her shoulder as she walked across the wooden porch.

Matt waved as he pulled away, but Renee was already inside and seated at her desk. She opened her lap top and glanced at Joe Fiddles who was busy formatting at the layout table.

Plugging in her headset, she adjusted the earphones, clicked on the player, and began transcribing, eyes locked onto the screen.

"Hello boys. Good to see you. This is Neil Kessler. He's FBI and a friend, a good friend. Neil, this is Bob Farley (Camp Verde Constable), Dickie George (Jerome Marshall), and Paul Randall (Camp Verde Marshall)." *Note: Take a close look at Kessler's briefcase. I think it's a surveillance rig. *"Neil is investigating the robbery on the Rez. The FBI has jurisdiction, but he could use our help. It's your show, Neil."* [Kincaid]

"Thanks. I've got a couple of things you might be able to help me with. (Kessler opens the brief case. *Note: Check his right hand movement.) We're looking for a Native American, Jay Cook. He's been missing since the night of the robbery. We have*

a hunch he may know something. According to his father, Jay and the tribal cops were close. [Kessler]

"*I've seen them together. They work the drums at the pow pows. [Farley]*

"*The Sheriff Department faxed us some material.*" *Note: Kessler passes out copies, closes the briefcase and sets it under the table. *"The John Doe's were wearing biker gear. A deputy found two burned bikes and helmets at Mormon Flats. No plates and the serial numbers were chiseled off the frames. According to the report, they found residue of crystal meth in the gas tanks. It isn't much but it's interesting that the casino video-tapes show three John Doe's wearing biker gear.*" [Kessler]*

"*That's it, Kessler?*" [George]*

"*Just about. The theory is that the bikes could have been dumped and burned after the John Does ditched their limo.*" [Kessler]*

"*It's thirty miles from where they burned those bikes to the casino, as the crow flies. You've got three men in biker gear plus the driver. That's four. What happened to the other two, Kessler? Did they hitch a ride? It doesn't add.*" [George]*

"*Sounds more like a drug deal that went wrong and someone got burned. Manure happens. As long as it is on the Rez, I couldn't care less.*" [Randall]*

"*I take your point, but I have a job to do. If they were dealing meth, they probably were using a local supplier. I was hoping you might have some ideas.*" [Kessler]*

"*Well, excuse me, Kessler, but meth labs stink. Camp Verde and Cottonwood are burgs. Anyone cooks a batch here, we get a dozen calls. In the county, they can cook it in a cave, in a trailer, in the back of a van, or they bring the shit in from Mexico. You think it all comes from here?*" [Randall]*

"*It's not Mexican. It's a different grade and some of the ingredients are new. If it is coming from here they need supplies. Maybe someone has noticed an oddball making unusual purchases.*" [Kessler]*

"Shit! Like have we seen anyone carting cow manure, or hauling rubber tires and lead batteries from the junkyard? Or buying cases of alcohol and brake fluid at Wal-Mart or a couple of hundred pounds of rock salt from the feed store? [Randall]

"Look, I'm just on a fishing expedition, boys. Like I said, I'm just doing my job." [Kessler]

"Sounds like you don't think that we're doing ours." [Randall]

"You call what we do a job, Randall? Hell, I'd work for free if I didn't need the money." [George]

"What money? Are you drawing a paycheck in Jerome? What you do ought to be against the law. You should pay the Council." [Randall]

"Who says I don't?" [George]

"Okay, boys. I get the message. Thanks for your cooperation. It's been a pleasure. I need to get on the road. You coming, Kincaid? [Kessler]

"No, not just yet. I'll stick around here for awhile. Give the Sheriff my regards." [Kincaid]

"Yeah, Kessler, say hello to Bucky for us.' [George]
Laughter. *Note: Kessler apparently forgot or conveniently left his briefcase under the table.

"Well, boys, you did a good job on Kessler. You laid it on with a trowel. Now he'll work on O'Neil. Bucky will jump at the chance to get some cheap publicity. He's running for Sheriff again. He won't share any glory with the Feds, so Kessler won't stick around long. If you have any leads about the labs, pass them on to Bucky; let him do the dirty work. We don't need the gumballs. In fact, they are drawing the Feds like flies. The FBI is here and the DEA will be next. The sooner the 'cooks' are run out of here the better." [Kincaid]

"We've got customers to feed. They pay the freight, don't they?" [George]

"Send the business over to Havasu. We need to chill for the next month or so. We've got our own product. It's reliable and we have to protect the source and our own asses. And we've got

to find that Indian, Jay Cook, before someone else does."
[Kincaid]

"Hell, maybe he went back to the Black Hills, the old reservation. He's got people there." [Randall]

"So check it out." [Kincaid]

"Kincaid, we got towns to run. Pioneer Days start next week. We don't have any men to waste." [Farley]

"You've got manpower, Kincaid. Why don't you use Hubbard?" [Randall]

"Hubbard is a pain-in-the-ass and he's straight. He's pushing me as it is to bring K-9 sniffers here to do drug searches. I don't want him looking for Cook." [Kincaid]

"He won't find the Indian if he doesn't want to be found" [Randall]

"He won't find drugs even with sniffer dogs. Everything is wrapped in bentonite and buried under a ton of cement before it's shipped." [Farley]

"It's not the drugs I'm worried about. It's Jay Cook. He knows too much and if he talks to the wrong people, we're in trouble. That means all of us." [Kincaid]

"You know, Kincaid, it looks to me like you're between a rock and hard place. You're looking for a guy who's got 100,000 square miles to hide in and you've got no manpower. So what are we supposed to do?" [Randall]

"Keep an eye on Sam Cook and his granddaughter. You boys can check them out in town and if Bucky finds him, we've got help in the dispatcher's office." [Kincaid]

"Too many chiefs, boss, to look for one Indian, and O'Neil's not stupid." [Farley]

"Yeah, well, I'm not looking for anybody. This isn't my problem. I want no part of it." [Randall]

"You're part of it, Randall, the before and after part. If anything goes wrong, we all go down together." [Farley]

"Whoa, boys! No one's going down. There're a lot of people involved that can't afford to take chances and let things get out of hand. Anyway, we're in too deep, all of us. I need to

*know if I can count on you, Randall. I have enough to worry
about at my end. So where are you in this?"* [Kincaid]

"What choice do I have? [Randall]

"Zero. You knew that from the get-go." [Kincaid]

*"Okay, you want me to cut the crap? Here's where I'm
coming from. I don't know a thing and I never did know anything
and I don't want to know anything. You guys do what you have to.
As far as I'm concerned, we've never seen each other except for
an occasional cup of coffee."* [Randall]

*"Good thinking, Paul. We stick together like my Daddy
said and this too will pass."* [George]

"When this is over, I plan on retiring." [Randall]

"It'll be over when the fat lady sings." [Kincaid]

"When's that going to be?" [Randall]

"I'll let you know." [Kincaid]

*"Hell, why worry, Paul? When it's over in Cottonwood,
you can have my job here in Jerome. The pay ain't much, but you
don't have to do anything."* [George]

"Up yours!" [Randall] Laughter.

*"Not to change the subject, but who's that Indian buck with
the good looking broad?"* [Kincaid]

*"He's the artist the tribe hired to do a sculpture. His name
is Matt Dillon."* [Farley]

"He doesn't look like an artist, Tom." [Randall]

"What are artists supposed to look like?" [George]

"Well, you know, kind of fagotty." [Randall]

*"Well, that fagot dragged Carbahol off his horse and
knocked him on his ass. I read Hubbard's report. Dillon handled
himself like a professional. He immobilized him, but he didn't
break any bones."* [Farley]

*"Too bad. That woman is Renee Royer, a reporter for The
Village Voice. I've seen her bring people here before, but I'd be
glad to check her out."* [George]

*Note: Kincaid used his cell phone; I couldn't catch it.

*"Who's that blonde kid on the bike? He's been eyeballing
us."* [Kincaid]

"Jesus! You're making me nervous. He's a customer, probably waiting for me. [George]

"So what does he buy" [Kincaid]

"Two K's a week. Runs it through his biker buddies." [George]

"Where do they distribute it?" [Kincaid]

"Anywhere but here. They buy it here and move it out to Salt Lake, Reno, Portland, even South Dakota, so they tell me. They don't mess with California or Vegas; the bikers say the street gangs play too rough." [George]

"How long have you been doing business with them?" [Kincaid]

"A year, some for two years. Jesus, you're a suspicious bastard, Kincaid." [George]

"Have to be. Don't take anything for granted. Feds come in all shapes and sizes." Kincaid answered his cell phone: He must be on quick time.

"My sources tell me that Royer is okay and so is Dillon. Come on, Farley, walk me to my car." [Kincaid]

*Note: Looks like the party's over. Kessler went first, then Kincaid and Farley. George just looked under the table and smiled at Randall and now here we go…here's Kessler. I knew that was a surveillance case. We're in luck; he's opening it. Whoops, he screwed in an ear plug. Don't think we're going to get anything. Wrong. Here we go.

"That's it boys, Kincaid's goose is cooked." [Kessler]

"Right along with our gooses, Kessler." [Randall]

"Relax. You're state witnesses. We made a deal." [Kessler]

"So, what do we do now?" [George]

"Do what you always do. Just sit tight. We might not even need this stuff or your testimony. I may be able to use Kincaid to pry the lid off this can of worms. If it works, you might even be heroes." [Kessler]

"I don't want to be a dead hero, hoss." [George]

"No worries. You've got my word." [Kessler]

*Note: Hang on. Kessler exited stage left. The Marshals are standing. They've turned away, but I think I can amplify.

"Seems like we've got everybody's word, Paul." [George]

"I wouldn't trust either of those bastards as far as I could throw them. Witness protection sucks." [Randall]

"It beats being dead or in prison. We could have gotten a lot of time." [George]

"It still sucks." [Randall]

"Life sucks, Paul." [George] *Final note: That's it.

Query -- *Do you want me to follow up on Kincaid, Jay Cook, and Farley? Also the biker referent spoke to Matt and me on our way out of Jerome. He is a possible lead.*

Query – *Matt Dillon: Matt is looking for Jay Cook. Carbahol, the Marshals, and Kincaid have made him. I have the feeling that Kincaid made me, too. In my opinion, Dillon won't be helpful. He's a loner, a loose cannon, and in his own words, "a gunslinger." He's a sitting duck and I don't want to be sitting with him. I recommend that you have the Arizona people pull him out immediately.*

Renee hit the send button. She stared at the ceiling for a few minutes and began writing. Thirty minutes later she finished the article and printed it. She went over to Joe Fiddles' desk and handed him the copy. Joe scanned the article.

"Front page, Joe?"

"I'd say so. You've got the touch, Renee. I'll format it."

"I already have. I back-paged your back packers' bonanza article. That's where it belongs."

"I knew that. So, is Matt Dillon chocolate or vanilla?"

"Hmmm. I'd say strawberry."

"Then you must like him. You love strawberries."

"We often crave what we are allergic to, Joe. Let me help you with the layouts." Renee turned on the table scanners. They bent their heads over the desks for the next hour.

"It's a wrap, Renee," Joe announced. "I'm going over to the Jaycee's office. Lock up for me, will you?"

"Sure. I'll catch up with my mail and then I'm out of here, too." Renee opened her computer and read an e-mail message:

"We will follow up on Kincaid, but we're staying out of the Kessler sting except to cover our asses. Same thing goes for the DEA. Your material will be forwarded to them later rather than sooner. We do work for the same Justice Department, don't we? Farley and Kincaid are off your radar screen. Keep your antennae tuned for anything you can find on Cook. Stick close to Dillon; let him take the lead. Don't underestimate him. According to his boss, he's one savvy hombre who operates on the theory that moving targets are hard to hit. If he's a gunslinger, he's the Lone Ranger. His boss is certain Dillon will find Jay Cook. He says he is motivated. EOM. It just goes to show you, Renee, I'm gettin' a handle on this Western lingo."

Renee typed a reply: *"I guess that makes me Tonto, which is better than being Jane. You're becoming a real pain in the saddle, ak."* and closed the computer.

CHAPTER SEVEN

Matt unloaded his supplies and carried them inside, creating a small Matterhorn in front of the fireplace. "Dem bones, dem bones, dem dry bones," He half-sang and half-muttered as he crammed canned goods into the single cupboard. "De head bone is connected to de neck bone," as he stacked the kitchen wares on the open shelf by the window. "De knives, de forks, go into de drawers and de cook stove goes on de counter and de lanterns go onto de table and de propane tank go under de sink and de clothes go into de closet where dey gonna hang around." He crawled up the ladder. "De sleeping bag and de pillow are going into de loft where I'm going to lay down and listen to de word of de Lord."

He sprawled across the sleeping bag and surveyed the room below. Two Mexican cane-and-pigskin leather chairs were tucked neatly under a matching table. A sofa with wire-stuffed cushions and wooden arms, Arizona porch furniture circa 1940, rested in front of the adobe fireplace with a half-moon-shaped tiled ledge providing extra seating. A blackened bucket held tongs, a poker and a shovel. Suspended from the ceiling by a thin chain on pulleys, a wagon wheel with candles and tin holders provided light. A Two Grey Hills rug lay near the fireplace and pair of silvered Mexican sconces and a mirror completed the room's decor.

"Tidy, very tidy. Well, almost." Matt stared at the battered ice chest which blocked the doorway. "Forgot the ice. So who's perfect?" Outside the window, a squirrel chucked loudly. He glimpsed a bushy tail as the squirrel leaped from a cottonwood tree onto the roof. He rolled onto his back and listened as a pair of squirrels chased each other across the roof. A bumble bee buzzed in and out of the door. Matt yawned and fell asleep, listening to the gurgling murmurs of the river.

The shrill cry of a jay broke his dreams. Sweat coated his arms and his back felt slightly damp. Outside, the Verde sparkled and glimmered in the late afternoon sun. A rainbow trout arced out of the water and landed with a splash.

"The fish are up." He crawled out of the loft, located the six pack and fishing gear, and followed a worn path that ended in a hollow surrounded by small boulders. A rough bench between two sycamore trees overlooked the shallow riffles and a sand bar. Matt spotted several trout at the head of the riffles, so he set his fishing gear on the bench and slid the beer into a pool of cold water. He stripped off the plastic blister that surrounded his fly rod and reel as he scanned the river.

After quickly assembling the rig, he opened the carton of mealy worms, selected a fat one, and worked it onto the hook. He pulled off a blossom from a wild buttercup and added it to the mealy worms. "The Midas touch. Eat your heart out, Isaac." Edging onto the sand bar, Matt made a couple of practice casts, and then waded into the river where a shallow ripple flowed noisily over smooth stones. He checked his footing, stripped some line, made a short cast, and flicked his wrist. The yellow butter cup landed neatly below a ledge upstream. The line drifted towards a pool above the riffles as he worked the line.

Suddenly, he had a strike. He tugged the line lightly and rapidly reeled in a trout that broke water and flapped wildly as he coaxed it through the riffles. Pulling a stringer from his pocket, he uncoiled it, and ran it through the gills. He tapped the metal stake into the sand bar and laid the trout in an eddy next to the bar. "Ten inches. That's street legal."

Standing in the shallow water, he stood rooted, staring into the swirl where the sunlight penetrated the shadows beneath the etched cliff where the river had cut a deep blue pool. The river sounds merged into subtler murmurs. A catbird called and a car rumbled over a distant wooden bridge. He felt the pebbles sucking away beneath his feet as he bent forward slightly from the waist, holding the rod where it mated with the reel in his right hand. His left hand tested the tense line which ran from the rod's tip into the murmuring green water. He slowly raised, then lowered the tip moving his left arm away from his body in a long careful arc, releasing it when his arm was straight out from his side. He leaned forward, shoulders hunched, head thrust out on his long powerful neck. His neck easing, his shoulders flexing, he began rapidly reeling in. Suddenly with a terrific lurch, his rod tip dipped nearly into the water and line screamed from the reel; Matt whirled, lifting the rod high just as the line collapsed and the rod lost its tortured bow, quivering as it straightened. He crouched, frozen and alert, and whispered, "Dammit!" over the hissing ripples. Moving back to the bank, he sat down on a warm rock, tied another mealy worm and buttercup to his line, and waded back into the stream.

In twenty minutes, three more trout were added to the stringer and he set four smaller fish free. Matt broke down the rod and reel as he sipped his can of slightly cooled beer. "Twenty minutes and I've got dinner. I'm going to like this place. Better get a license." He heard a tractor in the distance, but there wasn't a soul in sight. A pair of cliff swallows flitted down the river. When a raven landed in the sycamore and eyed the trout, He tossed a pebble in its direction. The raven thought things over and flapped away.

"Time for a swim." Matt peeled off his clothes, piled them in a heap on the sand bar. He waded in cautiously until the water reached his knees and then he pushed out into the main channel. His breath went out in a whish as the current tugged him down stream. Kicking hard and stroking even harder, he made his way to the far bank. He sat down on the warm sand, pulled his legs up under his chin, dropped his head onto his knees, and prayed that the warm sun would stop his shivers.

Suddenly a melodic voice, somewhere between an alto and soprano, trilled across the water. "One day I went down swimmin' where there were no women, down by the deep blue sea. Seeing no one there, I hung my underwear on a willow tree." Matt stared at the opposite bank. Something moved; someone was watching. A cowboy dressed in levis? No, a red-haired cowgirl stood beside his pile of clothing. "But someone saw me there and stole my underwear and left me with a smile." The lilting voice faded away.

Paloma picked up Matt's shirt, looked at it thoughtfully, grinned, and dangled it provocatively over the water. "Nice shirt. You want it?"

"Don't be cute, Paloma."

"And your pants." Paloma held them up. "Better come get them," she teased.

"Not on your life."

"You can run, Matt, but you can't hide. I've got eyes."

"I bet you do."

"What's for supper? Trout?"

Matt raised his head. "I caught 'em; you cook them."

"I caught you. It sounds like a fair trade to me." Paloma dropped the shirt and pants on the sandbar. "Come over around sundown." She picked up the stringer of trout. "You're safe. I won't peek," she shouted and disappeared behind a cottonwood tree.

After waiting five minutes, Matt jumped into the Verde, swam to the sand bar, gathered his clothes, collected his fishing gear and stomped back to the adobe.

Matt and Paloma rested their feet on the edge of the fire ring, letting the heat from the glowing coals warm their toes. Flickering light from the lingering flame danced around the patio and off the branches overhead, sealing them in from the veil of darkness. The sun had long since dropped behind the Black Mesa. A cool breeze shuttled down the Verde, causing the leaves to rustle overhead. An owl hooted behind them, followed by an answering hoot from across the river. He sipped the buttery chardonnay. "What a beautiful night. Is it always like this?" he asked.

Paloma refilled his glass and added some to her own. "Always, if you like night sounds, stars and full moons. If you like to listen to your heart beat and let your thoughts drift into the night, it's a good place to be. It gets lonely sometimes, but never boring. My birds and animals keep me busy."

Matt felt something tugging at his pant legs. An Aussie pup who had wandered away from his sleeping brothers and sisters was gnawing the bottom of his levis. Matt began stroking the puppy, which sighed contentedly and rolled onto his back, arching his paws upward, begging for more.

"He likes you."

"How can you tell?"

"When I hold him, he just squirms and wiggles until I have to set him down."

"What's his name?"

"Digger. I used to call him Beau before he dug up my flower plants and those vines along the patio wall. He's all energy. Excuse me, Matt, I need to check the cages and feed the bats and owls; they're night feeders. I'll be right back."

"I'll go with you."

"No, stay put. Keep Digger company."

Matt watched Paloma walk down the path. In a few minutes, a light went on in the infirmary and he turned back to the fire, absentmindedly stroking the puppy. She soon returned and sat down. "You keep long hours," he said.

"It goes with the territory. Actually, I get a lot of support from the birder organizations, mostly volunteers. They feed them, nurse them, and clean the cages. Most days, I'm on the telephone answering distress calls and giving advice. I lead day trips and give talks to schools and civic groups. Sort of a Bird-and-Pony show, but the kids are fun. They love birds. But I'm really tied down. I can't get away for more than a day or two."

"Is that your biggest problem?"

"My biggest problem is with cattlemen. Some believe the only good animal is a dead one. They shoot coyotes and hawks. And then the rodent population explodes so they put out poison and the birds eat the carcasses and round and round it goes. The cow piles pollute the steams. The river is in danger. Phoenix wants the Verde water, which means more dams, and the developers want the land and water. If they get their way, we could lose the habitat for over 200 species of birds. It's an uphill battle, but we're slowly

95

making headway. The bald eagle is coming back. We have 18 pairs on the Middle Verde this season. They feed on the fish, raise their young, and migrate north."

"That trout we had tonight, did we steal someone's dinner?"

"I watched you fishing. You could be classified as a menace." Paloma laughed. "Fortunately, we have a hatchery at Page Springs. But a dam would end that. Warm sluggish water supports sucker fish and gunk, and the ecosystem goes bust. Not just the game fish, everything changes. Sorry, I'm off and running, again."

"How did you get involved in the first place?"

"You mean, how did a poor little city girl end up on a feather ranch?"

"No, seriously."

"Well, seriously, I grew up in Columbus, Ohio, the biggest backwoods city in America."

"Like Cottonwood?"

"Hmm, yeah, but bigger. I had a crush on my high school teacher. He had a passion for ornithology, so I naturally boned up on birds. I even joined the birdwatchers' club. I actually enjoyed the field trips."

"Sounds promising."

"Right. Well, nothing happened, not really. The guy just didn't seem interested and I sort of got aggressive."

"And?"

"Don't laugh, but uh, he was gay! He was a wonderful, kind person. He helped me get a free ride to OSU. But I wasn't a serious student. I applied for the veterinary college. Got turned down. I switched to the college of nursing. Held my own in anatomy, but it wasn't for me. Summers I worked at the Columbus Zoo, so I switched to zoology. They put me in charge of aviaries and then I just wanted something else. My parents divorced and I came here."

"And?"

"And I absolutely love it here. I'll never leave. Look at the stars. It's paradise." Matt looked skyward. The summer triangle -- Deneb, Vega, and Altair -- were almost directly overhead. "You can't see stars like this in Columbus. Look! The Pleiades, the Seven Sisters, and the Big Dipper, or do you call it the Big Bear?"

"My mother told me once that her people knew it as the Revolving Male and the Pleiades was known as the Seven Dancers and the Little Dipper, heh, oh, that was the Revolting Female. I mean the Revolving Female."

"Sounds like something a man would say. I guess we can be revolting."

"Altair," Matt pointed "is the brightest in Aguilar, the eagle constellation. He carried Zeus' thunderbolts. My mother's people thought he caught arrows in his claws. Sagittarius, the Archer, was the hunter in some tribal legends. Totally different cultures, but sometimes their myths parallel each other."

"You're really into astronomy, Matt."

"Not really, but I've spent a lot of nights camping out in my van thinking about meaning and purpose, like everyone else. That's what artists do or try to do, Paloma. You look for inspiration everywhere – the stars, myths, legends. Whatever inspires, whatever pushes your creative button. There is an Indian legend that the Creator set the stars into little patterns in the sky and all their knowledge and wisdom for us mortals to share. But coyote, the trickster, scattered the stars, and created chaos and mischief. We've been on our own ever since, trying to make sense where there is no sense."

"You're a poet, Matt. A dreamer. That's good. Most people don't even look at the stars."

"How can they? The stars are mostly washed out by light pollution. And, besides most people have their hands full just trying to survive."

"Maybe we're the lucky ones. We get a chance to do more than survive. If I had known about the eagle legend, I would have called Igor, Aguilar. Which reminds me, we're going to release him tomorrow. Would you like to help?"

"When?"

"We'll get started at daybreak. We'll move his cage down to the riverbank. Let him settle down, see how he likes it. Bob York is bringing kayaks and J.R. Taylor is coming over to help. The cage is a load."

"Sure. I'd be glad to help. I'll be there. Why do you need a kayak?"

"I'm hoping Igor will head down stream. That's where JR found him. Anyway, I want to follow him in case he's not up to it. We might have to retrieve him."

"That could be interesting."

"If he grounds on the river, we'll be all right. But if he goes to Eagle Rock, it could be a hassle. Jay Cook had a scare up there last year."

"What happened?"

"Jay was collecting eagle feathers for ceremonial purposes, asserting his rights as a Native American, at least that's what he claimed. The female ran him off. She dove for his head and Jay jumped into the river. And the female kept after him. She was defending her nest. Luckily, Bob and I were there. We saw the whole thing. It was a real show." Paloma laughed and slapped her leg. "Every time Jay raised his head out of the water, she made a pass at him. Jay had to duck. We had a whole party with us, Audubon people. We dragged him out onto the shoals on the other side. Boy, did they give him hell! But Jay didn't back down. I felt sorry for him and told him if wanted eagle feathers to come see me. About a week later, he showed up and I told him about the Portland group. They have preserved eagle specimens. Most Native Americans aren't aware of it, but the group will give them feathers, talons, beaks, a whole bird, whatever they want. Jay couldn't believe it. I told him you don't need to risk your life or disturb their nests. Send off for an eagle. I told him an adult eagle has seven thousand feathers. I asked if that would be enough."

"Knowing Jay, he'd want two."

"Jay asked a lot of questions about birding, falconry, and pollution in the river. He seemed really concerned. He asked

98

about the dead birds. I gave him my whole pitch. He thanked me and left. A few weeks later, he showed up with a present. Don't move. Digger is asleep." Paloma got up quietly and went into the cottage.

She returned a few minutes later and handed Matt a bracelet. He held it close to the fire: two cast silver eagles with outstretched talons surrounded by silver and abalone inlays. "It's beautiful. Jay gave it to you?"

"Yep. All he said was, 'This is for you. You're no White Dove, you're an Eagle Lady.'"

"Have you seen him since then?"

"A couple of months ago, Jay and JR Taylor brought Igor here. They found him on the flats just beyond the Big Bend."

"I'd like to meet Jay."

"I heard he left town. Someone said he went to Washington and didn't come back. You could ask Jen, his sister. I'm not sure where they live, but I see her at the flea market from time to time. I could ask around."

"No need to, Paloma. I was just curious."

Paloma touched Matt's arm. "It's been an extraordinary night, but now I have to go in." She lifted her glass.

Matt touched the rim of her glass with his. "It's was an extraordinary afternoon and a very special evening."

"Mi Casa is su Casa. Am I forgiven?"

He laughed, "You're forgiven. Next time, I'll wear a swimming suit."

"Wait until July and I'll join you. The water's warmer."

"And you'll be wearing a suit?"

"Depends on the weather. If it's really warm and dark enough, I might chance it. July is a ways off yet," Paloma sighed, "and tomorrow comes early. Are you coming with us?"

"Are you kidding? I want to see Igor fly."

"Take my flashlight and take Digger with you. I think he's made a friend."

"Are you sure?"

"He needs socializing. You both do. Don't worry. He's paper trained."

"Am I supposed to learn something from Digger?

"Good night, Matt. See you in the morning."

Matt waited until Paloma closed the door. He cradled the puppy carefully in his arms as he beamed the flashlight ahead to go back to the studio. When they accidentally bumped up against the aviary and Igor hissed and flapped his wings, Digger tried to leap out of his arms, but Matt was able to hold onto him.

"We're safe, Digs." After putting the puppy on the couch, he found the lantern, pumped up the pressure, struck a match and opened the valve. The silent hiss and pop as the mantles caught the flame startled the puppy. When Matt dimmed the lantern, the pup yawned and put his head between his paws. He watched sleepily as Matt spread a few sheets of *The Village Voice* in front of the door. "Do the classifieds work for you?" Digger barely managed a wiggle with the stump of his tail and fell asleep.

Matt climbed the ladder to the loft, undressed and crawled into his sleeping bag. A heavy gust of wind blew down the river, followed by a flash of lightning and a clap of thunder. Branches of a cottonwood scraped the roof top and an owl screeched near the window. When a sound like a cat being strangled echoed eerily from the hill behind the studio, Digger yelped and growled. Matt heard a thud and then water drizzling on paper. Digger whined and sniffed the bottom of the ladder. Sighing, Matt got up, and backed down the ladder. The puppy squirmed as he scooped him up in one hand, and pushed Digger into the loft.

When Matt crawled into the sleeping bag, Digger found his free arm and snuggled in beside him. A drenching rain storm swept down from the mesas. "This has been an extraordinary day, wouldn't you say, Digger?" There was no confirmation; Digger was fast asleep. The wind whining under the eaves and the warmth of the snuggling puppy lulled Matt back to sleep.

CHAPTER EIGHT

A warm, soft tongue, gently lapping his ear and neck, woke Matt. He opened his eyes just as Digger crawled onto his chest and began gleefully licking his face. Matt lifted the puppy up over his head. "Is it breakfast time? Time for me to get up, is that it? Or do you have to go potty? Give us a kiss."

Matt slid down the ladder. Digger tottered on the edge of the loft and then leaped. Matt caught him and put the puppy on the newspaper. "I'm going to have to teach you to climb. Do your thing." Matt opened a can of tuna, scraped it onto a paper plate, and set it on the floor with a flourish. "The breakfast of champions!"

The pup sniffed the tuna and began to wolf it down. "Dig in Digger." Matt stepped outside. The morning star, encircled by a sliver of moon, hung over the Black Mesa. Birds hopped into the open and shook off the clinging rain drops as Matt stepped into the open shower. He braced himself, turned the tap and clamped his eyes shut. The shower sputtered and gurgled and Matt howled as a sheet of icy water splattered his face and upper body. A watching coyote yelped and slinked up the hill. Matt adjusted the shower head from a drizzle into a needle spray.

"Holy, holy, holy. Sweet Mother, that's enough." Matt turned off the tap, noticed another handle on the side, and twisted it. Instantly, warm water, not tepid, but warm enough flowed. "Solar. Why didn't I think of that sooner?" He opened his shaving kit, unwrapped a bar of soap from the Pair-a-Dice Hotel and lathered his face, arms, and legs. "Shaving cream is for sissies," he said into the mirror on the shower wall. After shaving, he toweled off in a patch of sunlight that was inching across the patio. The smell of strong coffee, mingled with the aroma of biscuits and bacon, filled the morning air.

"Come on paint, let's get where we ain't." Matt dressed quickly, ran his fingers through his hair, pulled on his ball cap, picked up the puppy papers, and crammed them into a trash bag. "Let's go. I'll race you!" Digger nipped at his heels as they ran down the path to Paloma's yard.

A pink Jeep with a pink-and-white striped surrey top was parked near the river's edge. Behind the jeep, a carry-all trailer held a rack of kayaks. A large pinto horse that was browsing under a cottonwood tree, lifted its head and whinnied as Matt crossed the yard. "Here comes the sleepy head, boys," Paloma said loudly.

Matt grinned sheepishly. "I thought I was early."

"Early here is when there's not enough light to see your shadow. I'm J.R. Taylor. Everybody calls me JR. Pleased to meet you, Matt. This is Bob York."

Bob, an angular sunburned freckled faced man with curly auburn hair tied into a que, didn't get up. He wiped his hand on a bright yellow vest. "Sorry about that," he grinned and offered his hand.

"Bob's afraid he'll miss a bite," JR said.

"You've got that right, JR," Bob forked another load into his mouth.

"Come and get it, Matt, before these boys have seconds." Paloma handed him a tin plate. "Eggs, bacon, potatoes, sausage, and biscuits. Help yourself."

Matt filled his plate while Paloma poured him a cup of coffee. "Careful, it's hot," she warned.

Matt sat down beside Bob, who didn't look up. He was too busy wolfing down his breakfast. Paloma joined them. "Don't mind me. Dig in boys."

"Who's minding?" Bob said without slowing down.

Matt flinched as he lips touched the cup's rim, but managed a swallow. "God, that's the best cup of coffee I ever had."

"The coffee is great, but God, can you cook, Paloma! What's in these biscuits?" Bob asked.

"Apricot marmalade. You ready for more?"

"Just a couple."

"Can't let these go to waste, boys." Paloma piled more biscuits onto Matt's and Bob's plates. "They must not feed you boys at home."

"Home? Whose got a home, JR?" York said. "I live in a tent. That's my office." He pointed at a pink cell phone that was lying at the end of the table. "It floats. That way the kayakers can send out for a pizza." He laughed.

"Sun's up. You boys carry down Igor's cage and I'll put this stuff away," Paloma ordered.

"We moved Igor while you were fixing breakfast. Thought it might work better if we gave him some time to think things over," JR said.

"Then finish your coffee." The men refilled their cups and walked down to the river. The sweet sour odor of guana emanated from the cage. Igor was hopping back and forth, stretching his wings.

"He acts like he knows what's coming," JR said.

"He just might. Do you think he'll fly?" Bob asked.

"He'd better. Paloma's heart will break if he doesn't. You hear that Igor? You better make it." JR tapped the cage with his fist.

Paloma joined them. "Let's do it," she said. JR opened the cage door and stepped behind the cage. Igor eyed the opening.

"Should I prod him, Paloma?"

"Better wait. Let him think it over," she said.

"Hold up, JR, let me set up the camcorder," Bob said and ran back to the jeep.

Digger and Jolly Roger climbed up onto the boulders. Jolly growled when Digger tried to join him. "Jolly Roger sure is a bold puppy," Paloma said.

"Same initials as mine and just as ornery," JR said.

"I've got two kayaks in the water. Are you going, JR?" Bob interrupted.

"I'd rather ride a greased bronco bareback than get into one of those pink coffins."

"How about you, Matt, ever do any river running?" Bob asked.

"Some. The Upper Rio Grande, above Portales and a couple of rivers in Oregon. It's been awhile, though."

"Oh, hell, you'll be fine. The Verde doesn't offer much in the way of white water until you get to Beasley Flats. March and April are the best months." York sounded disappointed.

"Jolly Roger, get back down here," Paloma said. The puppy was crawling out on a ledge. He ignored her, looked over the edge, lost his balance, fell into a back eddy of water and started yelping. Digger leaped off the ledge, grabbed Jolly Rogers in the rear, and tugged him out of the water. Paloma stepped into the eddy and picked up both pups and handed Jolly Roger to Matt. "Did you see Digger go after him? He's only eight weeks old, my hero." She gave Digger a hug.

"Hell, I could've done that," JR said. "It's only four inches deep."

"Ki, ki, ki, kaa, kaa," Igor cried. The eagle sprang out of the cage, unfurled his wings, and launched himself off the bank. Igor dipped down over the river, and then climbed upward.

"He's flying! He's flying!" Paloma's wide-brimmed straw hat fell off; tears streamed down her cheeks. "My, God! Look at him!"

Igor rose abruptly, caught an updraft and circled effortlessly overhead, his seven-foot wing span casting an enormous shadow. Igor tilted his snow-white head. "Keeeeerrrrr," he screamed as he flew over them.

"He's heading for Eagle Rock," Paloma wiped her cheeks. "Did you get it, Bob?"

York was motionless; the camcorder hung uselessly by his side. "I missed it. Sorry, Paloma."

"It doesn't matter. We saw him, didn't we?"

"We saw him fly, Paloma. You did it!" JR said.

"I told you he would fly south. We better hurry. He might not make it."

"Keep your shirt on, Paloma. He'll make it. No worries," Bob said as he handed Matt a wet suit. "Try these on. They're the biggest I've got. They should work."

"Thanks. I'll be right back." Matt went back to the adobe, struggled into the wet suit, pulled on a pair of scuffs, and trotted back to the river bank.

"They fit?" Bob asked.

"A bit snug, but they'll do."

"Inflatable boats are best for here, Matt. You might catch a level three or a level five rapid and maybe some debris. No real problems. I don't think you'll have to portage through the shoals. Stay away from the undercut on the Big Bend."

"We'll be fine, Bob," Paloma said.

"I'll pick you up at Beasley Flats, okay?" JR offered.

"Okay. JR, thanks. See you tonight?" Paloma asked.

"I'll be there."

Paloma settled herself into her kayak as it drifted downstream. She waved at York and JR and began paddling with a will. They picked up the pace as they rounded the bend. JR stood up in his stirrups and waved, while York's pink jeep was already crossing the wooden bridge.

Neither of them spoke as they drifted idly past some up-scale homes, agricultural fields, and green fenced pastures bordered by willow, cottonwood, and sycamore trees. A blue heron rose up from a gravel bar and flapped downstream. The Verde turned east and the sun warmed them as they drifted closer to the Black Hills. Swallows darted in and out of nests carved in the river bank. Thrashers, flycatchers, and yellow warblers flitted among the sycamores. Red-winged blackbirds mocked them when they entered a marshy area choked with reeds. A peregrine falcon hovered over a clump of grass, waiting for its prey.

"Two hundred species of birds inhabit or migrate through the Verde, Matt. That's why we have to save it. From Sullivan's Fork to Horseshoe Dam, it's all endangered. The river has to flow freely. More housing and dams will crash the whole ecosystem. You put in a dam, and the water temperature rises, the fish can't spawn, the river silts up, and pollutants like lead, arsenic and phosphates increase. A dam strangles a river."

"I thought this area was a scenic preserve."

"Only the middle Verde. The upstream, downstream, and Cottonwood areas aren't protected. If the developers win, the Verde will become an Obsenic Preserve. Bad joke," Paloma laughed. "Come with us to the meeting tonight. Everyone's invited. It will be the typical obfuscating free-for-all as JR says. Everyone wants a piece of the Verde. I'll make my usual 'Conservation through Education' pitch, but no one will listen." The river quickened as they drifted out of the marshy area.

"Come on, Matt, white water ahead. I'll race you!" Paloma dug in with her paddle and shot ahead. Cold water ran down Matt's arms as he straightened the kayak. He was gaining on Paloma just as she disappeared over a drop, screaming at the top of her lungs. He yelled and stroked hard as the kayak lifted and then slithered over the edge. He straightened and guided the kayak through a narrow trough that widened into "duck pond," a deep pool of calmer water.

"That was it?" Matt asked, sounding a little disappointed.

"You didn't expect the Niagara Falls did you?" She splashed him with her paddle and pulled away before he could retaliate. They turned northeast, paddled around a wide bend and turned back to the south, alternately paddling and drifting around a series of bends. When a blue heron took off and flapped its way southward, Paloma yelled, "He's staying ahead of us. Blue herons are good luck."

Towering 200 feet above them, a chimney shaped rock had split apart from the mesa. "That's Eagle Rock," Paloma said and drove her kayak through a riffle and nudged it onto a gravel bar. "Let's take a break." He brought his kayak alongside Paloma's. "We're lucky. The river's really up today. No portaging. It's probably good all the way to Beasley Flats."

"How far is it?"

106

"Another thirty minutes or so. Take a look." She handed Matt the binoculars.

He scanned the rock. "Where?"

"Up there on your left."

He shifted his gaze to a huge pile of sticks that looked like it had been glued to the side of the cliff. A young bird sat precariously on the edge, lifting its wings to cool itself. Circling overhead, the mother bird glided to the nest, braking at the last moment, and landed behind the fledgling.

"This is a super riffle, Matt. The eagles depend on it for fish. No riffle, no spawning, no fish, no eagles." Paloma pointed skyward. "There's Igor."

"Where?"

"Way up to the right of the pinnacle."

He shifted the binoculars and saw a large eagle circling above. "How can you tell it's him?"

"I painted his talons with purple nail polish."

"You what?"

"You know, purple nail polish." Paloma giggled.

"His wife must like that."

"She's probably more ticked off that he hasn't been around to help feed the chick." Igor dropped down below the rim and soared down the riffle, his purple talons barely brushing the riffle as he snagged a fish. He flapped his wings, and worked his way skyward, and then glided to the perch. After ripping a piece of fish and swallowing a large chunk, he eyed the chick as it scrambled towards the catch. Then he turned and stared disdainfully down at Matt and Paloma.

"Look at him, Matt. He's majestic. He looks like an emperor on his throne. I'm so happy. I think I'm going to cry. Don't laugh."

"I won't laugh. You're riding a wave. Go ahead and cry."

She rested her head on Matt's shoulder. Neither moved until Igor lifted himself up, spread his wings and launched himself off the perch. Igor caught a thermal and slowly spiraled higher and higher where he was joined by his mate. They watched as the sun inched its way overhead and Matt finally stirred.

"I don't know about you, but I'm beginning to cook in this suit." He waded into the river, opened the zipper down to his waist and lowered himself until the water touched his chin. "Yow!" he bellowed.

Paloma followed him into the water, modestly turned her back, unzipped her top, ducked under water and came up beside him. "It's not that bad, Matt."

"Sure, if you are an Eskimo." They raced across to the far bank and did a slow crawl back. Paloma put on her life jacket, got into the kayak and pushed off into deeper water. Matt's kayak flipped over as he tried to get in.

"You are something, Matt." Her laughter echoed across the river. A magpie joined in with a raucous caw.

"They don't call me the king of the rafters for nothing." Matt straddled the kayak, slid his legs inboard and picked up his paddle. Just beyond the riffle, a small stream coursed over some rocks, creating a small waterfall before it entered the Verde. "It's beautiful," Matt said.

"Indian Creek. It dries up in the summer until the monsoons come. Stinking Springs, an old Anasazi site, is further up the canyon. There are cliff dwellings up there, or so I've been told. I've never seen them."

"Want to take a look?"

"It's not a good idea. Bob took a party of rock hounds up the canyon and the owner came to their camp with a couple of weirdoes armed to the teeth. They fired some potshots around the canyon and told Bob to clear out. That was in the middle of the night. Bob says it was real spooky. So, he packed up his party and came back to the river."

"Who's the owner?"

"Monty Arnold. He's a recluse, a real nut case, Bob says. Calls himself a survivalist. He prints a newsletter, rants and raves a lot about the apocalypse, guns, gold, government conspiracies, UFOs, and illegal border crossings. Far, far right stuff. Claims he

108

has a paramilitary organization with several thousand members. More like 300 or 400, Bob says. At least, that's all the online subscribers. No one really knows. Last winter Bob flew his ultra light over a bunch of them dressed in camos and boots having a paintball war. He thought someone fired at him, so he took off."

"With a paintball gun?"

"No silly, with a rifle. Luckily they missed. Bob checked his ultra light for holes, but he didn't find any."

"Lucky Bob."

"Anyway, he doesn't want me to go up the canyon."

"I have no problem with that."

They paddled and drifted through two large bends in the river, turning east, then north and back to the southwest. The elevation dropped; palo verde, creosote bushes, white thorn acacia, jojoba, and desert hackberry and cactus began to dominate the low lying scrub hills and flood plain.

"Beasley Flat," Paloma announced as they passed a pair of isolated lava formations. "There's our ride!" York's pink jeep was parked at the edge of the pull-out.

"How was the river?" Bob asked.

"It was a breeze. Placid. Matt only flipped once," Paloma said.

"You flipped over?"

"I was reaching for a paddle and just kept going. The water was fine."

"Let's get out of here before you broil in those suits. Should have packed a change of clothes for you. I forgot."

"Some tour guide. Did you bring sandwiches?" Paloma asked.

"Yep, but they looked so good I ate them."

"Bob, you didn't."

"Nah. They're in the Igloo."

"I'm starved." Paloma scrambled into the back seat and opened the Igloo while Matt and Bob put the kayaks onto the roof rack and stowed the paddles. She tore open a sandwich wrapped in tinfoil. "Bob, not peanut butter and pickles again?"

"The safari special. The tourists love it. You can't believe the requests I get for recipes, Matt."

"Drive," Paloma said and handed Matt a sandwich. She started to pull out the pickles, but changed her mind and began wolfing down her sandwich. "Pull over here, Bob."

Bob brought the jeep to a stop. "That's JR's spread," Paloma pointed to a tall windmill, its vanes spread to catch the wind, turning slowly west to northwest. "There's always a wind through here." The windmill towered over a grove of cottonwoods. "It used to be cattle country, but JR switched over to llamas." Paloma handed Matt her binoculars. "You can see them there beyond the corral."

Matt lifted the glasses and saw JR loading hay into a trough. Heads erect with curious expectancy, a small group of adult llamas was edging closer to the trough.

"I'm so proud of JR for that," Paloma said.

"The llamas were Paloma's idea, Matt. JR's water company is sitting on top of an aquifer. The 11th commandment according to her is 'Thou Shall Not Pollute.'"

"He owns a water company?"

"Yes. He supplies the Verde Village. This whole basin is an aquifer."

Matt pointed to a pair of windmills to the south. "Are those JR's wells?"

"No, they belong to John Cooper. Don't ask who John Cooper is," Bob said.

"John Cooper is a lying, self-promoting charlatan who's trying to divide the locals and the Indian tribes into groups of haters. His cows pollute the Verde and his wells," Paloma interrupted.

"I warned you Matt," Bob grinned, "he's a polluter."

"You're damn right he is. I wouldn't drink a drop of water from his water company. It isn't just water he pollutes, he pollutes everything he touches. You know I'm right, Bob; tell him."

"No way, Paloma. Matt doesn't want to hear this."

"John Cooper publishes a gun and ammo magazine. He fancies himself a fast draw expert. He's a John Bircher, or he used to be. See those buildings there?" Paloma gave her binoculars to Matt. He scanned the buildings. Two men with holsters were lounging in a doorway near the main building. There were two others sitting on a fence near the gate. "See anything?"

"Well, I see four cowboys with guns."

"Only four? Well, golly, keep looking. There's probably a dozen more. The structures are fake. The whole place is a training ground for urban warfare. He trains people for the government."

"The U.S. government?"

"Yes, and anybody else. Covert operations people come here all the time. Business executives, bodyguards, paramilitary types, anybody who wants to shoot something or someone. This is the place. It's true, isn't it, Bob?"

"Of course, it's true."

"Bob and I have watched them. They hold maneuvers. Some Sundays it sounds like the Fourth of July."

"Where do they come from?"

"Who knows? He runs ads in all those mercenary and adventure magazines. He's got a lot of irons in the fire. He brings in executives from big corporations. Calls it stress management training. He scrapes a few yards of bentonite out of the old Indian burial grounds with a back hoe, and these guys dig through the clay to find a pot. It's private land, so it's all legal. They get up at dawn and run obstacle courses. Then they play cops and robbers. We heard that he gets $5,000 a pop per week."

"Sweet Mother," Matt said.

"And his cows poop in the Verde. He doesn't fence them off. And he overgrazes."

"Well, there you have it, Matt. If the cows didn't crap in the river, Paloma probably wouldn't care."

"No way, Bob. He trashes ecologists, calls us cactus terrorists in his magazine. He encourages people to kill wild animals, not just for sport, but to kill anything that walks, crawls, or flies. I'm sure he, or one of his groupies, shot Igor. He's evil, Matt. Cooper hates everyone. You can see it in his eyes."

"Well, Matt, now you know who wears the black hats. Welcome to the neighborhood."

"Are Arnold's and Cooper's properties connected?" Matt asked.

Bob gave Matt a calculated look.

"Matt wanted to hike up the canyon. I told him about the run in you had with Arnold," Paloma said.

"Not that I know of. Arnold's a loner. But he keeps company with the wackos," Bob said.

"Some neighborhood." Matt took a bite of his sandwich. "This is great."

"You hear that Paloma? A man after my own heart."

"Men are crazy," Paloma said between bites. "They'll eat anything."

When they finished eating, Bob snaked the jeep up a goat trail and crossed the flats where the sandy basin turned onto a secondary gravel road.

"So, did you see Igor?" Bob asked.

"Bob, you wouldn't believe it. He was there on Eagle Rock. So was his mate and a fledgling. We should have brought the camcorder."

"You should make a documentary. Maybe you'd get funding from the Discovery Channel," Matt said.

"Oh, do you think so? Bob, we have to go back. I took a lot of film after we caged Igor."

"Matt's right. There's your Foundation money. We could put in some pink jeep footage and exploit the hell out your eagle: Igor the Great Flies Again."

"Don't be an ass," she replied.

"Seriously, you could do something with it."

"Seriously?"

"Cerealsly. Kellog's would back us."

Paloma groaned.

"Really, it's a good idea. You and Matt could take some river footage and I could do a fly-by with the ultra light for aerial takes. Do some editing. I know a distributor."

"Really?"

"Yes, Paloma." Bob pulled in behind the infirmary. "Are you with us?" he asked Matt.

"I'm with you."

They piled hands one by one on top of the other.

"Let's do it," Bob said.

"All right." Paloma hugged them both and got out of the jeep with Matt. "Are you coming to the meeting?" she asked Bob.

"I'll put in my two-cents worth. Are you coming, Matt?"

"Yep. Everyone tells me that its a chance to meet the locals."

Bob raised his eyebrows. "There'll be all kinds of people and they won't all be locals, probably more politicians than rednecks."

"I'd better change out of this wet suit."

"No worries. Bring it with you tonight. Got to go, Paloma. See you, Matt." Bob drove off.

"Matt, that was fun. I have to run now, too. JR's picking me up at 6:30 and I need to feed the birds, run the dogs, and get dressed. You can ride in with us."

"I'll let you know. I might want to drive around town before I go. You don't suppose I could borrow Digger, do you?"

"Sure, great. He could use some company." Paloma grinned. After entering the run, she was immediately surrounded by yapping and leaping puppies. She picked up Digger who lavished her with kisses. "Here you go."

Matt took the pup, scratched his chest, set him on the ground and started down the path. Digger hesitated and looked back at the other puppies. When Matt whistled and clapped his hands, Digger made up his mind and raced to him.

"I think you've got a bud, Matt."

"Think so?"

"Definitely. Have fun you two."

CHAPTER NINE

VIEWS DIFFER ABOUT THE
VERDE VALLEY WATER SHED
By Renee Royer, The Village Voice

All the usual suspects were present at a town meeting Wednesday evening at the Cottonwood Community Center. County Supervisor Ted Ackers chaired the meeting and introduced representatives from USGS, Arizona Department of Water Resources, Yavapai County Water Resources Advisory Committee, the Tri-Village Mayors, directors of the Tri-Village private water companies, and our U.S. Senators.

The local tribal councils were present as were representatives from Nature Conservancy, Audubon Society, Friends of the Verde Valley, and independent concerned citizen groups. In fact, there were nearly as many representatives on the dais as there were people in the audience, nearly 200.

Ted Ackers started the ball rolling by announcing the Senators' recommendation to create a partnership of federal, state, and local representatives to promote sound water management. Funds would be provided to conduct ongoing studies of the watershed. Then he offered to field questions.

"Why should we form another group and spend more on studies? The Verde was declared an endangered river ten years ago. The USGS did a four million dollar study. Every group here has done studies. It's time to act, not to waste more time and money." Bill McGovern sat down to a round of applause.

Sonny Strickland, who represents the YCWARAC, stood up to defend the recommendation. "Times have changed since those studies. We need the money for the science and recommendations of the federal experts to create and sustain a viable long-term plan that balances competing uses for water."

"There you go again, Strickland, you mean a viable plan to sustain the Tri-cities, Phoenix, and your water company. You want to pump the Paulden aquifer dry," an unidentified member of the audience challenged, receiving mixed applause.

"We've got to have residents speak up and be at the table, not just special interest and advisory groups."

"Speak for yourself, Barb. No one else will."

"I just did," Barbara Colburn said.

"It would be nice if the federal government would just provide the money without any strings," Jerome Mayor Stephen Frietschle said.

"The Senators will never go for it," Edie Wyckoff, their representative, said. "It's one thing to provide funds, but we need to know what we are getting."

"The Salt River Project will get its way no matter what we do. They always do. We pay for the water coming and going. While we wait, we'll pay double rates to the private water companies," Ed Meacham from Verde Village commented.

"If you want water, you have to pay for it. You folks don't have any water of your own. You've got too many people up there. I'm having to drill deeper every year," Sonny Strickland answered. "Tell them, JR." He called on JR Taylor, rancher and water company director.

"Well, folks, I hate to agree with Strickland on anything, but there are too many people in the county. Prescott is already draining the Paulden and Big Chino reservoirs. We have to stop these land exchanges. They overload the whole system. You won't know you're thirsty, until you turn on the tap and it's dry or it's too polluted to drink. I'm not drilling any deeper, because we're already at the level where we'll be piping up lead and arsenic. Your towns are considering expensive heavy metal treatment plants, and that's not good for the river. The Verde is the last wild desert river. It's the last stand for hundreds of species and wet lands. This whole ecosystem is endangered, and we're all part of

115

that ecosystem Some days it may not look like much, but it's all we've got, and we can't allow it to be dammed up, diverted or just sucked dry by land developers, the Salt River Project, the tri-cities or Phoenix. Comes a 20-year drought and they are finished anyway." JR Taylor sat down, receiving a standing ovation.

"At least five endangered species -- the river otter, desert bald eagle, southwestern willow flycatcher, peregrine falcon and leopard frog-- live in the corridor that the river supports and wild turkeys, bobcats, and lynx are making a comeback. In addition, the Verde has one of the highest breeding bird densities of any North American habitat," Paloma Patterson informed the audience. She urged us to pass more stringent pollution controls.

Things got a bit sticky when Ed Stalcup, a Camp Verde resident, accused the Apache Tribe of polluting the river with their gravel and cement operations. Tribal representative Ben David defended them, saying the tribe was a major employer in the Valley and that the plant complied with all federal regulations.

"When was the last inspection, Dan? Or the first, for that matter?" Willie Norton wanted to know. "And, Dan, what fools on the Council authorized a new car wash for Cottonwood?"

Judy Blake said that many people are dissatisfied with the political log jam of too many committees. Several speakers followed her and engaged in a verbal free-for-all, most of which isn't worth reporting or fit for printing.

Barbara Colburn said she was disillusioned by all the name calling and hot air. "It's not going to help anybody."

Roger Mudd suggested a vector agency, warning that encephalitis from deer mice and mosquito-born West Nile virus were potential threats in Central Arizona. He urged that we consider environmentally safe controls.

Bob York commented that the recent high water flow cleaned out debris and detritus from the Upper Verde. He urged the forestry department to allow only licensed rafting companies and that private individuals be required to obtain permits.

Marvin Douglas responded with a tirade about how the federal and state governments are regulating us to death.

116

Someone suggested loudly that he should leave the meeting and the Valley if he didn't like it here.

Reverend Adams pleaded for reasonable discourse. Cottonwood Mayor Jake Nelson suggested that the federal government should deny the tribal application for developing a mall on the Indian trust lands. Bob Davis from the Apache Tribe insisted the conversion of the freeway property to trust land was legal and the tribe could develop the property.

Strickland said the deal represented unfair trade practices. Not only would the tri-villages and state be unable to draw taxes from the trust land, but local businesses would be unable to compete.

Tom Fallon, the Apache Tribal Manager, defended the proposal, saying that the proposed stores would improve the local economy by creating employment, lowering prices, and cutting transportation costs.

Their dispute was interrupted by boos and catcalls. Ted Ackers pointed out that these disputes would best be served by all parties working cooperatively within the framework of the proposed Verde Valley Partnership.

Ted Williams of the U.S. Forest Service said that the forest rangers were overwhelmed by the amount of dumping in the national forests. He asked for volunteer groups to assist in clean-up operations and asked the audience to report violations.

Ed Meacham wanted to know if the proposed land swap of the I-17 corridor property for land on the Upper Verde would result in more development there. Edie Wyckoff said that the Secretary of Interior was in favor of consolidating forest lands and that no consideration would be given to lease holders to develop housing. But consideration would be given to organizations, such as the National Land Conservancy, to protect wildlife refuges.

Dan Cunningham, the National Land Conservancy spokesman, responded by saying that, if the Verde is sacrificed, there will be nothing to protect.

Mayor Nelson of Cottonwood announced a follow-up town hall meeting.

Darlene Mitchell reminded everyone about the Saturday flea market.

Ted Ackers concluded the meeting by stating that the Verde is a unique and irreplaceable riparian resource and, to transcend competing and self-serving interests, some federal and state involvement is essential. We need to work together, and creating the Verde partnership is the best place to start.

Renee opened the window by her desk, turned the computer towards the shadowy figures sitting on the wooden porch in front of the Chamber of Commerce office, and began typing the conversation.

"She's a looker," Sonny Stickland said.

"That she is." John Cooper agreed.

"She's working late again."

"Biddles struck gold when he found her."

"You could use her to edit your rag magazines."

"Too much trouble. She has a built-in crap detector."

"Biddles wouldn't let her go. He knows a good thing."

"Biddles doesn't know squat, John."

"He prints what we want him to."

"Hell, he prints everything, all sides."

"That's what we want, John, just keep stirring the pot. Look what happened at the meeting. They're all polarized. The Secretary will push the BLM to act soon. He has to head off the Senator's recommendations."

"We don't need him or the agencies or that twit of a Governor either."

"We'll get the water rights. Leave it to me. The politicians are going to fall flat on their asses. They will stall, point their fingers, and clear out. They have to get re-elected. Don't they?"

"I don't care about water rights; I've got all the water rights I need. I want that God damn mountain!"

"The bentonite?"

"That and more. I can hide enough ammo up there to outfit an army and I will when I'm ready."

"Sometimes you scare me, John."

"You just don't get it, Sonny. There's trouble coming and when it comes, we will survive. When the brown material hits the twirling blade, we got everything we need here: water, cattle, good land and a good climate. We've got the manpower. My people can control the valley and we can blow the highways at both ends of the valley. No one comes or goes. You'll see." "What about that taxidermist?"

"That nutter does what I tell him to. We've packed enough ammonium nitrate and diesel in the bentonite up there to blow up the valley."

"You'd blow up the highways and start up a redneck nation. I hope I don't live long enough to see that."

"If you had it your way, you'd cram this valley full of retirees. Hell, you'd sell your soul to pave this valley with malls and when you run out of water and jobs, you and these people will turn on each other. Hell, you'll be the first one to kiss my tokus."

"Save that crap for your paramilitary nut cases, John. You're going to create you own Armageddon if you're not careful. Where are you hiding that stuff?"

"You don't really want to know, Sonny. If someone finds it, they'll regret it. Since we're asking where everything is, where are you keeping the gravel and sand contracts?"

"In my safe."

"Well, you better burn them!"

"Where I haul gravel is my business."

"It's my gravel you're hauling and, if one of these eco-nuts wants someone to pay to clean up the Verde, let the Indians pay for it. I'm not going to. As far as you're concerned, you didn't get one yard from my side of the river."

"I didn't keep a record. Most of that rock was quarried on BLM land. That dry bed of yours was an afterthought."

"The hell, you say. That afterthought is where that Indian found lead and arsenic. Are you leasing your trucks to the tribe?"

"Yeah, so what? They paid me good money to haul rocks from the Rez."

"Where are they hauling now?"

"I don't know, maybe Phoenix, Vegas, Havasu. I just track the mileage."

"Hauling gravel that far doesn't make sense, does it? But the tribe doesn't run the business, do they? The syndicate runs it. And Fallon tells me some of those loads go all the way to Salt Lake, Portland, and Seattle. That didn't make sense to me either, so I had one of my boys keep an eye on the operation. He's washing trucks. He tells me there's bentonite on the bottom of every one of the rigs. Personally, I'd say they're running drugs. Not that I give a damn, but half of those rigs are mine. I want you to pull them out. Break the leases and get rid of those records."

"And if I don't?"

"Look, if you want to put your ass in a sling, that's your problem. But you're not putting mine there. Just do what I tell you, or I'll do it for you."

"Fallon won't like it. He wants the Indians to fry. They'll lose their water rights."

"If the Indians fry, you're going to get burned, and Fallon too."

"Well, like the man said, you've got to know when to fold them, and it's past time."

"It's time to fold the cards, Sonny."

Renee sat quietly at her desk and waited until Strickland and Cooper drove off. After making several copies of the article, she put a copy on Fiddler's desk and stuffed the others in her bag. She shut down her computer, turned off the lights, and closed the door. Across the street in front of the Q & Brew, pickups were lined up like horses at a hitching rail.

Renee crossed the street, stepped onto the wooden porch and peered through the window. She could hear the click of billiard balls. A long line of pool tables marched from the doorway to the bar in the rear. Shuffling his feet in the wood shavings that covered the floor, JR leaned over to make a shot. York grinned as the cue ball hit the eight ball and caromed into the side pocket. JR and York hung their cue sticks in a rack decorated with burned-in cattle brands and joined Paloma and Matt, who were sitting at a round table, their backs to the wall.

"Are you just looking or are you going in?" Startled, Renee turned. Billy Berger, the biker from Jerome, was sitting on a bench at the far end of the porch.

"Going in." Renee straightened her hair and pushed through the swinging doors. The billiard balls ceased clicking as she ran the gauntlet past the row of tables and players to join the group at the table.

"We saved you a seat," JR pulled out a chair for her.

"Thanks. Must be losing my touch," she said to Paloma.

"You don't have to worry. The last time we were here, JR had a friendly talk with the boys, like cowboy to cowboy." Paloma grinned at JR.

"I never was a cowboy or a cow puncher. I was a cowman, but now, I don't know what I am."

"You're a llama breeder. You need to trade in that Stetson for one of those Peruvian felt caps," Renee said.

"That'll be the day." A weathered-looking blond barmaid in tight jeans and a pink checkered shirt brought them four cans of Budweiser, picked up their empties, and moved to the next table.

"Cora, why don't you stock Sedona Red?" JR asked.

"Cause cowboys can't read, JR. They buy what's on TV." Cora dumped her tray into an overflowing trash can.

"You're just in time, Renee," JR said. "That table's empty and Matt here is itching to play. Bob and I showed him a thing or two, but I told him that you might be more his speed. Why don't you give him a whirl?"

"Sure, why not?" Renee passed around copies of her article. "You can read it while Matt and I play pool."

JR looked at his copy. "It'll take longer to read this than the game will last."

Matt selected a cue stick from the rack and stepped to the side of the table. Renee took her time and chose a maple pool stick with a red star, hefted it carefully, and moved to the front of the table as Matt racked the billiard balls.

"You're not going to let her shoot first, are you? I'd make her draw for the first shot," JR said.

"Ladies first," Matt grinned.

"In that case, let me point out that the loser buys the next round," JR added.

"Oh, JR, let go of it. Let them play. Go for it, Renee," Paloma said.

Renee smiled. "Okay." She placed the cue ball on the left side of the table, smile fading as she focused to hit the rack with force. Balls whizzed around the table and the cue ball slowed to a stop in the middle. The two and six balls fell into corner pockets and the seven ball rolled slowly across the table and dropped into the side pocket. The players at the nearby table stopped their games to watch. The cue ball never left the center of the table as Renee moved around, picked off the one, three, four, and five balls in rapid succession, drawing the cue ball down the rail on her last shot. After making an easy drop on the eight ball, she looked up and asked, "Double or nothing?"

"You're joking," Matt said.

"I never joke when I gamble."

"Hell, you're not gambling, Renee. You're just putting notches on your cue stick," JR said. "Better quit while you're ahead, Matt."

"I'm game," Matt said. "Rack 'em."

Renee racked the balls and put the tray under the table. Matt positioned the ball on the right side of the table, turned his cap around, drew the cue and snapped a shot. The six and seven balls fell into the corner pockets while the one ball covered the four ball. After studying the layout, he arched the cue high and jumped the cue ball over the four and dropped the one ball.

"I'll be damned," JR said. "He made it." The noise in the room quieted to a low buzz.

Matt used a bridge to bank in the two ball and then banked the three into the side pocket. "Eight ball in the side pocket," he said as he tapped the pocket with his cue stick.

"How's he's going to do that, Bob?" JR asked quietly.

"Watch."

Matt banked the four ball down the length of the table. It edged by the five ball and kissed the eight ball into the side pocket. The buzzing stopped.

"Nice game, Matt," Renee said.

"Two out of three?"

"I don't think so. Let's just call it a draw." Renee racked her cue stick, sat down at the table and stared at the ceiling. JR slapped his leg and guffawed loudly.

"We set you up, Renee. Matt's quite a hustler. You fell for it, hook, line, and..."

"Yeah, I know, and sinker."

"He's quite the fisherman, too. Did Paloma tell you that Matt landed some trout with a candy-assed rig. Tell her, Paloma."

"You tell her, JR. It's your show."

"Well, Matt used buttercups for flies, and mealy worms. He landed four trout in ten minutes." Renee stared at Matt suspiciously. "And he got so hot and bothered...,"

"Drop it, JR," Paloma warned and colored slightly.

"Don't be shy, Paloma. I'm just repeating what you told Bob and me at breakfast."

"Well, I didn't think you'd spread it around."

"Tell me, I'm all ears," Renee said.

"Well, as I was saying. Matt got all heated up from fishing and decided to go for a swim, except he didn't have any trunks. So, he spread his clothes on a sand bar and went for a swim."

"That's enough, JR," Paloma interrupted. "Drop it."

"Go on, JR. I'm interested," Renee said.

"Thought you would be. Well, Paloma here, found his clothes and hid them behind the boulders. Poor Matt. Here he was buck naked, high and dry on the other side of Verde."

"It was a joke, JR. I shouldn't have told you."

"I think I've heard this before somewhere. It was a song, something about Running Bear and Poor Little White Dove." Renee's and Paloma's eyes locked, flashed fire and then twinkled. Paloma barely suppressed a smile.

Matt stood up and stretched. "I think I could use some air," he said as he walked towards the front of the saloon. JR laughed and slapped his thigh.

"Poor Little White Dove. You mean Poor Little Running Bear. There he goes."

Outside of the Q & Brew, Matt looked through the window and saw Paloma talking and gesturing and everyone laughing.

"Long time, Matt." the biker, who was waiting at the end of the porch, said. They shook hands warmly.

"It sure has been, Dick. What are you doing here?"

"Same ol'. Same ol'. Only it's not Dick Radcliffe now. I'm Billy Berger this time around, remember?"

"Oh, yeah, Billy Berger. It's got a ring to it."

"These boys think I'm the son or grandson of the old man – the leader of the pack. Anyway, he's dead and they don't know any better."

"What's the same ol', same ol'?"

Dick looked around the corner. "Amphetamines. The bikers are packing it out of here. The fix is in with the local law."

"So where is it coming from?"

"Mexico. It's a pipe line. Some of it's local. I'm looking for the faucet, but I'm not making much progress. There's a laundry here, but I haven't figured it out. My cash is dead-ended. No trace and we've dropped a lot."

"The casino?"

"Maybe, but if they are washing money, it's cute."

"Offshore?"

"Like I said, it's cute. A whole lot of money going round and round. But it isn't coming out around here. They are layering it off somewhere else."

"Who are they?"

"I don't know, Matt. Couldn't tell you even if I did, but it's probably a Columbian deal. You back to work?"

"Sculpting. I'm doing a piece for the Apache Tribe."

"Excuse me, what a coincidence. It just happens that the tribe owns a casino and you just happen to work for the Arizona Gaming Commission. I checked."

"It was that easy?"

"A revolving door, Matt. You're wide open, without a cover."

"I don't like this, Dick. Fallon, the tribal manager, knows I'm here and so does Sam Cook. He asked me to come."

"You're not covered, Matt. It looks like a set up to me. You're bait, my friend. If the casino management starts digging, kiss your ass goodbye."

Matt kicked a beer can with his boot, picked it up, and tossed it against a building. "You're probably right, Dick, but I'm not leaving. I'm looking for Jay Cook, Sam's grandson. He's a friend and something's happened to him."

"Well, don't look too hard. It could happen to you, too. Do you have something I can write on?" Matt took off his cap and pulled a card from under the brim. Radcliff scratched a number on the card and handed it back. "Call me. I'll back you up if you get caught short. It looks like I've got more friends here than you do."

"Same ol'. Same ol'."

"You still shoot a mean stick. That Renee's a knockout. I've seen her at the casino."

"She works there."

"Yeh, if she works for that bunch, I'd check her out. By the way, I'm pretty sure that case she carries is a surveillance rig."

"You sure?"

"Yep, I'm sure. It's a custom job, not a government issue. How about the red head? What does she do?"

"She runs a bird refuge."

"You be careful; you don't want to get plucked."

"She's a lady. What happened to your hair?" Matt asked as Dick strapped his helmet over his red bandana.

"Had to shave it off."

"How come?"

"Took my helmet off, ran into some bees that stung the hell out of me. Take care." Radcliffe fired up his bike and eased out the alley onto Main Street before flipping on his lights.

Matt waited until Radcliffe turned the corner. He thought he saw the Venetian blinds shut in the *Village Voice* office across the street. When Matt joined the group in the Q & Brew again, Renee handed him a copy of her article. She drank her beer slowly and studied the cattle brands that were burned on the walls and the ceiling. Paloma finished reading first.

"That's good, Renee. You've caught the spirit of the meeting and you left room to read between the lines."

"You don't have to read between the lines, Paloma," JR said. "These meetings are a damn waste of time. They can make all the noise they want. Right now Strickland thinks he's got everybody eating out of his hand, and he's probably right. He's got the votes, if it comes to that, and SRP's got the money and money talks."

"What do you mean?" Renee asked.

"I mean that SRP is getting court orders to stop the ranchers from using Verde water, calling us thieves when they're the thieves. It's an old trick. I'll fight them if I have to. My land is grandfathered under the Groundwater Act, but if SRP can shut the private water companies down, they'll squeeze everyone and sell to the highest bidder. Time is on their side, and the Verde Valley Water Association and more damn studies work for them. We're just seeing the beginning! They'll legislate us out of existence. I hate to say it, Renee, but with bad press from the local papers, Phoenix will make it look like SRP is doing everybody a favor. Nothing but a damn bunch of manipulating bastards."

"What's the real problem?" she asked.

"Same old thing -- greed, ignorance, and too many people. The mines exploited the Valley ranchers, the ranchers overgrazed, and now it's overdeveloped. When I was a kid, we used to picnic at Slide Rock. It was beautiful! And now people from Phoenix wash their kids' diapers in the pools. It's so polluted they shut it down every summer, but they still blame the ranchers. The mine tailings were never cleaned up properly because the state was paid off. Since the highways zip you right to Prescott or Flagstaff, people never see the river; the Agua Fria is dried up all the way to New River. Oh, it runs in the monsoons and SRP takes credit for saving the housing down stream – flood control, they call it. The cattlemen and the agricultural interests used to run things in Arizona. Now we're being out-lobbied by the special interest groups: the utilities, the urban developers and, let's face it, by the Indian casinos. According the McCain-Lieberman bill, they can contribute all they want to political campaigns. Kind of curious, but their home states, there are 12 casinos in Arizona and 22 in Connecticut. Money talks. The pesticide companies don't give a damn about the rivers, or the water we drink, or the air we breathe. Same with the mining industry. Trying to separate lobbyists from politicians is like trying to wipe gravy off a deck of cards."

"You sound more and more like an ecologist, JR," Renee said.

"Hell, I've always been an ecologist. Most ranchers are at heart."

"Ranchers shot, trapped, poisoned and overgrazed the west from the Mississippi to California," Paloma said. "You know it's true. They annihilated the west in some ways and in other ways they saved it. But times have changed. Private ranchers are doing their best, but the BLM and the Forestry Department are screwing it all up. Controlled logging management is just another name for strip logging."

"What can be done?" Renee asked.

"Done? Fight fire with fire? Join the Green Peace movement? Become an eco-terrorist? We have to start somewhere. If we can't save the Verde River, we can't save anything. Print that in your paper, Renee and give everybody something to think about." JR stood up. "Well, I said my piece. Time to go."

"Don't go just yet," Paloma begged.

JR gave her a hug. "It's been a long day, dear. I'll see you tomorrow." JR walked past the pool tables and pushed through the swinging doors. The billiard balls didn't start clicking until his diesel truck fired up and he pulled away.

"Whew! JR is pissed. I didn't know he was that upset," York said.

"He cares, Bob. He truly loves this valley," Paloma explained.

"If you stick together, you have a chance," Renee ventured.

"Here's to us cactus huggers!" Paloma said, and they toasted and drained their glasses.

"I've got to go." Renee stood up.

"Me, to," Matt added.

"Party's over. I'll drive you home, Paloma. You two take care," Bob said as he and Paloma got up from the table.

"Matt, I've got some clippings you might be interested in. I'll get them for you," Renee offered. He waited for her by her car while she went into *The Village Voice* office. When she returned, she laid her laptop on the hood of the mustang, opened it carefully, and handed him a folder.

"Thanks,"

"It's not much."

"I'll get it back to you."

"No need. There's more, but it's pretty dated. It would take awhile to pull and print."

"How long do you keep back issues?"

"Everything nowadays is archived on the web, state of the art. But Joe didn't get into the swing of it until last year."

"When you came?"

"Yes," Renee laughed. "The *Voice* was stacked full of deadheads. The place was a fire trap."

"What happened to the old issues?"

"Joe warehouses them in a storage unit, 'for posterity,' he says. Why anybody would keep a record of the comings and goings in this sandbox is beyond me."

"What did you think about the Senator's recommendation?"

128

"That it is just a recommendation. Nothing will come of it. It cost him nothing in Phoenix while he gets some local votes. JR is spot on -- money talks.

"I agree. I'd like to come over sometime and do some browsing."

"Browsing? What are you looking for?"

"Oh, just general stuff. Since I'm doing a sculpture that represents the community, I need Verde Valley history, like the General Crook Trail, the Camp Verde fort, and the Indian ruins."

"The bookstore and library have a lot of that material and you can use the Internet, of course."

"Uh, I don't have a computer. I still use a typewriter. Maybe I could borrow yours."

"SOL, Matt. I've got to run."

"Me, too."

"Back to poor Little White Dove? Opps, there I go. Sorry. Couldn't resist it. Paloma is a great gal."

"And me?"

"All men are Running Bears. That's what cold showers are for. Good night."

"Good night." Matt waited until she drove off. He glanced at *The Village Voice* window, started the engine, and followed her to the first stop sign. Renee turned left; Matt turned right and took the back road to the bridge.

He parked outside the fence. Since a light was glowing from the front window of the studio, he walked across the flagstone patio and entered the adobe cautiously. Light from the kerosene lamp on the table flickered off the walls. As he opened the door wider, Digger barked, growled and wagged his stub of a tail. Matt scooped the puppy up and they exchanged kisses.

Matt surveyed the room. There was a water bowl and a dish on the papers by the door. "Looks like you've been fed." Matt picked up a note on the table:

"I thought you might want some company. I'm sorry. I shouldn't have said anything to Bob and JR. They were

129

so tickled about your fishing with buttercups. I couldn't resist. I'm just a big mouth. Forgive me. Paloma."

"Let's take a walk. Time to do your business." Matt led Digger down the path to the river. The half moon was almost straight up, reflecting on the silver water. Matt had a vision of himself standing in a canoe looking shoreward. He could see the shore, his reflection in the water, but the canoe was empty. He felt that he was seeing an echo of a past life, a trace memory, or was it the present? "Just we three," he thought, "my echo, my shadow, and an empty canoe."

A light flicked on in Paloma's bedroom and she walked in and began to undress. He watched as she draped her blouse on a chair, sat down, removed her boots, stood up, took off her jeans, folded them, and laid them on the chair also. Barely breathing and mesmerized, he watched as Paloma unpinned and began brushing her copper hair which glimmered in the lamp light, contrasting sharply with her porcelain white skin.

"A figure to die for. Titian, eat your heart out," Matt's throat constricted as Paloma slipped on a thin robe, closed her window and turned out the light. "The shades of night were falling swiftly, but the highwayman got a good look anyway." When an owl hooted and a coyote barked, Digger scooted closer to Matt. "Finished your business? Time to do mine." Matt went inside the adobe, picked up his cell phone and punched in a number.

"Vance here."

"It's me, 007."

"Cut the crap. Where have you been? You were to check in daily."

"After I got settled, you said. It took a while to look into the Cultural Center. That Fallon set-up was too cozy."

"So where are you?"

"I've got a cabin with a studio along the Verde. It's convenient. I can see who comes and goes."

"We had you, in let's see, the Pair-a-Dice Motel, the casino, Camp Verde, Montezuma's Castle, Jerome, Cottonwood, some place called Tutzigoot. Where the hell is that?"

"It's a monument. I was sightseeing."

"Sightseeing?"

"Gathering local color. Studying impact. Don't worry. It didn't cost you anything."

"Okay, Matt, fine, fine. Impact is our thing. You need to get going."

"I've got some ideas. Let me give you some names. See what you can get me on Col. Ken Kincaid, Arizona DPS. He's on the Governors Committee.

"I can't go there, Matt."

"And I'm interested in a Constable Farley from Camp Verde, a Marshal Dick George from Jerome, and a Marshal Paul Randall in Cottonwood."

"I can't go there either."

"There must be background checks at the Yavapai County Sheriff's department."

"Okay. What have you got?"

"Just a hunch. They had a meeting at lunch yesterday."

"Give me a break."

"Arm or leg? And while you're at it, there's an undercover DEA agent here, Dick Radcliff or maybe Billy Berger. I've worked with him before. I want to know what he's doing here, and there's an FBI agent here, too. His name is Kessler."

"Matt, I can't work this."

"Then find someone who can or I'm walking. This deal is a can of worms."

"Okay. I'll check around."

"Do that and while you're at it, check into a John Cooper."

"Who's he?"

"He's got a ranch here, supposedly trains undercover operatives for the CIA and hustles paramilitaries on the side."

"This is crazy. Where's the connection to gambling interests?

"Something's not right in paradise."

"Well, let's get back on focus. You need to plant some dollars."

"I put some in the slot machines on Monday. I'll feed the kitty tonight."

"It's important."

"If you say so."

"I'll see what I can find out."

"Thanks, Chester. Make it fast."

"Oh, yes, one more thing. We lost you yesterday afternoon."

"I was cruising down the river."

"What?"

"Kayaking on the Verde. I went fishing."

"Oh. Is that it?"

"Guess so. When can I reach you?"

"We're here 24/7."

"Is that Atlantic or Pacific Standard time?"

"Good night, Matt."

CHAPTER TEN

The children sat on the floor, arms folded, legs tucked under like miniature smiling Buddhas. "Who was Ha-vik?" Jen asked.

"The Eagleman!"

"Is the Eagleman scary?"

"Yes!"

"What did he do that was so scary and dangerous? Who can tell me? Angie?"

"He swooped down and captured Corn Maiden."

"And what did he do with her?"

"He took her to his cave!" the children chorused.

"Who can tell me how Ha-vik became an Eagleman?"

"Toary, the witch, made him drink Kool-Aid and he grew feathers," Tommy shouted.

"It wasn't Kool-Aid. It was a magic potion with poison in it," Cierra said, shaking her braids.

"Well, Kool-Aid is poison. Everyone knows that!"

"That's an interesting idea, Tommy. What makes you think Kool-Aid is poisonous?"

"Well, it's not exactly poisonous, but it's not good for you to drink. That's what Miss Burns told us. Unless it's made with the stuff that's in sugar-free gum."

"Kool-Aid sucks." Angel grinned. "If you drink it, you'll grow feathers. My brother drinks Kool-Aid with sugar and he passes out. He does it on purpose to make my mother mad."

"Tommy, would you ask your brother to see me after school"

"Are you mad at him?"

"No, I just want to talk with him. Now, where were we? Who can help me remember?"

"Corn Maiden is in the cave," the children chorused.

"And then what happened? Jimmy?"

"The hunter came and fired their arrows at him, but Eagleman caught them in his claws. They couldn't kill him!"

"So what did they do?"

"The Chief sent for Elder Brother, and he climbed into the cave, and turned into a fly, and when the Eagleman came back, he changed back into a man, and he cut off the Eagleman's head, and threw his body over a cliff, " Cierra gushed before any of the other children could interrupt her. "I'm out of breath!" she added.

"That was wonderful, Cierra. There's just one more thing I want to know. Who can tell me why the witch turned Ha-vik into an Eagleman in the first place? Angel?"

"Because he told lies to the people and cheated them."

"Okay. Who else agrees with Angel?"

"I do. I do," the children yelled.

"And what will happen if you lie or cheat?"

"A witch will poison you with Kool-Aid," Angie shouted.

"Well, not exactly, but something will happen if you become a liar, won't it?"

"People won't like you!" Cierra insisted.

"And what else?"

"People won't trust you. Sometimes when you tell the truth, people don't like you either," Angel explained.

"That's a very important point. Did you all hear what Angel just said? Is it more important to be liked... or to be trusted? Don't answer me right now. I want you to think about it. We'll talk about what it means to be trusted tomorrow, okay?" Jen picked up a set of gourds and shook them. "We need to practice our dance. Girls first. Pick your gourds and form a big circle. Boys, wait your turn." The girls squealed and shouted as they rushed to the table.

"Form a circle, a big one. Bigger; that's right. Now you boys get your weapons and hide behind the table." The boys pushed and shoved their way to the table. "Boys, slow down. Slow down." Jen waited. "Now, be still. Shh...hush... Are we ready? Are we really ready? All right, here we go!"

Jen began, "One, two, and three. Shake, that's right. Remember you lead, Angie. That's right." Slowly Angie led the girls in a wide circle and then turned inside. The circle evolved into an S as they began to shuffle their feet and shake their gourds. "Now, start the song." The children began chanting as they moved around the room. Jen picked up a drum and began tapping it slowly and increased the tempo.

"Where is Eagleman?"

"He's hiding on the mountain," the children answered together.

Matt stepped to the edge of the loft. "Krrrr...Krrrr.." he whistled. The children looked up at the balcony.

"Look! The Eagleman! He's up there!" Jen pointed.

Matt jumped out of the loft and landed on the table with a thud. He spread his arms wide "Krrrrr...," he whistled and hopped around the table and jumped to the floor. When Matt scooped Cierra into his arms, she gave a delighted scream and tried to wiggle free. The other girls screamed and ran to Jen.

"The Eagleman has captured Corn Maiden. Get him boys!" Jen yelled. Charging from behind the table, the boys pretended to shoot arrows at Matt while Angel swung his rubber hatchet wildly. "Be careful, boys."

Matt set Cierra down and twisting and dodging, pretended to catch the arrows.

"You're dead!" Tommy yelled.

"No, I'm not." Matt pretended to snap an arrow in his hands.

"I'm Elder Brother," Angel shouted as he rushed towards Matt, who picked him up and held Angel over his head.

"You are very brave," Matt said as he set Angel down, "and very heavy."

"All right, children. It's time for lunch. Put your things on the table and line up by the door. I'll be with you in a minute."

The children piled their gourds and weapons on the table and raced towards the door. "Don't run!" Jen clapped her hands. "You're no I'itoi, Matt, but we desperately need a replacement for Jay."

"I can't dance," Matt protested.

"The Eagle Dance is just a buck and a wing. You can do it!"

"Let me think on it."

"Class!"

"All right. I'll do it."

"Promise?"

"I promise, cross my heart."

"Matt has promised class. We'll practice here every week."

"I'll be here."

"Okay, I'll hold you to that."

"That's the last time I jump off a balcony."

"Don't blame me. You asked for it. I've got to take the children to lunch now. Jay keeps his costume upstairs in his locker in the lavatory, and I think he's got a video-tape of last year's gourd dance. Check it out. Can I bring you something from the cafeteria?"

"Yes, some Kool-Aid, full strength. Fry bread with lots of karo syrup. I'll need energy if I'm going to grow feathers."

"If you eat that junk, you'll be a cross-eyed eagle and your tail feathers will fall off." She turned to the class. "Line up in two rows, children. Are we ready?" she checked the rows.

"I'm ready," Angel said.

"All right, let's go."

Matt scratched his head as Jen and the children filed out the door. "Why do I do these things?" he asked himself as he went upstairs to the artist's quarters.

He opened the door and flipped on the light switch. A partitioned wall, with a row of lockers attached to it, separated the kitchenette from the dressing room and shower. The first locker was empty. Renee Royer's name was inked on a strip of tape on the second locker. When he shook the lock as if he expected it to open, nothing happened. He opened the third locker which had

Jay Cook's name taped on it. A black and silver ball cap with an Oakland Raiders badge and a pair of dark sunglasses were on the top shelf. On a hook in the back, a matching Raiders jacket hung limply. On the floor was a cardboard box, lid half open, resting on stacks of video tapes.

Matt began laying out the contents of the box on the dressing bench. An eagle tail feather and beaded headband were on top. Matt took out some woven armbands, deer bone anklets, and two gourd rattles trimmed with leather strips. When found a rabbit fur and leather bodice with kit fox tails attached to the back, he placed it against his thighs. "It just might fit." He sat on his haunches in front of the locker and examined the labeled tapes. He pulled out three that looked promising: *Gourd Dance, Deer Dance*, and *Camp Verde Pow-Wow.*

He carried the tapes to the AV room, located a VCR, inserted the *Gourd Dance* and sat down in a swivel chair. "No titles," he mused as a group of young women dressed in blue beaded dresses trimmed with yellow fringes danced in a circle. Behind them, under canvas-covered trade stalls, onlookers pressed against a yellow tape which separated them from dancers.

A dozen young men sat in a circle, their sticks flashing in the sun as they pounded a drum and chanted. A heavy bodied, yellow-faced, green-armed, red-legged male dancer entered the ring and shook his brightly painted gourds menacingly at the spectators. Raising small clouds of dust pounding the ground, he pursued the gourd dancers who fled in mock alarm. Suddenly, warriors with wooden hawk masks and armed with bows and arrows entered the ring and circled the dancer.

"I can do that." Matt hit the pause button. He went back to the dressing room, kicked off his shoes, quickly stripped to his shorts, and began putting on the eagle costume. He adjusted the eagle feather on the headband and lowered the tight armbands. Fortunately, the anklets slipped on easily. He examined the fur bodice. "No problem. One size fits all," he muttered as he wrapped it around his waist, cinched it and looked in the mirror.

His shorts showed below the bodice. "Shorts are for white men. Me Indian Brave." He pulled off the shorts and began jumping around. "Indian brave need jock strap. Pale faces will think I'm a primitive bastard." Matt returned to the AV room, rewound the tape, hit the play button, and increased the volume.

He circled the room, moving to the beat of the drums. Step, whirl, step, step. Curl, crouch, step, step. He arched his arms high over his head and, in a swooping movement, raced around the table. Circling the chair, he threatened it with his gourds, pirouetted and began a series of stiff-legged side steps, anklets clinking. "Krrrr....," he whistled as the drum beats rose to a crescendo and stopped suddenly.

"Ta da, bravo, encore!"

Startled, Matt turned. Renee was standing at the doorway, smiling and politely clapping her hands. He glanced at the VCR screen and saw three hooded men getting out of a black limo. He hit the stop button. "I was practicing for the Eagle Dance."

"Oh, I see. I thought you had gone native, rediscovering your roots."

"Funny. Very funny."

"I'm sorry. I shouldn't have eavesdropped, but I don't see a half-naked hunk prancing around the AV room every day."

"Sort of made your day, huh? Well, if you'll excuse me, I'll just get into something less risqué." He curtsied and picked up his gourds.

When Renee started giggling, Matt shook the rattles and disappeared into the dressing room. He changed his clothes, put Jay's gear away, and banged the locker shut. When he walked back to the AV room, Renee was staring thoughtfully down at the main floor where Jen and her students were working at the large crafts table.

"She's pretty, isn't she?"

"Yes, she is."

"Now it's my turn to change, Matt. Don't go away. I'll be right back." Renee left the room.

Matt turned the VCR on, pushed the fast forward button and pushed play. A black limo pulled into the breezeway where Carbahol and two other tribal police were handling cash bags. Three men in parkas, one with a hood over his face, stepped out of the car. Two pointed their shotguns at the security men and the other pointed his shotgun at Carbahol, who quickly undid his holster and laid it on the ground. The hooded man picked it up, tossed it into the limo, and motioned to Carbahol to lay face down on the ground and lock his fingers behind his neck. On command, a security guard began passing the bags to the other guard, who stacked them inside the limo. When they were finished, one armed man gestured with his shotgun and the guards got into the limo. The robbers quickly climbed in behind them and the car pulled away. "Four men, unless someone else was inside," looking at his watch, Matt added, "in less than four minutes."

He watched further as Carbahol got to his feet and dashed into the casino. The counting room door opened and a man wearing a black ball cap and dark jacket peered out and went back inside. Then, tape blanked out. Matt ejected it, laid it on the table, and walked back to the dressing room.

With one foot elevated on the dressing bench, Renee straightened the seam of a netted stocking that reached to her thigh and smoothed her white beaded dress.

"Sorry. The door was open," Matt said softly.

"Don't be. Do you like it?" Her lips curved into a soft smile and she smoothed the front of her dress again and turned. "Are my seams straight?"

"Yes. You look great, Renee. It's a beautiful dress. But I'm more interested in this." Matt picked up her laptop and set it on the table. "Mind if I have a look?" He pushed the release button and the lid popped open. Twisting a knob, he asked, "How does this interesting thing work?"

"Don't touch that," Renee ordered as he turned a second knob. "Here, let me." She pushed a slide on the lid. "It's a telescopic video recorder and it's a computer. No secret weapons."

"You didn't get this at a spy store, Renee. This is government surveillance gear. So who do you work for? The FBI? DEA? Or maybe the Company?"

"Do you always come on like gangbusters?"

"Only when I need to. And I need to know now." He glared at Renee. "Or I make some phone calls." Matt picked up his cell phone and punched in his code.

"All right, you win. I'll talk." Renee playfully raised her hands over her head, sat down, crossed her legs, and rested her chin on her hands. She appraised Matt with her eyes. "We have a situation here. I could tell you that a friend bought me the case, that I'm a reporter. That it's useful."

"Sorry. A reporter from *The Village Voice* needs a custom surveillance device?"

"All right. No games. I'm a federal agent. I'm on an assignment, period. That's all I can tell you."

"Which agency?"

"Sorry, I can't tell you that."

"Can't or won't? You just said, no games."

"I can't unless I get it cleared. I'm in a bind here, Matt."

"So am I. You know what I'm doing here, don't you?"

"Yes and no. I know you're working for the Arizona Gaming Commission and that you're investigating illegal activities. On your own, you're trying to find Jay Cook. That's about it."

"So where do we go from here? Maybe you should check with your supervisor and I'll check with mine."

"And we both know where that's going, don't we? I'll get pulled. The trouble is that I'm staying. Let's say I've got unfinished business here."

"I was afraid something like this would happen when you were posted here. You're at the wrong place, at the wrong time, and doing things in the wrong way. No offense, Matt."

"You mean I have no suave or deboner?"

Renee laughed. "Let's just say it's another case of the left hand doesn't know what the right's doing. You could upset the apple cart. Six months of my time and effort would be a complete waste. Sorry, it's not your fault, but I'm requesting to have you pulled. I have no choice. May I have the case, please?" He reluctantly handed Renee the laptop. She turned on the computer, inserted a key, and began to type.

Matt walked to the edge and stared down at Jen and the children working at the craft table. When she looked up and waved, he waved back and then went back to the VCR, and inserted the tape. "What did you say?" he asked Renee when she finished sending her report.

"I described the situation and requested instructions."

"So, what's the situation?"

"Oh, shut up!" Renee got up and began pacing around the room. "I wish I had a cigarette."

"You smoke?"

"Never, well almost never." She moved beside him. "What do you have on that tape?"

"You saw it while I was changing clothes."

"Yes, I saw it. When did you figure out that I was an agent?"

"When we had lunch in Jerome, when you were taping the cops' conversation."

"Was it that obvious?"

"It was to me."

"So, tell me about the tape." Renee walked over to the recorder and they watched the replay. "So what do you make of it?"

"Well, someone filmed the robbery and I'm guessing it was Jay. He must have installed a surveillance camera in the breezeway. I don't know how or when or why. Maybe it was already there. Jay designed this AV Lab; maybe it was overlooked when the casino set up their surveillance."

"Go on."

"Whoever planned the robbery had inside information. Look, the security guards walk out the door with the cashier bags and the limo pulls in at that exact minute. It's all over in less than four minutes. They had to know when the cash was coming."

"You're right, Matt. It's like a military operation."

"Who would know when the guards open the breezeway door?"

"Salvatori. He phones the limos and personally clears the hallways. Normally he would greet the guests."

"Only Salvatori?"

"A couple of times he's asked me to accompany him. When they leave, he escorts them back to the limos, along with the cash bags. It's routine. The guards load and unload them. I'm sure that the security team was caught off guard. They thought it was just another cash and carry delivery. After all, it was their money and limos."

"Do you believe that the casino is being used to launder money?"

"It's complicated, but a lot of cash is being moved here. Sometimes more bags go out than come in."

"How do you know that?"

"I move around. There's a restroom in the hall. Sometimes I go back to the kitchen. I watch the players at the tables. I can't check each time. Sometimes they spend a little, but usually, they just eat something and pack up."

"Bags in and bags out. Who are they?"

"Well, some high-rollers, but not many come here. Most of the people in limos are foreigners -- Asians, Filipinos, Chinese, a few Columbians, and twice, I think, a group of Peruvians."

"Drug lords?"

"Obviously. Why else would they be here? Occasionally an Italian bunch from the East Coast shows up and Salvatori gives them the royal treatment."

"The East Coast?"

"Accents, topcoats, dark hats, and sallow complexions. They dress and speak like they're trying out for *The Sopranos*. Blue topcoats in the desert, for God's sake. They even wear them inside the casino. Salvatori takes them up to the Eagles Nest and fawns over them. He's disgusting. They never stay long; then he escorts them out the front door, and they leave in a different limo. I know because I've checked the plates. They never take any cash and, as far as I can tell, they don't bring any in either. Matt, I shouldn't be discussing this. I'm been dropping markers. So far, the cash that is brought here stays here or it shows up at the Arizona Central Bank. Only one of my markers turned up in Shanghai and another in London."

"Some lead! Are they skimming?"

"Of course. The cashiers lock their boxes with the slips inside. The boxes are stacked in the counting room so they can switch before they count. There's a small room with no surveillance inside the first room because it can't be seen from the counting room. Even if there was an auditor in the room, you could skim and swim. If you want to beat the system, it's easy. The counting room is a bank; they wire transfer credit anywhere, even to the Federal Reserve...."

"And the limos?"

"Better than Brinks."

"So, what's the bottom line?"

"Whatever the Rez's percentage is, they're paying the tribe more than they take in, so go figure."

"Look at this, Renee." Matt hit play again. A shadowy figure appeared in the counting room, picked up a small box and walked out the side door. A security guard moved through the room, stepped outside as the video stopped. "What do you make of that?"

"Whoever he is, he saw the robbery. He must have known he wouldn't be seen on the casino cameras. He had to have been watching the counting room, but from where? And, he had a key. Where could it be?"

"I'm thinking," Matt said impatiently.

When her laptop beeped, Renee typed in a series of numbers and opened the message as Matt looked over her shoulder:

"R2D2 advise: If gunslinger agrees to participate on a need-to-know basis and not to notify his sponsor and acknowledges that our sponsor is to be protected, we are willing to cooperate. If gunslinger agrees, respond now."

"Matt, it's your call," Renee said over her shoulder.
"I agree."
"Are you sure?"
"I'm sure. Go for it."
"*We have a go,*" Renee typed and hit the send signal. The reply was immediate:

"The welcome Matt is out... that's a pun. I warned you not to underestimate him, R2D2. Please cooperate until further notice, anka."

"Oh, goodie! We get to work together," Renee said sarcastically.
"Yeah, wonderful. Who's anka?"
"He's my supervisor. I've never met him and I don't want to know who he is."
"Do you trust him?"
"To a point. So far he hasn't let me down."
"So, what's next?"
"I'm due on the floor; we're staging a bowling tournament. I'm off at six. Why don't we meet at *The Village Voice* at say, seven? We can talk things over. I'm late." She grabbed her laptop and sprinted down the staircase. Matt removed the tape from the VCR and returned it to Jay's locker.

CHAPTER ELEVEN

"Jesus, she's hot! She was buck naked." Shorty ejected the video tape and slipped it into his brief case, next to his desk on the surveillance room floor.

"Burn it, Shorty, before you get all our asses into a sling."

"What about the chief? What the hell was he doing in there?"

"Getting ready to go on the warpath, stupid."

"I mean with that video tape?"

"He probably found one of your porn tapes, some of the crap you tape in the restrooms. They are animals, and so are you, Shorty. You give surveillance a dirty name."

"Survey this!"

"Knock it off and dump that tape."

"Not on your life. It goes in the locker. The night crew will love it."

"If you want to be a jerk-off, it's your funeral."

Matt looked down from the loft. Jen was arranging strings of coral, cobalt, and glass beads on a Navajo rug. She eyed one critically, shook her head, and put it carefully into a cardboard box.

"A keeper," Matt called. She looked up.

"Too good for tourists. Come look. Help me decide."

"Be right there." He half-slid, half-jumped down the pole ladder.

"It's a good thing the girls are gone. Don't you ever use stairs?"

"Not if I can help it."

"You're setting a bad example. I'm trying to teach them manners."

"I've got manners."

"You know what I mean. They already want to be eagles and fly like you. They were leaping and jumping off the jungle gym after lunch."

"And you want them to be good little girls?"

"I don't want them to break an arm or a leg imitating you. You're their hero. Kids love to see adults acting up."

"Well, wait until they see me in Jay's outfit."

"You found it?"

"Yes. I tried it on and it fits okay."

"Great!" Jen held up a coral necklace. "Cierra strung it and made the clasp."

He looked closely at a small silver frog with bulging eyes. "Nice. Are you teaching them sand-casting, too?"

"Yes. I want them to do more than just string beads, but bead work is becoming a lost tradition. Even a few years ago, everything was decorated with beads, especially the women's ceremonial dresses and the men's shirts. So I'm teaching them beadwork, and how to make jewelry and to sew."

"What do you want, Jen?"

"I want to create things, to be an artist, like you and Jay. Jay says artists are born, that you can't teach someone to be an artist, you can only learn technique. He says if you're doing crafts, you're not truly an artist."

"He's partly right. Crafts make our lives better, more beautiful, and often more meaningful. Talent at craft-making is a gift. I don't define creativity the way Jay does. I think the real test is the feeling you get from what you're doing."

"I feel bored, especially when I'm polishing Jay's production pieces."

"I'm with you, Jen. I hate polishing anything At least you have a great work space here. Who designed it?"

"Jay and Dennis Decomble; he's a Native American architect. They were so enthusiastic that it was exciting to watch. Neither of them wanted the Cultural Center to be just another museum filled with pots and relics. A *kivascape* was what they called it – a place to mix, mingle, and connect in small groups and forums. They wanted an atmosphere where people could work, play, and communicate beyond cultural boundaries. You need to talk to Jay. He explains it better than I do."

"Well, it works. The Center has the feel of a kiva."

"It works, but it's not what Jay and Dennis had in mind. Cultural Centers aren't money-makers like casinos. Sam and Jay tried very hard to convince everyone to keep the Center, but the tribe voted to convert the main building into a casino."

"Money talks."

"I guess it does, but we're adding more space to the Cultural Center. It's a start, but it's not the same."

"Who designed the AV room?"

"That was Jay's idea. It was meant to be a television studio because Jay wanted to make educational and training films. He planned to install a satellite hook-up with Native American schools and colleges so speakers and trainers could conduct interactive television classrooms."

"Do you know where Jay is? I'm a friend, Jen. I know he's in trouble and I want to help, if I can."

"I'm not sure he wants help. Jay's changed. He went to Phoenix, started drinking, and came back here. Something happened, but I'm not sure exactly what. He says it's better if I don't know. He wouldn't even tell Grandfather, and then he just disappeared again."

"Have you seen him?"

"I'm sorry, I should have told you earlier, but Jay wants to see you. He wants you, me and the girls to go together on the Verde Canyon Train."

"When?"

"Tomorrow afternoon. He says we're to sit in the back and he'll find us." Jen dabbed her eyes with a tissue. "I'm so scared. I'm afraid something bad is going to happen." Matt put his arm around her.

"Nothing bad is going to happen, not tomorrow afternoon. Jay wouldn't take a risk that might harm you or the girls. Besides, I'll be there with you. Okay?"

"Sure. Okay. I know you're right. Jay's friends will be on the train, too. But I'm still scared."

"Don't be. How are you getting to the station?"

"Sam's driving us."

"Does Sam know that you're going to meet Jay?"

"No, I haven't been honest with him either and he's so worried. But Jay says I can't tell Grandfather anything because it will just upset him."

"Jay's right. Let's just keep it quiet until we discover what's on his mind. I have a hunch that things are going to get better."

"But they could get worse."

"Maybe, maybe not," Matt suggested. Jen began putting the trays away. "Can you handle it?"

"Yes, I can."

"Do you know why Jay is hiding?"

"I truly don't know. He hasn't told me or Wally."

"Wally has seen him?"

"Yes, Wally takes him food."

"Wally was packing that extra burro with food for Jay, wasn't he?"

"Yes."

"Where was he taking it?"

"I don't know. He says Jay moves around a lot."

"One last question: Did Jay keep any blueprints or sketches of the center?"

"I'm not sure, but Dennis would have them. He has offices in Sedona and Phoenix. You could ask him."

Matt saw Renee watching them from the stairwell above. "Excuse me, Jen. Renee is going to give me a tour of the casino. I'll meet you at the station tomorrow."

"Sure, Matt, see you then."

Matt joined Renee and they walked into the hallway. "Sorry to interrupt you. What was that all about?"

"Jen is worried about Jay."

"Is that it?"

"That's it."

"Well, I'm free for a half hour or so. Do you want the grand tour?"

"Let's do the short tour. Can you get me into the surveillance room and the counting room?"

"Hmm. Never tried that before, but they know me. Let's see what happens." Renee knocked on the door of the counting room. A security guard undid a chain and stuck his head out. "Hi, Bill. Is Loren available? We'd like to look around."

"Sure. Come on in."

They stepped inside and Bill re-bolted the door. "Wait here. I'll get him." He walked past a row of counting machines where two clerks were loading stacks of bills into metal trays. On the other side of the room in three small office cubicles, women were busily scanning computer screens. Cables for the surveillance cameras, monitors and sprinkler system cluttered the ceiling. Due to the constant hum of the air conditioning units, the room was always exceptionally cool and noisy.

At the far end of the room, Bill was talking to a pink-skinned, bald man with thick glasses who was hunched over a wide desk. "The gnome," Renee whispered. Loren gestured to them. "Let's go."

Stepping outside his cubicle as they approached, Loren peered over his glasses at Matt and nodded. "Renee, what a pleasure," the short, squat, unattractive man said.

"Loren, this is Matt Dillon; he's our sculptor. Vince wanted him to meet everyone, including you. That is, if you have a moment."

"Delighted to meet you, Matt. Renee rarely includes us on the guided tour." Loren led them down the aisle. "There's not much to show you. The money from the cashiers comes here and we count it there. We keep the cash boxes in the walk-in safe. Very secure." He waved at two large, open doors. "The girls record every transaction for the auditors and we ship the overage to the central banks."

"You make it sound easy."

149

"Oh, it looks easy, but it's actually very complex. We handle several millions of dollars every year. That's not profit, of course. Keeping track of every penny isn't easy, but I run a tight ship. Isn't that right, Darlene?" He said to a wisp of a clerk who looked up over her glasses.

"He's a slave driver," Darlene agreed.

"That's my girl. Darlene's in charge of money transfers, credit lines, deposits, and withdrawals. Actually, Matt, most of our business is via credit links since no one carries cash anymore. Big winners don't walk out the door with a bundle. Too risky. An old-fashioned thief might take it. We're the new breed; we just take their credit cards. Bad joke."

"Thank you, Loren. Let's go upstairs, Matt. I'll show you the surveillance room."

"My pleasure, Renee. What are you going to create for us, Matt?"

"Huh, maybe a silver eagle, if you can spare a few coins for the foundry."

"You wouldn't get a silver eagle out of this trash; in the old days, maybe. This stuff is mostly copper and brass."

"I could do it in plastic."

"You'd be right with the times then. Come see me anytime, Matt," Loren said as he ushered them to the door. "Take care, Renee." Bill closed the door behind them.

"We should call him the ogre or the troll instead of the gnome," Renee said as they walked down the hall. "He gives me the creeps." Renee paused beside the restroom door. "Check it out."

Matt opened the door to the men's room and stepped inside while Renee stood behind him. It was a plain, no frills lavatory with two steel cubicles, two porcelain urinals, a towel rack, a wash basin, a long mirror, an electric hair dryer and several wall mounted dispensing machines. "Lovely."

"Check the dispensers."

Matt stepped inside. There were units for condoms, combs, and scents. The last machine dispensed heroin needles.

"We're heroin-friendly," Renee said as Matt stepped back into the hallway.

"Why?"

"Convenient cover when tainted money shows up. There's a unit in all the restrooms, especially in the suites. I wouldn't use a needle there though, unless I didn't mind being on camera. Over at Lake Havasu, some customers were robbed in the restrooms. In Vegas, too. No security in a restroom, no privacy either," Renee said as they walked up the stairs.

The door to the surveillance room was open. Shorty was waiting for them at the top of the stairs. "What a surprise! Matt and Renee, doing a tour are we? Welcome to the black room. Let me show you around. Come on in," Shorty beckoned. Matt blinked as he stepped into the room. An aura of blue light cascaded from the wall of mounted monitors. "No need for a walking tour. You can see everything from here." Shorty adjusted a dial. "Watch the big screen, Matt."

An enlarged view of a soda fountain appeared on the monitor where two animated boys were eating ice cream. "Give me an overhead," Shorty said to one of the controllers. Matt was looking straight down on the boys. "Close up." The lens zoomed in on the ice cream cup. A caramel sundae with a half-eaten maraschino cherry popped up. "Count the change." The camera zoomed onto some coins laying flat on the counter: a quarter, dime, and two copper pennies. The camera zoomed again. The caricature of Lincoln's face filled the screen. "1988," Shorty said and turned to Renee, as if he expected applause.

Getting no encouragement, he shrugged and requested, "Bowling alley." Four different views of the ten-lane bowling alley filled the monitors. A crowd of mostly male spectators was watching several scantily clad girls dressed in Dallas cheerleader outfits. Zooming in on a bare-waisted, large bosomed blonde juggling a bowling ball, the camera focused on her short shorts as she bent over and lobbed the ball down the alley. She turned and giggled as the ball slid into the gutter. "Gutter ball," Shorty said.

"Thank you, Shorty. Your mind's always in the gutter."

151

"My, aren't we snippy today?" The screens came back on. "We've got everything covered, Matt."

"How many cameras?"

"Company secret, but enough. We can spot a cheat while he's thinking about a move. You can see it in their body language. It's state of the art, from the parking lots to the kitchens. We see everything. If they have a record, we've got them: non-desirables, card counters, and cuppers. All the casinos have a black list and we exchange data about VIPS, whales, losers, and compulsives. You're on file, too, Matt."

"That's good to know."

"Everything under the federal gaming laws is legal. In fact, it's illegal not to use surveillance."

"Well, you're sure not breaking the law here."

"That's good. Most of what you see, we only hold for a week. The problem stuff we keep in storage."

"Are you guys going to be looking over my shoulder when I work on the sculpture?"

"Not possible. Except for the entry doors, the craft rooms aren't covered. We can see who comes and goes, but otherwise, it's out of bounds. The Tribal Council meetings are strictly taboo, too." Shorty refocused a camera on the beaded tassels on a cheerleader's costume.

"I don't know who planned the Bowling Babes Tournament, Renee, but I'm sure glad they did."

"I bet you are, Shorty."

"You can say that again."

"Why bother? C'mon, Matt. What a bunch of creeps," Renee said as they stepped outside the surveillance room.

"Be careful. They can read your lips."

"I hope they do," Renee made a face at a camera. "At least I know where the cameras are."

"I wouldn't be too sure of that."

"I've got to get back to the floor. I'll see you tonight."

Matt dialed his controller as he pulled away from the casino. "Chester, do we have a good connection?"

"I hear you loud and clear, Matt. Where are you?"

"I'm on I-17, just ready to drop into the Valley. What have you got for me?"

"Not much. Radcliffe is on a thirty day administrative leave."

"For what reason?"

"Unclear, but he apparently refused an opportunity to advance his career. The DEA wanted to pull him. Get the picture?"

"Yeah, at least, I think I do. Someone wanted him out of here."

"Could be; maybe, like I said, he's just a pain in the butt. They haven't heard from him and that, as far as they knew, he was in the Puget Sound area visiting his sister."

"What about Royer?"

"Unknown. She's not with any federal agency that I checked, but I didn't use a whisk broom. She could be deep cover, but there should be an entry level record. She's using her real name. She is who her resume says she is, and the Gaming Commission vetted her."

"I'm not buying it, Chester. She could be private."

"She could be working for another syndicate. They're competitive as hell. It's a cut throat business. If you can discover the competition out of line, you squeeze them and take over. It happens, not often, but manure happens. Are you there, Matt?"

"I'm here. Just thinking."

"Well, think out loud."

"Two possible agents, neither connected, both here in Camp Verde. Something's wrong with this picture."

"I see what you mean. I'll go back over the tracks. Give me a couple of days. Meanwhile, I filled out your laundry list. You ready?"

"I'm not taking notes, Chester. What have you got?"

"Well, let's start with the Marshals. Farley was with the San Diego Police Department for 17 years, primarily with the beach patrol. He apparently got tired of giving citations to skate boarders and under-age drinkers. Two CID investigations, but he was cleared. Signed on with the Border Patrol and, three years later, retired. Took the job at Camp Verde five years ago. He's a pensioner; so are the others.

"Randall was with a K-9 unit in the LAPD for 23 years, reached the rank of sergeant. He quit after a methhead shot his dog. He took the Cottonwood job seven years ago. Received a citation from the DPS for assistance rendered during a high speed chase that resulted in the death of civilians.

"Dick George is an interesting case. USMC military policeman, honorable discharge, Mesa Community College, criminal justice major. No degree. After that Phoenix police academy, nine-week dropout, martial art instructor, security guard, and rodeo circuit rider. Joined Yavapai Sheriffs posse and is a member in good standing. He became Marshall a year ago."

"That's it?"

"It doesn't take much in Jerome. Two charges for assault, both dropped, and one for public indecency in Benson, probably wasn't wearing a Stetson."

"Right."

"You asked about Kincaid. The story is that he made a bid for the Governor's office, but didn't get past the primaries. The Governor doesn't trust him, so she puts him on committees where she can keep an eye on him. She's also put a choke collar on his budget. Also, put a couple of watchers on him. They have a sort of a hate-hate relationship that goes beyond niggysob. I'm been told some of it goes way back, but that's before my time."

"How long have you been with the Gaming Commission, Chester?"

"Five months and one week and four days. If I make six months, I'm taking early retirement. This job is a bitch. Tribal gaming is just a political football. If you're associated, you're going to get your ass kicked; everyone wants a piece."

"The Governor?"

"Hell, she's a trip of the worst kind."

"What kind is that?"

"The sincere my-way-or-the-highway kind. Forget it. It's my problem, not yours. Which brings me to Cooper. He's trouble with a capital T."

"What have you got?"

"What haven't I got? Two real Purple Hearts, a Silver Star, and a Navy Cross from way back when he trained Navy seals for ultra-covert operations. He was a flyer, a helicopter pilot and a demolitions expert. He left after the first Gulf War and took jobs hustling arms and munitions and training agents all around the Middle East. He worked as a military advisor for the Moroccan Government and for the CIA in Iraq and Panama."

"Sounds like a nice guy," Matt interrupted.

"There's more. Cooper's an ultra-right winger, publishes paramilitary rags. The scuttlebutt is that he trains covert operators for the CIA. You don't want anything to do with him. He's one tough nut and he's protected."

"Tell me something I want to hear, Chester."

"Well, he shot himself in the leg during a fast-draw contest."

"You mean, he's human."

"Not exactly. He finished the competition before he let someone send for an ambulance."

"Is that it?"

"That's it."

"Thanks a load, Chester. I mean it. You got more than I expected."

"Anytime."

"Hey, what about Jay Cook?"

"De nada. I've asked, but everyone clams up. I get the feeing that I'm not supposed to get anywhere. I'll keep looking. Welcome to Happy Valley"

"Thanks," Matt replied and hung up.

CHAPTER TWELVE

Matt mingled with the tourists in the boxcar gift store. He picked up an H-O model engine, an exact scale replica of the Verde Canyon Railroad's vintage FD-7 with Doug Allen's bald eagle logo that was waiting on the tracks outside the depot. He set the replica carefully back on the miniature train tracks. Eagle novelties, toys, teddy bears, tee shirts, western hats, shot glasses, and other specialty items filled the shelves of the spacious room. On impulse, he bought two pressed pennies and wandered into the Railroad Museum. Inside, an intriguing exhibit of photographs and memorabilia helped him spend a pleasant half hour reliving the history of one of America's company towns.

Matt went outside and waited on the platform. The white bald eagle logo contrasted vividly with the metallic blue of the diesel driver. It appeared ready to take flight as the depot shuddered from the blast of air horns mounted atop the cab. "All aboard!" the conductor shouted as he stepped out of the first car. Walked to the end of the platform and passing by the closed air conditioned cars, Matt opted for the open-air viewing cars at the end of the train.

"Over here, Matt." Jen and several young girls, lunch boxes in hand, were standing outside the Copper Spike Café. "What do you say, girls?"

"Good afternoon, Matt."

"Good afternoon, girls."

The air horns blasted twice. "Last call! All aboard!" the conductor shouted.

An attendant approached them and said, "We're ready for the girls, Jen."

"All right, girls. Go with Amy. Behave yourselves. Remember, you are the Gourd Girls."

"I'll remember," Cierra promised as the girls filed up the steps into the train.

"Come get me if you need me. I'll be in the back."

"No worries, Jen. We'll keep them busy," Amy smiled.

"Let's get on, Matt, before someone gets the rear seat." He followed Jen back to the last car.

"Plenty of room," he said as they found a seat in the last row of the empty open observation car.

"I like it back here; you can see the whole train when it curves around Sycamore Hill."

The whistle blasted three times. As the train jerked and pulled slowly away from the depot, four heavy-set Indian men, wearing dark blue shirts, dark blue denim pants, black boots and black Stetsons, stepped off the end of the platform and climbed into the front of the car.

Picking up speed as it moved through the flats, the train passed the Old Clarkdale smelter and its forty-foot-tall slagheaps. Mingus Mountain towered majestically above as the train turned into the white limestone-ringed chasm of the Verde Canyon. The canyon walls were an intricate and brilliant patchwork of color: black basalt blocks supported enormous vermillion sandstone cliffs ringed by a white limestone ridge.

As the train rumbled across a trestle, above them a series of Sinagua dwellings, tucked into the cliffs, loomed over the tracks. "Awesome, isn't it?" Jen asked.

"Astonishing." Below them the light played on the crystal clear water of the Verde River. Prickly pears, larkspur, Spanish dagger, mesquite, ocotillo and Indian paint-brush colored the canyon floor. Cottonwoods, Arizona walnuts, and sycamores spread their canopies over the river. Overhead a pair of bald eagles soared and disappeared over the towering red-rock domes and cathedral-like spires. A pristine canyon appeared magically from which a surge of water escalated downward, tumbling over a block of basalt before it made its way to the Verde.

"SOB Canyon -- Sweet Old Bill. Don't ask me who he was," Jen said.

The pair of eagles returned, riding thermals, and circled patiently overhead. "That's Turtle Rock," Jen said. "Our people believe it guards the entrance to Sycamore Canyon. This canyon has been a home to Indian people since time began. But, like all the land that was ours, it's for sale." She pointed at several For Sale signs on the western side of the river.

"That can't be. You can't put homes here. That's a sacrilege."

"It will be unless the land swap is approved. The Forest Service would acquire it and supposedly add it to the Sycamore Wilderness unless..."

"Unless what?"

The train whistled. "That's the tunnel, Matt. I'll go check with the girls." Jen made her way forward. On the way, she spoke briefly to one of the men. The other three were sprawled in their seats, totally relaxed or asleep. When Jen entered the coach, three of the men stood up and moved inside the door, blocking Matt's view. The fourth man went down the steps, looked forward as the engine disappeared into the entrance to the tunnel. The bright light of day turned black and then the black turned to brilliant sunlight.

"Good to see you, Matt." A solidly built Indian was standing in the rear stairwell.

"Jay!" Matt stood up and the two men grabbed each other, swaying as the train rocked beneath their feet.

"Did I surprise you?" Jay laughed.

"Nothing you do will ever surprise me, Jay."

"Well, you look surprised."

"I was watching for you, but I wasn't expecting a bat out of a cave."

"Let's sit before we fall down."

The men who had been blocking the vestibule returned to their seats nonchalantly.

"I see you brought lunch." Jay pointed to the box lying on the seat, so Matt handed it to him. Jay flipped open the lid. "Pastrami and German potato salad – soul food. Thanks. So, how do I look?" Jay asked while wolfing down the sandwich.

158

"A little leaner. A few grey hairs, otherwise, you look about the same."

"Lots of meat, beans and corn meal, and I sleep under the stars. It's good for me."

"Where are you staying?"

"In a cave in the cliffs. The miners used to store dynamite up there. It's dry. I spent one night in an old cliff dwelling. Too wet, too many scorpions, and I was afraid some pot hunter or ranger would find me, so I moved up here. No one comes up here." The train rumbled across a long trestle. "All the conveniences. I even built a sweat lodge," Jay said as he picked up a fork and jabbed into his potato salad. "I'm glad you came, Matt. I'm in a tough spot, between a rock and a hard spot. A real foul-up."

"So, why have you been hiding? Who's after you?"

"Well, the short of it is, uh, did you find the video of the robbery?"

"Yes."

"Could you recognize me?"

"Possibly. Nothing that would stand up in court, however. I saw a heavy-set male wearing a Raiders cap and jacket."

"I was afraid the casino cameras got a better shot, so I split."

"I hate to ask, but, just in case, were you involved?"

"That's what Salvatori thinks."

"Why were you in the counting room?"

"Coincidence."

"You just happened to be in counting room when the robbery was going on?"

"The other way around, Matt. I saw the robbery from the AV room. I was watching the counting room. When those guys grabbed the money bags, I saw my chance."

"How did you get inside?"

"There's a space between the AV ceiling and the counting room. You can enter it from the AV room. I opened the baffle and just dropped in. I put it back, but I couldn't go back that way. I

159

grabbed a box of discs and a couple of tapes, and I split, just walked away. I just wanted proof."

"What kind of proof?"

"That Salvatori is laundering money and they are skimming. The Gnome records every transaction before they transfer funds. It's all on the discs: whales, drug lords, and big spenders. Salvatori even filmed the pay-offs to the tribal council. I hope I got the right tapes.

"So where are the tapes?"

"I gave them to Tom Fallon."

"Why?"

Jay looked over his shoulder at the men sitting in front of the car. "I wasn't thinking straight. I didn't know what to do, so I went to Tom. He told me that Carbahol said the robbery was an inside job and Salvatori wanted him to find me. Tom asked me what was on the tapes and I told him what I hoped was on the tapes, but I didn't know for sure. Tom just blew up! He told me that I was a fool, an idiot, and I guess he's right."

"You're no fool. At times you act like an idiot or a man with a cause, which is about the same thing."

Jay laughed and pounded Matt's shoulder. "Oh, man, am I glad to see you! I haven't felt so good since that time we super-glued Dr. Muriel's glasses onto her drawing board."

"That didn't work out too well, did it?'

"No, but it was fun. But this is a real screwed-up foul-up."

"Why didn't you just turn the tapes over to the FBI?"

"Lots of reasons. As Tom explained to me, and he admits he's no lawyer, they will probably put my ass in jail. They just might try to prove I was in on the robbery. Even if I have evidence of some kind, it wouldn't be admissible in court, would it? They'll claim it was tampered with by a drunken Indian. Even if I could prove the syndicate is bribing the tribal officers or skimming, Tom says that the Governor or the Feds would close the casino and the tribe would go down the tubes. That's not too swift, is it? And, Tom says, Mr. FBI Kessler is working with Salvatori. He's right. I've seen them wheeling and dealing, and Mr. DPS Kincaid is covering the drug operation. They're running drugs through the cement plant. So if I go to the cops, I'm a dead duck and the tribe loses everything."

"So, Tom told you to hide?"

"He told me to hide in the hills until you got here. He said you'd find a way to smoke them out without putting the tribe in jeopardy. In fact, he insisted we shouldn't do anything until you got here and until the land swap took place."

"Tom didn't tell me any of this," Matt said.

"I told him not to. I told him it was better if you had time to look around and see what's going on at the casino for yourself. I hate what the council's doing, but my father's dream is coming true. We're halfway home. We're out of poverty. We've got a chance to buy our homeland back. But we've got to stop the syndicate, and the council has to go, but I don't see a way."

"Well, this isn't the way, Jay."

"I know, but we have to get the syndicate off our backs and find a way to keep the money."

"The White Buffalo. Where have I heard that before?"

"From me. I know the white man's money won't set us free. But we can't throw it all away. We can't go back to being noble poverty-stricken Rez Indians. Look, those are my brothers up in front. Three years ago they were meth heads, alcoholics, just like me. We're all drum men now. We're clean. We are sweat lodge brothers. I just wanted you to see how things were before the house of cards collapses."

"Why me?"

"You're not a Rez Indian. You're Chief Comet, fiery crusader; you're Super Indian."

"Is that the way you see me, Jay?"

"No, not really. But you're smart; you can think. I also know you care about our people, and you don't tolerate fools."

"Well, maybe I'm about to start. First, tell me how much Jen knows?"

"That I've been video-taping the counting room and that Salvatori is looking for me. She typed my report on the lead pollution. She knows there're lead and arsenic on the 80-acre parcel we want to develop. It could be coming from our gravel operation. But I'm guessing it's spread all around the valley. The land is toxic where we built the housing complex. And Fallon said he wanted a second opinion before he told the Council. No need to panic, he said. I have a hunch that the original sources are the mine tailings in Jerome and in Clarkdale."

"Where's the report?"

"I don't know. I got to the airport to go to Washington and I got scared. I just couldn't get on the airplane."

"What did you do?"

"I got drunk. I woke up a week later in a Phoenix motel and went the rehab clinic."

"Where's the report now?"

"I gave it to Fallon, and he mailed it to the Secretary of the Interior."

"Are you sure?"

"Pretty sure. Sam got a card back thanking me for my contribution." After pulling into Perkinsville, the train came to a halt and the passengers began to debark.

"So who are your body guards?"

"They're the hawks, my rehab buddies. They are all Rez firemen, except Ray, who's a cop."

"That's good to know."

"They come up here from time to time. Wally brings supplies and we're searching the caves for the cash bags."

"Why up here?"

"They found the bikes up here. I think they stashed the bags in the canyon somewhere. We have to be careful because Farley shows up now and then. Nothing else to do, so we search the caves."

"That's it?"

"For now. I'm just trying to survive until you come up with something."

"Don't count on it."

"C'mon. I'll introduce you." They joined the men who were talking and joking among themselves at the end of the platform. "Matt, this is Ralph, David, Nathan, and Butch. They are sons of Geronimo. This is Matt, our friend and brother." Matt shook hands with the men.

"Sons of Cochise sounds better, Jay," Nathan said.

"Well, we're all sons of somebody," David spoke up.

"We are that," Jay said.

"Welcome, brother," Ralph said, and the men shook hands again.

"Matt tells me, promised me, that he will find a way to get the casino monkeys off our backs and soon."

"I didn't exactly say that, Jay."

"But that's what you intend to do, isn't it?"

Matt looked away and then at the men. "Yes. I will do what I can."

"Yaeeh," the men chorused quietly.

"I may need your help before this is over." Matt looked at each man squarely.

"Whatever you need, brother. We are ready." They raised their fists.

The train whistle blasted a warning. The conductor shouted, "All aboard!"

"We're staying, Matt. Going to take in the sights of lovely downtown Perkinsville." The men laughed. "Take care," Jay said and they disappeared behind the train depot as Matt climbed into the open car.

Jen settled the Gourd Girls in the midsection of the open car and joined Matt in the rear. "You're doing a good job with the children, Jen. They need you," he said.

"Just as much as I need them. They are my teachers, too." The train rattled along as light and shadows cast from the cliff walls and sycamores danced over the cars, lulling the girls to sleep. "The children are our future, Matt. I want them to become our doctors, lawyers, teachers, and artists -- our voices. They can make a contribution."

"Here in the Valley?"

"Yes, here. Why not?"

"They would still be on the Rez, wouldn't they? Or in the pipeline to an inner city ghetto or worse." A shadow flicked down a canyon wall, crossed the railroad car, and flashed over the streambed. They looked up just in time to see an eagle disappear over the mesa.

"I want us to be free, just like that eagle, with that kind of freedom."

"We're not eagles, Jen."

"You are. I want our children, my children, our people to be free. I want us out of the cage."

"You are mistaking something about me. I'm not free. I'm an outsider, an outside man, as my father used to call me. I'm my own experiment in living. I value my isolation, my privacy, even my loneliness. But I'm not free, none of us are. Creative activity, fruitful activity, my father used to say, is the only way through the maze. Freedom is somewhere on the other side. Right now I'm stuck between two worlds – the white man's and the red man's. I help out where I can, like you do, but then I lose my way and have to start all over. Sometimes, I think I've found what I'm looking for, but the trick is to know what do about it, and I'm not sure what I should do, Jen."

She sat thoughtfully until the train swept towards the station. Then she took his hands and held them tightly. "You know Matt, for you, for me, for all of us, love is the only answer. You are a creator, not a destroyer. You must become a bridge between our reality and the white's. If you want to be alone, that's your road. But any action you take to help end social injustice is an act of love and compassion, and that's what connects us. We need your help." Jen squeezed his hands. "I must get the girls," she said as the train eased into the depot.

Matt sat in the empty sunlit car and watched Jen march the girls across the platform. The song "The Windmills of my Mind" ran through his head as he adjusted his cap, stepped off the train, and walked across the parking lot to the Kombi.

164

CHAPTER THIRTEEN

Matt parked in front of the library, a building constructed from limestone blocks with large glass windows shaded by ancient cottonwoods. He went through the front doors to a cool, spacious room which felt almost subterranean. He located a row of computers just beyond the check-out counter and went to work. Two hours later, he staggered out with copies of BLM annual reports, USGS surveys, US wildlife Department monographs, Yavapai County zoning codes, the McCain-Fiengold bill, a history of the Yavapai-Apache tribes, a review of ranching, mining, and water rights legislative enactments from 1878 to 1941, and a library card.

Afterwards, he drove to McDonalds and picked up a burger, fries, and a shake. "Soul food," he thought as he parked under a cottonwood tree at the edge of town to eat his dinner. When he closed a geologic survey file, it was nearly dusk. "There's more than gold in them thar hills," he said aloud as he turned onto a back road to Camp Verde.

Renee's red Mustang was parked in front of the *Village Voice*. After hanging a u-turn, he parked in front of the Q & Brew, got out and crossed the street. Renee was sitting at her desk, obviously waiting for him, with the door to *The Village Voice* office open. He took off his cap, ran his fingers through his hair. "Are we ready?" he asked himself. "I mean, are we really ready?" and he stepped through the door.

"Hi, Renee. How was your day?"

"Very interesting." She handed him a copy. "Here, read all about it."

Wayne Parrish

Governor Visiting Verde Valley Villages

*Cottonwood. Governor Marylou Gray will host the first
wildlife conference during her three-day visit to the Verde Valley.
On Saturday she will be the guest of honor for the Pioneer Day
Parade. Today she presented a check from the Water Finance
Authority to help Yavapai County develop plans for wastewater
treatment plants. She held a public conference with tri-village
officials and the water advisory committee, and said she has
concerns about forest fire endangerment, unrestricted growth, and
water policy. During a brief Q & A period, the Governor stated
that it is surprising that a substance so inert as water can be so
volatile. But the solution is to develop a sound management plan
with the assistance of the Arizona Department of Water Resource.*

*Ed Meacham of the Concerned Citizens about Development
(CCADG) one of the several alphabet-soup groups representing
environmentalists and conservationists, said that CCADG was
concerned about the flawed estimates. According to him, the goal
of recharging the aquifers is not being met and is in direct conflict
with sustaining the Valley's goal of sustainability for the Verde
River. He concluded that at the present rate of usage, the springs
that are designated as headwaters and the Upper Verde will dry up
in the next twenty years.*

*These figures, once again, caused an uproar between the
various interest groups, and the meeting was disrupted by name-
calling and insults hurled by the participants.*

*The Governor voiced her dismay over the disruption,
exhorted calmer heads to prevail and expressed the interesting
viewpoint that things couldn't be quite as dismal as Meacham
reported. In fact, she had been assured that the ADWR were
upgrading their studies, and were encouraged that the recent rains
and snowfall, while increasing the danger potential, were
revitalizing the aquifers. More importantly, every citizen in the
Verde Valley should be reassured that the quality, not just the
quantity of the river, would be enhanced by water treatment plants.
She said that one of the primary reasons for coming here is to urge*

166

the Apache Tribe to clean up their act and get with the program. It's time they provided a treatment plan for their reservation and developed safeguards for their cement plant. They need to share the burden and the responsibility to encourage economic growth and development, just like everyone else who lives here. The audience response was a mixed bag of applause, jeers, and headshaking and, in some cases, stunned silence.

At this point, your reporter pointed out that it was unfortunate that no tribal council members were present, but it was clear that the Governor was unaware of the vast economic, political, and philanthropic contributions of the tribes. I'm certain the tribal councils will be interested in the Governor's visit. All in all, it was an astounding performance, certainly not an outstanding one. The repercussions should provide substance for the debate for several years, and seriously disable Yavapai County's water advisory plans. The Governor left the meeting to take her public policy road show to Prescott.

"I'm losing my objectivity if I ever had any," Renee said after Matt read the article.

"Taking sides becomes you."

"Not in this case. It's a lose-lose situation. Progress vs. preservation."

"No. It's common sense. It's simple: the Valley can't support another metropolis."

"Not to change the subject, but how are we going to work this out, Matt? I didn't attend a sidekick seminar."

"I'm not comfortable with this either."

"So, why did you agree?"

"Curiosity, I guess."

"Go on."

"Like, who are you, Renee? And who are you working for and what do you know about me?"

"You agreed. I don't want to spar with you."

"Why not? The referee is on your side. I think he suggested that we cooperate."

"Does that mean what I hope it means? If I show you what I've got, you'll show me what you've got?"

Matt smiled. "I think I could go that far."

"You show me yours first."

He turned his pockets inside out. "Nothing, zip, de nada. Your turn."

Renee moved closer, running her hands down her dress. "No pockets, but for openers, I work for the Federal Gaming Commission. I'm doing an impact survey."

"That's it?"

"That's it."

"Excuse me, but wasn't the impact study completed last year? I don't remember a follow-up on compulsive gamblers. Renee, I signed a blank check. Call your guy and tell him to tear it up." He made for the door.

"Wait, Matt. Where are you going?"

He turned. "I'm calling my bank to put in a stop order."

"Come back. Let's talk. Please sit down." Matt sat gingerly on the edge of the desk. She continued, "Look, I'm sorry. I'm just pissed. I've been here six months and haven't accomplished a damn thing. Oh, I've picked up a lot of loose ends, but nothing that makes a case. The casino is laundering drug money, but I can't prove it. I put up with Fiddles and do all his work and then put in a shift at the casino and, when I get home, I file reports on that damn machine. I haven't got time to investigate, and now you're here!"

"Are we having a pity party?"

"Oh, shut up! What would you know?"

"Look, I'm sorry." Matt impulsively wrapped his arms around Renee. She let him hold her for several moments and then shrugged her shoulders and stepped away. "I'm okay." She sat down, looked at him thoughtfully, and said, "Okay, we're in this together, whatever this is, but I don't know where to start."

"Try the beginning."

"In the beginning, I did work for the Federal Gaming Commission."

"Go on."

"Well, I moved up the ladder and my old boss put me on the impact study. It was interesting, fascinating, really, and I learned a lot. But I didn't like the Washington scene, the whole bureaucratic bit. I finished the report for the Commission on problem gambling and moved on. I always wanted to be a writer. So I quit, moved to Flagstaff, and enrolled in journalism courses at NAU." She breathed deeply. "I wrote an article on gambling addiction. Want to see it?"

"Sure."

"It's there on my desk. It's that piece under the glass top." Matt leaned over the desk. *One in Five Gamblers Commit Suicide* had been highlighted with a yellow marker.

> *The effects of problem gambling are devastating.*
> *The suicide rate for pathological gamblers is much*
> *higher than for any other addictive disorder.*
> *Nearly half of gambling addicts have considered*
> *suicide. The compulsive gambling population has*
> *grown by at least 50% in the last decade and has*
> *doubled in populations within 50 miles of a casino.*
> *The impact of gambling on a community includes*
> *increased divorce rates, child neglect, and crime.*

Dad was scribbled across the article.

"Your father committed suicide?" Matt asked softly.

"Yes, but not until he sold all of our belongings while my mother was in a hospital. After my mother died, I got a scholarship to LSU. I was on my own and doing fine. He came to the dorm one day, tired, broke, and hungry. I gave him ten dollars, but he also stole twelve dollars from my roommate's wallet and some quarters from a jar we kept for the coin laundry. That was the last time I ever saw him."

"Renee, I'm sorry."

"Look, it's no problem, Matt. Writing that piece helped me to what, detach? That's the way I want to stay -- detached. No, don't interrupt, please." She raised her hand to silence him. "A prof encouraged me to do an internship with a newspaper, so I came here and I like it here. I've never lived in a small town before. I picked up a job at the casino as a cocktail waitress. Salvatori liked me and offered me the hostess job."

"Whoa. I thought your job was a cover. You weren't working for the Gaming Commission then?"

"Nope. It was a real job."

"So how did the Commission contact you?"

"They didn't. I called my old boss and told that there was a lot of funny business going on at the casino. Frankly, I needed the money. He was delighted to rehire me and turn me over to Anka. The rest is history, but, as I said, I was making no progress, so I requested a transfer back to my old job. Then the casino was robbed, and Anka asked me – no, told me -- to stay put. But now I'm ready to quit again. I want out. How about you, Matt? Want to join me? We can ride into the sunset together."

"I'd like to; I dig riding off into sunsets. But before we go, why don't you show me your tapes?"

"What tapes?"

"Your laptop, Renee, is not exactly an ectasketch, is it?"

"Was it that obvious?"

"Not unless you know what to look for."

She opened her case and tapped the escape key. "Use the scroll." He scanned through the typescript twice and then picked up a pad and began making notes while she turned on a desk lamp and pulled her chair closer.

"Very interesting," Matt said. "It's nice to know that I'm kind of fagotty…"

She laughed. "I knew that would bother you."

"What's your read on this?"

"Well, Kessler's running a sting on Kincaid. He's squeezing George and Randall. The Marshals are dealing meth, Kincaid is obviously providing protection for a bigger operation, and I'm guessing that Kessler is reaching for the sky. He wants the traffickers."

"What does Anka say?"

"Told me he'd cover it, since he thinks there's no clear connection to the casino. It's Kessler's sting and he wants me to back off."

"And?"

"I don't agree. Kessler is investigating the casino robbery and, obviously, Kincaid. The casino is laundering drug money. Kincaid has been to the casino at least twice this year. Salvatori gives him the royal treatment, but he never gambles."

"How about Farley?"

"I've never seen him inside the casino."

"He wasn't with Kessler. He left with Kincaid."

"Farley is Kincaid's weasel."

"I agree, Renee. I had Vance run a pedigree on the Marshals and Kincaid. The Marshals are flakey. Basically, they are pensioners, except for Dick George, so they don't get big salaries. Should we check with the IRS?"

"I already have,. They're clean, too clean. That's what the laundry business is all about. They don't even bank their salaries."

"The bad news is that Kincaid checked us out while we were having lunch, which means he's connected somewhere, and he ran a line on Billy Burger."

"I'll need to warn him, Renee. He's a friend."

"He's the biker you talked to in Jerome, and you met him outside the Q & Brew, right?"

"How did you know that?"

"I peeked out the restroom window. I am a snoop, you know. So who is he?"

"His name is Dick Radcliffe. He's DEA, or he was DEA, could be something else now."

"Oh, God. Who's on first?"

"And Why's at home plate? We need to know why."

She stared at the ceiling. "Cooperate, the man said." She punched up a file. "Try this. Welcome to Happy Valley."

He read the item marked *Cooper-Strickland.* "Crunch my buns," he said when he finished. "I don't believe it. When did you get this?"

"After the town meeting. They were talking on the porch across the street."

"What did Anka say?"

"I haven't sent it yet." She crossed her legs. "I was going to, but I came over to the Q & Brew and I just got to thinking that it was a good time to walk off into the sunset."

"Give me a half hour to pack my things. I'll go with you."

"That's comforting, Matt. I'm so glad you're here. Like I said, welcome to Happy Valley."

"You'll need the cavalry to sort this out. A paramilitary basketcase who owns a water company, wants to blow up the valley, is tied to Strickland who owns a water company, and they both suspect, hell, they *know* the cement plant is a drug warehouse for the syndicate."

"There's more. Trucks and limos are leased to the tribe by Strickland, and Cooper wants out."

"And Strickland wants the water rights."

"And Joe is a dupe or a stool pigeon, and he's my boss," Renee added.

"And Salvatori and Anka."

"You've got it. So why don't we just go as we are?"

The street lights had turned on. Trucks were lined up across the street in front of the Q & Brew. They sat quietly in the gloom of the darkened office. Matt was about to say something when an explosion rattled the windows and doors. They instinctively dove for the floor, cracking their heads together in the process.

"What the hell was that?" he sputtered. There was another explosion, stronger than the first. The front window of the *Village Voice* sagged and cracked as Matt scrambled to his feet and pulled Renee up. "Outside."

Renee beat Matt through the door and onto the boardwalk. People were spilling out of the Q & Brew and someone shouted,

"The laundromat's on fire." Black smoke was billowing out the windows of a small white frame building.

"Oh, no! Maybe someone's in there," Renee shouted.

"Call 911!" Matt took off running towards the laundromat. The smoke was clearing, so Matt looked inside. Small flames were creeping up the wall of a closet when Radcliffe joined him.

"Anyone inside?"

"I don't think so. Let's take a look." Matt tested the door knob, but it wouldn't budge easily. So he forced the door open with his shoulder and stepped inside.

Radcliffe followed close behind, pulled a flashlight from his jacket, and played it on the walls and floors. "It's clear. It doesn't look like anyone was inside."

"It must have been a gas explosion."

"Check that hole. That must have been the second explosion."

Matt stuck his head through the opening. The back wall of the office was on fire. "Give me the flashlight." He beamed the light around the room. Taking a chance, he stepped through the gap. Then a siren wailed and an airhorn blasted and cut out.

"Let's go, Matt. There could be another explosion."

Matt went over to a filing cabinet that had a gaping hole on one side. He glanced in the open cabinet and saw that files had been ripped out and tossed on the floor. Since scattered papers were beginning to curl and ignite, he stepped back through the hole. "No one inside," he yelled. "Everybody out. We've got fire. Let's go." Radcliffe shooed everyone outside just as a fire truck pulled up.

"Out of the way, folks. Get off the street," a burly fireman shouted at the crowd.

"You've got a fire in the next building," Matt shouted at the fireman. "I didn't see anyone inside. But you'd better check."

"Thanks, buddy. Go take a look, Martin. Elmer, bring me water. Sweet Jesus! Get out of the street. Where's the damn Marshall? About time," he muttered as a Camp Verde police car pulled up behind the fire truck.

173

"Get these people off my back, Farley. Elmer, where's my water?"

"Right beside you, Chief!"

"Well, turn it on and get in there. What are you waiting for?"

Elmer muttered, turned the handle, and pushed through the door.

"Get me another hose up there on the roof," the Chief shouted.

"Let's get out of harm's way, Matt. Let the boys do their job," Radcliffe suggested. They crossed the street and joined Renee, who was scribbling madly on a yellow pad. He looked over his shoulder.

"Was there anyone inside?"

"No. No bodies. The front door was locked. The laundromat must have been closed."

"That's odd. They keep it open until midnight." Renee said.

"Well, whoever set off the pipe bomb must have locked the door," Radcliffe said.

"There was a bomb?"

"A pipe bomb," Matt said. "It was attached to the file cabinet."

"You saw it?"

"Someone broke through the wall to get into the water company."

"Uh oh, we've got company. I think Bucky wants to talk to us," Radcliffe said.

"Here comes Honest Abe himself," Renee said. Sheriff O'Neil's coarse nose, thick eyebrows, dark eyes, unruly mane of hair, and solemn look gave him a Lincolnesque appearance.

"Who says he's honest?" Radcliff asked softly as Bucky strode purposely across the street.

"He does. Almost looks presidential."

"Good evening, folks," O'Neil said with a smile parting his thick lips. "Getting it all down, Renee?"

"Just the highlights, Sheriff. I need the details."

"Well, I'll get them to you as soon as I figure out what happened here." He turned to Matt and Radcliffe. "Elmer tells me that you boys were inside the laundromat when they got here?"

"We heard the explosion, the first one, and we ran outside after the second one broke the windows. Matt ran to the laundromat and I called 911," Renee answered.

"You went inside?" Bucky asked.

"Yes, Sheriff. The door was locked, but I couldn't be sure if someone wasn't inside. There was still a lot of smoke. He followed me in," Matt nodded at Radcliffe.

"I was shooting pool at the Q & Brew. I thought a bomb had gone off. I went outside and saw the smoke. Same as him. I thought somebody might be inside."

"Well, you boys took a chance."

"Why was the door locked, Sheriff?" Renee asked.

'Well, I don't know."

"It's never been locked before midnight."

"How do you know that?"

"I do my laundry there."

"Every night?"

"No, but regularly."

"Did you see anyone on the street?"

"I don't think so, but I wasn't really looking," Matt said.

"See anything inside?" O'Neil asked Matt.

"I stuck my head through the hole in the wall. The fire was spreading so we got out."

"And you?" turning to Radcliffe.

"I didn't look inside. I started to think there might be another bomb and I cleared out."

"Who said there was a bomb?"

"Had to be. That was one hell of a bang, Sheriff."

"The fire chief thinks a gas leak under the floor of the Laundromat set it off, a spark, maybe. Gas could have seeped under the water company building. It's too soon to say."

"What about that hole in the wall, Sheriff?" Renee asked.

"Could have been a pipe bomb."

"Three pipe bombs in one day? That's no coincidence; that's news."

"I don't see a connection. This was a break in while the other two were meth labs. The trailer outside Page Springs was booby trapped with a shotgun with a hair trigger aimed at the front door. In the other situation, the guy had a pipe bomb wired to the light switch in that crack shack in Dewey."

"You were lucky, Sheriff."

"Not lucky. Only a fool would go through the front door of a crack house."

A Camp Verde patrol car pulled up. Constable Farley got out one side and a pale, visibly shaken Sonny Strickland got out the other. "Well, I need to take care of business. I don't think I need a statement, but would you mind letting me see your ID's just for the record?" Matt and Radcliffe fished their driver licenses out of their wallets. The Sheriff copied the numbers onto a notepad. "Thanks for your help," he said as he handed them back.

"Sheriff, how about…." Renee asked.

"Renee, I'll give you what I've got as soon as I know. You can scoop *The Prescottonian*."

"Great. You promise?"

"You've got my word."

They watched as the Sheriff strode like a long-legged crane across the street. "He looks like Wilt the Stilt," Radcliffe said.

"That man could leap tall buildings," Matt added.

"Don't let him hear you say that. He'll put it in his press release."

"Faster than a speeding bullet?" Radcliffe asked.

"That's already there. He's been involved in high speed car chases this year. He used a rifle left-handed, out the window, twice. He stopped one driver. The second time, two people in an oncoming car were killed. They couldn't get out of the way, crashed into a ravine on Cherry Road. He's a grand stander, one arrogant SOB."

"Well, hats off to the local law. I'm glad they are on the job. I'll buy," Radcliffe offered.

"You two go ahead; I'm going to stick around and see if I can talk to Strickland," Renee said.

Except for the barkeep, Matt and Radcliffe were alone in the Q & Brew. "Time to talk, buddy." Radcliffe took a look pull from his can of beer and looked at Matt expectantly.

"I agree, Dick. What do you know about Renee?"

"I'm just guessing, but I'd say she is working for the Federal Gaming Commission or someone like that."

"Good guess. But Kincaid is curious about her and you. He checked you both out."

"Well, he won't find anything on me. I'm not sure about Renee. Too many leaks in that agency. It's too political. Salvatori, and I'm guessing, is laundering money for the drug dealers. They are using that cement plant as a drop for Mexican meth. It could be Salvatori's deal, but I bet, the syndicate is backing it. I'm sure Kincaid's providing protection."

"And Kessler?"

"FBI. Squirrelly guy. He's doing a job on Kincaid and putting heat on the Marshals."

"I can confirm that. Renee taped Kessler taping Kincaid when we were at the café in Jerome."

"Happy days. Now we have an explosion and O'Neil's torching the local meth labs. It's a Chinese fire drill."

"So, what are you going to do?"

"I'm thinking. I'm thinking." Radcliffe finished his beer. "Life is an adventure, and an adventure is a badly planned trip. I do have a plan, but the best laid plans aft gang awry, or something like that." He grinned. "How about you?"

"I don't know, Dick. I just got here. The usual stumble, fumble, and curse. It's something more than drugs and money laundering, but I'm not sure what. I'll check out Jeff Cooper. He may have something to do with the explosions tonight."

"Whoa, buddy! That man is a certified nutter. I'd keep my distance."

"Is he dealing drugs and making meth?"

"No. Those guys don't go in for that. He was CIA and they did the Contra deals, but it was for the cause. Hell, they get high on patriotism. You know, Matt, you ought to get in your bus and get the hell out of here."

"That's the second time tonight I've been told that."

"If Renee made me an offer, I'd take it. Another beer, Billy, if you please. How about you, Matt?"

"No thanks. I'd better get back to Renee. We have some things to work out."

"Let me know if you need a helping hand."

"I think your hands are already full."

"You're right. If the crap hits the fan, I'll send up a flare. You too, buddy."

"If I can. See you." Matt made his way through the Q & Brew which was filling up since the street show was over. He crossed the street and stood outside *The Village Voice* office. Renee closed her computer, turned off the light, and locked the door. "What did Strickland tell you?" he asked.

"He played dumb. He says some drughead must have been after the petty cash drawer."

"So, what do you think?"

"He's lying and he's spooked. The cash drawer wasn't touched and his shirt was soaking wet with sweat."

"How about Cooper?"

"Who else? You heard what he said on the tape. That wasn't an idle threat. Cooper meant what he said. I can't show the Sheriff the tape. I can't let him know I'm taping conversations. Bucky's no fool, and Strickland isn't going to say anything, not yet."

"Later might be too late. I'm not going to sleep tonight. Wrong. I am going to sleep tonight if my ears ever stop ringing."

"Do you want to go over this tomorrow? I think we need a fresh start."

"Why don't we drive up to Sedona? You said we ought to get away."

"Sedona's not far enough. I was thinking maybe the Tonga Islands. What's in Sedona?"

"I'd like to meet with an architect there and a Land Conservancy guy who knows something about the pollution problems along the Verde."

"Interesting. Well, let me think. Joe's been after me to do a piece on Sedona tourism. It works for me, and I suppose we could hassle with this other stuff tomorrow."

"Why hassle it? Let's give it a rest."

"You're on, Matt. I'll let Anka know."

"Why not give Anka a rest, too?"

"You know, I think you're right. Why not?"

As he walked Renee to her car, he said, "I'll pick you up here in the morning. Is 9:30 okay?"

"Sure." Renee backed out and turned her Mustang north on Main Street.

Matt watched her taillights until they dimmed. A meteorite carved a blue streak overhead, split in two, and disappeared over Cleopatra Hill. "I hope that not an omen," he whispered.

CHAPTER FOURTEEN

"The green pinions and junipers contrasted vividly with the cloud-dotted blue sky and the red rock formations that rose spectacularly from the base of the Mogollan Rim. A picture-perfect sunrise against Thunder Mountain greeted us."

"What are you talking about? It's almost noon," Matt remarked.

"There will be a sunrise tomorrow. There always is." Renee continued speaking into her headset. "The moon, still white in the brightening sky, dangles over Bell Rock, a silent rust-colored sentinel bursting with electric energy from the red earth vortex beneath the dome. Cathedral Rock is an excellent place to bask in and absorb energy from the surreal light of the early morning sun. Along with the airport vortex, these vortexes create an enormous grid of energy."

Renee continued dictating into her headset: "A native legend tells that a newly married couple argued day and night. The woman complained that he never helped her out around the cave and that he would never listen to her. He complained that she nagged him all the time and never appreciated the game he hunted. The argument went on endlessly. One day they appealed to their God for a solution and He responded by placing them back to back so that they each would retain their vision and direction."

"God is great," Matt offered. "What happens after dark?"

"They're stuck, back to back."

"I knew there had to be a catch."

"Always is."

"So, what's this vortex stuff all about?"

"Well, a vortex is a site where the earth's invisible lines of power supposedly intersect." Renee read from a brochure: "In 1980 Peg Bryant, a New Age channeler who lived in Sedona, determined there were at least four vortices, though the locals call them vortexes. The term is more symbolic than literal. Her adherents believe that electrical and magnetic energy flows upward through the domes. Bell Rock and Boynton Canyon are electrical male energy. Cathedral Rock is female magnetic energy. The airport dome is male and female energy combined. It's more balanced. But the energies are so subtle, they can't be measured scientifically."

"So, it's all New Age malarkey?"

"That's what skeptics say. The Yavapai and the Apaches considered the rocks sacred, as well as the Navajo and the Hopi, especially Boynton Canyon. Only the bravest chiefs and medicine men were allowed to visit the sacred shrines. Pilgrims come from all over the world to visit Sedona now. It's a Mecca for the New Agers, crystal healing electromagnetic field therapy, tarot readings, angelic healing, channeling, meditation services, vortex tours, retreat centers, and spiritual goodies. It's all here." She tossed the brochure aside.

"What do you think?"

"I think that there are a lot of psychically, spiritually, and emotionally damaged people. There's a world of hurt out there which will take something more than aromatherapy to balance. But I have to believe that if you come here with an open heart and open mind, you won't leave empty-handed, and in your case..."

"In my case?

"Invest in a crystal. Align your chakras. Balance your yin and yang. Consult a tarot reader. Revise your mantra. Learn to chant. Buy a new hat."

"A new hat? What's wrong with my hat?"

"Well, for one thing it makes you look like a very serious Frisbee player."

"You mean a sincere Frisbee player?"

"No, I mean I'm sincerely seriously starving. Pull in at the Coffee Pot." A large dome-shaped rock which vaguely resembled a campfire coffee pot, overshadowed a restaurant and parking lot packed with campers, vans, and motor homes. Matt turned off the highway and stopped at the end of a row of vehicles.

"If you're in a hurry, Renee, this isn't the place."

"They have a take out. Be right back." Renee jumped out of the van and dashed across the parking lot.

"101 omelets, only fresh eggs anything but the chipolatas," Matt thought as he read the 100th selection posted on a billboard above the restaurant.

Renee opened the door and slid into the seat beside him. "I got a chipolata omelet." Matt felt his face tighten. "For me," Renee quickly added. "And a strawberry kiwi that's really delightful for you." His shoulders eased. "Go to the Y and turn left at the traffic light and then hang another left at the second driveway."

Catching the light, he executed the turns and parked under a sycamore tree. "You live right. I never find an open space anywhere near Tacky Placky."

"Where?"

"Tlaqueplaque."

"Oh."

When they found a bench overlooking a meandering arm of Oak Creek, Renee divided the omelets and handed Matt a fork. "I'll be right back." She scurried down a cobblestone street that separated two massive grey Mexican colonial structures and darted into an arcade. Reappearing moments later, she smiled radiantly as she set a pair of tall goblets on the bench. "Sparking Chablis. It cuts the chipolata and sweetens the strawberries."

"Mucho gracious," Matt said as he gratefully swallowed the wine.

A light breeze swept down the canyon, rustling the leaves. When a Rufus humming bird darted in front of Matt and hovered fearlessly inches from his face, he casually removed his sunglasses. The hummer, satisfied that he had threatened his rival away, spiraled skyward and disappeared over a rooftop. "The Rufuses are incredible bullies. They are like bumble bees," Renee said. They ate quietly as the creek sang its song and the Rufus returned again and again to dance overhead.

"That was terrific," Matt said. "Finished?"

Renee handed him her plate and he dumped them in a trash container. She locked her arm in his. "C'mon. Let's look around."

For the next hour they visited swank art salons and humble shops filled with trash and treasure from all over the world. Stalls featuring curried rice, barbequed ribs, and Italian ice cream lined the streets. On a side lane, jugglers, clowns, and mimes competed with time share touts for their attention.

A bottled blonde with enormous cleavage partially concealed by strings of quartz crystals on silver chains was holding court next to a crystal kiosk. Her twanging voice extolled the virtues of prisms and healing power from the vortexes, and promised in a rehearsed spiel that the magnetic lines of the force enhances male and female energy, and, lowering her voice, forestalls, even prevents, breakups. Holding up an amethyst prism, she told the small crowd standing in front of her, "These crystals clarify sounds. You hear bell sounds if you carry these up Bell Rock."

"Do they clink or clank?" Matt asked and Renee shoved an elbow into his ribs. The blond stepped close to Renee and dangled a crystal. It swung like a pendulum back and forth and it began to swirl round and round, making larger and larger circles.

"You have a pure heart, honey." Then a frown creased her face and the blond hesitated. "But you have a very short heartline. You need this crystal." She grasped the crystal and stopped it in midswing. "Why don't you try it on?" she asked while she opened the loop and placed it over Renee's neck. The crystal pendulum settled snugly between her breasts and over her heart. "Feel the power?"

Renee brightened. "I do feel something. I really do. It's kind of, well, vibrates." She looked at Matt thoughtfully.

"Keep it, honey; it's a gift."

"Oh, I couldn't," Renee protested. "How much is it?"

The blond put a hand on her hip. "For you, thirty dollars. It's pure pink amethyst."

Renee started fishing through her purse. Matt reached for his wallet and found a twenty and a ten. "You're a lucky man, sir. Your lady is a treasure. She has a pure heart," she said as she snatched the bills from his hand. "Peace."

"Peace," Renee said and tugged at his arm to lead him around the corner. Once out of sight of the tourists, she said, "My hero!" as she hugged Matt, laughing uncontrollably.

"All right. What's the joke?"

Renee laughed again. "You're so serious. I'm afraid to tell you."

"So tell me."

"You promise not to get mad?"

"I'll take Kings X on this one."

"Well, Annie is a friend. She's a dealer at the casino. We call her Cosmic Annie. Whenever I come to Tacky Placky, I shill for her and she buys lunch."

"You're a trip, Renee." She held the crystal in front of Matt. It swung like a pendulum and moved from his heart to hers. "It's no problem. Annie will give me back the money."

He put the crystal in his shirt pocket. "I think I'll keep it for awhile. I have a feeling that I'm going to need all the psychic energy I can gather today."

"That was sweet of you, Matt," She squeezed his arm. "Be right back," she said and slipped away.

Matt idled down the street, eyeing the street vendors' wares and dodging several time share touts. He stopped in front of kiosk that displayed a variety of trade junk: ceramic pieces, saguaro magnets, tin wily coyotes, and miniature Navajo wedding ollas. On impulse, he purchased a small string of ceramic chili peppers and a map of the vortexes. He paused in front of a book stall that specialized in Western titles. Picking up a worn-looking novel, he skimmed through it, and handed the clerk a five dollar bill. She put the book in a plastic bag and handed him his change as she smiled pleasantly at Matt and said, "Enjoy."

He crossed to the shady side of the street and stood under the awning of the Wild West Emporium which displayed a wide variety of Stetson hats in its window. The huge domed Stetson popularized by Dan Blocker in the television show *Bonanza* dwarfed the ten-gallon hat labeled "The Gus" that Robert Duvall wore in *The Lonesome Dove* and the black "George Strait" Stetson. Matt went inside.

An elderly, gray-haired man was dusting the glass shelves. "Looking for a hat?"

"Not sure. Just looking."

"You live around here?"

"Camp Verde."

"If you live around here, you got to have a Stetson. You don't have to be a cowboy. Everyone wears Stetsons nowadays -- entertainers, movie stars, even Presidents. We sell more hats to Germans and Japanese than we do to the locals. Can't go to a dance without one, but they aren't cheap."

Matt found a white one that he liked, put it on, and stepped in front of a mirror. "That looks good on you. I mean it; it looks great," Renee said from the doorway. He adjusted the brim and put on his sunglasses. "That's a serious hat. What do you think?"

"Looks good. Feels good," he said.

"Then seize the moment, as my Daddy used to say."

"How much?" he asked.

"Like I said, they aren't cheap. That's 100% 100X shaved beaver. It's the Sidewinder. It's also called the Denson Pinch and, now, hold onto your hat, 'cause it's $1200. Like the lady says, it's a perfect fit."

Matt took the hat off and gingerly restored it to the shelf. "Thank you. I was just browsing."

"Browsing is across the street, but if you're looking for an entry level hat, they're in the back."

"Let's go, Renee." He reached for her arm and led her outside.

"It did look good on you, Matt."

"Are you shilling for this guy, too?" He reversed his John Deer cap. "Polyester with a nylon adjustable strap. Five dollars at Wal-Mart. It keeps the sun off my head and the rain off my neck."

185

"But not your ears."

"Giddy up, Renee. Let's get going." They got into the VW. Matt draped the string of chilis and the prism around his rear view mirror. When he spun the crystal, a myriad of hexagon rainbows danced merrily inside the van. "Thank you Cosmic, uh…"

"Annie."

"Thank you, Cosmic Annie. I didn't remember her name, but I never forget a face."

"You mean a bosom." Renee punched his arm. "That's what souvenirs are for!"

"So I can remember her name or her bosom?" Renee punched his arm again. "Where to?" Matt asked.

"Oak Creek Canyon – slide rock. Turn west at the Y." Matt trailed a caravan of pink jeeps through the light. Two miles up the canyon, the jeeps turned onto a forest service road and they had a clear road ahead. Renee clicked on her tape recorder:

"Oak Creek bubbles through the canyon. It curves in the sheer cliffs surrounded by towering ponderosas and twisted junipers. Oak Creek Canyon is a chasm of stupendous views, side canyons, creeks, picturesque red rock monoliths, limestone and sandstone cliffs, a place of silence, peace, and tranquility. The scenic highway is not only a getaway but a gateway that connects to the planet's spiritual nature. A back door to the mythological universe." Renee clicked off her recorder. "How does that sound?"

"It sounds like a sound bite for a pink jeep tour."

"Really? That bad?"

"Like I maybe should paint the van pink and decorate it with yellow daisies and red pentstemons and golden poppies."

"Red what?"

"Pentstemons. They're roadside flowers. You need a total assault on the senses, Renee. Let your readers feel it, taste it, touch it, smell it. Stir their imaginations, their memories, their desires. Tell them about yourself. Let them in on your secrets before you hit them with your list of hotels, restaurants, and bargain stores."

"Hmmm. You're saying that my article sucks."

Matt pulled the VW to a halt behind a long row of cars parked on the side of the road. "No. You're a good writer. So was Zane Grey." Matt reached into the plastic bag and handed Renee a copy of *Call of the Canyon*. "Read it. He wrote a lyrical, idyllic piece about Oak Creek. The man was an ecologist, a prophet. He knew what was going to happen here. What he didn't do was urge Teddy Roosevelt to declare the Red Rock Country a national park and declare his heroine Sedona Schnebly and her Inn national disasters."

"Matt, you are amazing. That was truly passionate."

"Feel their passion, Renee. Let it go through you and pass it forward to your readers." He waited until a large SUV pulled out from the long row of vehicles that were parked along the edge of the highway.

"See? The crystals do work!" Renee said as he nosed the van into the space.

He closed the window curtains and waited in front of the van while Renee changed her clothes. Across the road, Oak Creek burbled through a series of pools and then gushed down through a series of narrow channels. The white water splashed against slippery red rocks, forming a natural slide. Life-jacketed children screamed with abandon as they clutched their crotches and sides, waiting to catapult down the chasm. Sunbathers were sprawled on a red ledge that rimmed the creek. Hikers poked their way upstream along a trail that led deeper into a narrow canyon.

"Next," Renee said, and stepped out of the van. She had slipped on a white smock covered with large yellow daisies, which set off her dark hair and brown-toned skin. She stuffed a small pixel camera and her recorder into a raffia bag. "I'll wait for you across the street."

Matt opened the side doors, checked for stray hikers, and, seeing none on his side of the highway, changed quickly into a pair of shorts and slid on thongs. He grabbed a towel from a rope rack and tossed it over his shoulders. After a string of cars passed, he sprinted across the highway. Renee was aiming her camera at a small boy teetering on the lip of the rock slide.

The camera clicked as the boy made a leap of faith and screamed his way down the thirty-foot shute worn smooth by a billion bottoms and the camera clicked again as the boy's father pulled him from the pool and held the laughing boy triumphantly over his head. "Good show, David!" the father yelled.

The camera clicked again as the father passed the boy to his mother and opened his arms wide, encouraging a doubtful-looking blond girl to join him. "Come on, Trish!" The camera kept clicking as she went headfirst into the shute, only her head and shoulders above water. She shot out the shute and collided with her father, who gathered her in his arms and deposited her on a shelf.

"Can we do it again, Daddy?" the children cried.

"That's my story," Renee said. "*Mother Nature's Slip and Slide*. Let's stay on this side, Matt. It's less crowded and the sun's coming our way." They crawled over a rock wall and spread their towels on a sun-drenched sandstone bench. Renee lay down and rested her chin on her arms. Matt sat down, crossed his legs, rested his arms on his knees and turned palms up. "Are we going to meditate?"

He closed his eyes and sat silently. Fifteen minutes passed and then twenty. When he opened his eyes, Renee was resting on her side, one hand holding her chin, staring at him.

"Good to see you're still here. What has the swami decided?"

Touching his forehead, he said, "The swami needs to refresh himself in the slip and slide." The sun had drifted to the edge of the canyon as they walked down to the creek and made their way to the edge of slide rock.

"You go first."

"No, let's go down together." He sat down on the lip. Renee sat behind him and wrapped her legs around his waist, circling her arms around his chest and he pushed off. The ride was smooth and surprisingly swift. They landed together in a circular basin of water. Renee still clung to him as they stood up.

"Warm enough for you?" Matt asked.

"Exquisitely brisk. Let's do it again." They climbed back to the top. "Let's go head first. Me on top."

Matt lay down on his stomach and she pressed her body on top of him and wrapped arms around his shoulders. He was conscious of her warmth as they sped down the shute. He arched his body as they hit the pool and glided across. She slipped off and swam to the next slide. He followed her as they slithered through a series of smaller slides.

"That was fun. Let's do it again. We can play horse and rider," Renee said as they clambered up the ledge.

"This horse is headed for the corral."

The sun lowered and the shadows changed direction. creating new shapes on the red rock ledges and outcrops. The warm colors bathed the canyon as the sky dimmed from a pale yellow to a hazy orange. The day campers had fled, replaced by a flotilla of ducks scouring the edges of the ponds for left over tidbits, which reminded Matt that he was famished as he waited impatiently for Renee to finish changing. Exiting the van with a door slam that echoed off the cliff walls, Renee appeared, wearing a short plain white shift with an embroidered peasant blouse and white leather sandals that accented her dark skin. Her ebony hair glistened in the sunlight.

"So?" she asked, "What's next?"

"Back to work. I have to see a man – Dale Cunningham."

Neither of them spoke, keeping their own private council as they drove back to Sedona.

The National Land Conservancy Office was located in a small courtyard sandwiched between two open air art galleries filled with bronze statues of horsemen, Indian warriors, women, babies, and goddesses. An angular-jawed man with blue eyes and a shock of red hair looked up from his desk when Matt stuck his head over an open Dutch door and peered inside.

"Come in," the man waved. Matt opened the bottom half of the door and they entered a small office with walls lined with topographical maps.

"Can I help you?"

"I'm Matt Dillon. I'm looking for Dale Cunningham."

"You've found him and you are....?"

"Renee Royer."

"Please have a seat. Can I offer you some coffee?"

"Yes, black, thank you," Matt responded.

"I'll have the same," Renee added.

Dale went over to an antiquated coffee urn, found mugs, filled them, carried them over, and set them on the desk. "What's Jay up to this time?" he asked as he settled into the chair, "And how do you fit in? The reason I ask is that the last time Jay was here, he declared war on the Racquet Club at the mouth of Boynton Canyon. Sacred land. He got headlines at a time when we didn't need any. The Land Conservancy is non-confrontational. Having said that, we would like the pink jeep pimps and the Racquet Club out of the canyon." He grinned. "Jay's concerned, as I told you, about the water rights the tribe has retained on the Middle Verde Reservation and about stream pollution. And there seem to be some other interested parties. By the way, what's your interest, Matt?"

"The tribe hired me to do a piece for the Cultural Center. Jay's a friend and he asked me to look into it for him."

"Just a friend of the family? Well, so am I. I called Sam Cook and he asked me to help you anyway that I could and that's good enough for me." Dale opened a desk drawer, pulled out a manila folder, and spread the contents on the desk. "USG summaries, surveys, reports, congressional mandates, litigations, and recommendations. It's a witches' brew. But let's cut to the chase. What it boils down to is that the land swap which gave the tribe the new reservation and the 80-acre parcel where they want to develop a mall is by any measure illegal, even though the Secretary of Interior approved it."

"How is it illegal?" Matt sat forward on the edge of his chair.

"Well, you have to trade contiguous property and the 80-acre parcel isn't contiguous, obviously, and, equally obvious, you

190

can't retain four twenty-acre parcels and water rights in the old parcel you have traded. The whole deal could be, will be, challenged by someone -- cities, the state, the Sierra Club, environmental groups, the SRP, even us. It's a wonder it hasn't been challenged already."

"Why hasn't it?" Matt asked.

"That's the nub of it. A couple or maybe three reasons." Dale got up from his chair and walked over to a topographical map. "On his way out of office, Bill Clinton made a grand last gesture. He declared millions of acres of federal land to be national and state parks. The states, the Forestry Department, and BLM got the hiccups trying to digest his largesse. He opened a can of worms. Forestry is trying to connect the dots and the BLM is trying to scatter them. Developers, ecogroups, everybody is getting into the game. The 1880's mining acts are being attacked, as they deserve to be. But this is a free-for-all -- the city of Prescott is after the Paulden Reservoir. Everybody is holding their breath to see what happens. But down here," Dale touched the map, "the Chinese are after the Black Hills."

"Who?"

"Good question, but *why* is a better one. It could've been anyone. But the answer is cement. There's a world-wide shortage and the Chinese are building on an unprecedented scale. The whole Upper Verde is a limestone bonanza. High grade sitting at the top of the mesa just waiting to be strip-mined and here you have a railroad all the way from Perkinsville to Ashfork which can connect to San Diego, LA, and China. Comprehend? It's no secret. The Commerce Department sent a U.S. trade mission to China. The Chinese are eager for our business and want to cut a deal. Ford and General Motors want to open assembly plants. Philip Morris wants to sell cigarettes, and China wants cement to construct buildings and highways. Can you imagine what the world will be like a few years from now when a billion cigarette smoking Chinese are creeping bumper-to-bumper in their Ford Exploders and Saturns on the Peking-Shanghai Expressway? Talk about second-hand smoke and the ozone layer! We'll all be toast."

191

Dale went back to his desk and picked up the manila folder. "A Peruvian company wants to purchase the land after the deal is approved. A friend of mine says the company is owned by a family of former aristocrats who are associated with a drug cartel, and another source has told me that their proposal is on the Secretary's desk."

"Why don't you do something about it?"

"What's to do? Like I said, the National Land Conservancy isn't confrontational. In fact, we aren't even aware of the situation. They are not responsible; I'm not responsible. In fact, I resigned a month ago. This office is moving to Prescott as soon as we can find a volunteer. Nobody's responsible in an election year."

"Somebody has to be responsible."

"Then I guess you are." Dale handed Matt the folder. "I've planted some hand grenades, but don't count on their amounting to much. Tell Sam that he'd better get to Washington and do some jawboning before the tribe runs out of funds. He may not be the Chairman, but he's respected. Tell him I'm going fishing in Alaska and picking a fight with an oil company. Just give him the folder, Matt; he'll know what do with it. Say 'Hi' to Jay for me," Dale said as he ushered them to the door.

Matt and Renee sat down on the edge of a fountain outside the office. She dipped her hand into cool water and said, "This is surreal, Matt. What are you going to do?"

"What can I do? Look it over and give it to Sam."

"What can he do? He has no authority. He can't go to the Council."

"He may not have to. He can make a case in Washington. He's not shy."

"And he's not young, Matt."

"Are you saying that I should go?"

"Who would you go to? You're a gaming investigator; so am I. What's this got to do with gaming? Anka would file this in his waste basket. Nothing's happened yet; none of these land deals may go forward."

"There is a problem with the water rights. You know that."

"Sure, everyone wants the water. It doesn't matter who wins; everybody loses. There's nothing I heard in there that I could print and Fiddles wouldn't touch it with the proverbial pole. Let's get an ice cream cone. There's a little shop down the street."

They bought Italian ices and sat down on a bench. Renee licked her cone slowly, deep in thought. "What makes us do what we do, Matt? It's a beautiful day. We're in a beautiful place. Why can't we just be two normal people?"

"I wouldn't know how, and neither would you. And neither would any two normal people, if there is such a thing, and if they knew what we know."

"And what do we know?"

"That the world's on fire."

"And we're going to put out the fire?"

"Yep. We're the fire brigade, one bucket at a time, if that's what it takes."

CHAPTER FIFTEEN

The Blue Owl café sat on the rim of the mesa, separated from the golf course and the sandstone boulders. The café's rails and posts supported a rough shingle roof capped by a rusty roadrunner wind vane, turning west to northwest and back again.

"I have a sense of de ja vu," Matt said as they sat in willow chairs at a table near the end of the porch, overlooking the golf course's rolling green hills.

"Did you see *The Angel and the Bad Man*?"

"With John Wayne? Yes, I vaguely remember it."

"This was part of the set. John Ford made a lot of movies in Sedona and Robert Mitchum filmed *Blood on the Moon* here. The owners bought this false front and the water tank. They broke it down and rebuilt it up here."

Matt noticed several petroglyphs scattered around the prickly pear cactus garden. A small owl, incised into the patina, guarded the steps. "Interesting piece. I wonder what it's trying to tell us."

"Probably that it's hungry. I think we'll have to go inside to order."

Inside, a blond waitress wearing a cowhide Stetson, a western shirt, tight levis, and a holstered six gun handed them a menu. "Tonight's special is crab salad, charbroiled New York steak, Chablis, and I can serve you on the porch." The waitress winked at Matt.

"I'll have mine medium rare," Renee said. "You get the wine, Matt. I'll find us a table."

The waitress brought him a bottle of Chablis and two glasses. "Enjoy!" she said as she smiled and handed him the tray.

He found Renee sitting at a table overlooking the river, legs propped on a porch rail. He sat the tray on a cowhide-covered table and filled their glasses. She picked up her glass and took a sip. "It's good. Do waitresses always wink at you like that?"

"Not always."

"Do you always wink back?"

"Actually, I usually wink first."

"Does it work?"

"Depends on which eye I use." He winked at her with his left eye and then his right. "The double whammy. It's a sure thing."

"Doesn't work on us city girls."

"Never?"

"Well, almost never."

"Want me to try again."

"Yes, take your best shot."

Matt blinked his eyes twice, and then rolled them. "How's that?"

"You got me. That went straight to my heart." Renee put one hand over her heart and sighed.

The sun had set when the waitress brought their food. When they had finished dinner, the moon and Venus were rising. Renee went to the van to get her recorder and leaning against the building, she composed. "The evening breeze seductively whispers 'Sedona' as the moon and Venus, the only lights in the sky, rise over the towering purple spikes in this light-friendly village." The recorder clicked off. "That does it. Let's go for a walk. Bring the Chablis."

Matt picked up the bottle and their glasses and followed down a flagstone path that ended on the golf course. She walked onto the green and kicked off her sandals and danced across the grass. "It is so soft. Take off your sandals." He slipped out of the thongs and wiggled his toes in the grass. Renee stretched her arms moonward. "Come dance with me, Matt," she said, pirouetting and making a throaty howl that echoed eerily. Matt set the bottle of Chablis on the grass, raced across the green, dropped to his knees and slid to a stop in front of Renee.

"Sacrifice her!" he cried.

"I think we're high, Matt, at least I am." She sank to her knees, wrapped her arms around his neck and kissed him, a long, sweet, sensual kiss and a longer embrace. Matt felt he was sinking into the dark waters of a vortex. They kissed again and then again. Matt moved his lips to her cheeks, neck, and shoulders. Renee's lips found his and she drew him downward, deeper and deeper into the vortex.

Hearing an ominous click and hiss behind him, Matt turned just in time to be hit in the face with a stream of water. He sputtered while Renee screamed.

"They've turned on the sprinklers!" He was hit by another stream of water. Renee grabbed her sandals and scrambled to her feet. "Here they come again. Run!" she yelled as she sprinted back to the flagstone path. Matt calmly picked up their glasses, the bottle, and his thongs. "Run, Matt, you'll get soaked!"

"I'm already soaked," he replied, swallowing his glass of wine. "Unfortunately, I'm not drunk." Back at the van, Matt toweled off, changed into Levis and crawled into the front seat. Renee was waiting for him, a towel wrapped like a turban around her head. Removing it, she began brushing her hair. "That wasn't supposed to happen, Matt."

"Which? The kiss or the cold shower?"

"Both – neither – you fool." They broke out laughing.

"Are you a night owl?"

"What do you have in mind?"

"I think we should follow up on the Land Conservancy. We need to connect the dots between water rights, land swaps, and pollution to the tribe's involvement, if there is a connection."

"How do we do that?"

"Let's go to my office."

"And do what?"

"Research."

Matt groaned. "Not exactly what I had in mind."

"C'mon. Let's go."

He groaned again and started the van.

The stars shone brightly as they drove from Sedona to Cottonwood. Outlining the research plan, Renee said, "You do the timber, mining and grazing and Verde Valley stuff. I'll do the water rights and local ecological stuff. Two computers are better than one. Then we'll tie it together, but first, stop at the Night Owl Café. We need refreshments."

"How nice. Is this your idea of a slumber party?"

"Who needs sleep?"

"That's what I meant."

"Coffee and yesterday's donuts were all I could get," Renee said as Matt parked in front of the darkened office of *The Village Voice*. He waited while she searched for her keys.

"Pretzels and beer across the street. We could shoot a game of pool."

"I'd beat you." She opened the door. "I think I'll start with coffee."

Matt sat down in front of a computer and waited as she logged him online. Renee sat with her back to him and logged in.

"Why does this remind me of Cathedral Rock?" he asked.

"How's that?"

"Oh, a man and a woman with different purposes and direction sitting back to back."

"Oh, I gotcha. I'll clean the cave and provide the coffee and donuts while you go hunting."

"Right." Matt sipped his coffee, stared at the ceiling and began playing tentatively with the keyboard. Gradually he became absorbed with his task, hardly noticing Renee as she occasionally went back and forth from her computer to the deadwood files.

The dark night had yielded to the soft pre-dawn blues and grays when Matt switched off his computer, picked up half a donut, inspected it, and returned it to the paper plate. Swallowing some cold coffee and swiveling in his chair, he saw Renee staring at him, leaning against the front door with arms folded..

"What is it?" Matt asked.

"Depressing, isn't it?"

"Cold coffee and stale donuts?"

"No. The human race."

"Oh, I thought you were talking about the rat race."

"Same thing, isn't it? So what have you got?"

"Let's see. I'll go from the specific to the general and start with logging. The Forestry Department creates 'managed' forest, an euphemism for logged forests. That means managed for the logging companies. Smaller trees fill in where the large valuable ones were removed, which adds to the fuel density, and then you get a drought and bark beetles. Then you get arson as opposed to lightning. The Rodeo-Chedeski fire burned 284,000 acres of Apache Reservation land and 176,000 acres of National Forest. There are 2,145 miles of logging roads that are supposed to make good fire breaks paid for by tax payer's money, which benefits the timber industry. The fire swept over them like they didn't exist. Interestingly, the politicians and loggers turned the fact that logging increases fire danger, not lessens it, claiming the environmentalists blocked timber cutting, resulting in massive fires. The environmentalist's blamed the tribe when they couldn't block forest management, which brought in the BIA, DPA, wildlife protection lobbyists, eco-scientists, NRA, hunters, and the Sierra Club. 'Eco-tourism' and 'Save the spotted owl' become catchwords."

"So what's the bottom line?"

"The bottom line is that the Forestry Department does a land swap. It takes over urban-facing forests that it can protect with modern apparatus. The public sighs with relief and doesn't realize that the former forest land is turned over to the timber industry to manage. The next problem is grazing, or subsidized munching. Some wealthy corporations and a few small ranchers pay a monthly fee to graze their livestock on public lands. The federal grazing program costs 150 million and probably more to subsidize 3% of the nation's cattle raisers. It costs more than money though. The overgrazing leads to erosion, the loss of wildlife habitat. But in riparian areas, like the Verde, cattle pollute by removing vegetation, trampling banks, increasing sedimentation, and depositing wastes in the rivers, including those that flow into reservoirs like the Bartlett Dam."

Renee picked up the theme. "There goes the fish habitat, the pygmy owl, and the Southwestern fly catcher. A songbird meltdown. The Audubon clubs, the Center for Biological Diversity, and the Friends of Smokey the Bear aren't going to take this lightly, nor the Navajo sheep herders, who claim they have a sovereign right to overgraze. If they allow their lands to be strip-mined or to become a toxic dumping ground, that's okay. It's one option to escape overwhelming poverty. Now, any well-intentioned forest or BLM employee who tries to help either side is called an eco-terrorist, eco-communist and other not–so-polite labels. Meanwhile back at the ranch, grazing permits are cancelled or restricted fees are raised to prohibitive levels. So, change the laws, raise the taxes, and swap lands. The Native Americans get urban land. The land is privatized. The ranchers move further out. The BLM takes over and provides roads, water, tanks, and eco-tourists. The developers get the patent lands for a song, divide them into small lots and resell them for a fortune. The cities and states get a tax windfall. Everybody's happy. The mining companies get off the hook. The taxpayers clean up the tailings, and build lead and detoxification plants. The towns incorporate, take over the private water companies, discover they can't afford maintenance, and sell them to the utility companies. The small fry pay fines, and the big ones do as they please. Triple the water rates, and the Native Americans and the eco-nuts are the fall guys. Everybody blames the politicians, and the reformers bite each other in the butt and disappear."

"Renee, the Secretary is responsible for policy. The President's policy, supposedly, but you have Congress to deal with. There are all kinds of committees and divisions involved with overlapping and often conflicting recommendations."

"Somebody has to pay for all this. Move the ranchers, miners, and loggers out and move people, malls, and developers in. When you bring more water, more roads, more power, and more services in, you pollute and destroy the vegetation and the wildlife

199

habitat, including the riparian streams. The effect is synergistic, cumulative systemic and systematic."

"Disgusting, isn't it?" Renee tossed her notes onto the table.

"It's all about what Zane Grey wrote in the *Call of the Canyon*. The Red Rock country, the Verde Valley, and the Southwestern streams should have been designated national parks then. Surviving World War I, he foresaw WWII and overpopulation, famine, and genocide. He didn't see the bureaucrats, lobbyists, and regional agencies with their conflicts of interest. Greed, blame, and error. Total ecocopalypse."

"My God, Matt. You make it sound hopeless."

"Maybe it is. It's all online where anyone can read it. They don't need *The Village Voice*. Find the polluters and sue them. Kill the cattle and sheep. Stop drilling oil wells. Drill more wells in Alaska. Stop immigration. Send the white man back to Europe. Send the Blacks back to Africa. Build more prisons. Open more casinos. Eliminate video games. Of course, we'll always have the Arabs and the French. Better yet, blame the Indians. After Custer, they could have pushed the white man back to Chicago, at least." Matt stood up and did a war dance.

"You're terrible!" Renee laughed.

"Let them have Chicago and LA, and we sure didn't want Boston or New York.. So what have we got?"

"Well, I can turn the telescope around. The Verde Valley is a microcosm of what you're saying." Renee picked up her notes. "The three villages want to incorporate. They want to privatize the water companies. JR, Fallon and Cooper are going to fight. The Apache Tribe exchanged their reservation for the new rez, but they kept their water rights. As Dan said, it is an illegal deal. The Apaches have petitioned that the 80 acre parcel be declared a trust land and the tri-villages are appealing to the Governor and to the Interior Department. The forestry wants to interface with the villages, and the Upper Verde tract is up for grabs."

"Where is it located?"

"Interesting question. Next to Cooper's and Tom Fallon's property. I have nothing to tie this to the tribe or the casino except that the immediate impact of the casino has been to boost the local economy and improve the general welfare of the tribe. The long-term effect of developing the trust lands is to reduce the city revenues, unless the tribes agree to a new taxation process -- in other words -- give up some of their sovereignty. There's going to be a lot of court cases; it will get nasty. In my opinion, the tribal government isn't up to this. The syndicate controls the casino, runs the cement plant, and will control the trust properties."

"Well, let's see how this all works out. The Upper Verde tract is worth maybe four to five million, if we assume an acre is worth $640. And the I-17 property is worth three to four hundred million dollars at $275,000 per acre."

"Where did you get those figures?"

"From Strickland's real estate website."

"That's a great deal of money for the Forestry Department."

"Except they are trading it for land in Prescott, Paulden, and Flagstaff worth, say, two to three million dollars at $640 per acre, and the water rights."

"Well, that sounds about right for a forest service trade. Who's responsible for that?"

"The Secretary of the Interior."

"What a surprise! The taxpayers are shafted once again. The tribes are just pawns, Matt, and there's nothing anybody can do." The morning sun bounced off Renee's forehead as she stared out the window.

"Maybe yes and maybe no, Renee, but we can try. The question is, Who controls the tribe? The syndicate? Fallon? He arranged the land swap and, thanks to you, we know he has a stake in the water rights and who knows what else? I'm going to talk with him and Sam Cook. And the Queen Bee knows something, probably more than I realized. Then there's the tribal council. Maybe the public would like to call their senators, representatives, and the Governor about the shaft they are about to get."

201

"How Matt? With what? My boss isn't going to go along with this – for God sake, he's already told me to back off of the impact studies."

"What about the stuff you taped?"

"I've been thinking about that. Kessler obviously has enough on Kincaid to lock him up, but he wants to link him and the drug traffickers to the casino. He might be working on the money laundering angle. Your friend Radcliffe is DEA, and they both know the cement plant is a warehouse for...."

"Latin American druglords who want to obtain the Upper Verde to quarry limestone."

"Which is upsetting Cooper, because he wants the mountain as a refuge for his loonies who are ..."

"Preparing for Armageddon," Matt finished.

"So Cooper blew up Strickland's records to disassociate himself from Strickland, Fallon and perhaps, I hate to say it, JR."

"JR? No way!"

"Why not? Everyone in this county is involved somehow. They all have a dog in the fight: the mayors, the Marshals, the tribes, the water companies, the Sheriff, my God, even the Governor, possibly the senators, congressmen, and Secretary of Interior. It's a web of dupes, dimwits, and do-gooders."

"My God, Renee, you make it sound hopeless."

"That's my line."

"Well, it's true, isn't it?"

"What about Anka?"

"I haven't a clue. He's already told me to back off, remember?"

"I'm thinking we should bypass him and my controller. I'll be right back."

"Where are you going?"

"Across the street to Mail Box Etc. to copy these." Matt walked across the street and entered the store. "I need ten copies," he said to a white haired clerk, "and ten envelopes." The clerk took the manila folder and went back to a copy machine.

"Any particular order?"

"Nope, just run them as is." The clerk pushed several buttons while Matt began addressing ten mailers. Twenty minutes later, the copies had been addressed and stamped. He paid the clerk and asked, "When does the mail go out?"

"Pick up is at 8:40. Nice doing business with you. Come again."

Matt went next door and stuck an envelope through the mail slot at the water company. He crossed the street, stopped at the VW and stuffed the extra mailers in the overhead rack.

Renee was waiting for him inside. "What took you so long?"

"The copier had some problems. I need some time to think, Renee, and some breakfast and a nap. How about you?"

"Breakfast first." They went next door to the Night Owl Café where Joe Biddles was sitting at a table. Matt and Renee sat down next to him.

"Good morning, Renee. Glad to see you got an early start this morning," Joe said.

"An early start to what?"

"Press day. Same as always."

Renee groaned. "Coffee, orange juice, and toast, dry," she said to the waitress.

"Take your time, Renee. I'll start with the features," Joe said as he got up and left the cafe.

"I'll never survive this, Matt. I'm due at the casino at 8:00. What are you going to do?"

"What else? Eat breakfast. Go home and take a nap."

"You just try," Renee made a face.

"Well, at least one of us has to get some sleep."

"Just try. I've got your cell number."

"Thanks for the warning. I'll leave it in the van." He kissed her on the forehead. "Thanks for a wonderful day, evening, night, and breakfast. I'll call you."

CHAPTER SIXTEEN

"It's a beautiful day," Matt decided as he drove down the General Cook Trail which led from Old Fort Verde to Old Fort Whipple on the edge of Prescott. He pulled off at Young's Farm to pick up some early peaches which Paloma had requested. "Stop and visit. It's the kind of organic farm I want someday," Paloma had told him.

He went inside the big barn and bought some cheese and a round loaf of fresh bread. He added a flat of peaches and a pair of cantaloupes to his cart. On impulse, he added a quart box of strawberries, a small cherry pie, and two quarts of fresh apple juice.

"It's a shame they are closing this place," a middle-aged woman said as he joined the line in front of the cash register. "It will be a real loss to the community."

"Why are they closing? It looks like they are doing well."

"They have for twenty years, but it's something about water and taxes. It's the developers. They want everything they can get their hands on. Who needs them? We sure don't, but nobody asked us." She shrugged her shoulders as she rung up his purchases and stuffed them into a recycled paper bag along with some health pamphlets. Matt dropped his change in a jar labeled Donations for Friends of Charlotte Hall Museum.

When he returned to the Kombi, he spread the contents on the back bench and tried some cheese, tore off a chunk of warm bread, and watched the traffic. It was turning warm. He opened the apple juice and drank some. "Bread, cheese, and apple juice. Where is the thou?" He picked up a thumb-sized red strawberry and ate it slowly, savoring its sweet juiciness. "Thou are sweet. Thou are enough." He repacked the bag, stowed it under the bench, and put the apple juice on the front seat.

When Matt turned west onto Highway 89, the two lane road widened into six lanes with sprawling suburbs and tacky frontage road shops lining both sides of the highway. Topping Bushwhacker Hill, a thumb-shaped butte dominated the skyline above Prescott. On his left, a shopping mall was flanked by the Yavapai Casino. Matt caught the light and turned up a ramp, a steep incline that led up the side of a hill. At the top, a parking lot surrounded the Prescott Resort and Bucky's Casino. He drove around the main building and parked the Kombi in a space that tottered on the edge of a steep drop. Directly beneath him, Highway 89A turned north, a direct route to Ashfork, Williams, and the Grand Canyon. Across the road, a dozen or more white framed building with blue shutters flanked a parade ground. "Old Glory" hung from a white flagpole over Fort Whipple. Beyond the fort, a set of painted white rocks demarked the edge of the Yavapai Reservation.

Matt entered through Bucky's Casino side entrance. Inside, the ching, ching, ching of the slots swallowing coins, flashing neon lights, and the vacuous voice of a Kino caller reminded him of the penny arcades of his childhood. After purchasing a roll of quarters from a cashier, he found a cup, dropped a few coins in a poker machine, and walked out the main entrance into the hotel lobby.

A magnificent 15-by-20 foot oil painting of the Grand Canyon dominated the lobby. Beyond the lobby, oil paintings, mostly Western landscapes and classic gilded frames, lined the hallway. Two classic sculptures by Waddell and Sorenson bestowed a rare grace and elegance to the space. He sat down on a leather bench across from the pieces when a round pink-cheeked blue-eyed man with fringes of white hair capped with a leather beret, sat down next to him.

"Max, how are you?" Matt slid over to make room for Max's bulky frame.

"Some days are better than others," he wheezed. "The air is better up here. I can breathe most of the time, except in late summer. Tree pollen gets worse after the monsoons."

"So, what's on your mind?"

"Plenty. Your report confirms what we've suspected, but we need proof. At one level, the casino is making political wampum utilizing tribal accounts to launder soft money into hard money -- thanks to the McCain-Feingold loophole. The reason your marked bills aren't turning up anywhere except the banks is the casino isn't placing for the small drug dealers. It isn't turning in small bills for large. Your boys aren't interested. Besides, we're making it harder to launder the small stuff. We're busting casinos in Florida and Canada. The cement plant is a shell, Matt. Illegal money from China is coming in. Those Chinamen you spotted harvest forests, smuggle illegal timber out of the Philippines, Papua New Guinea and Indonesia. They are shipping up to 23 boatloads a week to China. They are stripping the rain forest for wood products, mainly Marabou flooring which they sell legally in the U.S., even if we know it's made from illegal timber. Same with the cement, except it's going the other way. The Chinese want influence and they are juicing our politicians. Meanwhile, they supply legal dollars to the casino that transfers the funds electronically to private banks in Belize, Belarussia, and the Philippines. They surf it right through the pipeline with high speed cybernetic transfers. Then, they layer it all over the world to shell companies and the "dirty money" pays off the lumber smugglers, the drug smugglers, and the terrorists who put it back in the pipeline and layer it all over again."

"You're saying that the Black Mesa Casino is an electronic clearing house?"

"Exactly, for Chinese dollars, drugs, cement, and lumber. Thanks to the Gnome. He's a genius, Matt. He runs the show for the Brits who operate one of the syndicates."

"Who do they work for?"

"It could be anyone on the planet, terror-friendly Middle Eastern despots or narco-tyrants trying to pump their billions into the white economy. Illegal narcotics," Max added, "account for one-tenth of all world trade. My guess is some corporate head of an insurance company who's acting as a go-between the black and white economies. They take in money and everybody gets a piece,

206

except you and me. Hell, we're probably working for them, but we're too dumb to figure it out."

"How do we stop it?"

"Too big to stop. Trillions of dollars daily pass through the Euro banks and the Federal Reserve. They let the illegal money go through; it's only a fraction of the known transactions. You'd have to shut down the world economies, legal and illegal, to chase their transactions. And you'd have to close down our own illegal money transfers. We can't go there."

"I give up. What do you want from me?"

"What would happen if we enlightened the folks around the state about all the money laundering that's going on in their back yards? Matt, if we conducted a survey, the general response would be that people have no clue that money laundering is a scheme to disguise the nature, source, ownership, location and disposition of property derived from criminal activity, anonymously. If we told them that it's been going on big time in America since prohibition, they would probably blink, then go on about their business. To most people, it's a victimless crime. It doesn't have the drama of a murder or a robbery or a drug bust. It's an invisible problem and that's what makes it so difficult to stop."

"So you're saying that Money Laundering 101 for the general public doesn't work."

"Right. The druglords make Al Capone and the old mafias look like small-time crooks. Today, money laundering is slight of hand... a magic trick for wealth creation... the life blood of drug dealers, fraudsters, smugglers, arms dealers, terrorists, extortionists, and tax-evaders. Dirty money is the world's third largest business."

Max handed Matt a small metal device. "It's a flash drive. You said you could get into the counting room, right?"

"Yeah. I'm pretty sure I can," Matt said as he examined the device.

"Simply insert the drive into a computer. Unlock, unplug, and walk away. Return the key to sender. The whole world will be grateful. My Big Enchilada gets the casino data. Everything the casino's got, every laundering transaction to other casinos, and every money layer transfer on the network will be downloaded. We will knock out their whole cybernetwork with one stroke of a key." Max beamed. When I recruited you at ASU I knew someday, we would pull it off. The New Mexico, Oregon, and Texas operations were just practice. We can do this, Matt."

"What do you mean 'we', White Man?" Matt grinned.

"We're home free. It's a dream of a lifetime."

"What about the tribe?"

"No worries. The Gnome runs a clean shop. The tribe will keep their dollars and casino, but they'll have to sign on with the state and play by the rules, like everyone else." Max chuckled. "For you and me, it's the dream of a lifetime. We can run a money laundering consulting service. Every bank, insurance company, and CEO in the world will want a clean bill of health."

Matt stood up. "No thanks. I don't want a part of that future. You really set me up this time, but it's over. I'll bug the computers for you, but after that I'm done, and I'm doing it for my own reasons, not yours."

"Of course you will. You're a dreamer. I counted on that."

"Don't count your chickens. There's a real risk."

"Yes, there is. If it doesn't come off, we'll try again with some other casino."

"I'm going to pull it off. But it could backfire because you're not the only duck in the pond. The Arizona Gaming Commission might respond to this big time."

"Your controller, Vance, is a bureaucrat. He and Johnson don't have a clue as to how things are really done. They won't know what's happened until they read about it in the newspapers. Somebody will have to tell them what to do. Peace offering." Max handed Matt an envelope. "It's the skinny on Cooper. He worked for Bush I and ran the rope ladder on Noriega. They went up and down it a few times before they slipped a noose over Noriega and dragged him to Miami. Serial fiascos. The others were two-bitters. It's all there, for your eyes only. Do you think they're the bunch that robbed the casino?"

"It's a possibility. I'm just curious."

"Well, you know what curiosity does to cats. Don't touch them until you clear the computers. After that, it's no skin off our noses. In fact, it might help. The CIA might have to pull in their ears again."

"You tapped my cell phone?"

Max laughed. "Of course. What did you expect? "

"I thought it was Vance."

"You mean, you hoped it was Vance."

"Is anyone else listening?"

"Just us."

"Max, when this over, I'm out."

"You want out? In this business, the fat lady never sings."

"See you." Matt walked away as Max offered his hand.

Outside the casino, Matt sat in the Kombi and stared at Thumb Butte. He thumbed through his brochures, stuck them in an overhead net, and started the van. The ramp led down to Highway 89; he took the Prescott exit and turned off onto Gurley Street. After following Gurley to Montezuma and turning left onto Whiskey Row, he found a parking spot in front of the Palace Bar. He got out the van, fed a parking meter, and went into the Worm Map and Bookstore next door.

"Can I help you?" an amiable balding man with thick black eyebrows and deep-set dark eyes asked.

"I need some Arizona topographic maps."

The man led him to a large wall map. "Any place in particular?"

"Yes. The Verde River Valley."

"That covers a lot of territory." He picked up a pointer and traced a line down the river. "We've got topographic maps for these sections; GSD overlays, plat maps, prospector maps that cover old mines and mining camps; and I even have a ghost town map. If you're interested in real estate, we're linked to the county's assessor's office. I can pull down property owners, tax defaulters, assessor records, and county recorder deeds."

"You can do all that?"

209

"Right here, section by section, or plat by plat. Two dollars each." Matt picked a target on the map. The clerk walked over to his computer. "We can start here. Pick your section. Zoom in, pick your plat. Zoom in again, and pick your lot. A piece of cake." The man stepped away from the computer and pushed a stool in front of the screen.

"Thanks," Matt said. "Can I borrow a pencil and pad?" The clerk found a pad and pencil on the table and handed them to Matt. Then he looked over Matt's shoulders as he located Cottonwood and zoomed in on the Verde River. Matt zoomed in on Sycamore Canyon, and located a plat map.

"You're doing fine," the clerk said. "Call me if you need help."

Matt spent a half hour tracking plats on the Verde River, from Paulden and Big Chino through Perkinsville to Camp Verde. He stood up, stretched, and handed his list to the clerk, who briefly scanned it and typed in the numbers.

"We have most of these in the racks." He pointed to the map drawers. "Some of these will take me a few minutes." He pushed some buttons and the printer hummed. "Color?"

"Yes, please." Matt picked a pamphlet on interesting things to see and do in Prescott -- the Smoki Museum, the George Phippen Cowboy Artists Gallery and the Charlotte Hall Museum. A special section listed thirty or so antique shops and promos for Whiskey Row. "Where's Whiskey Row?" he asked.

"You're right in the middle of it."

"How about the Smoki Museum and the Phippen Gallery?"

The clerk handed him a local map. "Here, take this. The Smoki is on your way out of town and the Phippen is about seven miles out on Highway 89A." The clerk put the local map on top of the plat maps and slid them into a thin plastic bag. "That will be $37 even," he said cheerfully.

Matt paid. "Where can I get a good cup of coffee?"

"St. Michael's; it's on the corner. They have a great reading lounge where you can spread out your maps. Come back soon," the clerk said and handed Matt the sack. The cowbell clanged as the door behind him.

The clerk picked up his cell phone. "Hello. It's me....Barney. Some guy was just in here and picked up some plat maps. Thought you'd want to know. Yes. That's right, Coopers...JR Taylor's...right up the Verde to Fallon's piece. A big guy, Indian. I don't know; he paid cash. Anytime."

Matt went inside St. Michael's Internet Cafe, an old fashioned place that had been converted from a saloon to a coffee bar. It wasn't crowded. A thirtysomething, thin male with a dark goatee and black leather cap was reading a worn-looking paperback. Three coeds looked up as Matt walked to the bar. One girl sucked on a straw as she checked him out and rolled her eyes at the other two girls, who laughed self-consciously. After the waitress took his order, he laid the maps on the long, empty table by the front window. Two hours and three cups of coffee later, he finished and stuffed the maps back into the plastic sack.

On impulse, he used at one of the computers to search the Defense Department records. He keyed in several names and linked them to service records, duty stations, ranks, citations, and discharge dates. After cross-referencing the data on Cooper with the Panama, Noriega, Contra Costa, Somalia, and Kosovo, he said aloud, "Why am I not surprised?" He printed the documentation, closed the computer, and looked around.

The coeds had been replaced by two women dressed in flimsy apparel and wearing long strings of beads, and a large man with a spectacular crown of white hair. The women glanced at Matt as he stood up and stretched, and then they dropped their eyes when he stared back. He left the café, crossed the street at the light, and walked east to the Courthouse Square. He stopped in front of a statue of Bucky O'Neill, a rough rider astride a horse. While he read the inscription, an oddly dressed white-haired woman in her early eighties approached.

"How are you today?" her voice rang cheerily.

"I'm fine," Matt said, "How are you?"

"Fit as a fiddle and ready for love," she said and did a quick two-step. "That's my Bucky. He was a Rough Rider, a real hero. Not like our Sheriff Bucky O'Neil. His family came from the wrong-side-of-the-tracks O'Neils. They got the 'l' knocked out of them." She fingered the plaque. "The real deal O'Neills, have two 'l's,' see?"

"That's interesting."

"Well, I've got people to meet. I come here every day. Maybe I'll see you again." She walked away, swinging her hips and humming to herself.

Matt stopped in the front of the war memorial, a dozen cast bronze miniature figures. Their size bothered him, too small in stature to match their deeds. He sat on a bench and watched the squirrels chase each other across the lawn and up into the treetops. After studying his notes for awhile, he got up and walked back to the van. He drove around the Courthouse Square, turned west on Gurley, and turned off when he spotted a Smoki Museum sign attached to a light pole.

A block later, he pulled in front of odd-shaped building, actually an oversized hogan. Matt got out the van and climbed the several flights of flagstone steps, admiring the mature shrubs, bushes and trees which shaded the building. Inside, a cavernous room was supported by peeled pine poles and old worn, blackened and polished flagstones were on the floor. Indian pots were casually scattered around the room. Beaded shirts and squaw dresses were hung on the walls. It was cool and eerily silent as he walked past tastefully displayed Sinaloa, Anazasa and Mimbras artifacts, pot shards, stove tools and Indian baskets in cases.

Matt carefully studied the Cherokee pipes and Plains Indian drums and flutes, thinking, "A world of our own and all that's left is hanging on these walls and displayed in these cases, a morbid reminder of what we were." He signed the guest book, scratching a thank you beside his name. Looking, but not finding an attendant, he stuffed several bills in the donations box, walked outside to the van, and checked his map.

Matt followed Gurley Street back to the Y and turned north. A few miles down the highway, he pulled over at Watson Lake to admire a thousand stalagmites which grew out of the cerulean water, reaching for the cerulean sky. The only sound was a lone kayaker paddling across the lake until a roar of a truck broke his reverie.

Stopping at a sturdy, but modest, wooden building across the highway, he bought a New Guinea Bird-Wing, a florescent blue butterfly, expertly mounted by a short dark man who volunteered his French ancestry. "Good choice. They aren't going to be around much longer," the proprietor volunteered.

"Why is that?"

"Their habitat is disappearing. It's getting harder to get permits, but that won't stop the logging companies from turning the rain forests into a sea of mud." The short, dark proprietor shrugged his shoulders. "In fifty years, the only specimens left will be in museums."

"Who's responsible?"

"Don't ask me. "'The enemy is us, as Pogo said," he laughed bitterly.

Back on Highway 89A, Matt drove through the Granite Dells with its mounds of boulders, Tom Mix country, turned off the highway and drove up the hill to the George Phippen Cowboy Artists Hall of Fame Museum. The parking lot was empty except for a single older blue sedan. A woman sitting outside under a wide porch put down her book to greet him.

"Good afternoon," she said. "I'll turn on the lights for you." He followed her through the doorway and entered the darkened room. The attendant flipped several switches and overhead rows of track lamps glowed down from the barn-like rafters. "I'll be outside if you need anything. The gift shop is open."

"Thank you," Matt said and walked slowly around the room. It was a veritable feast of Western art by George Phippen, Remington, George Naggle, Joe Beeler, Ray Swanson, Fred Fellows, and Olaf Wieghorst as well as lesser known and almost forgotten talented artists. A sepia-toned pair of sketches of bronco busters had a sculptural quality, as did some caricatures of seraped sheepherders drawn by Willa Sparks.

Near the exit, he stopped to read a plaque: "The George Phippen Museum is dedicated to the painters and sculptors who skillfully portray the throb of desert heat, the smell of work and sweat, and the crunch of boots in the sand, the mystery of riding herd, the courage of warriors, pioneers, cowboys, and frontiersman. The wonders and majesty of the west with passion and accuracy. To paint like it was, like it never was and most of all like it would never be again. Impressed, he fed the donation box.

"Kind, of quiet here," he said to the docent on his way out.

"That's why I come here," she smiled. "I like it that way. But it gets busy in May when we hold the Hall of Fame show. Mr. Matt Dillon, you should enter something. We have a have a category for Western sculptors."

"How do you know my name?"

"You signed the guestbook. I recognized your name and looked you up. I've seen the cougar you did when you were at Shidoni. You have talent, young man, and I'm a good judge of talent. It runs in the family. So what are you working on now?"

"I'm planning a piece for the Apache Tribe in Camp Verde."

"Let me see your sketches."

"I didn't bring them with me."

"Don't go away," she said, went inside and came back a few minutes later. She handed Matt a large sketch book and a box of charcoal sticks. "George always said 'It ain't nothing if it's in your head. It only counts when it's on paper.' Bring it back when it's full."

"Well, thanks. Uh..."

"I'm Louise. I'm here on Wednesday afternoons. Adios, Matt Dillon."

"Well, thank you again." He removed his cap. "It was a pleasure meeting you."

On the way back to Camp Verde, a local radio newscaster interrupted the country cowboy songs with a news story. "The Governor is planning a series of meetings with local government officers, Chambers of Commerce, and tribal officials. She is concerned," the spokesman said, "about planned growth in rural areas such as our Verde Valley communities. Land use and water conservation are high on her agenda, as is creating a fair and equitable taxation scheme for the tribal gaming casinos."

Matt pulled into the overlook above Tuzigoot, got out of the Kombi, sat at a concrete table, opened his stack of notes and began reading.

"You were there, Cooper," he thought. "Iran Contra, Noriega, drug trafficking, arms smuggling, money laundering, fraudulent elections, coups, counter coups, murder, assassinations, Casey's blunders, Powell's attempt to prevent the military option. The Keystone Cops. You and Casey built him up and tore him down. Yo-yo foreign policies and you were a player in Iraq and in Bosnia until Clinton dumped your gang, and so were my friends. Somebody had to keep the peace, move the arms, shipments, distribute the drugs, fly the planes, and count the bodies, didn't they?" He jabbed the pages with his finger. "So were you, and you. And God help me, so was I. And who else was there?" Tossing the papers in the air, Matt picked up his sketch pad and began drawing. The breeze captured them and they drifted upwards, white scraps sailing towards Tutzigoot.

A DPS patrol car pulled into the turnout, cruised down the lane, and parked beside the Kombi. Officer Hubbard walked over, wiped his forehead with his sleeve and waved his cap at the desert vista. "Nice view, isn't it?"

"If you say so, Hubbard."

"You don't mind if I call you Matt?"

"Why not, Bob? I mean how often do I get a chance to be on a first name basis with a DPS officer?"

"There's a first time for everything and this is a first for me." Toying with his cap, Hubbard looked Matt in the eye. "I'm curious. I'm wondering what you and Renee Royer were doing in Jerome, in Sedona, and in Prescott?

"I'm curious too, Bob. What business is that of yours?"

Hubbard scowled and then smiled. "It all does get curiouser and curiouser, doesn't it? I mean, you're both there, and then I get curious and so does Kincaid. In fact, he got so curious that he ordered me to pull a complete profile on you both. FBI, CIA, Interpol. In a few hours, he's going to know a lot about you."

"Good for him. He could've asked me."

Hubbard laughed. "A lot of good that would do. I'm sticking my neck out here, but here's my story: Kincaid's a rotten cop who's infecting the honest cops. He's the big dog ruining the DPS. I've got 19 years in and he's the worst SOB I've ever seen. And, I'm going to bust him before I retire, and I've got a hunch, let's say, a big hunch, that you might help me." For a moment, his fingers worried the edges of his cap. "But I'll do it with or without anyone's help. Big dogs bark. I'm just a little dog, but little dogs bite."

"All right. I hear you. You're taking a risk and so will I. I'm an officer with the Arizona Gaming Commission. You can check me out with Chester Vance, but I bet, you already have."

Hubbard grinned. "Correct."

"And I don't have a thing on Kincaid, except that I know that he and Marshals are playing footsie, possibly dealing drugs. That's all you get from me except that if I find out that Kincaid is dirty, I'll let you know."

"He's mean and he's dirty, just like the Marshals, but proving it is something else. You don't have a lot of time, Matt. When Kincaid discovers who you are, he'll kick the can. You could get hurt, and Renee too. I threw a monkey wrench into his search, but it won't stick. You've got maybe a week before he wises up that your profile got lost in the paper shuffle."

"Thanks, Hubbard. I appreciate it."

"So, what about Renee?"

"I have no idea. She's not with the Gaming Commission or anybody else that I know of. I've checked."

"Well, that's good news. She's a sweetheart. The kind of gal you'd leave your wife for on Christmas morning." Hubbard put his cap on and offered his hand. "Keep the faith," he said as they shook hands.

Matt watched the patrol car until it was out of sight, then he got into the Kombi. "Yep. Curiouser and curiouser," he said as he started the engine. Five miles from Camp Verde, he spotted Hubbard writing a ticket for a semi-rig. He didn't look up as the Kombi crawled by and Matt turned onto the frontage road.

Driving to McDonald's, he bought a burger, fries, and a shake. "Soul food," he thought as he parked under a cottonwood tree at the edge of town. It was nearly dusk when he closed the geologic survey. "There's more than gold in them thar hills."

Taking a back road to Camp Verde, he saw Renee's red Mustang parked in front of *The Village Voice*. He hung a u-turn, parked in front of the Q & Brew, got out and crossed the street. Obviously waiting for him with the door open, Renee was sitting at her desk. He took off his cap, ran his fingers through his hair. "Are we ready? I mean, are we really ready?" he asked himself and stepped through the door.

"Hi, Renee. How was your day?"

"Not very interesting. How about you?"

"I've been doing some digging." Matt handed Renee his notepad, sat down, and stared out the window as she skimmed through his notes.

"So?" she asked when she finished.

"So, the Verde Valley towns estimate of water usage is incorrect. They are using much more water than projected. The goals of recharging the aquifers are not being met. At the present rate of usage, the Upper Verde will dry up in the next 20 years, maybe ten, if the present drought continues. There's going to be a real struggle to control the water rights and…"

"That's not news, Matt. Progress vs. preservation. It's a lose-lose situation. It's common sense; the Valley can't support another metropolis."

"Probably not, but it explains why a lot of people want to get control of the tribe's water rights."

"What exactly are you saying?"

"I'm saying whoever controls the tribe gets control of the water rights."

"The syndicate?"

"Could be. Or Salt River Project."

"Or anyone who could make a buck if the casino fails. A drug cartel or a water company."

"Well, let me put it in a nutshell for you. The casino is controlled by the syndicate and the only reason it's here is to launder money. What the tribe makes up front, they keep. The profit goes into a face account which the syndicate is 'back dooring' through the wire room. The regs are getting tougher on Native American gambling casinos, but they are meaningless. If the tribe develops a mall, with a Wal-Mart, restaurants, and a car wash, the syndicate will be able to wash even more money. If it all comes out, and it will sooner or later, sovereignty won't protect the tribe from seizure and forfeitures of their land or water rights. So, I want to turn over their rocks now and let it all hang out."

"You're mad, Matt!"

"Hey! There's your book, Renee. Call it *Dirty Money*, throw in some sex, prostitution, illegal gambling, extortion, and you've got a bestseller."

"Be serious."

"I am. You said you wanted to write; you've got your ticket."

"You have away about you, Masked Man. What are we going to do? Me, Tonto."

"Well, Tonto, here's the plan." Matt spoke quickly.

Renee's face darkened. She folded her arms across her chest and paced the room. "That's it?" she said when he finished.

"It's called KISS – keep it simple, stupid."

"I agree with the stupid part. You're certifiable."

"Well, I may be crazy, but I'm not stupid."

"Wrong, You're certifiable *and* stupid."

"Hey. If it doesn't work, I won't go in. All they'll have is a series of irritating, but plausible, distractions."

"And I'm the main distraction, right?"

"You're not the only one. It's possible nobody will even notice you, right?"

"Yeah, nobody, but Shorty, who'll probably sell the tapes."

"He might. If they are any good, I'll buy one."

"Promise?"

"Sure."

"In that case, I'll do it."

"Are you positive?"

"Why not? If Hubbard told the truth, I'm out of here anyway. That, plus my report to Anka, which I haven't sent, guarantees it. So, when's show time?"

"Tomorrow night," Matt said. Renee picked up her hand bag. "Where are you going?" he asked.

"Shopping, where else?"

"What for?"

"Something slinky, easy to get on and off, and a fresh can of pepper spray. Good night. Lock the door behind you." Renee marched out, leaving a bewildered Matt standing in the doorway. He felt a twinge of guilt that he had not told her about Max as he watched the Mustang turn the corner. He shrugged his shoulders and sat down at the computer.

"Ahron, it's Matt. I need a pass key. Unlock, download, lock, load, and ship."

"What's the address?"

"I want an APB. Everyone that counts, Feds, markets, punters, hacks, anyone with a grudge."

"That's everybody, all right. Like, you want a magic wand? I have one. It will pull cryptographic, blind signatures, and download all casino accounts and transfers."

"I need a virus."

"I have one we call Armageddon. Banks, security brokerages, currency exchange houses, insurance and loan companies, travel agencies, issuers of travel checks, real estate companies, casinos."

"I don't want Armageddon, only illegals."

"Plug in the flash and give us a few minutes." Matt inserted the flash guide and waited impatiently until Ahron signaled. "You have a Trojan horse. We can peel off the layering like you peel an onion. Okay, what do you want us to do?"

"Move decimal points, create John Does, and transfer funds to charities, children's funds, wildlife organizations, women centers, and the Friends of Sharlot Hall. In fact, the Friends of anyone... Friends of libraries, museums, the Dalai Lama, and animal shelters."

"Whoa. I think I get it. I'll use the works."

"Send out the press releases, and the hard data goes to all federal and state agencies, and county government courts."

"How long do we have?"

"You can start Saturday morning, your time. You have 24 hours and then pull the plug."

"You have a name?"

"Call it Eagle Feathers. Ciao." Matt removed the flash, turned off the computer, and locked the office door behind him.

Cobalt on cobalt, space on space, sky meeting sea, a broken line of breakers thinly separating the spheres, endlessly washing ashore, greeting the warm yellow sand, and palm trees swayed gracefully where Ahron Meszaros sat with his laptop jacked into the Internet. "Aloha and peace, brother bloggers...."

CHAPTER SEVENTEEN

Prisms of light danced across the porch as the sun reflected off the hubcaps. Wally was shoving kindling under an iron box, sending a wisp of smoke skyward. When Matt peered over the ocotillo fence, the burros looked up from their feed trough and raised their ears expectantly.

"C'mon in Matt," Wally said in his rasping voice. "I'm getting old. I'm shrinking, talking to the burros, and then forgetting what I've told them. You're just in time for breakfast." He set a small blackened coffee pot half filled with water onto the coals. Pulling a heavy murderous-looking knife from its scabbard, he began cutting slices of ham and dropping them into an already hot iron skillet. As they sizzled, he emptied two heaping tablespoons into the coffee pot and scraped coals off the lid of a dutch oven as Matt peered over the ocotillo fence..

He then went to the porch and opened a cupboard. He set blue enameled tin plates and cups and substantial-looking knives, forks, and spoons on the table, and added a jar of honey, salt and pepper shakers, sugar, and a can of tinned milk. He went back to the fire, checked again on the biscuits, turned the ham slices and stirred the potatoes. "Bring the plates," he said.

Matt held the plates as Wally carefully ladled ham and potatoes onto them. Wally removed the pot with the biscuits from the fire and looked inside. Satisfied, he scooped them onto the plates. "Let's eat. I'll bring the coffee," he growled. "To hell with the comforts of civilization, Matt. In the city, waiters serve you a meal. It's a transaction. It has no significance, just something you hurry through. Up here, it's something you've earned."

"What brought you here?

221

Wally swallowed some coffee and leaned back in his chair as he watched a red-tailed hawk sail overhead and disappear over the thin band of green cottonwoods below. "For thirty years, I was a geologist, consumed with solving geological mysteries. It was satisfying, demanding, engaging, and frustrating. I went to far away places with strange-sounding names. Had some great years and plenty of penniless ones, and I found glory holes for a lot of companies. I woke up one day, my youth gone, regretting helping mindless, greedy corporations destroy the planet. So I switched sides. I fell in with some off-the-wall eco-nuts who were as power-happy as the CEOs. I married one, but she wanted me to lead her to riches, fame, and prestige. I did the talking and she did the walking, meaning she sold my soul to the company store. The pay-off was a big house in Pacific Palisades. I was an eco rep for an oil company. One fine day, I walked away. I preferred the loneliness, heat, hunger, thirst, the freezing and ungodly wind of the desert and mountains to living with her and working for the combines. It isn't romantic, but its beats dying in bed. My heart aches at the mess I helped make."

Matt swallowed some coffee. "Maybe I should feel sorry for you, but somehow I just can't," he said to the bearded burly prospector.

"Why should you? I've got a whole world of my own that most people don't even know exists. No people. No cars. No malls. Just me and the critters. It's empty out there, Matt. The prospectors are all gone; so are the Indians and the sheepherders. The wildlife is coming back, at least in places where the government doesn't manage. When you wake up in the morning out there in the Big Empty, you're alive. My God, you're alive and that's all that matters. That's the real gold, Matt. And besides, I've got my glory hole, enough money to keep me and the burros."

"You found gold?"

"No!" Wally winked. "A company pension. More coffee?"

"Yes, thanks." Wally poured another cup and sat down.

"What's on your mind?"

"Limestone. Water rights. The Verde River." Matt hesitated. "The gaming casino. Jay and Sam. The tribe. I met a man yesterday who thinks a combine wants to buy the Old Rez, convert the Upper Verde into a mining operation, and ship the cement to China."

"Who's 'they'?"

"I don't know."

"Uhumm… well, maybe I can find out. I know some people."

"Thanks. It could be helpful."

"What will you do when you find out?"

"I'm not sure yet. It's a real mess, but if the tribe loses control of the casino, it could lose the water rights too. If that happens, I think the Verde is finished. I don't see how to prevent it. In fact, I may end up helping the very people who want the water rights!"

"How's that?"

"Exposing the corruption at the casino may force the tribe into bankruptcy."

"Sounds like you're in pretty deep, between the proverbial rock and a hard place."

"You've got that right." Wally swished his coffee and finished it in one swallow. "Let me tell you a story. One evening I was sitting by the fire and I watched a wasp crawl slowly across the rug. My dog, who was resting on the rug, started to sniff it, kind of curious-like. But I shooed him off. I was tempted to step on it, but I let it go. That wasp made it to a corner and crawled into a spider web. The next thing you know, a little black spider popped out of a crack in the wall and went after that wasp. He bit him, I think, and danced backwards and then he came back, started spinning threads, and wrapped up that wasp. The more it struggled, the more threads that spider spun. I started feeling sorry for the wasp; wasn't a thing I could do for him. Then I started feeling sorry for the spider. Life's not easy for spiders either." Wally paused.

"What did you do?"

223

"Well, I took off my shoe and splattered both of them. Put them out of their misery. Sort of made it safe for everyone to walk around barefoot. Sometimes you have to do what you have to do."

"That's a cheerful thought." Matt finished his coffee. "Thanks for a great breakfast."

"Next time you're here, we can eat at Ruth's. She's not a bad cook, but she talks too much. See you around."

"Yeah. Thanks, Wally."

Matt sat for awhile in his van, staring blankly at the blank sky. Then he reached into the glove compartment, pulled out a card, studied it for a moment, and dialed his cell phone. "Yo," a gruff voice rasped.

"I need a favor. Care to lend a hand?"

"What do you need?"

"A distraction. A small disturbance at the casino."

"When?"

"Tomorrow night, in one of the lounges, at 8:45 on the button. I'll need six to eight minutes."

"Can do. What's up?"

"I can't say. I'll probably end up with my pants on fire. Won't be the first time."

"We should talk; maybe shoot a game of pool."

"For sure. Maybe after the prom. Take care."

"Yo. You too, man."

Matt made his way up the ninety-two steps to Sam's lodge. Jen was waiting for him at the top. "I was just coming to get you," she said. "Grandfather wants to see you. He is waiting for you in the sweat lodge."

She led him down the path to the circular lodge hidden behind a huge outcrop of rocks. Inside, a high nasal voice was chanting a song. Jen opened the flap "Grandfather, Matt is here," she said, interrupting the singer.

"Come and join me, Matt," Sam said. "Undress over there. Drink from the jug on the bench. You better take it in with you. You'll need it." Jen bushed and fled back around the rock.

Matt quickly stripped to his shorts, found the jug, and drank deeply. He opened the flap, stooped, and slid inside the sweat lodge. Sam was sitting cross-legged in the back of the lodge.

"You better sit near the door. It gets close in here if you are not used to it." Matt closed the flap, sat down in front of the fire pit, and crossed his legs. Sam tossed a gourd of water on the hot rocks. A cloud of stream filled the room, rising up and soaking the sheets and blankets there were covered by a plastic tarp. "It's an Indian sauna, Matt. We were using sweat lodges long before the Romans and Greeks. And today, I need it. My bones, and even my brain, aches. I've made my chaotic last trip to Washington. I have to cleanse myself before giving my report to the Council."

Sam threw more water on the rocks, filling the lodge with steam. "The news is not good. The Senator will speak from a new bully pulpit next year when he takes over as Chairman of the Committee on Indian Affairs. And he is still in control of the Commerce and Science and Transportation Committees. The Council sees this as an opportunity to flex their muscles. They are going to use the gambling revenues to hire lobbyists and make political contributions. Russell leased a box at the sport coliseum for our congressmen, and the money wasn't reported to the federal elections committee. The Governor is no stranger to the power Indians can wield. She wants a new gaming compact. She's already visiting the tribes. She is coming here for Saturday's parade. Last week she spoke with the Queen Bee, who's furious. The Governor asked when we were going to get our act together and behave like normal citizens. You can get the details when you see her. She's been asking about you."

"Does she know why I'm here?"

"If she doesn't, she has guessed by now. If we play the game, we're going to lose our sovereignty. We will lose our culture and our spirit and, in the end, our land. We don't control the casino; the syndicate does. We are like dummies sitting in their laps. The Water Settlements Act and the Senator's recommendations for a watershed commission will cost us our

225

water rights. We will lose them to the politicians. If we lose the Verde, the state and cities will swallow it. They will 'mine' the water and the minerals, and we get drugs, alcohol, and pick-up trucks in exchange. I don't know what to do. I'm too old to fight and too proud to run."

"What do you want me to do?"

"The future is up to you young people -- you, Jen, Jay, and the Hawks. You will all have to decide soon if you are Indian or White. I'll leave you to think on it. I must get ready for the Council meeting." Sam got up and left.

Matt heard Sam run the shower and walk off. He found the gourd, tossed more water on the rocks, listened to the sizzle as the steam filled the room. As he sat quietly in the dark lodge, he remembered the day his mother dressed him up as an Indian, with a feather in his hair, moccasins, and a rubber tomahawk. She told him, "In your heart, you are a warrior. You don't need a magic feather to give you courage. Trust in your strength. If you ever have to go to war, don't carry a rubber tomahawk. Your weapon is here," and she touched her forehead to his. It was the only reference she ever made to their Indianness.

"How could I be an Indian?" Matt wondered, and began to rethink his plan.

He emerged from the sweat lodge and waited while his eyes adjusted to the sunlight. Everything appeared so vividly alive -- the vast valley, the infinite bright sky, the thousands of square miles of bare mauve earth, the stark red rocks, lonely mesas, shadowed canyons, and the green ribbon of the Verde River. He could feel how big and empty this world is, and he instinctively knew that white America didn't have an explanation for this wonder. He understood the white man's need to cram it full with tenements, factories, and highways. Feeling the conflict between the old beliefs and the modern viewpoints he wondered if the crystal people have it right after all. This is a magical land, a place of earth, energy, and convergence.

He recalled the vision he had in the stuporous steam of the sweat lodge. In his mind's eye, he had seen a majestic bald eagle, the American symbol of lonely grandeur and freedom, the regal bird on the American Seal, clutching arrows and ringed by stars and stripes. A symbol of the great two forces in life -- the destructive and the constructive.--on one side, greed, selfishness and materialism; and, on the other side, generosity, sacrifice and freedom. Which side will prevail, he wondered.

After showering, he dressed quickly and walked back to the hogan. Jen and Sam had already left for the council meeting. Matt skipped and hopped down the steps and met Wally, who was waiting by the gate.

"Heard you were doing a sweat. Learn anything?"

"Yeah. Don't do a sweat when you're full of ham and biscuits."

Wally laughed. "You're lucky I didn't fill you with beans. You'd have blown a hole in the side of that lodge."

"You're right about that, and, hey, thanks for the advice."

"You're welcome. What was it I told you? I forget."

"I'll remind you next time, Wally. Take care."

"You, too."

Matt got into his VW, turned on the ignition, and waved at Wally as he turned north on the frontage road and headed for the reservation and the meeting.

He slipped unnoticed out of the side door of the auditorium and stood on the porch. On the lawn, Jay's Hawks were sitting in a circle, pounding a solitary drum, a ragged chorus of hoarse voices wailing a monotonous song.

Inside, the rhetoric continued, interrupted at intervals by strong dissenting voices. Matt left after the Queen Bee had spoken eloquently, her words resonating as he strode towards the singers. "There're a few, a handful, who see the corruption we are living. Most of us are in denial that we have accepted the White Man's way of life, which we don't really understand. The casino culture is our white buffalo. The money relieves our poverty, but it destroys our spirit. It is our own people who oppress us now. Our leaders pay themselves large amounts of money they do not deserve because they lack education and experience, and they are deaf and dumb to our spiritual ways. Therefore, they practice evil ways." She had pointed a finger at the Council members.

"It is time we wake up and rid ourselves of these Eaglemen, for they are boastful, corrupt, and foolish. It is time to end their wrongdoings and strive to return to our almost forgotten values of the past. If we are to become a sovereign people, we must develop lawyers, doctors, educators, and scientists to guide our people who also know and practice our traditions and will sacrifice to protect the earth that nourishes us. We must rid ourselves of fast-talking, lazy men. I have spoken." The room had quieted, and then the denials and orations began again.

Matt waited until the drumming and chanting stopped. He lowered his eyes and spoke simply. "I need your help"

"What do you have in mind, brother?"

Matt outlined his plan. The drummer nodded. "No worries. When do we start?"

"Tomorrow night. It's our best chance."

"It is time to act, brothers," Ralph said.

The singers looked at each other and smiled. "Maybe we should dance." The drummer began beating the large drum. Matt joined in as the Hawks formed a circle and started dancing, each man bending, bowing, weaving, shuffling, and circling clockwise around the drummer. When they finished, the drummer said, "Jen was right. You dance like an Indian, Matt. You dance with your body. White men dance only with their feet." Matt's spine tingled when they clasped hands. "I must go," he said. "Thank you."

Conscious that the young men were watching as he walked to the casino, he entered through the side door, walked across the casino's main floor, and saw Tom in the Eagle's Nest. He went up the ramp and sat down facing Tom. The waitress approached, but Matt waved her away.

"Good to see you. Making any progress?" Tom asked.

"Possibly, but I've got a few bees in my bonnet."

"Shoot."

"I had a talk with Jay."

228

"And you're wondering why I suggested he should get lost?"

"That and some other things."

"Jay's a drunk. He's not reliable. A child really. He jumped into a hornet's nest. A big mistake. He grabbed some video tapes and brought them to me. He was panicked and, frankly, so was I. He was probably caught on a surveillance camera, and…"

"And what?"

"I told him to hide. That he'd be tied to the casino robbery and no one would believe a drunken Indian. I said he'd go to prison or worse if Salvatori thought he was involved, and that the tribe would get a black eye."

"What's on the video tapes?"

"Nothing, absolutely nothing. Well, not quite. Three tapes were blank and two were of the women's toilets, women taking care of business. Apparently somebody in the surveillance room is a voyeur. I put them in the locker upstairs with that other crap."

"You knew about that stuff?"

"Yes, Jay showed me some. Look, Matt, I want the syndicate and Salvatori out of here. That's no secret, but there's nothing on the tapes that would help. Frankly I was hoping you would discover something useful. We need to break the contract without disclosing anything that could possibly close the casino. You do realize what's at stake here?"

"I'm trying to, Tom. I need to know if the council members are being paid off."

"I don't think so. Oh, they get a free lunch, but that's not the end of the world. What's on your mind?"

"I've been focusing on illegal gambling, money laundering, and skimming, but I have a nagging feeling that I'm overlooking something."

"Like what?"

"Let's go back a little. Jay mentioned a pollution report he was supposed to hand-carry to the Secretary of Interior's office."

"That report was a joke. Jay had a grant. He took some soil samples, sent them to the Ag Department at NAU. A grad assistant wrote up the report for him. No news there. There's lead and arsenic all over the Valley, always has been and always will be. With the mine tailings everywhere, you don't need a geologist for that. The tailings are part of the problem, but they were cleaned up years ago. And the increased ratios in the wells and aquifers are due to better record keeping by the EPA."

"How does that affect the water companies? What's the impact?"

"Boy, you do have a bee in your bonnet. You sound like an ecologist. The answer is zilch. More development will require deeper drilling. If the well ratios climb, the EPS will demand that the tri-valleys install heavy metal purification plants. That's their problem."

"And the tribe?"

"As far as I know, they have no plans to utilize their water rights. If they try, there will be litigation. SRP and the Metropolitan Water Company will step in. Everybody wants a piece of the Verde, and the winner is whoever spends the most money influencing the legislators. The bottom line is that the tri-cities will still need heavy metal processing plants."

"And if the tribe loses the casino?"

"I see where this is going: No casino, no influence, no water. It could go that way, but I don't think it will if the tribe regains control of the casino. The big 'if' is if they agree to pay a percentage of the profit to the state. It's the only way to go, Matt."

"What about sovereignty?"

"That's a dead horse. Frankly, no one gives a damn. Hell, the tribe doesn't even know what it means. Do you?"

"I'm not sure, but some people here care."

"The Queen Bee and her 'Save the Vanishing American' bit? The council members don't care. As long as they're in charge, the people stay on the dole. Everyone has their hands out, including the kids."

"Well, I care, Tom."

"Good for you. Hope you come up with something, but history and time are against you. You have anything else on your mind?"

"Yes, the Rez land swap was illegal. That was your project, wasn't it?"

"To a degree. Old lands for new. Freeway land for wilderness land. It's working. No one will go back on it."

"Why would anyone give up land on the right-of-way and, if they did, how do they benefit? What's in it for you?"

"Me? Nothing. I have no part of it. It's not my deal."

"But the land abuts your property. You have two holdings with access to the upper aquifers. What do you have in mind? A possible pipe link? A dam? And the railway goes through it, doesn't it? They could ship cement to China via San Diego."

"Cement?"

"Sure, from all the limestone ledges. Or didn't you know about the cement?"

Matt handed him a manila folder. "You wanted a progress report."

Tom rapidly scanned the pages. His hands shook as he read a few lines more carefully. "You SOB."

"Takes one to know one. Now, you take care."

Tom watched Matt walk down the ramp and then picked up his cell phone. "Sheriff, this is Tom Fallon. We need to talk."

CHAPTER EIGHTEEN

Matt parked the Kombi next to the corral where thirty or so dun-colored llamas were waiting around the feed troughs, their long-lashed brown eyes fixed on JR and Paloma. He heard soft humming sounds and chortles as Paloma shooed away a sturdy male who was trying to nibble her straw hat while she hand-feed pellets to a fuzzy reddish-colored baby llama. After pouring pellets into a trough, JR waved his hat in the face of a large male and backed away as the llama drew back his head, baring his teeth.

"Back off, you smelly bugger."

"JR, don't do that. He'll just spit on you."

JR grunted. "Come to see the stock, Matt? They're all totally worthless, smelly critters that spit."

"I heard that," Paloma spoke loudly. "That's not true; they're beautiful." The llamas chewed their food, gazed at her with wide eyes as she put down the tin pail and walked over to the men. "They are not worthless, JR. You're making money and you know it."

"Well, they are not exactly cash cows, Matt. They are more like mules in sheep clothing and just as ornery."

"They only spit on people they dislike, like ornery, smelly cowboys."

"I just spit back," JR grinned as a curious llama approached Paloma and snatched her straw hat. It trotted away quickly as Paloma, red hair streaming behind, tried to rescue the hat. "Now that's a sight, Matt."

"I hear you."

"Paloma's right. She usually is. The dude ranchers want llamas. It's the newest fad. They don't pollute like the cattle, and their wool is worth something." JR took off his hat and scratched his head. "I don't know; somehow, I'm still a cattleman at heart."

Matt handed him a manila envelope. "Take a look at this."

"Hmmm." JR dug into his shirt for a leather pouch, laid a line of tobacco down a thin blue paper, tightened the string with his teeth, creased the paper with a practiced move and licked the edge. Striking a match against a corral post, he lit the cigarette, took a deep puff and opened the envelope. His face revealed nothing as he read the report.

He finished, took a deep drag, held it and then exhaled. "Why am I not surprised, Matt?" He handed the report to Paloma.

Her lips moved as she scanned the report; her eyes flashed fire. "They can't do this, JR. It's not right. It's not fair. It's not legal!"

"The hell they can't. If it ain't legal, they'll make it legal and if it's legal, they'll make what we're doing illegal. Hell, that's what they've been doing all along. When push comes to shove, they'll desert us."

"The Cattleman's Association won't let it happen."

"The hell they won't. We've been sitting on our butts since the Sagebrush Rebellion because everyone was scared the Arabs would buy up the land. Now it looks like these Peruvians need a place to squat." JR pinched out his cigarette and looked tired. "We don't own the land, Paloma. We come and go. Now maybe it's someone else's turn."

"Your family has been here for a hundred years!"

"Maybe so. I'm slowing down, but the Taylors aren't quitters." JR looked at Matt. "Where did you get this?"

"Some of it came from Dale Cunningham. The rest I found in the public library."

"The National Land Conservancy guy? Have they got a dog in this fight, too?"

"Don't think so. They are non-confrontational. Dale's moving to Alaska."

"Well, I'm going to get confrontational."

"That's what I had in mind," Matt said.

"What else did you have in mind?" JR spoke very slowly.

"I gave Strickland a copy at breakfast and one to Fallon. He didn't take it well. I put a few in the mail. Renee is working on an article, and I thought I'd hand-deliver copies to you and Cooper."

"You figure you're going to smoke everyone out, me included. Is that the plan?"

"Something like that."

"And I gather there's more to it?"

"You're right."

"What's the rest of the story?"

"I work for the Arizona Gaming Commission, JR. They sent me to check on possible illegal activities at the casino. I was also to survey the impact the casino has had on the tribe and the Verde community. I just stumbled into this."

"Well, you're sure doing your job. The casino is sure making an impact," JR said. "Are you really a sculptor or is that just a cover?" Paloma asked.

"Yes, Paloma, I am really a sculptor. I'm sorry if I've disappointed you."

"Don't be sorry," JR said. "Hell, this won't be easy, but it's going to be exciting. What you brought us may be a godsend, Matt. C'mon, let's go see Cooper. I want to see his face when he reads this. We'll be back soon, Paloma. Don't worry."

JR climbed into the Kombi. "Just go straight across the flats, following that track."

Matt approached the row of false-fronted buildings from the south. Two men dressed in khaki and camos were watching; the taller man was aiming a telescoped rifle in their direction. As the Kombi neared the fence, the man leaned the rifle against a post, and hunched his body over the top rail. The other man went inside the barn.

"That's Cooper. Let me do the talking," JR said as he opened the door and slid off the seat. Taking off his hat, he wiped his forehead with his arm, and put his hat back on, lowering the brim.

"I could have picked you off at 200 yards out, JR," Cooper said.

"Now why would you want to do that, John?" JR asked Cooper, a lean broad-shouldered man with a black patch over his left eye.

"Well, you never know nowadays. All kinds of whackos come out to the flats. Shooters, dopers, trash." Cooper took his foot off the rail. "You ain't wearing your piece, JR. Shouldn't go anywhere without your piece." He patted his holster and glared at Matt with his good eye.

"Matt's a friend, John. I'm showing him around."

"You don't have a piece either, son. You ought to get one if you're going to hang around out here."

"He doesn't need one. Matt can take care of himself," JR said.

"We all need our guns. This country will go to hell when we stop carrying our guns. Are you a shooter, Matt?"

"It's been a while."

"Well, c'mon back. Let's see what you can do." Cooper led them around the side of the barn. "On your left, that cluster is a replica of Little Saigon, a street in L.A. Could be anywhere. On your right is a Columbian village. You choose."

"I'll go for the village."

"Lend him your pistol, Fred, and a spare clip." Fred handed Matt his Glock and a clip. "Fred will do the pull-ups. Follow the blue footprints. JR and I will just step inside the bunker while you walk through."

Matt glanced down at a painted wooden footprint that had been laid into the clay. "There's good guys and bad guys, Matt. Try to shoot the bad guys," Cooper laughed.

"I'll try." Hunched his shoulders, he flipped the safety off, started down the path, peered around the edge of the building and disappeared around the corner. A shot rang out, then several in succession. A scattering of shots followed another round of rapid fire. Matt was waiting in the center of the street when Cooper and JR came in from the far end. Cooper checked the targets in the doorways and windows of the building. Matt handed him the Glock and the empty clip.

"That was real nice, Matt. Fifteen targets, JR, all chest shots. You didn't learn that in the Army."

"Navy Seals. We had a shooting range, but not quite like this layout."

"Well, I'm sure Matt is impressed, John, but he isn't a recruit. He won't be signing up for one of your camps."

"Why not? He looks fit enough and he can shoot." Cooper offered the pistol to JR. "Want to give it a try?"

"No, thanks. I don't shoot at paper targets."

"If you change your mind, come by anytime."

"John, I brought you something you might want to look at." JR took the set of papers out of his pocket and handed them to Cooper, who unfolded the papers, scanned them and scowled. "Give you any ideas, John?" JR asked. "I mean, as how you're into survival and all that."

"Where did you get this?" Cooper asked, his forehead sweating lightly.

"Found them in my mailbox – maybe there's some in yours. They are all over the place. Well, you take care, John. If you get any ideas, let me know, you hear? Let's go, Matt. I've got horses to feed."

"You ought to paint the bus with camo, son," Cooper said. "It would be harder to see. That red and white paint stands out like a sore thumb."

"That's the general idea, sir," Matt said.

"Not a good idea." Cooper picked up his rifle and walked towards the barn as they got into the Kombi.

Matt swung the VW in a wide circle and headed back to JR's ranch. "What happened to Cooper's eye?"

"I heard it was self-inflicted. He put it out trying to commit suicide."

"Are you kidding me? How did he survive?"

"He was using a sling-shot." JR slapped his leg.

"You're a case, JR."

"That I am; that I am. Did you see him sweat? He's shook up and then some."

"What do think he'll do?"

"Well, we'll have to wait and see. That's what you wanted, wasn't it? I'll keep an eye on his place. Maybe he'll call in his cuckoos. Who knows?"

Paloma met them at the gate, holding binoculars. "So, what happened?"

"Absolutely nothing. Cooper sweat a little, that's all."

"What did you expect? You're lucky you didn't get shot."

"What for? We just delivered the mail."

"You know what for. He wants your ranch and he wants your water company. He's an evil man."

"Honey, he only wants the land next to his. There's plenty like him. But he won't get it." He took off his hat and scratched his head. "So what's next, Matt?"

"I don't have any answers, but I'm going to find some."

"Some things take time. Meanwhile, I'm going to make some calls. It might help."

"The more the merrier, JR."

"What are you going to do?"

"I've got some errands to run. Saturday, I'm going flying with York to video your eagles, Paloma. That is, if you still want to go along?"

"Of course, I want to, but I can't on Saturday. JR and I are going to be in the Pioneer Parade."

"York told me to tell you that we're going up in the afternoon."

"Oh, I want to go with you. What about the horses, JR?"

"We'll take the horse trailer straight from the parade grounds. No problem."

"Great! I've got to run," Matt said. "Take care." He turned the Kombi in a circle, followed the gravel road and crossed over the cattle guard.

"Can we trust him, Paloma?"

"He's as straight as they come. He has a good heart, JR."

237

"Well, he better have, because I sure as hell have dealt myself in." He took off his hat again, and scratched his head. "I need a cup of coffee, and then let's get the appaloosa groomed for the parade."

Outside the studio, Matt felt naked and alone with the heat burning his shoulder blades. Falling at sharp angles, the sunlight washed the mesquite bushes with a bright yellow and washed the arroyos with a soft gray. The monsoon winds were pushing clouds from one rock mesa to another. The baked breath of the sandstone ledges reached upward, trying to grab the phantom rain to quench its thirst. Soaring high overhead, a bald eagle raced its shadow across the mesa wall. The current of his mind also flowed over the gentle shoals of the Verde and onto the serrated outline of the Black Mesa.

"Life," he thought, "even when people are in nature, is overlooked, worse it's unnoticed. We are sleepwalkers, eco-zombies. Natural life is off our radar screens. We don't see the connection between the destruction of forests, streams, and oceans to the death of all of us, and our planet. Even if we are partially wake, we won't surrender our comfort and convenience. Who's willing to give up their car, television, cell phone, refrigerator, or hairspray to save a woodpecker or an owl? Or for ground squirrels or a stream full of trout or blue sky? No one, not even those who live here, let along city dwellers for something they've never seen. No one, not even me," he concluded guiltily.

Inside the studio, the air smelled recently swept, as if the night wind had somehow blown a frenzied cleaning. Whistling, he sized up the room and absentmindedly reached down to scratch Digger's head. "This is a good place to itch and sketch." The pup barked softly and wagged his stubby tail. Matt sat down at the table, opened a pad and began to draw.

When he finished, he studied the sketches in the fading light: an old woman standing beside Bucky O'Neall's statue; Max, in his beret, holding a key in his outstretched hand; Paloma, in a turned-up straw hat, feeding a baby llama; JR rolling a cigarette;

238

Cooper sighting down a rifle barrel; Renee seated in her Mustang, eyes challenging, almost accusing looking over her shoulder; Old Wally, shoe in hand, peering at a bee and a spider; Digger asleep on the floor with his head resting on his bowl.

Matt felt light headed and his eyes ached. His head nodded, his mind stopped, and he dozed off. He felt, but didn't hear a voice deep within him say, "Be still. You are capable of doing much more than your dream of. What you search for is in yourself. Be like a buffalo -- face the wind and go through the storm. Adversity. Survival. Adaptation."

CHAPTER NINETEEN

"Rosey Rosenkratz sat deep in a blue leather chair, gazing out of the glazed windows at the Tempe Buttes. The other ten men at the table shared his graying hair color, except for two who had lost theirs altogether. They all wore sport coats, slacks, loafers, and sport shirts, except for Rosey, who wore a white collared shirt and a bolo tie with a large polished agate shaped like the state of Arizona. They all had the appearance of upstanding business men, but something in their weary, cold eyes and the way they flicked their cigar ashes suggested they were accustomed to making deals to steal from others.

"So, what do you think, Bud?" Rosey asked Bud Gordon, the "faucet" to the state commerce and water resources subcommittees.

"The Salt River Project people are going to take a keen interest in this. The statutes regarding surface water define the term as water of all sources, flowing in streams or in the definite underground channels. This underground channel is often referred to as the subflow of the stream. The lateral extent of the subflow of a stream has recently been clarified by the Arizona Superior Court 'as the saturated Holocene alluvium.'"

"What the hell does the mean, Bud?" Rosey snapped.

"Generally, it means the loose gravel and sand that lies beneath and adjacent to a stream, that has been laid down during the Holocene period – the last 10,000 years or so." Bud smiled, paused for effect, "And that means that the water in the subflow is subject to the surface water statutes, or prior appropriation by SRP or any claimant."

"Where's this going, Bud?" Rod asked peevishly.

Bud grinned. "And that means that a number of wells in the Verde Valley, both public and private, are drawing presumably surface water that they do or do not have a legitimate claim to. There is going to be some considerable litigation over parcels with water rights attached." Bud paused and looked at the men around the table. "Water rights are attached to the land not to the owners. It's confusing," he added smugly. "Arizona's surface water is based on the 'right of prior appropriation.' To cut to the chase, JR Taylor's land water claim in the Verde predates the 1919 'Drop Dead' date in which a surface water claim must have been made in order for it to hold water. That's a joke," Bud laughed, but no one else at the table laughed with him.

"Oh, well. The Fallon, Strickland, and Cooper properties have changed hands numerous times, as have the properties of the land developers. The SRP will probably dispute those claims and the Indian claims as well. Naturally, they will have to substantiate that they have made use of their irrigation rights, which they probably did at some time or another on the original reservation, but their recent claims for the new reservation won't hold up, in my opinion. I don't know what SRP's intentions are but whoever sent out that report knew what he was doing. He's stirred up a hornet's nest.

"What's your read on this Rod?"

"The Senator, as usual, has positioned himself well on the Verde Valley referendum. He's proposed something we can control; the utility companies will come out on top. They buy out the private water companies or we regulate them out of business. If we have to, we confiscate. In fact, we could confiscate John Cooper's holdings and we could condemn J.R. Taylor's property, but we might not have to. Tom Fallon is a pushover who's double-crossing the tribe and thinks Cooper is double-crossing him and that other water company jerk, Strickland. So Fallon crossed Cooper. They're all after the water rights. Fallon thinks that, if he exposes Cooper's robbery and the casino's money laundering scheme without revealing his role, he'd have a shot at the water rights and the limestone. Now, he's running scared without a clue that he's backed into a buzz saw. Fallon doesn't know that we bailed out the Tribes Helping Tribes project that the Apache Council sponsored. They're out; we're in."

"What about the Senator?"

"The Senator has a bully pulpit. He's the Chairman for Indian Affairs and the Commerce Committee. He's making a big mistake. Politics and gambling don't mix."

"Is that so?" The men around the table laughed loudly.

"I meant not in the open, where the public reads about it in the newspapers."

"What about the Governor?"

"She benefited from the gambling compact that drew the Indians into the voting booth and from their campaign contributions."

"Hell, she'll never survive the scandal. She's cut a deal with a tribe run by a syndicate that's running drugs, laundering money, and polluting the Verde River. And Kincaid, even although she hates the SOB, was her pick on the public safety committee and on the Gaming Commission. He'll finger her and she'll dump on him. Hell, they'll both have to resign."

"I don't think I like this, Rosey. Kincaid could drop a load on Enterprise. He knows that we put up the money."

"What are you suggesting, Rod?"

"I'm thinking that this is a good time to get rid of Kincaid. He's played both sides long enough."

"Who do we put in there?"

"We'll cross that bridge when we come to it, Rod. Someone honest and stupid. Someone who'll clean house on the DPS and get the Feds out of the valley. Sorry, Kessler, nothing personal, but that's how it is."

"I understand," Kessler responded.

The men waited while Rosey poured a glass of water, opened a vial, and tapped two pills onto the mahogany table. He swallowed one and laid the other on the table. Rosey patted his stomach. "Neil, what's your read?"

"There's a lot of if's that I don't like, but if Bucky finds drugs at the cement plant and if he finds any records of shipments, which won't tell us anything more than trucks here and trucks there, and if we can tie to anything the DEA's got, and if they share what they have... But there probably won't be enough evidence beyond proving malfeasance. The syndicate will have a backup story and a fall guy, probably Salvatori."

Kessler waited as Rosey swallowed the other pill. "Your best shot is to let Bucky raid the casino. If he finds proof of a money laundering operation, the casino is finished. The tribe will be bankrupted and Enterprise will be the beneficiary. And if your newspapers push this, you'll get slots and maybe more if the other tribes have to fold or at least come under stronger regs and taxes."

"That's a lot of 'ifs'," Rod said.

"That's what's called free enterprise, Neil. Gentlemen, we should give some thought to picking up the limestone properties, diversify. How about you, Tom? One of your friends, as I recall, has a cement company in Phoenix. Would he be interested in doing business with China?"

"Too big a reach, Rosey."

"Well, maybe we can reconsider that later. Does anyone see any problems?"

"The President isn't going to be happy if his Secretary of Interior gets caught by the short hairs," Rod spoke up.

"And what if Bucky screws it up?" Bud asked.

"Even if he does, he'll get re-elected. Hell, last year the voters in California elected a dead man for Sheriff."

"Knowing Bucky, he probably will, but even if he gets it half right, we win," Rosey said.

"And what's the other half?"

"No crap falls on us. We didn't lift a finger. We're not involved."

"What about Kincaid?" Bud asked.

"He has no loyalty to us or to the syndicate. He works for himself. As I said, the sooner he goes, the better," Rod said.

"No need for that. Just sweeten the pot," Bud said.

"To hell with that," Rod replied.

"Do we all agree?" Rosey asked. The men around the table nodded. "Then I think we should adjourn." The men stubbed out their cigars and exited through a side door of the Pima Room. Neil opened the front door and beckoned to Bucky. He entered the room and closed the door. Rosey stood in front of the table waiting. "Bucky, let me get straight to the point. You've got a green light. If you deliver, we'll support your bid for Governor. We will make a significant contribution, indirectly of course."

"Does that mean party support?"

"Absolutely. You have my word. But I'm telling you up front, if this turns into a fiasco, if you bungle this, we never heard of you. You will never call on us again. Understand?"

"I hear you alright."

"Now we need insurance. We want you to take Neil with you. He will back you up. You need an FBI presence, especially on the Rez."

"The hell, you say, and who gets the credit? Me or the FBI?"

"I'm just along for the ride, Bucky. No worries."

"And you will bring Kincaid along?" Rosey insisted.

"How am I going to do that without giving a reason? If I do, he'll tip them off."

"I'll take care of Kincaid." Kessler said.

"I hate to suggest this, but if Kincaid doesn't come back, it would be better for everyone; perhaps he could have an accident," Rosey said.

"I want no part of anything like that. No deal, Rosey."

"Well, that's up to you, Bucky. Think it over. Let Neil know what you decide. I have to run. Would you mind waiting outside, Sheriff? Neal will be right with you." Bucky paled and walked out of the room. Kessler closed the door.

"Neal, what do you see in your future?"

"I'd like the Director's job."

"Ha! You're a rare one. Well, we might be able to help you. I'll keep it in mind. It was Rod's idea to bring you in, not

244

mine. We probably shouldn't have, but I don't think we could manage without your help. Can you handle it?"

"I can manage it, Mr. Rosenkratz."

"What do you get out of this, Neil?"

"Satisfaction. Kincaid is too ambitious and so is Bucky. I'm not a politician, but I do want the Director's job."

"You're ambitious, too," Rosey said as they shook hands. "Be careful with Bucky. He's a loose cannon." He winked at Kessler and left through the side door.

Neil went into the hall and stood next to Bucky, who was staring out at the Buttes. "I didn't bargain for this, Neil."

"Relax, Bucky. If that's all that's holding you back, I'll take care of Kincaid. I know him. He'll talk his head off."

"And if he doesn't?"

"Bucky, I've got enough on Kincaid to put him away for 99 years, twice. I'll let you take his confession. C'mon, let's get out of here. Too much second-hand smoke is unhealthy."

CHAPTER TWENTY

Shorty rocked back and forth in front of the surveillance monitor, moaning softly and squeezing the palms of his hands together. "What's going on?" Ken asked.

"It's that Renee Babe. Jesus! Look at this!" Ken moved closer to the monitor. Renee raised her arms, allowing her pale blue dress to fall to the floor. She reached slowly behind her back, unhooked her bra, and dropped it beside the dress. She wiggled out of the half-slip. "Oh, Jesus!" Shorty said.

A blue light began blinking on and off. "Fire in the hole! Station 23. Two guys are going at it in the bowling alley." On screen, a leather-vested heavy-set man with tattooed arms was sparring with a scrawny, mustachioed blond male who aimed at the larger man's groin. Side-stepping the kick, the larger man pulled his opponent's tee-shirt over his head, locked an arm around his neck, and began pummeling him on the head and shoulders. Two security men closed on the brawlers and finally separated them. The scrawny man, freed from his assailant, pulled his shirt off and swung wildly, knocking down one of his rescuers while the other man grabbed the other security guard and wrestled him to the floor. "All security to the bowling alley."

Three uniformed guards, carrying P47 batons, moved in lockstep through the doorway, pushing through the patrons who were frantically trying to flee. A biker roll-blocked the guards from behind, knocking them to the floor as another biker grabbed and threw their batons down the bowling alley.

"Jesus, it's a free-for-all," Shorty said. He jabbed some console buttons.

"What are you doing?" Ken asked.

"What do you think? I'm locking the cashiers' cages."

"Call the boss, Shorty. And you, Tom, get your ass out there. You, too, Bill. Cover the counting room."

"Should I take a weapon?" Bill asked.

"No, just go out there and direct traffic."

"Yes, sir," Shorty said. "It's a brawl. The cages are covered. I've sent for back-ups. Should I call the tribal police?"

"Yes, sir, right away." The monitor screen revealed a slender nude figure stepping into the shower as Shorty punched two numbers. "Oh, Jesus! Sorry, sir. I'm trying the chief's office right now." Shorty redialed the numbers. "We have a fight in the bowling alley. We need back up."

In the kitchen, a short order cook lifted a cast iron skillet clumsily from the heavy duty range, spilling grease onto the burner and starting a fire. He dropped the pan into a large sink and turned on the faucet; a fire ball forced him to back away. He pulled off his apron and tried to smother the fire. He yelled as it burst into flames. When the fire sprinkler system alarm bell sounded, a helper grabbed a fire extinguisher off the wall, aimed it at the fire, and pulled the release.

"It's broke," he shouted as water cascaded down from the ceiling. "Get out of there. The sprinklers will put it out." He shoved the man out of the door and tossed some greasy rags onto the apron. He looked back and smiled as he closed the door.

"What's happening in the kitchen?" Bill asked.

"We got a fire. You better clear your people out of there." Bill hesitated and then pushed the kitchen door open. The greasy rags flamed and smoke poured out into the hall. The cook pushed Bill away from the door and slammed it forcefully.

"You fucking idiot! You want to burn down the whole building? Get your people out of here." The cooks ran down the hallway to the back exit. Bill ran to the counting room, opened the door and stuck his head inside.

"Everybody out. We have a fire in the kitchen. No panicking, please, but move it!" Ken and three brown-suited men walked out the door and into the hallway.

"Shouldn't we shut down, Ken?" Bill asked as five firemen rushed through the back door, carrying extinguishers. One man peered through the windows of the kitchen and down the hall.

"I need a number two hose. Get those people out of here and shut those doors." A fireman waved them down the hall, pushed them into the casino and locked the doors. The two firemen by the kitchen door turned on their extinguishers and a white cloud of mist sprayed through the hallway.

"That ought to do it." They opened the kitchen door and stepped inside. A fireman entered the counting room and inserted a flash drive with a USB interface into the computer. As it downloaded the files, he checked the status bar and his watch: two minutes. The status registered 87%. Ten seconds later, he executed a program, and twenty seconds later, ejected the four gigabyte flash drive and stuck it into his pocket. Firing a mist from the fire extinguisher at the ceiling, he walked backwards out of the door, and followed the other firemen out of the casino.

"Watch out!" a fireman shouted. Forcing the firemen and the security guards to leap out of the way, several men on motorcycles raced through the breezeway, thundered across the parking lot and disappeared over the far embankment. "Jesus, who are those idiots?" he asked.

Matt stood behind a dumpster, stripped out of the fireman's rig, and handed it to a fireman. "Did you get what you wanted?" an Indian fireman asked.

"I've got it." Matt looked at his watch. "Six minutes, maybe four for the counters. You can let them in the building now."

One of the firemen unblocked the entrance hallway. Obviously flustered, Salvatori walked down the hall, followed closely by Ken and Bill. He tried the knob, then slipped his pass card into the slot, opened the door, and stepped inside the counting room. Salvatori pushed into the room after them.

"Get Shorty!" Salvatori yelled. Bill punched his cell phone and handed it to him. Shorty turned away from the monitor.

"Give me the status on the counting room."

"Okay, sir. No one in or out."

"You sure?"

"I want you to check on the bowling alley hallway and the kitchen tapes for anything, especially any unauthorized people."

"The hall was empty, sir, nobody but the firemen and the cooks."

"Check again."

Shorty replayed the shower tape, pulled it out of the player and took it to the locker room. "See you later, babe," he said, putting it on the stack inside his locker.

"What do you want Carbahol to do?" Bill asked.

"For Christ's sake, call the DPS. I want those bikers picked up," Salvatori replied.

"What about the security team?"

"Get their statements and fire them."

"Should we do that?" Bill asked.

"I want them fired and blacklisted. Have Carbahol's men finish the shift."

"What about the cooks?"

"Ease up, Bill. Let's go see the damage." Inside the kitchen, two cooks were standing in a pool of water surveying the mess. Wall fixtures were dripping water and open tins of cocoa, sugar, and flour were oozing down the cabinets.

"What happened?"

"Grease fire. Those iron skillets got too hot to handle, boss," a cook answered.

"And you shoved them into the sink?"

"My fault, boss. I didn't think."

"You're not supposed to think. You're supposed to react."

"Sorry, boss."

"Sorry, boss, my ass." Salvatori turned to Bill. "Get the janitors here. Send everyone to the front kitchen. Shut down the Thai Room and the Kiddie Fountain. It's going to cost two grand to clean this up. I want it back online tonight. You guys are staying until this mess is cleaned up." Salvatori glared at everyone.

"I'll be in the Eagle's Nest. You keep an eye on these guys." Salvatori joined five Asian men with high pants that exposed their white socks sitting on the edge of their chairs.

"Is everything all right?" one man asked anxiously.

"Perfect," Salvatori said. "We just had a fire drill, a practice."

"Is that necessary?"

"Oh, it's always necessary. We run a tight ship here," Salvatori said and drank from his tumbler of Perrier.

A dark figure opened the door to Queen Bee's office and began draping rolls of toilet paper over the file cases, desks, and furniture. Satisfied, he opened a pack of matches, lit a cigarillo, puffed on it, inserted it behind the row of matches, and closed the flap. He set the matchbook carefully on a small mound of tissue, closed the door and walked out.

Matt walked back to the bar when Radcliffe motioned to an empty stool. "Been saving it for you. What'll you have?"

"Tequila. Make it a double," Matt said. The Q & Brew was packed with bikers and cowboys, an unlikely combination. The bartender set the tequila, a slice of lemon, and a salt shaker on the bar. Matt took it straight down, bit into the lemon, shook some salt onto the back of his hand, and licked it off. The lemon and salt put out the fire in his throat.

"I didn't know you drank the hard stuff, Matt."

"I don't, except on special occasions."

"Is this an occasion?"

"I sure hope so. It better be. I'm way out on a limb."

"Did you get anything?"

"I don't know yet, Dick. But I emptied their computers."

"The syndicate won't like that. What if they figure it out?"

"They won't have to. I left a bug that has the whole wide world in its hand."

"Oh, oh. I wish I'd known. That could be trouble for me. I've got something going down."

"When?"

"Saturday morning I'm swapping spit for drugs."

"A sting? Where?"

"The cement plant. We're using the Pioneer Day celebrations for cover."

"What are you after?"

"The casino has a sharp shooter in tow -- money laundering. We're hoping he'll put the money in the hopper."

Matt looked at his watch. "If he's going to do it, he'll have to plug it in before eleven."

"Thanks, Matt; that'll work. Give me a tequila too, bartender."

"Make it two." They drank their drinks quietly. "What about your people?" Matt asked.

"Charlie's pissed that he got a black eye. They're at Denny's now. Farley was in here, looking around and the DPS drove by. The town's crawling with bikers for Saturday's rally. The jails will be full of guys with black eyes. No worries."

"Good. I've got to run."

"Unfinished business?"

"Yep. I've got more roads to travel."

"Is this a great business, or what? No rest for the wicked. Bartender, I'll have another, please."

"You aren't going to get on your bike, are you, Dick?"

"Hell, no. I'll stay here and keep an eye on things. I'm staying in the motel down the street. Not to worry."

Matt slipped out the side door. After his head cleared, he made his way *The Village Voice* office. Renee's Mustang was parked in front and her desk light was on. When he rapped at the window, Renee opened the door wide. She stepped out onto the porch, her arms crossed over her chest. The light from the gibbous moon cast a blue sheen on her black hair as she tossed her head, her flashing blue eyes contrasting with her bronze coloring.

"I hope you're pleased," she said irritably. "You're a disaster, Matt. Do you have any idea of what you've done?"

"Nope, not really, but I have the data." He held up a key ring. "Want to check it out?"

"You're certifiable," she said as she snatched it out of his hand and marched into the office. She plugged the key into the computer port and waited while it downloaded. "This better be good. You didn't tell me you were going to burn down the kitchen and the Cultural Center and start a riot in the bowling alley. Salvatori's going crazy. He's firing everyone, and I think he's got his eye on me too. My boss will kill me. Our whole operation is shot. Salvatori is going through the tapes and he's calling in his computer gurus. It's insane, Matt. You've lost it, and you've blown my job."

"Whoa, slow down some. Are you sure there was a fire in the Cultural Center?"

"Of course, you set it or had your firehouse buddies do it. The tribal records were destroyed, or at least Queen Bee's files were. She's been blaming everyone."

"When did that happen?"

"Right after the casino kitchen fire. Luckily the fireman were still around or the whole Center would have burned down and probably the casino, too. We're talking arson, Matt. You had no right..."

"I didn't have anything to do with it. I left as soon as I could."

"It must have been the bikers."

"They were gone, Renee. They were over the hill before I left. Who would want to burn the records?"

"Well, it sure wasn't Salvatori," Renee bit her lip. "He had me soothe the wise Oriental gentlemen while he lit into Annie."

"Cosmic Annie? What does she have to do with this?"

"Salvatori thinks Annie helped Tom Fallon scam the casino while all hell was breaking loose."

"What?"

"Fallon took the casino for $300,000 at the blackjack tables. He said that Fallon was sitting up in the Eagles Nest just waiting for a chance, and he got it while Salvatori was running

252

around with his head cut off, putting out fires. I was with the
Chinese and Fallon took advantage of Annie. Fallon's no gambler,
Matt. That's obvious."

"So, did Annie help him?"

"She's not very smart, but she's not that stupid."

"How did he do it?"

"He went to the open table. He made three $50,000 bets
and then doubled up. He won $300,000, walked away from the
table, and cashed out. He didn't even leave her a toke. She was so
stunned that she just sat and waited for Ken."

"I suppose you think that I set Fallon up, too?"

"Oh, shut up! It's Annie who's in trouble. I couldn't care
less about him."

"It'll be interesting to see if Tom shows up for work
tomorrow. I sure as hell wouldn't." The computer cleared, so
Renee began playing the keyboard. She scrolled through several
files. She tensed up and leaned forward, her brows tightening.
She pursed her lips, frowned, and then her face relaxed. Her blue
eyes sparkled and a smile formed at the corners of her mouth.
Renee clapped her hands. "Oh, Matt! We've got the SOBs! They
are dead in the water." She tapped the keys. "Oh, oh, dear God!
We own the laundry, Matt!"

"Is that a pun?"

She jumped out of her chair, grabbed Matt, and kissed him.
"Ugh!" she said. "Tequila breath!" and stepped back. Then she
kissed him again. "It's over. It's finally over. I'm out of here. No
more casino nights. Oh, my God! What am I going to do?"

"Wire your boss."

"Oh, no, not yet. I need to think about all this."

"So, I'm not an insane klutz after all?"

"No, no, Matt. You're my hero, the Lone Ranger,
remember? You did it." Renee closed the computer, started to put
the key in her purse, changed her mind, found some masking tape
and tapped it under her chair. "I don't want that on me. Let's get
out of here. I'm so happy. I'm so scared." She closed the door.

"Want to go for a ride?" Matt asked her.

"No, Matt, not tonight. I've got to talk to Annie. How about tomorrow?" She ran to her car. "I'll call you."

Matt crossed the street to a pay phone, lifted the receiver, slid in a pay card, and dialed a 011 number. "Mala Resort, Vava'u," a silky voice answered. "Bonga, bonga, bonga. I don't ever wanna to leave Tonga. You can keep civilization. I'll stay right here."

"Send the mail, Ahron."

"Worldwide? You better duck for cover. Why not come here? You can catch the bamboo express."

"Maybe later. I have things to do."

"Take care, then. I do mean – take care!"

"I definitely will." Matt put the phone on the hook and walked to his car.

CHAPTER TWENTY-ONE

The Governor and her entourage were seated in box seats in the center of the bleachers along with the Yavapai County Commissioners, the mayors of the tri-villages and their guests. Sheriff Bucky O'Neil stood at the side of the grandstand with DPS Colonel Kincaid, Sgt. Hubbard, and a DPS patrolman.

Dressed in their finery, a contingent of Native Americans representing the Yavapai, Apache, Hopi, and Navajo tribes filed past the grandstand, followed by the Sheriff's posse, dressed in red cowboy shirts, blue demins, white chaps and white calfskin boots, with six-guns in holsters. They raised their white Stetsons high over their heads as they passed the reviewing stand. The Governor stood and waved her lavender handkerchief.

"Only in Arizona," she said as she sat down.

"They all vote, Governor, and they vote for us," her aide said quietly.

"Who is that?" the Governor asked.

Riding an appaloosa and dressed in blue riding skirt, a white blouse with a collar, and red hair trailing down her back, Paloma smiled and waved as the crowd cheered.

"She's the Colonel's Daughter. It's a tradition. The commandant of old Fort Verde brought his daughter out west with him. It's quite a story. Someone even wrote a book about her. Knocked the troopers for a loop."

"Well, if she looked anything like that woman, I can understand why."

A mounted file of troopers wearing post-Civil War cavalry uniforms saluted with drawn sabers as they passed in review. They were trailed by the Mingus Mountain Marching Band playing a spirited rendition of "She Wore a Yellow Ribbon."

A truck-drawn float packed with Jen's Gourd Girls, wearing beaded dresses, costumed tribal drummers and flute players paused in front of the Grand Stand. The Gourd Girls opened small beaded pouches and blew pollen dust into the air.

"Now, that's what I call a blessing," Bucky O'Neil said. "Suitable for the occasion, I hope." He peered down Main Street as the Sheriff's posse was turning the corner.

"All hell's about to break loose, boys. The posse is going straight down Second Street and right on to the cement plant. A little surprise party, Colonel."

"They are going to do what?" Kincaid exclaimed.

"They are going to raid the cement plant. I got a tip. They're running drugs right under our noses."

"Now? In the middle of a parade?"

"Thought you'd like that, Kincaid. It's a great cover. They'll never see us coming. Hell, they'll probably be watching the parade. Wouldn't want to leave the DPS out of this bust, would we? I've got a patrol car behind the grandstand. Let's go. You don't want to miss out." Bucky took the Colonel's arm. "Hubbard, you, and your buddy better keep an eye on the Governor. Wouldn't want anything to happen to her, would we? Oh, Hubbard, better keep your eye on the Marshals, too. My people are going to arrest them, but uh, keep it quiet for the next hour or so."

"Have you lost your mind? You can't pull this off," Kincaid said, pulling his arm free from Bucky's grasp

"The hell I can't and I don't need any back-ups. I've got all the help I need. It's going to go slicker than a whistle. No one will even notice. But you could put some of your people on the highway just in case. C'mon, you can use my radio phone. Keep your hair on, Hubbard." Kincaid looked at Hubbard, shook his head and followed O'Neil.

Bucky drove down Third Street, turned onto Front Street, and parked behind a telephone utility truck. A lineman lowered the safety bucket as the men got out of the cruiser.

"What's happening, Barney?" O'Neil called to the lineman.

"Not sure, Sheriff. We've got outlaw bikers in the yard. One guy went inside and two limos drove inside. The front doors are locked down."

"How many people?"

"Two men at the side door, five bikers in the yard, maybe a dozen people inside."

"Wouldn't you know it! We're going to need back-ups after all. What can you get me?" Bucky turned to Kincaid.

"Great!" Kincaid said. "Nothing close. I'll get on the horn." Kincaid got into the cruiser and picked up the Sheriff's radio phone. "I want two patrol cars at the freeway exit. Bring the Flagstaff units to Cordes Junction and call Hubbard. We have a screw up here. Talk to me. Okay, then send the Prescott unit to Jerome and the Prescott Valley unit east to Cordes Junction."

Kincaid looked over his shoulder at O'Neal and then punched his cell phone. "The Sheriff's busting the cement plant. You've got maybe thirty minutes. I'll try to buy more," he said and got out of the car as a white unmarked vehicle pulled in behind the Sheriff's cruiser.

Neil Kessler and a man wearing a blue FBI vest over a flack jacket got out of the car. "Where's the party?" Kessler asked Kincaid.

"On the other side of the bank at the cement plant. What are you doing here?"

"I got a call from O'Neil. The cement plant belongs to the tribe, so he invited us." Kessler smiled. "How about you?"

"He told me ten minutes ago."

"I guess Bucky didn't want any competition, Kincaid."

"It's a screw up. He wants me to back him up with ten minutes' notice. I don't have anybody close."

"Well, it's his party then, isn't it?" Down the lane the Sheriff's posse had dismounted and were putting on flack vests and visored helmets.

"What have we got?" Kessler asked the lineman.

"It's hard to say. Some bikers in the yard and more people inside. What's Bucky going to do?"

"Who knows? Looks like the Charge of the Light Brigade," Kessler said as the Sheriff's posse tied their horses.

Inside the cement plant, Radcliffe opened a pair of saddle bags and handed several packets of 100 dollar bills to the Gnome who broke open two packets and began typing the serial numbers into his laptop.

"I ran it through the casino at Laughlin. It's clean." Radcliffe waited while the Gnome checked the dollars and closed the laptop.

"And so it is. Let your people come in one at a time."

"I want to check the ice," Radcliffe said.

"What's to check? It's premium Belize. No Mexican crap. You've seen it before and the C's pure Columbian, Peruvian actually. Yes or No?"

"All right."

"Put the cash in the back seat, Dicky." The Gnome signaled to the Marshal. "Open the front door. Let's get this over with." The metal garage clanged upward as a biker entered through the side door and walked over to the table.

"Grab a six pack, Marv, and take off," Radcliffe said.

"Well, gentlemen, we'll leave first, if you don't mind," the Gnome said.

"I want my people out of here and on the highway before the parade breaks up. I'll feel a lot better if you stick around," Radcliffe said.

The Gnome looked at his watch. "If you insist. How long?"

"We'll leave in five minute intervals. Thirty minutes."

The Gnome's cell phone rang. He flipped it open. As he listened, his face turned red, then gray. "Close that door," he shouted. "It's a bust!" His bodyguard reached inside his jacket and pulled out an automatic. "Everybody stay put. Start the crusher, please. Do it!" He spoke sharply to the shop foreman. "You know the drill."

The foreman nodded and pulled a lever. "Just add these packages to the conveyor belt. Uh, you," the Gnome motioned, "give him a hand. All of it. Quickly." The second bodyguard cleared the table and loaded the meth onto the conveyor belt as the foreman climbed a ladder into the loft and began throwing bulk packages into the hopper.

"Ask the others to come in quickly." The bodyguard went to the limo, brought the packets of cash back, and dumped them on the conveyor belt. "That's ours!" Radcliffe shouted.

"You're either stupid or you're a narc," the Gnome snarled. "It doesn't matter, does it? Either way, you lose." A bugle sounded somewhere outside the cement plant.

"What the hell was that?"

"Go look!" the Gnome rasped, and shoved Dicky George. Radcliffe watched helplessly as the briefcase full of cash moved up the conveyor belt and dropped into the hopper.

"Now, flush it," the Gnome said and the foreman pulled a pair of red-knobbed handles. The sludge from the hopper poured into a conduit.

"It's on the way to the river," the foreman said.

"What's going on out there?" the Gnome asked.

"There's a whole army of guys on horseback. The bikers are splitting," Dicky said.

"Well, let's go wait in the office and, uh, open the front doors."

"What about me?" Radcliffe asked.

"I suggest you join your friends, if you have any. Use the back door."

Matt walked out onto the tarmac of the Cottonwood airport. Bob York was fueling the pink candy-striped Challenger ultra-light. "Just topping it off, Matt." He finished, and strapped the empty can onto a rack in the pink jeep. "She has a 52 horse power rotax, but I get the same performance as the big boys with the 90 HP 912. It's a fine engine, but it costs an extra $12,000, 50% more per hour to operate plus the extra weight of the 912 is like carrying another ten gallons of gas, except you can't use the gas! Let's fly!"

Matt crawled into the cockpit and strapped himself in, thankful his knees were only shaking slightly. Bob tossed a handful of dirt into the air to check the wind direction, got into his seat, checked the flaps and rudder, and touched a Buddha that hung from the control panel. "Here's to no crosswinds, no tailwinds, and no thermals," he said as he turned the switch. The engine kicked in and he ran the throttle up and backed it down; satisfied, he checked the runway, applied power, and released the brakes. After Bob pushed the throttle forward, the plane picked up speed.

Matt glanced at the air speed indictor; it read 45 mph as the Challenger lifted into the air. Bob put the nose down and eased the throttle. "Yeeoow. Houston we're airborne." He turned the plane and slowly circled the runway as they climbed to 800 feet.

"Where can you get an airplane that will land on wheels, floats or skis? Gets off the ground in less than 100 feet, stalls out at 24 miles an hour, can cruise all day at 85 miles an hour and climb to 14,000 feet and gives helicopter visibility in all directions, even in turns?" Bob asked as they headed east towards Sycamore Canyon.

"I don't know, but I hope we don't have to use the skis."

"No worries. If the engine cuts out, this bird turns into a glider. Of course, that limits your landing options."

"Where did you learn to fly?"

"Started with hang gliders. Built my first ultra light when I was fifteen. You didn't need a license then; you still don't."

"You don't have a pilot's license?"

"Not for these babies. Flying is all about freedom, Matt. This is as free as it gets. Relax. I have a multi-engine license. I flew helicopters in the Gulf War." Spires and towers of the red rock country loomed on the horizon. Bob flew the plane parallel to the white limestone escarpment and then came in low over the mesa. Some men in camo suits were scattered among the rocks. A few looked up; others lay motionless on the ground; some appeared to be firing weapons.

"Looks like Old Man Arnold's got company."

"What the hell are they doing?"

"Cooper's troopers must be having a paint ball war, war games. Nut cases." Bob made a shallow turn and dropped to less than 100 feet. "That's Farley and that's Cooper, maybe the neighbors are complaining." He turned the plane and Eagle Rock loomed up on the south. "And we've got an eagle. We've got two! Get the camcorder, Matt."

Matt opened the case, extracted the camcorder, and flipped the button. The battery light blinked on, then off.

"It's ready, Matt. I set it up this morning. Holy Moly." Two eagles were chasing each across the sky, diving and rolling. The larger bird made a mock attack, presenting its talons and rolling away. The smaller eagle climbed rapidly, folded its wings, and dived. The larger bird followed him downward. Both birds braked, locked talons and tumbled towards the earth, only to break free a few feet above the ground. Bob circled at slow speed while the eagles circled beneath them, riding a thermal and climbing upward.

"Did you get that, Matt? God, I hope so."

"Let's give them some space." A flock of ducks soared upward as they slid by some contoured fields and turned east. Below them, JR was flapping his hat rapidly up and down next to a pink jeep while Paloma was swinging a kayak paddle over her head and pointing skyward.

Goosing the throttle and circling the plane, Bob brought it in low down the canyon. "Who the hell's that?"

"It's Wally," Matt said.

"Who are those guys on the rocks?"

"Apaches from the Rez. I know them."

The men were waving their hats and pointing upward at the rim of the mesa. Bob nearly stalled the ultra-light as he turned on a dime and came back low and slow. The men below pounded their chests and pointed again to the top of the mesa while one man put a stick to his shoulder and aimed it at the ridge.

Bob dipped the wings and pulled on the throttle. "Whatever it is, it's on the mesa."

261

Matt saw someone, a blurred figure of a woman in a blue dress, just inside the opening to a cliff house.

Bob headed east and then banked to the north. "Let's see what's going on." He flew over the ridge and slowed the Challenger. "Too low. Can't see." He climbed higher. When they approached Arnold's adobe, someone began firing, rounds ripped through the starboard wing. "Those aren't paint balls, Matt. They're firing automatic weapons." The engine quit and the prop slowed and stopped spinning. "We're hit."

"How about the airport?"

"Too damn low. I can make the flats, maybe." Matt looked over his shoulder, watching for muzzle flashes. "Damn psychos," Bob yelled.

As they passed over JR and Paloma, Bob turned off the switch and started his approach, aiming for a flat space between two trees, one about 75 feet and the other about 50 feet tall. The air speed was reduced to 30 mph as he set the plane down on the brush covered flat, slammed the brakes, and came to a stop in less than 150 feet. They unbuckled their seat belts and scrambled out of the plane. Impulsively, Bob ran to the rear of the plane and kissed the tail. "You are one sweet bird. Are you OK, Matt?"

"Yeah. I think so, but my pucker factor is off the wall."

JR and Paloma pulled up in the pickup. Paloma jumped out and ran to Bob. "Are you all right?"

"We're fine. Matt's a little tight."

"What happened?" JR asked. "Your engine give out?"

"No. The locos up on the mesa shot us down. Look there and there, holes in the starboard wing. Look there." Bob was shaking. "Christ, they hit the prop and the engine."

"We'd better clear out," JR suggested.

"Do you have a radio?" Matt asked.

"Not in the plane and the jeep doesn't have one either."

Matt tested his cell phone. "No dice. It has a GPS, but I don't know if anyone will respond." He tossed it in the plane.

"We better not wait here," JR said. "Those guys may come looking."

"I'm sure they will," Bob said. "I need to get to a phone; we'd better get to town."

"You can use the phone at the ranch. That's twenty minutes closer," JR said.

Bob put his hands in his pockets and walked around the Challenger. He rested one arm on the prop blade, stared at Matt and JR, and said, "This isn't probably the best time to tell you folks that I work for the ATF. We've been watching Arnold and Cooper. We think they have ammo and explosives stashed somewhere on the mesa, or maybe in the adobe. This doesn't look good; something's gone wrong. I don't have any choice; I have to call in the bomb detail."

Matt noticed that JR and Paloma seemed to take Bob's revelation in stride, that maybe he had made the announcement strictly for his benefit. "How long will they take to get here?" Matt asked coldly.

"An hour, maybe more. There's a team at the Prescott airport."

"The Sheriff's closer; so's the DPS."

"They aren't equipped to handle this, Matt."

"Well, why don't you get started Bob? I'm going back up the canyon. Wally's up there and so are some friends of mine."

"Take JR with you. He knows every rock and crack in that canyon."

"That's jake with me," JR said. "We'd best get going."

"Wait for my team to get set up, Matt."

"Wait for one or two hours? That's too long. Get Bucky, the sheriff's posse in town and, here, call this guy. His name is Radcliffe. He's DEA. He might be able to help."

"Christ, the posse is on horses!"

"Just get them. Bucky's got a helicopter. So does the DPS."

"We've got time to do this right, Matt. They aren't going anywhere."

"I saw a woman standing inside the cliff house when we flew by. I think it was Jen."

"Are you sure?" Paloma asked.

"I can't take the chance," Matt answered.

"Bob, we have to do something," Paloma agreed.

"We will, Paloma," Matt grabbed a coil of nylon rope from the back of the jeep. "Get going, Bob." Bob jumped into the pink jeep and Paloma scrambled in beside him. Then he spun gravel and headed across the flats.

"How far to those cliff dwellings?" Matt asked JR.

"Twenty minutes of fast walking if you follow the wash, less if you go over the ridge."

"Let's do it. You up to running?"

"These boots weren't made for running, but let's go." The two men starting jogging down the flats, reaching the base of the ridge in five minutes.

"I wish I had my horse," JR puffed. "We can cut across here." He slowed to a fast walk as he led the way up the ridge. "I take the pony through here." A narrow saddle separated a string of boulders and led down to a wide wash. JR stopped to catch his breath. "Follow the streambed 'til it bends to the right, Matt. You'll see a boulder with some Indian sign on it. Go to the top of that rise. You can see the cliff dwellings from there. Don't worry about me. I'll catch up as soon as I get my wind. Go on."

"If you say so."

"Get going...."

Matt trotted up the wash, adjusted the coiled rope over his shoulder, and settled into a ground-eating jog until he reached the bend and slowed. A large boulder covered with petroglyphs was resting in front of a low ridge covered with scrub mesquite bushes and a solitary ironwood tree. A large spiral was incised in the center of the glyph and it was topped by an arrow and a pair of eyes. Matt half crawled and clawed his way through the bush, startling some quail which scattered in front of him.

A pack of javelinas broke through the bush and dashed, squealing, down the wash. Picking up a track that angled uphill, Matt climbed and paused to catch his breath. He spotted JR walking at a steady clip a few hundred yards down the wash.

264

Directly below, Wally was crouched under a rock wall, near a ledge of rocks that formed the base of the cliff dwelling. He stared at the opening where he thought he had seen Jen, but there was no movement. Going down the slope, Matt spotted a rattle snake, leaped over it, lost his footing, and slid down the slope, landing a few feet from Wally, who was brandishing a skillet.

"Matt! You scared the hell out of me. Where did you come from?" Wally lowered the skillet.

"Up the wash. What's going on?"

"It's a Chinese fire drill. Jen and Jay went to Arnold's. Jay wanted to get down into the cliff house."

"Why?"

"Because he thinks Arnold and Cooper hid the casino's stolen money up there. Jen was going to distract Arnold while he looked around, but something went wrong. Jen yelled and we heard shots. Then you boys flew over. Where's the plane?"

"Someone put a hole in the engine and we had to ditch. Where are the Hawks?"

"They went up the wash to help. There's a cut that leads to the top."

"How long ago?"

"Hell, I don't know, maybe twenty minutes. I heard more shots and then it got quiet. It's trouble, serious trouble."

"Bob went after the Sheriff. JR will be here soon. How do I get to the top?"

"You can try the cut, same as the boys did. It ain't easy. You better wait until the Sheriff gets here. If the boys can't help Jay and Jen, you sure can't."

"Maybe there's another way." He studied the canyon wall.

"You ain't going up that face. That rope might get you down, but it won't get you up. "

Matt walked over to the rock face. He focused on the petroglyphs and pictographs, scratches of an earlier people who had depicted their wars, conquests, and tragedies. One panel showed an eagle with a human-like head and outstretched talons clutching arrows. Gazing up at the tremendous red mountain wall, his eyes slowly swept across the ledges, seams, cracks, fissures, and niches that were choked with growth. Above that, a blank wall 50 feet high stretched for a thousand yards, broken only by a scattering of caves, large and small, which housed the remnants of the ancient people who once made their homes there. He pressed down the wall and pushed his way behind a juniper tree where a faded petroglyph of a warrior shooting an arrow at a giant bird figure and a directional arrow pointed upwards to a carefully incised drawing of a cliff house.

"What are you doing, Matt?"

"Looking for a ladder. Give me your knife." Wally pulled his knife from its scabbard and handed it to him. Matt stepped inside a fissure and started scraping the rock face. As the dirt loosened, a hand hold was revealed.

"It's a ladder, Wally!" Matt scraped out several more steps. Then he gripped the top step and pulled himself up, hung on with one hand, and scraped out another handhold. When JR joined them, he had worked his way 20 feet up the wall.

"What's he doing?" JR panted.

"He's going after Jen on his Jacob's Ladder. It looks like it runs up to the cliff house."

"Can I help, Matt?" JR yelled.

"You know where the cut is? Wally says the boys went that way."

"I know where it is. I've been up it."

"See if you can find them. Maybe you can distract Cooper. Be careful. They are armed."

"So am I. Give me thirty minutes."

"Take your time," Matt paused, bent his head, and wiped the sweat from his forehead as JR started running up the wash. "Wally, go up to that rise. If you see anyone in the cliff house, bang your skillet."

"Sure."

"Be careful, there's a snake up there."

"I can take care of snakes. You take care of yourself."

Matt inched his way slowly up the cliff face, his lungs burned, his muscles ached, and his shirt was soaked with sweat. He gripped the base of a juniper and rested a yard or so from the edge of the cliff house. The stones of the cliff dwelling looked loose, and the rocks below were unforgiving. Dead trees had toppled down the cliff, littering the ground. Matt slipped Wally's knife carefully into a loop in his belt, steadied himself, stretched sideways, and grasped a large rock on top of the ledge which came loose and clattered down the cliff face. Matt kept pulling on the rocks. It was twisting, treacherous work. He gripped a rock at the base, tugged, and pulled again. It had a solid feel.

"A leap of faith," he thought as he let go with his left hand, swaying perilously until it joined with his right hand. Legs dangling over the face of the cliff, he hung for a moment, heaved himself over the ledge, and tumbled inside the cliff house. He leaned over the parapet to catch his breath and looked out at the valley below. It was like standing on the edge of the world with endless white sky touching the endless sandstone and shale of the red-tinted mesas until they plunged into the Verde River. "God's view of the earth, the eagles' view," he thought.

In the distance, he saw men on horseback; their dust smeared the heat-hazed wash like a vast sea fog. "Here comes the cavalry. I hope they get here by nightfall," he said aloud.

A helicopter raced by like an angry dragonfly and disappeared over the mesa. Matt waved his arms. "They didn't see us," Wally yelled. "Are you okay?" Matt pumped his fists up and down.

Matt heard a sound deep inside the cliff house, like a cat slowly being strangled. He followed the sound, stepping quietly across the hard-packed dirt floor, avoiding scattered pots and shards. A shaft of light beamed down through an opening in the corner of the room. He scaled a pole ladder that led up to the upper floor of the cliff house and stuck his head and shoulders through the opening. Two people were lying on the floor. One was moving, twisting and writhing; the other was motionless.

Matt climbed into the upper room, a storeroom filled with packing crates and plastic buckets. Several bags were piled beneath a stairwell. Jen was lying on the floor, her arms and legs wrapped in duct tape. She twisted and moaned. He touched her face and whispered, "It's Matt. Be quiet." He used Wally's knife to cut through the duck tape, freeing her hands and feet. Jen sat up and ripped the tape from her mouth.

"Oh, Matt, it's you! Thank God!" she said softly and hugged him.

"It's okay, Jen. It's okay." He turned to Jay, who was laying on his side, his legs drawn up in the fetal position.

"Jay's hurt, Matt. Cooper shot him."

Matt knelt beside Jay. "He's breathing, but there's a lot of blood."

"We've got to get out of here, before they come back. Cooper's going to blow up the mesa," Jen whispered. "I heard him say he was going to take care of the fuses. He's going to blow us up and Arnold too." Her arms and legs were shaking.

"Where is he?"

"Up those stairs. He knows the Sheriff is coming. I heard him say that Arnold will take the fall. He's going to kill us. He told the man who tied me up that, when the Sheriff shows up, he'll say that they came up here for maneuvers and the lunatic panicked and committed suicide."

"Stay put," Matt said, and went up the stairs. He tested the door with his shoulder and came back. "I can't budge it. It must have a bar across it."

"I'm scared."

"Don't worry. We're going to be all right. We have to get out of here before Cooper comes back for the cash. He won't leave without it." Matt stooped beside Jay, uncoiled the nylon rope, and looped it around Jay's shoulders. "Help me with Jay." Lifting Jay into a sitting position, Matt looped the rope behind him, tied a double bowline knot, and formed a sling. He put his arms around Jay. "Take his legs, Jen." They carried him to the opening. "Climb down, Jen. I'll lower him to you." Jen grabbed the pole and slid down to the floor below. Matt put Jay's legs through the opening, grasped the rope in both hands, nudged Jay's shoulders with his knees, and then lowered him through the opening.

"I've got him!" Jen said. "Hurry! I can't hold him." Matt slid down the pole, put his arms under Jay's and steadied him. "Grab his legs, Jen." They lifted him over to the ledge.

"That was the easy part." Matt went back, picked up the pole ladder, carried it to the ledge and laid it in front of the gap. He waved at Wally, who was watching them from the top of the ridge. Matt motioned with his hand and Wally started down the slope. "We'll have to lower him."

"We can't, Matt; he's hurt so bad."

"We don't have a choice. He'll die here if we don't." Matt looped the nylon rope twice around the pole ladder. "Feet first, and then his shoulders." He sat on the floor and braced his legs. "Push, Jen." Jay's legs went over the side and his body eased over the ledge.

"Wally's there," she said. Matt let the rope slide through his hands. "He's clear, Matt. Keep going."

Matt alternately slackened and tightened the ropes. "How he's doing?" he asked. His face was tense; the muscles in his arms were bulging with knots. Sweat was burning his eyes.

"He's okay. He's about six feet from the bottom."

"Where's Wally?"

"He's there." Matt slowly lowered Jay another three feet. "Wally's got him." She announced and Matt collapsed on the floor.

"Good thing." He rested for a minute, rolled over, and stood up. "Now, let's get you out of here."

Jen started to go back into the cave. "The money's up there; so are the records."

"We don't need them. Let's go."

"You're too late, my friends. You should have gone while you could." Cooper was watching through the opening in the floor, his head, one arm and shoulder protruded through the opening. Gesturing with a Glock pistol in his right hand, his left hand was locked onto the edge of the opening. "Move over here. You first,

Matt. Come this way. Slowly." Matt walked slowly back to the opening. Cooper peered down at Matt like the one-eyed cyclops. "You should brought have your piece."

"Now, you, Jen." He gestured with the Glock.

Two shots echoed like cannon fire in the small room. Matt reeled backwards as blue acrid smoke curled from Cooper's gun. He felt a sharp pain, like a bee sting, as Cooper dropped through the opening and hit the floor with a thud. Matt picked up the pistol and stuck it in his belt, and rolled Cooper over.

A look of shock and disbelief spread across his face. "Don't leave me," Cooper whined. "I couldn't find the detonators."

"That's too bad. You shouldn't have come back."

"It's too late," Cooper said. He pointed at the stairs. "He'll blow us up."

Matt stepped up onto the ledge and looped the nylon rope under his arm and his right leg. "Jen, wrap your arms around my neck and your legs around my waist. Don't look down."

Cooper rose to his knees, and started to crawl towards them. "Wait! You don't...," he whispered and fell forward on his face. Matt pushed off the ledge and began rappelling down the cliff face. Wally was waiting for them when, seconds later, they dropped to the ground. So were several men from the Sheriff's Department.

"How are you all doing?" a concerned, stooped grey-haired deputy asked.

"We're fine," Matt said warily.

"Are you sure?"

Matt touched his scalp gingerly. "I think I'm okay."

"Let me look." Matt let the Deputy examine his scalp. "Not even a crease. You got a new part in your hair, but no blood. We've got a helicopter coming. Your friend is all right, but he needs attention. Is he your brother, Miss?" the Deputy asked.

"Yes," Jen said numbly.

"He's going to be fine."

270

"Sheriff, Jeff Cooper's up there. He said something about detonators."

"Cooper's still up there? My God! That ATF guy told us there's a mountain of ammonium nitrate up there. Call them," he said to a deputy, "and tell them to clear their people out of there. We'd better get out of here, too. Come on . Let's move."

A helicopter descended slowly and landed in the wash.

"Move where, Captain?"

"Where else? Down the wash to the helicopter. You two. Pick him up."

"Maybe we shouldn't move him."

"He'll get hurt a lot worse if we leave him here." Two deputies lifted Jay, slung their hands underneath him, and started down the wash. When they arrived at the helicopter, Jen stayed with Wally as the medics lifted Jay inside.

"Is he okay?" Matt asked a medic who was checking Jay's pulse.

The medic removed his stethoscope. "He's on the live side of dead. Let's go, Charlie!" Matt stooped and backed away as the helicopter lifted off and sped north.

"You're kind of pale, Miss," another deputy said. "Would you like some water?"

"Yes, a gallon, please."

Matt smiled. "Make it two gallons for me, Sheriff."

A huge bang roared down the wash, followed by a concussive rush of air. A   cloud of white smoke poured down the cliff face and bits of paper flitted through the air. The cliff houses let loose their burden of stones, and an avalanche of rocks cascaded downwards causing everyone to duck for cover behind the boulders. Overhead, an eagle screamed and soared towards the river.

No one moved because they waited for a second explosion. When none came, like flowers opening their petals, everyone uncurled and they stood up slowly and self-consciously checked to see if any body parts were missing.

"You saved us, Matt." Jen pointed at the cliffs. "White smoke! You are I'itoi!" Jen kissed him hard and held him close. The posse members looked away.

"Who the hell is Eetoy?" one of them asked another.

"I don't know; sounds Injun to me."

"It's an Indian legend," Wally said, his blue eyes squinting at the deputies from beneath the brim of his water-stained Stetson. "It has to do with an Eagleman. He was a gambler who went south. A witch poisoned him and turned him into an Eagleman. Then this Eagleman found a cave and tormented the people and one day, he captured Corn Flowers. She was a gourd girl and the braves shot arrows at him. But it didn't do any good. He just caught them in his claws. So they sent for this I'itoi fellow, who crawled up into the cave and rescued her and blew the bastard to bits. Ask Jen. She tells it better than I can." A smile tugged at the corner of Wally's mouth.

CHAPTER TWENTY-TWO

Salvatori entered the surveillance room. "What have we got, Ken?"

"Better sit down, boss." Salvatori slipped into a chair, leaned forward and brought up an image. "This is the fight in the lounge. It's a show, boss. These bozos are just sitting on their stools. The one guy keeps looking around like he's waiting for someone. Then, look, the bartender goes to his station. The guy spills his beer, says something to another guy, and they start whacking each other. It don't happen that way, boss. Now look. They're toying with each other. The bartender dials security and this guy isn't even watching because he's checking out the door. Here's the security team. The little guy lets them go by, and then roll blocks them. The crowd rushes the door and these two guys block the entrance. It's a set-up, boss. Now we got a fire in the kitchen and everyone comes running. The sprinklers go off, we clear out the kitchen, the hallway, and the counting room."

"I was there. Cut to the chase."

"This is complicated, boss."

"So uncomplicate it for me. "

"Jesus, Sal. Look. We got five firemen in the hallway. The big guy comes straight in, opens the door to the counting room. He's got a card key and goes straight in. Now here he is coming out five minutes and thirty-six seconds later, spraying that fogger and leaving."

"Who is he? What was he doing inside?"

"Nothing as far as I can tell. Everything is Jake inside. Maybe he just checked it out, boss. There are only four firemen on duty. After the fire, there were only four hanging around. The chief says he has only four men, but we got five!"

"Where are they?"

"They all left the Rez this morning. No one's seen them."

"Well, find them. If they brought in a ringer, I need to know what's going on, Ken. Now!"

"I've got Carbahol looking."

"We'll send our people."

"They're with the Gnome. They left over an hour ago."

Salvatori looked at his watch. "Okay. They'll be back in, say, forty minutes. I want the Gnome to check out those computers."

"There's more, boss. Let me show you something else." An image of Renee flipped on the screen. Salvatori watched as she disrobed and slipped into the shower. "Renee isn't taking a shower, boss. It's a striptease. Look, she ain't even wet."

"Where did you get this?"

"From Shorty's locker. It's my fault. I let the boys have their fun. It gets boring, so they play their little games."

"I don't pay those guys to play games, Ken."

"Boss, it's lucky we got this tape. Renee set us up."

"Yeah, maybe. But for what?"

Ken smiled. "Here we go." The image on the screen flipped to the Eagle's Nest. A time sequence panel ran underneath the image. Tom Fallon was sitting at a table. Salvatori watched as Fallon walked down the ramp, crossed over to the blackjack tables, and found a seat at the no-limit table where three Asians were playing. "Watch this, boss. Four hands. The Asians are betting 50K, throwing their money away." Salvatori looked at their expressionless faces as Fallon placed his bets. "Fallon looks spooked. He keeps watching the lounge. Four bets, boss. He picks up 300K and walks away. He didn't even leave a toke. This ain't no coincidence. They took us -- Renee, Annie, and Fallon. Nobody wins four hands on four bets and walks away. Annie cold-decked him. Look at the Wogs. They couldn't care less."

"Where are they?"

"Packing up."

"Where's Annie?"

"I sent Mark to Sedona to get her."

"And find Fallon."

"And, I got footage of Renee and Annie acting like they don't know each other. I think Renee's covering their backs. Maybe she set it up"

"Where is she?"

"In the interview room. Shorty's with her."

Salvatori paused in front of the office door, wiped his face with his handkerchief, and knocked. Shorty opened the door. "Wait outside, Shorty," Salvatori said as he stepped inside the small room. Renee was sitting in a straight chair in front of a desk. Her eyes flashed angrily as Salvatori took a swig from a bottle of Perrier water and set it down on the desk.

"What's going on, Sal?" she snapped.

"Well, that's what we're here to find out, isn't it? What was your cut, Renee – half or was it a three-way split?"

Renee tensed. "What do you mean?"

"Don't be cute. You, Annie and Fallon set us up. You took us for 300K."

"I didn't have anything to do with that." Her shoulders sagged slightly.

"I'm disappointed, Renee. If you needed money, I'd have helped you out. All you needed to do was ask."

"Sure, and what would I have to do for the favor? I don't need your money. I don't want it… I didn't set you up. If Fallon did, and I don't think he could, that's your problem, isn't it?"

"I don't have a lot of time to mess with this, Renee. We'll get Fallon. You and Annie will take a polygraph and then you'll spend a lot of time a room just like this." She crossed her legs and folded her arms across her chest.

"You're a real charm boy, Vince. Tell you what -- go get a warrant and the Rez cops. You arrest me and I'm going to sue your ass and the casino's."

"And if I don't?"

"You're still going to get sued."

Shorty knocked on the door and opened it. "Ken's says you got a call. It's urgent. He's waiting in the counting room, sir. Trouble." He handed Salvatori the phone. "It's the Gnome."

"All right. Send for that polygraph joker," Salvatori said as he stepped outside the door.

Renee opened her purse, pulled out a small bottle, flipped open the cap, and squeezed the contents into Salvatori's bottle of Perrier. Salvatori came back into the room, picked up the Perrier, gulped down half the bottle, and pressed buttons on his phone.

"Vince here. What's up?"

"The Sheriff busted the cement factory. We had to make a dump."

"What?"

"Vince, the Sheriff raided the cement factory. You got it?"

"Go on."

"We're about ten minutes out. I need to pull the plug on the computers and get the cash into the cage. Get Ken. Tell him to have the head cashier set up the cash boxes."

"What for?"

"I'll explain when I get there. Vince, listen, get Ken to shift the dealers' boxes, too. If the Sheriff isn't there, he won't be long. Kessler is with him and you better get those Wogs out of there. I'm calling Laughlin."

"Wait. Hold on."

"Vince, I'm calling Laughlin. You do what you have to do. I'm covering my ass. You better cover yours." Salvatori handed the phone to Ken.

"Get the trays, Ken. Load them with the Federal Reserve cash. Put a security team at the side door. The Gnome is bringing cash. We need a fast turn. I'll notify the cashier. Who's on deck?"

"Barney."

"Good."

"Did you find the polygrapher clown?"

"Yep, he was in the lounge. He went to get his gear. Then get going, Ken." Salvatori grabbed his bottle of Perrier and took another deep swallow.

"You're sweating, Vince. Something's going down? Maybe I can help," Renee smiled.

Salvatori shrugged, took another swallow, and set the bottle on the desk. "Nothing I can't handle, Renee. Keep her here, Shorty, and let me know when what's his face shows up."

"His name's Ted, sir. Ted Humphrey."

"Yeah, thanks." Salvatori went down the hall and stepped out into the breezeway. His eyes blurred. He grasped a steel support pole. His knees buckled, and he collapsed.

Renee pulled two cups from the dispenser, picked up the Perrier bottle and poured a cup for Shorty and herself. "I'm thirsty. Want some?" she smiled at Shorty. "I think we could both use a drink. We're both sweating." She laughed. "Here." She handed the cup to Shorty, turned towards the door, put the cup to her lips, tilted her head back, and swallowed.

She turned around, faced Shorty, smiled, sat down in the chair, crossed her legs and fiddled with the hem of her dress. "Tell me something, Shorty. Do you like seeing me getting undressed or is it better when I'm putting my clothes on?"

Shorty flushed, put the cup to his lips, and swallowed hard. "You know, Renee, I like it both ways, since you ask."

"If you like watching me so much, why didn't you ever ask me out? You're not shy, are you?"

"Don't mess with me. Your kind doesn't go out with guys like me. You don't even know we exist." Shorty finished the Perrier and tossed the cup into a waste basket.

"How do you know what kind of girl I am Shorty? I knew you guys were watching. Did it ever occur to you that I enjoyed teasing you?" She stood up, tossed her hair, and moved closer. "Would you like to touch me?"

"Don't bullshit with me, Renee." his eyes rolled back.

"Are you okay? Here, take my chair. You don't look too good." Shorty's legs buckled. Renee grabbed him by the shoulders, steered him to the desk chair and nudged him into the seat. "You're tired. Why don't you take it easy? That's a good boy."

Renee reached into his coat pocket, retrieved her cell phone, and hit two numbers. She waited and then said, "I have a problem. I'm in a side room, off the hallway. Tell Anka I'm going out the front door." She opened her purse, pulled out a can of pepper spray, put her bag over his shoulder, and stepped into the hallway, cell phone in one hand and pepper spray can in the other.

When the limo pulled into the breezeway, the driver and the Gnome got out. Ken was kneeling beside Salvatori. "What happened to him?" the Gnome asked.

"He passed out. I think he had a heart attack. I called the medics."

"Leave him. Get the bags," the Gnome shouted at the security team. "C'mon Ken. We can't waste time. You stay with him," he said to the security guard.

Gene Manring, the head cashier, was waiting for them. "Load the trays, Gene."

"I've got to make a count."

"Don't count it. Just load it and get it on the floor." The Gnome ran into the office and started his computer.

"I'll check on Sal," Ken said.

"Go ahead. I don't need you here."

Ken ran outside where a paramedic vehicle was parked in the breezeway. Two medics were kneeling beside Salvatori checking him out. "Is he okay?"

"Blood pressure is low, real low. Pulse is slow." One of the medics put an oxygen mask over Salvatori's face.

"Heart attack?" Ken asked as the medics peeled Salvatori's eyelids back.

"I don't think so. He's not a stroker, either." A helicopter whirled over the Cultural Center, circled, and began a slow descent to the helipad.

"Did you call the Sheriff?" Ken asked.

"No. We just got here. Someone else must have called."

Ken raced back to the counting room and keyed himself in. "Get the trays out of here, Gene. Get them on the floor. Put the rest in the cage. I'll be right with you," He ran to the Gnome's office. "We've got a Sheriff's helicopter on the pad."

"It's too late," the Gnome said and hit a key. "I cleared the board."

Ken hit the speaker button. "You've got a camera on the helicopter?"

"Yes, sir."

"What are they doing?"

"Talking to DPS, that Hubbard guy. The gate says three black-and-whites just came through. What's going on, Ken?"

"We're okay. Just keep monitoring them." Ken hurried back to the Gnome's office. "What's going on?" he demanded.

"Someone tapped our computers; our data is going everywhere: IRS, federal agencies, wildlife, fish and game, treasury, the Senate, casinos, and bloggers. It's all over the Internet." A stream of addresses swept down the monitor.

"Stop it. Pull the plug."

"Too late. It's a bug. Somebody planted a goddamn bug."

Ken hurried out the door, got his card key, and opened the door to the interview room where Shorty was slumped in the chair breathing heavily. Irritated, he stabbed the button on the house phone. "Have you seen Renee Royer?"

"She's on the helicopter pad, talking to a guy in a brown suit."

"Okay. Here's what you do. Pull the tapes and shred them or run a magnet over them. Burn them in the john. I don't care what you do, but get rid of them. Do you hear me?"

"We hear you, Ken. Look, uhmm, if you want to come up here and do it yourself...."

"You're fired, you bloody twits."

"Same to you. We just quit."

Ken picked up a cash box. "I'll take it, Gene." He made his way through the casino and walked out the front door.

"Have a good day, sir," the casino host said.

"You, too," Ken replied. He began to whistle as he made his way down the ramp. A black-and-white cruiser pulled up in front of the casino. Three deputies and Dick Radcliffe got out as Ken turned towards the parking lot.

"Excuse me, sir," Radcliffe said. Ken stopped, dropped the cash box on the ground, and raised his hands.

"What have we here?" the deputy asked as he picked up the box.

"He's the operations manager. Get the box and bring him," Radcliff said. "Keep everyone inside. Have this guy close and seal the doors," he pointed to a pale-faced guard.

Bucky O'Neil stopped in mid-stride beside the paramedics who were resuscitating Salvatori. The deputies waited beside him at the breezeway gate. "Go on." Bucky waved them inside. "What's his problem?"

"Passed out," the medic said. "Not sure why, but he'll be all right."

"He's just sleeping it off. I mickeyed him, Sheriff," Renee said to the medic, who raised an eyebrow.

"Who is he?"

"Vince Salvatori, the manager."

"Let me know when he wakes up. Read him his rights," O'Neal said to a deputy sheriff. "We need to get to the computers. After you." O'Neal tipped his hat to Renee.

She led Bucky and the deputies down the hallway. "Surveillance is up those stairs. The counting room is ahead on your left."

"You two, upstairs. Tell those bozos to cooperate or else. Let me know if there's a problem."

"Yes, sir." The deputies went up the steps two at a time.

"There's a man in the interview room. I drugged him, too."

O'Neal opened the door. Shorty was snoring. "Get a medic in here, for Christ's sake." He and Renee followed O'Neil to the counting room. When he pounded on the glass window, Gene Manring opened the door just as Radcliffe, accompanied by a deputy, Kessler and Ken, joined them.

"Sheriff, I've got a cash box and I need to look at the loading trays. This guy says the Gnome loaded the trays with cash from the cement plant into the cash boxes. I need access," Radcliffe demanded.

"I need access to the computers, Sheriff," Kessler said.

"Christ, who's running this show?" O'Neal asked, irritated.

"You are, Sheriff," Renee said sweetly. "Gene, help us out. Show us exactly what you did with the cash from the money bags."

"I didn't do anything wrong. I tried to stop Ken. We didn't even count it."

"Of course, you didn't, Gene," Renee patted his arm. "Just help us out. And, Ken, you're on a really slippery slope. I suggest you cooperate."

"Whatever you say."

"Where's the Gnome?"

"He's in the cubicle," the deputy answered. "He was hiding in the storage closet."

"I need room, Sheriff," Renee said and Kessler and O'Neal backed out of the cubicle.

"You won't find a thing but addresses," the Gnome giggled.

"You pulled the plug?" Kessler asked.

"I couldn't. Somebody planted a bug, the data is all over the Net."

Renee scanned the monitor. "Unfortunately, he's telling the truth, Kessler. It's spreading."

"How bad is it?"

"Right now the Salvation Army is getting an earful or should I say an eyeful? You've got an arrest, Kessler."

"You mean *I've* got an arrest," O'Neal said.

"I've got dibs on this guy, Sheriff," Radcliffe said.

"Why don't you two settle this in the hallway? I've got work to do." O'Neal and Radcliffe left. "Did your boy do this, Renee?" Kessler asked.

"Looks like it. I told you he was a bull in a china shop."

"No, you didn't," Kessler said.

Renee shot him an angry look. "I warned you. Anyway you look at it, the damage is done. This is a piece of art. It's a spiral. No way out. It's overseas now --South America, China."

Kessler joined O'Neil in the hallway who was barking orders to his dispatcher. "Who the hell is she? Mata Hari?"

"Worse, she's with the Federal Gaming Commission."

"Who was she talking about?"

"That sculptor, Matt Dillon. He's working for the Arizona Gaming Commission and for the Governor."

"We've got more cops than robbers here, Kessler." O'Neil walked down the hall, punched his cell phone, barked some questions, and closed the phone. "Hang on to your eyeballs, Kessler. An ATF agent by the name of Bob York sent an SOS to us and the DPS. Someone shot up his ultra light. Says that JR Taylor is there with Matt Dillon, that guy you just mentioned. Jeff Cooper and his loony tunies shot them down. York says Cooper has a load of explosives cached up there. I've got to get going."

"Wait. Matt's a friend of mine. I'll go with you," Radcliffe said.

"You find what you need, sonny?"

"In spades, Sheriff. The Gnome is toast; so is Salvatori."

Kessler sighed, "So am I. I'll get Renee. We'll meet you at the helicopter."

"Right! Bill, lock this place down until I get back," Bucky said. "Call the judge and tell her I want a dozen warrants. Make it two dozen."

"What charges?"

"Eh, try drug trafficking, fraud, illegal gambling, money laundering, kidnapping, pandering, illegal explosives, assault with a deadly weapon, smuggling, improper conduct in a public place, entanglement. Use your imagination, Bill."

"Renee, we've got a problem or two to take care of."

"Like what, Kessler?"

"Well, for one, we've got to get Washington to put out some fires."

"Why 'we,' Kessler?"

"Cause I'm Anka, Renee." He waited for her reaction.

"You? You're my controller?"

"That, and more. I report directly to the President. My material is for his eyes only."

"I see. Well, not anymore. Was that the bad or the good news?"

"The good news. The bad news is that Matt and an ATF agent named Bob York were shot down in their ultra light over Black Mesa." Renee covered her mouth with her hands. Her eyes widened, the color drained from her face. "He's all right. They crash landed in a wash near the mesa. York went for help and apparently Matt stayed behind to help someone in the canyon. Let's go. Sheriff O'Neal is going for a look see."

Kincaid was using his cell phone. He flipped it off as they approached the helicopter. "I thought we might need back-ups, so I called Hubbard."

"Well, call him back," Kessler said. "I want to talk to him." Kincaid looked at him, then at the Sheriff, shrugged his shoulders, dialed a number, and handed Kessler the phone.

"Hello, Dan. This is Neal Kessler. I need a favor. Would you pick up Dick George and Paul Randall? I want both of them placed in protective custody. That's right. They won't give you any problems. I'll keep your cell phone, Kincaid. It might come in handy." Turning to Bucky, he said, "You better cuff Kincaid. He's in this mess up to his eyeballs."

"I've got dibs on him too, Kessler," Radcliffe said.

"Sheriff, would you ask one of the deputies to escort Kincaid to a patrol car? I don't want him in the casino."

"You're arresting me?" Kincaid sputtered.

"Call it protective custody. A lot of people are going to be looking for you. You're about to become an endangered species."

"Where should I park him?" Bucky asked.

"Why not put him in the old jail in Jerome? It should be quiet up there. It'll give him time to think."

"You heard the man. Take him up to Jerome, Billy. Let's go, folks." The helicopter was airborne. It dropped over the edge of the mesa and headed north.

"Bring her in from the east, Jerry," Kessler said, as the pilot skimmed the treetops over Sycamore Canyon. Below, four Sheriff's patrol cars were climbing up the canyon road.

"That's York's jeep," Renee said. The pilot pointed the nose of the 'copter towards a clearing on the edge of the mesa.

"Who the hell are those guys?" Bucky asked when several men in camo suits ran towards the flat to their pick-ups. The Sheriff picked up the hand set. "We've got runners, Jim, coming your way. They are armed, so put your vehicles in the turnabout and take precautions."

"We've got company, Sheriff," the pilot said. "It's that government chopper from Prescott. They are setting down." They watched as the Huey hovered over a clearing. A squad of men in blue uniforms wearing flack suits dropped to the ground.

"Well, ain't that nice?" The Sheriff picked up his handset again. "The ATF has landed some people on the ridge, Jim. Just stay put till I tell you to move. I want to look at that ranch house." Jerry pointed the helicopter west.

"Kessler, I've got a bad feeling. I hope we don't have another Waco on our hands." Suddenly the adobe exploded, a plume of smoke belched skyward. Jerry turned the helicopter south and raced away.

"Matt!" Renee gasped.

A shock wave buffeted the helicopter, but Jerry was able to regain control and level it out. "I've got it, Sheriff."

"Take her back."

A thunder clap deafened them. "Another explosion, Sheriff," Jerry said as he turned the helicopter and picked up altitude.

"Set her down as close as you can get to the adobe. Jerry."

The men in camos were sprawled on the ground below. As the helicopter hovered closer, two men ran towards the trees while

284

a third, crawling on his hands and knees, tried to hide behind a boulder.

"Jim, get me some ambulances. We've got a Waco, and bring all your people up here. We'll back up the ATF boys. And get that government chopper. See if you can find out what's going on."

"Don't set her down, Jerry. Take me down the canyon instead. I've got a posse down there."

"Make up your mind, Sheriff. This bird isn't a yoyo," Jerry said and nosed the helicopter down the canyon. "Jesus! Look at that! The Indian ruins are gone! That was a helluva explosion."

O'Neil picked up the handset. "Jim, tell the dispatcher to give Cottonwood and Camp Verde the word. The people down there must be scared crapless. I'm going to touch base with the posse. Where are they, Jerry?"

"Right under your nose, Sheriff. Want to park it?"

"Yep, set her down." The helicopter landed on the edge of the wash. Renee scrambled out ahead of the others and raced across the flats. Matt stood up as she jumped into his arms and threw her legs around him. She pulled his head down and kissed him hard.

"What the hell is with that guy?" a posse member asked another. "She's the second woman to kiss him since we got here."

"Well, he's got twice as many as we do."

"Who's the Indian? What's he got to do with this mess?" Bucky asked Kessler.

"Matt Dillon. I think he already blew the whistle."

"Good. We'll hang him first." Bucky joined the posse. "Well, don't everybody talk at once."

JR stepped forward. "Cooper had Jay and Jen locked up in that cliff house, Bucky. Cooper shot down York's plane. Me and Matt came up here while York went for help. Matt, here, crawled up that wall and brought out Jay and Jen. Cooper shot Jay, and Matt dropped Jay over the side on a rope and then brought Jen down just as the posse showed up. Then the whole damn mountain exploded."

"For God's sake, slow done, JR. Run it by me real slow."

"I'm too damned excited, Bucky. Maybe Wally can tell you." JR motioned to Wally, who stepped forward.

"What happened here?"

Putting a hand to his ear, Wally answered, "I can't hear you, Sheriff. I'm deaf from that explosion."

A deputy stepped forward. "We're all about deaf, Sheriff, but I can hear you."

"Anybody hurt?" Bucky shouted.

"Jay Cook was shot."

"I know that. Where is he?"

"A DPS helicopter took him to the Cottonwood hospital," a deputy spoke up.

O'Neil looked up at the rock face. "How did he climb that?"

"He's Eetoy," another deputy said.

"Who the hell is Eetoy?"

"You better ask Wally, Sheriff. He tells it better than I can," the deputy said.

Wally shuffled forward. "I can hear you better now. Well, you see, Sheriff, there was this Indian gambler...."

"Excuse me, I don't have the time for this. Hanson, take your men up the canyon. We've got an armed militia up there. We don't want any stragglers coming this way. Leave five men here." Bucky looked around. "Kessler, let's go. Bring Dillon and the two ladies. We got room, Jerry?"

"I can squeeze them in."

"Then let's go." When everyone was inside the Huey, Bucky turned in his seat and offered his hand. "Pleased to meet you, Matt. We'll drop you off at the hospital. You can check on your brother, miss," he said to Jen. "Then we need to talk, Kessler."

"It's going to be a short talk, Sheriff. Renee and I need to get to Washington ASAP."

"I bet you do. And I need to get to Phoenix."

286

"The Governor's in Camp Verde, Bucky," Kessler pointed out.

"That's why I need to get to Phoenix." O'Neil winked at Kessler. "There's going to be a hallelujah trail and I want to be there first."

"I'm not going with you, Kessler," Renee said.

"You don't have a choice. There's too much at stake. Tell her, Matt."

"It's up to her."

"Right," Kessler responded sarcastically.

ATF agents wearing flack suits probed the smoking ruins of the cliff house while the sheriff's deputies ringed the edges of the gaping hole. "That sucker went off like the Fourth of July."

"They ain't going to find anyone alive down there," a posse member volunteered.

Bucky O'Neil gave up directing traffic and joined the onlookers on the side of the ridge. "You people look like you're a circular firing squad. Well, who's going to do the honors?"

"Bucky, let's do it the easy way. York and the ATF people are going to be sifting ashes for days. They aren't doing anything to help us. Radcliffe wants a piece of Kincaid, Farley, the Marshals, Salvatori and the Gnome. Is that right?" Kessler asked.

"That suits me."

"And so do I, and then some. So what I'm going to recommend is that you park them at County. I've put in a call to the attorney general's office. Let them sort it with the state and county. There're enough charges and credit to go around for everyone. Let's cut the crap and the red tape. You can hand out a statement to the press but "ongoing investigation" is as far as it goes, Bucky. Fair enough, Radcliffe?"

"Like I said, it suits me. If you'll excuse me?" Radcliffe walked away.

"Bucky," Kessler said sharply, "I don't want anything to happen to Kincaid. I need him, and the Enterprise bunch is going to feel some heat. There're going to be some political ramifications. You ought to distance yourself from that bunch, and, if I were you, I'd consider resigning in the next few days. You know, resign with honor while you can."

"You can't make me do that."

"I was there and, uh, I was wired. The best you could hope for would be a shot as a voluntary witness. Wouldn't look good. Save yourself a headache. Take a bow. Step down. One day, you can run for governor."

"In a pig's eye, Kessler. Your people will see to that."

"Times change, Bucky. This too shall pass. Keep your options open. I've got a plane to catch. See ya." Kessler made his way to the helicopter. "What a mess," he said as he slid into the jump seat and buckled up. "Sedona airport," he said to the pilot, who nodded. The helicopter lifted out of the clearing, circled the cliffs, and went north. Matt stared down at the smoking dead trees and piles of earth and rocks that littered the canyon floor.

"We don't have a lot of time. Renee and I have to get to Washington. What's out there?" Kessler asked Matt.

"How would I know? Whatever the Gnome decided to send."

"Where's the data going?"

"Everywhere and anywhere. If you're thinking of doing damage control, you're too late, Kessler."

"That's okay. We got the bad guys."

"You've got the little men. You weren't after the power players or the system. You wanted information to do some selective leaking and apply pressure. What about the tribe? What about the land exchanges and the water rights? Do you even give a damn?"

"Don't go righteous on me, Matt or you either, Renee. Did you know Matt was going to pull the plug?"

"I didn't have a clue," she answered.

"Well, Honest Matt took care of that. Tell me, Matt, what were you doing here? I mean honestly, before your hormones got in the way. Did you really come to help the tribe, to get the syndicate? Did you really believe you could pull that off?"

"Don't get personal, Kessler. I came to help Jay, Sam and Jen."

"You managed to do that, but you could have trusted us. I wasn't after Jay. In fact, I was trying to protect him."

"Right. And who would protect him from you?"

"Tell you what. Why don't you come to Washington? We might be able to work things out. In spite of what you may think right now, there are some smart people there and a few honest ones, too."

"No, thanks. I'll get off at Sedona."

"I could bring you along as a material witness in protective custody."

"You might regret that."

"You're probably right, but take my advice. You better be deaf and dumb."

"Oh, you mean be a good Indian?"

"Yeah, something like that."

"And what happens to the tribe?"

"I'd say they better play deaf and dumb, too. That would be a good idea." The helicopter dropped onto the helipad as a Lear jet was approaching the runway. "That's our ride, Renee." Kessler turned to the pilots. "I want you to pick up Salvatori and the Gnome. They'll be better off in Washington, just in case O'Neil makes a grand stand play. And be careful; the syndicate has long arms. Oh, and drop Matt off at the Cottonwood airport on your way back."

"I'd rather walk, Kessler."

"That's up to you. Let's go, Renee."

"Give me a minute to talk to Matt." Kessler shrugged and walked away. "Everything is going too fast. I don't really want to go with him."

"Then don't."

"Look, Matt. I know you don't want to go, but come with us. You can help."

"I already have. I turned over the rocks, remember."

"Yes, you did, and you may have done more damage than

you realize. Everyone's going to pay. You could have warned me."

"I thought it was better that you didn't know, Renee."

"So you were protecting me? From what? You didn't trust me. Is that it?"

"Did you trust me?"

"Against my better judgment, yes, I did trust you."

"And now you trust Kessler, your control? Three hours ago you didn't even know who he was, and now you're going to Washington with him. Why don't you ask him if he bugged your laptop, your cell phone? How long has he known about us, about the tapes? He set us both up. He doesn't give a damn about anyone but himself."

"Matt, it's my job. You set me up too, didn't you? I'm sorry. I didn't mean that. I have to see this thing through. I'm going to put Salvatori and all those creeps away."

"Renee, Bucky grabs the headlines, Kessler covers the beltway crowd, and you help them shaft the tribe, JR, and the Verde. Kessler burns the small fry and everyone else keeps right on truckin'."

"You're hurt and you're angry."

"You're damn right I'm angry. You know I'm right, and you're going along with them."

"Oh, God, I need time to think!"

"We need to get a move on, Renee," Kessler called.

"I'm coming." Renee gave Matt a hug, which he shrugged off. "I'll call you tonight." Kessler smiled at Matt and shook his head. "I promise," she said and ran towards the jet.

Matt climbed back into the helicopter. "Changed my mind."

"Where do you want to go?"

"Anywhere but here."

"We'll land you at the Cottonwood hospital. You're bleeding a little."

"I guess I am. I didn't know it showed." Matt took off his cap, ran his fingers through his hair, and probed his scalp gently.

The copilot got out of his seat and examined Matt's head carefully. "It's a scratch. A long one, but you'll live. What happened?"

"Near miss. A guy took a shot at me."

"These paramilitaries are all nut cases," the copilot said, returned to his seat and they lifted off.

Matt didn't look out the window until the helicopter put down at the heliport. "What kind of guy is your boss?" he asked.

"Who? Kessler? He's not my boss. He's just another brown suit, another cold fish. We don't pay any attention to them. We just drive the cab. Don't forget your case." The copilot handed Matt Renee's laptop.

Matt sat staring at the television in the waiting room. His cell phone rang. He flipped it open, thought about tossing it into a trash receptacle, but answered it instead.

"What is it, Renee?"

"It's Bob York. Radcliffe's been shot. They're bringing him in."

"Where are you?"

"I'm at the hospital."

"How bad is it?"

"An upper thigh wound. He went down hard."

"What happened?"

"Radcliffe tried to arrest Marshal Farley. Farley shot him, and then Radcliffe shot Farley. Farley's dead."

"Oh, my God!"

"I thought you'd want to know."

"I'm on my way."

A doctor in a surgical gown met York and Matt outside the ER. "He's stabilized. I'm sending him to Phoenix General Hospital while he's still sedated."

Radcliffe wiggled his fingers and smiled weakly at Bob and Matt as the medics moved the gurney down the hall.

Matt gave him a thumbs-up. "What's next, Bob?"

"The music goes round and round. I have to get to Washington. My people and Kessler want me there ASAP."

"You and everybody else. Kessler took Renee with him."

"What are we going to do, Matt?"

"That's easy. File a report. Then, I'm quitting. You do what you have to, but I'm through. I didn't help Jay; probably got him shot, and now Dick."

"How could you have stopped Cooper?"

"I should have brought Jay in when I met him on the train and I shouldn't have played games at the casino."

"What did you do, Matt?"

"Not much -- just planted a worm into their computers so their data banks went global."

"Sweet Mother!"

"So Kessler's fit to be tied and he took Renee to do damage control. Well, he won't be able to fly this, Bob."

"Couldn't you have sent the stuff to Renee or Kessler? You trust her, don't you?"

"Yes and no. I didn't know Kessler was her control. Even if I had, I don't trust him, and right now, I don't trust anyone."

"Well, you sure have rocked the boat. Put your foot right through the bottom. What are you going to do next?"

"I told you. Quit. Save them the trouble of firing me."

"Kessler won't let you get away with that. You're a material witness."

"He won't want me around. I'd be an embarrassment."

"If you say so."

"Any of your people get hurt?"

"We'll all be partially deaf for the rest of our lives. I'm joking." Bob pulled at his ears, "Well, almost. I thought we were goners when that adobe blew up. That phone call from the deputy saved our butts. We got out just in time, but barely."

"Did you find Arnold?"

"We didn't find anyone. No body parts, Cooper's or anyone else's. Who knows who else was inside? The cliff house must have been crammed with barrels of nitrate. That was the biggest explosion I've ever seen."

"There wasn't any in the cliff house, Bob. It must have been stored upstairs. I can't figure out why Cooper blew it up. He had nothing to gain."

"Cooper was a real nutter. All those paramilitaries are paranoid. He shot us down," Bob said bitterly. "Tried to kill us or his goofballs did."

"Cooper tried to tell me something. At least, I think, he was trying to."

"You saw Cooper? You talked to him?"

"I didn't really talk to him. He was pointing a pistol at me, then somebody shot him, and he fell through the trap door."

"Maybe he shot himself in the head. What did he say?"

"I'm not sure, something about the stairs. I think he said upstairs, behind me, something like that. I just grabbed Jen and jumped."

"Maybe he was trying to tell you about the charges."

"Maybe, but it doesn't matter anymore, does it?"

"I guess not."

The doctor joined them. "All's well that ends well." He clasped his hands together. "Your friend is going to limp for awhile. His biking days may be over, but orthoscopic surgery can do wonders. Jay lost a lot of blood, but there's no permanent damage."

"Thanks, Doc, thanks for everything. I'm glad you were here," Matt said.

"Just doing my job, but it's sure been exciting today. Take care of yourselves, boys."

"See you Doc. Thanks again."

"Matt, I've got to get going. I have to catch the redeye to D.C. Could you do me a favor? JR is going to tow the plane over to his barn. Could you lock her up? When I get back, I'll see if it can be repaired."

"Sure. When is JR going to move it?"

"Before dark." Bob handed Matt a key. "Don't forget the camcorder. Paloma wants to see if you got the eagles. Your life's at stake. You better hope you kept those birds in focus." Bob grinned. "It's been a helluva day. Don't get down on yourself, Buddy. You saved Jay and Jen's lives. I'll put in a word for you when I see Kessler. Right now, he's just hot under the collar, but he'll cool down. Hell, he's looking good." Bob clapped Matt on the shoulder. "I'll see you when I get back. Take care."

"That's for sure."

Matt stopped at the convenience shop and bought a can of cashews, a package of cheese, and some bottled water. He got into the Kombi and turned up the road to JR's without realizing how he got there. Somehow, the cashews and cheese had disappeared; empty wrappers were lying on the seat along with an empty water bottle.

Bob's plane was backed up to the door of the barn, so he parked the Kombi behind a back hoe. "You're just in time," JR yelled. "Help me push her inside."

Matt went back to the tail of the plane and lifted it. "I'll pull. You push."

JR put his hands on the canopy, "Ready?"

"I'm ready. Let's do it." He lifted the tail and tugged; the Challenger began to roll.

"Set her down. She's clear." Matt eased the tail down. "Wow! That was easy. You can help me move a piano anytime."

Matt examined the starboard wing and slipped a finger into the bullet holes.

"I looked her over. They can be fixed, but the engine is shot full of holes, probably an M16," JR said. "I'll close the doors. Monsoons are coming. At least it will be out of the weather."

Matt opened the passenger side of the Challenger. The rocker panel door was open. He looked inside and picked up some maps that were scattered around the cockpit along with some of Bob's spare clothing and gear. He wedged the locker side open, shoved the clothing inside and closed the slide bolt. He checked the floors and found the camcorder under the passenger seat. After filming the plane's interior and its damaged wing, he closed the locker door and bolted it shut.

Up front, JR was examining the engine. "You're lucky that you boys walked away."

"I guess we were."

"What's going to happen to all those monkeys?"

"They'll put them in the zoo, most of them."

"Well, Cooper and Arnold are goners. Bucky was sure upset. He wanted to arrest Farley, but Radcliffe shot that snake full of holes. Whatever he knew went with him, Cooper, too. He was strange, but in an odd kind of way, I respected him. I was joking about him trying to commit suicide with a sling shot, but he sure did kill himself."

"He killed himself a long time ago, JR."

They went through the side door of the barn. As they walked out into the feed lot, the llamas raised their heads expectantly. "What happened to Wally?" Matt asked.

"I'm not sure. He said he was going to find his burros. That explosion scared them off. He wasn't around when I got the plane, but a deputy told me that he'd seen Wally and the burros up on the ridge. I expect he's all right." JR shrugged. "What are you going to do now?"

"I'm going home to write my report and go to bed."

"Maybe that's best."

Matt put out his hand. "Thanks, JR."

"You're welcome."

"Here." Matt handed him the camcorder. "I almost forgot. Tell Paloma I filmed the eagles. I hope I got something useable."

"You could give it to her yourself."

"Not tonight. I don't need the third degree."

"I hear you!" JR laughed.

Matt headed home as the dark settled over Black Mesa and the constellations began their march across the sky.

Digger greeted him at the door. Matt filled the dog dish with puppy chow, added water to a bowl, and sat down on the couch. Outside, grey clouds gathered. At 9:00 p.m., the first rocket burst high over the rodeo grounds and reflected off the cloud cover. Digger jumped and began to shake. "It's okay," Matt said, stroking him. "It's just the Fourth of July in Happy Valley."

He opened Renee's computer, began skimming through the files, and making notes on a yellow pad. "So much for R2 D2," he said to Digger as he made a cup of green tea in the microwave. He drank it slowly while he studied the file that Chester Vance, his controller, had given him.

"Let's start with Farley," he said and he began brainstorming. "Now, let's take another look at Panama. Let's see what we've got." An hour later, he made another cup of tea, refilled the water bowl, and tossed Digger a rawhide chew. The pup settled down on the Navajo rug and began gnawing excitedly. "Well, I guess I can gnaw on this Noriega case -- Cooper, Kessler, the gang's all here."

Matt went directly to the Arizona Gaming Commission website and pulled the flag on the Black Mesa Casino. It took several minutes, but he was able to find the Gnomes' security check for the serial numbers on the cash Radcliffe had given him. He picked up his cell phone and punched in a number and hit the speaker key.

"Been waiting for your call," Max's raspy voice filled the room. "Figured it all out have you? It was all in that file I gave you. They were all in Panama at one time or another. It was just a question of time until Kessler took care of Cooper, and now his goose is cooked. Thanks to you, Matt, things are looking up."

"Who's running the show, Max?"

"We are...you can't trust the politicians. The stakes are too big to be left to them. You see, in democracies, there's a double standard. Crime no longer exists in isolation of the state, if it ever did. That's where we come in; we're the enforcers. We go after all the people who look the other way and the people who can't resist temptation, the bankers, lawyers, and administrators, the small fry and the big fish. Somebody has to be in command. Like I said, crime's too big a business to be left to the politicians, and we can't let the syndicates run the show, can we?"

"You're saying there's a shadow government?"

"Always has been and always will be. There has to be.

"You set up Kessler, Cooper, York, and Radcliffe. People died here and a lot more could have been hurt. Why Max? Revenge?"

"You could say that, but it's not my nature. I call it justice. They were lost in the scramble for their own gratification. Kessler had to go. He would have become the Director in charge of a ship of fools. They would have screwed up everything sooner or later. Greed was their problem. But you're no fool, Matt, and you're not greedy. I think it's time we talk about your future, Matt. We need a few honest men."

"And women?"

"Are thinking about Renee? She's smart enough and honest, possibly too honest. That might be a problem, but maybe we could work something out for both of you."

"You have a distorted sense of what's right and wrong, Max. Somehow you think that you've risen above it all. Anyway, save your breath. Have you ever heard of Radio Tonga?"

"Can't say that I have."

"It's a satellite station that broadcasts all over the world and to all ships at sea."

"What are you saying, Matt?"

"I'm saying I quit, and I'm saying that you're finished, Max. If anything happens to Renee or anyone else I know, you're going to hear the Fat Lady singing all around the world. A little off key, but I think anyone with a good voice recognition system will put it together, and there's something called the Moccasin Telegraph. Good bye, Max."

Matt hung up and began typing an email message:

Tonto, I'm sending you a silver bullet. See attachment.
Hi Ho Silver!

CHAPTER TWENTY-THREE

Matt began sketching eagles on the fifth of July. He drew eagles with fledglings in a nest; eagles circling overhead; eagles swooping with talons outstretched over riffles; eagles perched on crags. He tried earthbound eagles with folded wings and eagles with clutched prey. He even experimented with caricatures of eagles, comic eagles, ferocious eagles and symbolic eagles. He examined eagles online, using search engines. And, he borrowed Paloma's kayak and searched for Igor, but the birds had left, she guessed, for Montana.

The floors and the walls of the studio were covered with drawings. His cell phone rang on and off, but Matt ignored the silent messages. Digger came and went, and they shared meals. After dinner, Matt would swim until his broad shoulders ached as he butterflied back and forth across the Verde. Through the evenings and long into the nights, he worked at his drawings

On the fourth day, he took a sketch over to the window, examined it in the morning light, tacked it onto the wall, stepped back and surveyed it from several angles. "It's doable, Digs. Shall we do it?" Digger wagged his stub in agreement

"What's doable?" Paloma asked and scooped up Digger.

"This is doable," he pointed to the drawing.

"It's wonderful, Matt. It's alive."

"Wait till you see the clay model. That's when the fun begins." he beamed.

"When will you start?"

"Tonight. Dan's letting me use his workroom. Fewer distractions. Speaking of distractions. The river's warmed up." Matt grinned. "Are you ready for a swim?"

"You men all have a one track mind and memories like elephants when it comes to skinny dipping. All right. But just this once and it's just for a swim. You hear me?"

"I hear you."

They walked down to the river and Paloma disappeared behind a tall boulder. "Don't look!" she shouted, slipped surreptitiously into the water, and swam slowly, almost languidly, towards him, her pale skin glowing luminously under the water.

Matt peeled off his clothes and dove into the deep pool. Paloma tossed her red curls and stretched out her hands to Matt. They held hands as they drifted slowly with the current.

"This is silly, but it's fun. I like being with you."

"I like being with you, too, Paloma. You make me forget."

"Forget what?"

"That I'm angry at our folly-filled world, I guess. That we need distractions."

"Am I a distraction?"

"A very pleasant one."

"Distractions are habit-forming. It could be addicting."

"That would be nice," he said. Then they sank slowly to the sandy bottom and rested.

"I can't say that I haven't thought about it, Matt. I could fall for you. You have a beautiful mind, a gorgeous body, and a wonderful heart. And, most of the time, you are just, well, kind."

"Go on. I like this."

"Be quiet. You are also stubborn, aggravating, too intense, and a dreamer. You love your work, I think, probably more than anything else."

"Thank you, and, aside from the having the loveliest body I've ever seen," he glanced downward at Paloma's breasts and then quickly back to her wide blue eyes, "you have a wonderful, easy-going temperament. You love animals and people. You're gentle, caring, and sexy."

She laughed. "That's because you don't really don't know me. I'm a witch, a scold, a driver, a homebody. Just what men don't want."

"What do you want, Paloma? What's your dream?"

"It's not a dream. I want this stream, these hills, the bird sanctuary, a farm, a quiet life, children, animals, sunrises and sunsets. Peace. I want an acre of peace and…"

"And…"

"And a husband who loves me and who I can love back. A simple, solid man who loves nature as much as I do."

"Have you found him?"

"I think I have, but he's so slow on the draw that I'll probably have to propose."

"Do I know him?"

"Yes, but no more questions." Paloma splashed water in his face. "Let's go before I change my mind." She turned onto her stomach and kicked towards the river bank. While Paloma dressed behind the boulder, Digger grabbed Matt's towel and tugged it playfully as he was trying to towel off.

"I wish I could keep him," he said as he dressed.

"Why don't you? He yours if you want him."

"He belongs here. Living in cars, condos, and God knows where else is no life for a dog."

"It doesn't sound like much of a life for you either."

"I have many miles to go, Paloma," he said as they strolled up the path to the studio. Inside, the phone was ringing. "Damn it. There it goes again. They never stop calling."

"It's none of my business, Matt, but you need to take care of your business."

"I have. I've told them loud and clear that I want no part of their games, their power struggles. I've told Kessler and Vance that I don't know anything. I didn't see anything. I didn't hear anything. And I won't do anything to help them. They can't force me to cooperate. They know that I'd cause more headaches than it's worth."

"What about Renee?"

"Renee has her own agenda."

"She isn't on anyone's side. She loves you."

"Well, she's there, isn't she?"

"You know, Matt, you are more than stubborn; stupid is more accurate. I'm sorry I don't mean that."

"What do you want me to do?"

"You could go to Washington and see her."

"I could, but I won't. I'm not that strong, Paloma. If I went back to the craziness, I'd get sucked in and spit out. Renee and I are two different kinds of people. We'd end up despising each other. I shouldn't have gotten involved. No one to blame but myself. Now I just want my life back, doing what I want to do. "

"What's that?"

"I could say being creative, being an artist, but I'm not sure I can do that anymore, but I'm sure going to try. Mostly I want to be me, whatever that means, maybe just being free."

"Nobody's free, no matter how hard we try. The kind of freedom you're talking about is an illusion."

"Everything is an illusion, isn't it? It's all mystery."

"I agree with you there. Your journey is going to be a lonely one, but I won't feel sorry for you. And I still think you should call Renee. You're going to need a friend besides Digger."

"How about you? You're a friend, aren't you?"

"Yes, and one who loves you dearly." She gave him a firm, lingering kiss, turned and ran down the path.

He sat for a while on a boulder, staring at the stream and scratching Digger's ears. A trout leaped for a May fly, but he didn't notice. Matt sighed, "Come on. It's time to do the eagles."

Matt went back to the studio, packed his sketches into a portfolio, put Digger over the fence, and walked to the Kombi. The street was empty except for a gray sedan parked on the far side of the bridge. The driver looked away as Matt drew close, slowed down, and tipped his hat. "Not the social type, I guess," he said to himself. "I wonder if he's the only bird dog."

Matt parked by the side door and went inside the foundry. On his right were a miller tig welder, two arc welders, a sheet metal roller, three gas welders, and a kuhn air hammer. On the left was a large Campbell/Hausefield tilt furnace as well as a smaller casting furnace with a #40 crucible. At the far end of the room, two workers were shutting down the cupola furnace. Dan was waiting for him inside the clay room.

Opening the portfolio, Matt spread his sketches onto the table. Dan walked along the table slowly, casting an analytical eye. He picked up the sketch of the two eagles and whistled softly. "You drew it? It's pretty good, but can you do it?"

"I think so. Can you do it?"

"We can. We'll need the cupola furnace to handle the heat. It has a high melt rate, continuous operation. It's easier to handle and, hell, it's cheaper. Are you thinking of a single pouring?"

"I am."

"That will be quite a dance. Do you figure on doing it?"

"I do."

"What the hell, why not? If we do it right, the pieces will keep their integrity." Dan studied the sketches again. "We can join them with stainless rods. Bill's an artist with the arc welder. We'll do that part first. We'll need a forklift for this baby."

"But is it going to hang?"

"It's a beauty. It's going to fly, but the undercuts are really rather rough."

"Not if you do the wax and the ceramic shell right."

"Are you going cut it?"

"No way. One piece, no cuts, no joining, no sealing, as is."

"All or nothing, buddy. That's sure you, Matt. What if it doesn't pour?"

"Then we do it again."

"Money's no object, eh?"

"Let's say we can pour until I'm broke," Matt laughed.

"Knowing you, that won't take long. Do you want us to do the chasing and the patina?"

"I think so, but I'm going to be here just in case. The chasing is the easy part of this package. It's the patina that's bothering me some. I'm going blue on blue, some variation of black, and a blend of browns and golds. I don't want anything popping out."

"You're in luck. We've been running some limited editions for a California gallery. The artist specified rare earth oxides. It's a unique process that gives depth. It could work for that cloud, and the silver might illuminate it just right. Let me play with it, okay?"

"That's great, Dan. I've got some photos we can look at later."

"What about this other piece? Truthfully, I'm not impressed."

Matt laughed. "I didn't think you'd be. It's not what it looks like; it's what it says."

Dan looked at the sketch again. "It's not saying much to me. You don't intend to do this in bronze, do you?"

"I was thinking of a ceramic mold filled in with ceramic tiles."

"That would work. It'll save time and money."

"Jay and Jen are going to make the smaller pieces and make the ring in three pieces. They would have to work here."

"They can use my room, and I can help if they run into any trouble."

"Don't be too helpful. Jay will be here even if he does have one arm in a sling."

"I love Jay. It'll be good to have him here. When do you want to start?"

"Right now. I'll set up the wire frames."

"Okay. Go for it. There's an arc welder in the shop when you're ready." Dan went back to the foundry. Matt went to a bin, pulled out some stainless steel rods, and laid them on the work bench. Working quickly, he formed frames for the two pieces and bent and formed the upper frames also. After checking the sketches, he began adding lateral wires to the structures, shortened several pieces, shaped and narrowed the tops. Satisfied with the frames, he carried them into the shop. Dan joined him and they watched Bill as he tied the rods and wire together with the arc welder.

"That ought to do," Dan said. "We can add more rods to carry the weight later." Bill and Terry carried the frames back into the clay room and Dan pulled a black plastic wrap off two towering clay slabs. "I've added bentonite, like I told you, plus green powder. You can work it, but the moisture is nil, drying time is short. If you take my advice, you'll walk away from the clay when you're done. Bill can add the spruces and the gates and I'll do the plaster. In fact, it would better if you just stayed away until I call you."

Matt sliced off some slabs of clay, flattened them with his palms to squeeze out any pockets, then ran them through a press. He worked the frames from inside out, pressing, pushing, adding clay. His shoulder muscles bunched and flexed as he kneaded, pinched, shaped, and punched the clay. He formed the head blocks and added thin slabs of clay to the lateral wires, stretching and thinning, letting his hands do the thinking as he thickened the bases and worked the exterior sides. Gradually, the rough shapes and features began to appear and he added more clay for dimension. He stepped back to scrutinize the pieces, a fine sweat coating his back and arms and beads of perspiration dripping off his chin.

"They look like plaster castings for a pair of Maltese falcons," Dan said over his shoulder. He plugged in a blower and aimed it at Matt. "Here, this will cool you down. Now I'll blow-dry the birds."

"Not too much, Dan."

"Go on outside." He waved the blower at him. "Shoo!" When Dan was finished, he joined Matt on the patio. "I'm taking the boys out for a beer. Why don't you come along?"

"I think I'll just sit here for awhile. Get into the mood."

"Suit yourself. Are you going to work all night?"

"I expect so."

"Then I'll bring you an egg McDonalds."

"No thanks. I'll pass on that."

"Good luck then. See you tomorrow."

Matt watched the dust settle as they drove off. "Could've gone, should've gone, but didn't." He studied the surfaces of the clay mounds, picked up one of his sketches, found a small hammer and tacked it to a wallboard. At the table, he opened his toolkit, picked up a small silver spoon and stood in front of a clay mound.

"I mean, are we ready for this? Are we really ready?" He gripped the spoon in his long fingers, smelled the clay, tasted it, then placed his right hand on the top of the clay and let his left hand carve a curl. Focusing intensely, his fingers worked quickly, but carefully. A rhythm developed, and slices and curls fell on the table. From time to time, he paused, brushed them aside, rested his arms, stepped away, studied the figure and resumed work. Alternating hands, he occasionally applied a small trowel, a carpenter's chisel or a steel rasp. Outside the window, the sky turned red, pink, azure, blue and, finally, a deep black.

Around midnight, thunder rolled through the air and lightning forked across the sky, but no rain fell. Matt examined the eagle's head, the beak, and body. Toying with the outstretched wings, his hands hovered over the figure as he shaped the curves.

"That isn't so hard, is it? Why don't you tell me what you want to be?" Matt found a scalpel and formed the beak and the eyes.

He shaped the legs, laid the scalpel down, went into the darkness outside, and stood staring the night sky. He listened for the hoot of an owl, for the yip of a coyote, and for the honk of a horn, anything to diminish the silence and his yearning to go into town, to go to the Q & Brew, to hear laughter, and to see Renee in her white dress.

He went back inside and studied the eagle which was looking down at him disdainfully. "You're next," he said to the blank chocolate tower of clay. "Shave and a haircut, two bits. You're the angry one, aren't you? I would be, too, in your position." He picked up a mall and a chisel and carved a deep channel. "Take that," he said, and clawed at the clay. "Had enough? Well, you're going to like this." He picked up the spoon and caressed each side of the figure. He wet down the sides, sponged the base, and began making crosscuts with the rasp. He sliced and curled, found the scalpel and teased the tips of both birds' wings. "You have a tricky beak; don't toy with me. Polly wants a cracker?"

Matt began to hum and to sway as he worked. The dark sky faded to gray, the tips of the ridge across the river turned from azure to pink and then bright red as he kneeled on the table and coaxed the soft underbelly of the eagle. Outside, the sand turned bright white as he put the finishing touches to the eagles with the scalpel. "Relax. I'm not going to eat you," he said, as he applied a sponge. Moving his stool further away from the work table, he studied the eagles. From time to time, he applied the scalpel here, the sponge there, whittled a little with his rasp, and surveyed the pieces from different angles.

"I have you! When you're done, you're done. It's time to walk away." Matt scribbled a note and left it on the table for Dan: "I'm walking home. I'll be back to get the van and look the pieces over this afternoon."

Matt swept up the clay curls, dumped them in a trash can, turned off the lights and closed the door behind him. With his hands in his pockets, he walked down the dirt street, crossed the wooden bridge, and made his way to the studio. Inside, he poured a glass of orange juice and dropped onto the couch with a contented sigh.

Dan fumbled with his keys, opened the foundry door and stepped inside. "Jesus, Bill, look at this would you?" Bill and Dan moved closer to the eagles. "Don't touch them for god's sake!."

"They're awesome! There's nothing else you can say. My God, they're flying. I never saw an eagle up close, but man, they look real."

Jumping up and down, Dan clicked his heels together. "Come in here, boys. Look at this! We're going to do these pieces. We're going to be famous! We're the foundry that cast the Verde Eagles."

"Does the mean that we get a raise?"

"You'll not only get a raise, but you're going to get a bonus." He picked up the note. "Matt's gone home, to bed, I guess."

"He did all this in one night? I've never heard of anyone doing that."

"No one would, except Matt. That's the way he works. I saw him create an ice sculpture for a banquet once. He cut a 300-poind block of ice into a cow and calf in less than two hours, but this takes it all."

"Who's going to make the molds?"

"You are, Bill. Plaster, latex, grinding, and rough polish; it's all yours. I expect that Matt will do the finish. Hallelujah! Let's get to work, boys. Close the doors."

CHAPTER TWENTY-FOUR

Jay looked at the sketch. "I need a black 23." Jen nodded and handed him a ceramic tile. He squeezed an epoxy tube, coated the back of the tile, set it carefully in the ring with one hand, pressed down, and stepped back and examined it carefully. "Perfect. You did good, Sis."

"Thank you, Bro. I do the work and you have all the fun."

"It needs the master's touch."

"Hooey. Any idiot can inlay a piece that large."

"Not with one arm in a sling." Jay patted his injured arm.

"All right, you two. I'm not playing nursemaid. We need to finish this." Matt looked over at Jen, who was working on a small gold circular ceramic tile.

"Are you saying Jen and me are competitively impaired, Matt? I'm weak from hunger." Jay grinned and examined an empty bag of skittles. "A man can't live on pork rinds. I need some fry bread."

"I'll get lunch," Jen said. "I need to get away from you anyway. You help Jay, Matt. You'd better be finished by the time I get back."

"Hurry. I'm starving," Jay said to her back as she headed towards the kitchen.

"Find me a red twelve, Matt."

"How's the shoulder?"

"It aches. I think I've a got a touch of arthritis."

"You never did tell me what happened at Arnold's."

Jay sat back on his stool, rested his feet on the rungs. "I just did something stupid, like I always do. I thought I could get away with it. When we got there, Cooper's gorillas were playing fun in the sun with those paintball guns. The Hawks had already started down the canyon. I should have gone back, but good 'ol me, I didn't see Cooper, so we just walked right in the open door. I sent Jen to look for Arnold while I went down the stairs. The plastic bags were right there at the bottom, so were the tapes. I heard something up the stairs. When I looked up, Copper was at the top staring at me with that crazy eye and pointing a pistol. I thought he was going to shoot me with a paint ball gun. How crazy is that? Anyhow, I jumped off the stairs and he shot me."

Jay touched his shoulder and winced. "It knocked me down, Matt. I was stunned couldn't breathe. Then I blacked out. They told me at the hospital that the hot load should have killed me. Anyway, it's kind of cloudy, but I heard him dragging Jen down the stairs. I tried to move, but couldn't even raise my head. I opened my eyes and Cooper's bozo was standing right over me and he said that I was still breathing. Cooper leans over me and says, 'Can you talk?' I just closed my eyes and played dead. It didn't take much acting. Cooper says 'He isn't going anywhere. Tie her up.' That's when they tied Jen and taped her mouth. I could hear her moaning; she just kept moaning. My ears were ringing louder and louder, and then I heard a shot. That's when Cooper shot Arnold. I remember thinking someone's coming to help us. Everything was turning black. I couldn't hang on, so I just let go. When I woke up in the hospital, Dad and Jen were there. I was never so glad to see anyone. But to tell you the truth, I thought I was in the Happy Hunting Ground."

Jay laughed. "I didn't remember a thing. They told me how you crawled up the cliff, found us, and tossed me out the window like a sack of potatoes."

"You're lucky I had a rope. But if I hadn't, I would have taken a chance and thrown you out anyway."

"We were lucky, Matt, real lucky. If you hadn't been there and the posse and the Hawks, Jen and I would have been blown to bits, just like Arnold." He stared at the tiles. "Why did they kill him?"

"Cooper probably thought he had to. He wanted the mesa. Maybe he planned to all along. The paramilitaries were part of his paranoid vision to take over the Valley. Renee taped a

conversation he had with Strickland before Cooper blew up
Strickland's safe. Sonny panicked and told Fallon he wanted out.
Fallon ran to O'Neil, and the dominos starting falling."

"We were all flies on the wall, weren't we?"

"I guess we were. But you got swatted, Jay, near miss. Tell
me about Fallon. What soured him?"

"I don't know. I thought I knew him. He was my friend; he
stepped in when Dad and I fought. He got me into rehabs when
everyone else gave up. He gave me the job at the A-V Center, got
me the federal grant, and he talked Salvatori into buying my
jewelry. And, you know, I still can't believe he was selling out the
tribe. We all trusted him, even Sam and the Queen Bee."

"I'm not too sure about that. She's a wise old owl, but she
knows we're only human."

"You could be right. I was angry at her, jealous, I guess.
She had her fingers in every pot. I wanted to develop the ideal
cultural center, make it a national showcase. Let's face it; I wanted
to exploit the hell out of it, too. I wanted a great educational
center, an Indian television Mecca with a TV newsroom, a
clearinghouse, and an Indian town hall. A meeting place for Indian
artists, cultural pow-wows, but she was always interfering."

"I think Betty agrees with you now. She's offered you a
chance. You and Jen."

"You're right, Matt. What can I say? She used to say that
she couldn't trust me, not until I was sober."

"She was right."

"I know, and I'm sober now."

"And you've got the job, if you want it."

"Oh, I want it, but I want to earn it. I want the tribe to want
me."

"They will. They want you and Jen and the Hawks.
Speaking of the Hawks, how did you get started?"

"It just happened. Tom recommended me as a co-leader
for the drug rehab program since I had so much experience." Jay
laughed. "I sent out cattle calls for volunteers and the whole Fire
Department showed up. Every one of them had an alcohol or drug

problem. They taught me; I didn't teach them a thing. We went on a retreat together, sat out on that desert, and beat drums for three days and two nights. I swear I sweated off twenty pounds. I was so thirsty, Matt, I would have drunk my own urine, but I didn't have any left. We were ready to haul out when this flock of Harris hawks flies in and lands on top of the cactus. This one bird flies into the brush and startles a rabbit. Another hawk runs under the mesquite and chases it out. Then another bird flies off a cactus and pounces on it. They ambushed every rabbit on that hill in half an hour. I never saw birds cooperate like that. Then Ralph says 'There's our sign. It's an omen. We're like the hawks. We're Jay's hawks.' Right out of Batman comics." Jay laughed. "We're brothers, Matt."

"I envy you."

"Envy me? You're one of us. They love you, Matt. They helped you bust in the counting room, didn't they? Screwed with Salvatori, set the fire, rigged you in that fireman's outfit so you could ambush the bastards. They covered your tracks. God, I would have loved to seen that." Jay laughed so hard that his eyes watered.

He was drying his eyes with his bandana when Jen set a tray on the table. "I see you boys are hard at work."

"Hey, Jen, what did you bring us?"

"Blue corn flat bread, rice, beans, and fresh strawberries and lemon-flavored mineral water. Sorry, no Kool Aid." She grinned at Matt.

"Hey, that's what took so long? Grinding all that blue corn meal?"

"I ground it in the blender. Don't tell anyone." They dug in and ate silently. Jen surprised Matt and Jay by finishing first.

"My sister can sure finish a plate faster than anyone."

"Had to, with you and Dad around."

Jay waved his plastic fork. "I was just getting to the part where Tom set me up. He knew the cables in the audio-visual room were still tied to the casino surveillance room. He wanted me to watch the counting room because he believed the casino was laundering money, but he didn't know how. So I kept bringing him the video-tapes. In time, Tom figured out that Salvatori and the syndicate were bringing in cash and passing it on to the Asian bunch and the Peruvians, and that Salvatori was laundering their drug money and vice versa. Tom did some checking and learned that all casino money goes through the Feds."

"How can they do that, Matt?" Jen asked.

"That's not easy to explain," Matt said. "But, simply put, hundreds of thousands of transactions go through the Feds, the Euro and the Asian banks. Everyone is moving money in-shore, off-shore, legally and illegally, daily, including illegal money from our own government's illicit operations. Cooper knew that because he used illegal money to finance covert CIA operations. What Jay didn't know was that Fallon passed information to Cooper and helped him set up the robbery. Cooper wanted cash to buy Arnold's property, something he always planned to do..."

"Or kill for it if he had to." Jay finished the sentence.

"I don't get it. Why would Tom help Cooper rob the casino?" Jen asked.

"That's the nub. Both Fallon and Cooper owned the principal water companies in Camp Verde," Matt answered. "It was Tom's idea to obtain the tribe's water rights. It gets complicated, but Tom wanted to bankrupt the tribe. If he could embarrass the tribe and the syndicate with a robbery, maybe the casino would be closed. But he was also embezzling from the tribe. Queen Bee was onto to him and she also knew that the syndicate was bribing the Tribal Council. Tom searched her office several times, but her records were kept in that Choctaw shorthand of hers. When I broke into the computer room, Tom was ready. Carbahol overheard the Hawks making plans to start a fire in the kitchen and he passed it on to Tom. And Tom double-crossed everyone, as usual. He realized the sky was falling, so he spread a couple of rolls of toilet paper around Betty's office, lit his cigar, stuck it inside a folded match cover, and walked away. When the fire started, he and Cosmic Annie played their little game. Tom cashed in the chips, and they flew to Vegas, laundered the cash in a casino, and then flew to Mexico City and on to Belize. No extradition from there."

"Maybe we should try that, Matt."

"Not on your life, Jay," Jen said quickly.

"I'm kidding."

"No, you're not."

"Yes, I am."

"He's kidding, Jen. Trust me."

"I trust you, Matt, but not him."

"Jay was catching on to Fallon, Jen. He just didn't realize how deep a hole Fallon had dug for himself. Fallon arranged the land swap when the tribe traded reservations. The tribe got land for the new Rez, for the casino, and for the proposed mall. Two hundred and fifty thousand acres of freeway land for 8500 acres of wilderness, conveniently located next to his ranch. The whole area is a huge aquifer, Jen, and add that to the Indian water rights. Tom, Cooper, and Strickland would all be rich. They used Strickland to stir up trouble between the tribe and the townies. Cooper's rednecks did their part. Then Fallon urged the Tribal Council to lease their 80 acres to mall developers to stir the pot some more. A mall would kill the local businesses and the tribe retained 80 acres on the old Rez, which is strictly illegal. The key was that Tom got the syndicate to extort the Secretary of Interior to enact the trade. They were able to get to him because the Secretary was a compulsive gambler. The syndicate was holding a million dollars' worth of his IOU's and they squeezed him. He couldn't afford a public disclosure since he was a potential candidate for Vice President on next year's ticket. Salvatori and the syndicate had their eyes on the 8500 acres. Salvatori made an arrangement on his own with the Peruvian drug lords. They planned to strip the limestone, put in a pulverizing plant, and ship it out on the Verde railroad to Ashfork, then to San Diego and to China. There's a worldwide shortage of cement, Jen, and the Chinese need all they can get. The Peruvians, by the way, know the business. They own cement plants all around the world, and the Chinese are their biggest customers."

313

"How did you figure this all out, Matt?"

"I didn't. I had my head stuck in the casino operation. I was looking for illicit gambling and money laundering. Frankly, I wanted to prove the syndicate was bribing the council members and that's exactly what Tom wanted me to believe. Renee's tapes of the Marshals' conversation made good listening and Dick Radcliffe hinted that Salvatori was running a major drug operation. And I realized that Kincaid was a player, and I suspected Kessler. I didn't know what to do, so I pulled the string. When the casino records hit the oscillating fan, the world figured it out."

"You're not exactly on speaking terms with Kessler, are you, Matt?"

"I'm not talking to anyone in Washington, Jay, now or in the future. When we finish the sculptures, I'm out of the rat race."

"Are you saying that you don't want to be a bahana man?"

"Just want to be my own man. Skin color has nothing to do with it."

"So what's going to happen to the tribe?"

"The tribe's not yet out the woods, Jay. But things may work out for the best. Leave it to Sam and the Queen Bee." Matt put his arm around Jen.

"I promise." Jay took his arm out of the sling and crossed his heart.

"You better behave, Jay," Jen said.

"Or you'll what?"

"I'll break your other arm."

"Come on, kids, knock it off," Matt said.

"Time to do the donuts," Dan said as he approached them. Matt grinned and pushed his stool under the work table.

"Can I watch, Dan?" Jen asked.

"Sure, Jen, come on back."

"Can I help?" Jay asked hopefully.

"Sure, check our footwork; you know the drill. If we screw up, pull the plug on the foamer."

"You'll be all right," Jay said.

Inside the pour room, Bill and Terry were smoothing sand. Dan handed Jay and Jen goggles and leather aprons. "Put these on and stay behind the red line. Don't stare at the exhaust. Safety first."

"What if something happens?"

"If we drop that crucible, run like hell, Jen, and don't look back."

"Is it that dangerous?"

"Not if we take care of business. You can watch from the doorway if you want."

"I'm staying here," she said.

"That's my girl. Let's get dressed, Matt." They stepped into an alcove. Dan handed him a pair of aluminized carbon-Kevlar leggings with Velcro. "Nothing but the best."

"Sure beats blue denim and leather aprons." Matt put on a carbon-Kevlar coat and pants, and strapped on leggings and a pair of Kevlar spats over his safety shoes. After checking each other's rigs for gaps, the men walked onto the pouring floor. Wearing leggings, Kevlar aprons and hoods, Bill and Terry were standing beside the furnace doors.

"Let's dance, boys!" Dan and Matt pulled on their protective hoods. Matt tugged on his steel-reinforced gloves and took a stance on the right side of the furnace while Dan stood on the left. "Ready, Matt?"

"Ready." Dan pumped his arm.

Bill and Terry tugged on a bar and swung the gate open. A ball of hot gases belched outward and upward as the two men paused to let the exhaust escape. Bill attached a hook from the overhead crane to the lifting bail, waited as Terry closed the safety latches on the yoke swivels and stepped away.

"Teamwork," Dan shouted. "You lead." Matt nodded. Terry punched a button on his hand-held control and the fiery crucible lifted slowly out of the furnace. Bill steered it, with its orange red brew, to the center of the pouring floor, where it dangled delicately. Matt stared for a moment at the turbulent lava-like incandescence. Dan raised his hand and Bill attached a hook to the yokes that held the glowing ceramic shells. They cleared the doors and Terry steered them out of the furnace, then stepped back and used the hoist to guide them to the center of the pouring floor. Satisfied, he pumped a fist. Dan signaled back.

"You lead," Dan said and pointed his gloved fist at the crucible. Matt took over the controls and steered the lip of the crucible over the gate of the first ceramic shell. The crucible tilted. Dan reached inside with a long-handled scoop to clear the dross and slag on the surface as Matt began pouring. At the critical moment, he capped the gate, simultaneously reversed the tilt on the crucible, moved it over the second ceramic shell, paused, and then began the next pour. In less than thirty seconds, he eased the crucible away from the molds and handed the controls to Bill, who directed the crucible to one side and began pouring the surplus bronze into ingot molds.

Dan and Matt walked outside toward the work patio and began peeling off their gear. Jay and Jen joined them. "Well, what did you think, Jen?"

"Oh, it's was scary and beautiful."

"And hot," Dan said. "But it's hotter out here on this patio. I need a beer."

"What do you do next?" Jen asked.

"We'll let it cool a little. Then start the chasing process, clean it up, cut off the spuires and gates. Do a rough polish. Finally Matt comes back and smoothes the casting. We do the patina and waxing last."

"Can I watch?"

"You can mix my secret oxides." Dan draped a beefy arm around her shoulders and squeezed her close. "You can help too, Jay. It's time you got back into the business. What do you say?"

"Production work?"

"Hell, no. That's the bread and butter. We need studio pieces, Jay. This foundry has a reputation to maintain."

316

"You're on, Dan." Jen slipped away from Dan and hugged her brother as Terry and Bill joined them on the patio and began peeling off their gear.

"What did I tell you, boys? That was a dance wasn't it? Didn't I tell you that Matt could pour? If Matt poured a glass of milk to the brim, you couldn't lift the glass without spilling it. You're good, Matt."

"Dan pours like he was pouring beer in a glass. The head always spills over the rim," Bill said, shaking Matt's hand.

"We're going out for lunch, boss, while the furnace is cooling. Do we start the chasing, or is Matt going to do it?"

"I'm out of here," Matt said. "It's all yours."

"What about the shells, Matt?"

"Cut them."

"Are you sure?"

"I'm sure."

"Come on, Jen, we've got beads to string," Jay said.

"Thanks, Dan, it was fun. It was a great pour."

"You're welcome, Matt. But we're only halfway home."

"I know. I'll be back tomorrow."

"I'll buy you a beer."

"Later. I'll let you know."

Matt sat on the patio and thought about the pour, and about Jay and Jen, and about Renee. Then he went looking for Paloma. He stuck his head inside the infirmary door. She was holding a pair of needed-nosed pliers in one hand and holding Digger flat on his side with the other.

"Come in, Matt. You're just in time. You can keep him still." Digger looked up sorrowfully and tried to wiggle his stubby tail. Spiny quills extended outward from his muzzle, jowls, and mouth.

"What happened?" he asked, pressing his hands on Digger's shoulders and flanks firmly.

Paloma held Digger's head and began to carefully remove the quills. "He went after that old porcupine again. This is the second time," she said as she removed a quill. "Stop squirming!

The little quills are the worst. Open your mouth, baby." She squeezed Digger's jaws.

"I thought you said that Aussies are smart."

"They are. The first time, he was just curious."

"And the second time?"

"The second time, he was so damn mad, he didn't care." Paloma ran her fingers inside Digger's cheeks. "I think we got all of them." She swabbed Digger's wounds and the inside of his mouth with hydrogen peroxide. "Doesn't taste so good, does it?" Digger squirmed. "You can let him go." Matt released Digger, who stared at him gratefully and began licking his hands. "That's gratitude for you. I do the dirty work and your hand gets licked." Paloma huffed. "Bring him outside."

Matt set Digger down outside the door. The pup looked at them, put his nose to the ground, found a scent and followed it across the yard. "Is he going after the porcupine again?"

"I doubt it, but I wouldn't put it past him. Males are slow learners."

They followed Digger to the river and heard a frog croak. Digger scrambled up the side of a rock and stood very still. With one paw resting on the frog, he sniffed the air and studied the ground. "He's been after that frog for days."

"He's standing on it?"

"Naturally, all males are short-sighted. They can't see something when it's right under their noses."

"Boy, we are full of animal wit and wisdom today."

"Anybody home?"

"We're down here!" Digger raced to greet Bob and he gave Paloma a quick hug.

"It's good to see you, Matt," Bob said, and sat down on a rock. "Whew! I'm worn out, folks. Washington, Chicago, Boston, San Francisco. Committee meetings, hearings, debriefings, newspaper reporters. A three-ring circus and then some. The press wanted a Waco. It took some doing, but everyone agrees that Cooper was just a wacko. Now they are digging up his CIA connections, all the way back to Contra Costa. They'll worry that bone to death."

"You must be thirsty. I'll get us some iced tea."

"No need, Paloma. We'll come up to the house."

"You stay put. I'll be right back."

Bob shifted over to another boulder. "That's better," he sighed.

"Have you seen the ultra light?" Matt asked.

"Not since I helped JR tow it to his barn. The Bureau was going to get me a new one, but I took the cash instead. I'd rather fix it myself." Bob looked away and then back at Matt. "I saw Renee. In fact, I saw her twice. She asked about you. I told her I didn't know anything except that Paloma said that you were working on your sculpture day and night. She's worried about you, Matt. She said she's been calling you."

"Calling for me or for Kessler?"

"I don't know, both, maybe." Bob picked a pebble and tossed it into the river. "Kessler's kept her busy as hell. He's parading her all around the Capitol building. Right now, he's the President's golden boy. He's in the meeting rooms and the hallways, pulling strings all over the place. Water Commission, Interior, Gaming Commission, and Indian Affairs. And Justice. It ain't easy, Matt. You turned over a lot of rocks."

"And Kessler's doing damage control."

"He's doing more than plugging leaks. The President plans to visit Arizona, and I think, he's going to clean up this mess before he moves out of the White House and Renee, well, she's just doing her job, Matt."

"Some job."

"Matt, I hate to say this, but you started it."

"Are you blaming me for broadcasting what all these scumbags -- the syndicates, the lobbyists, the beltway boys -- are doing? Hell, forget it!" Matt stood up.

"Here's your tea, boys," Paloma interrupted. "Looks like you could use something cool to drink." Matt took the glass and chugged half of it down.

"Thanks, Paloma. I really was thirsty."

"I saw Dick Radcliffe, too, Matt," Bob said.

"How's he doing?"

"He's got a limp and a promotion, Bureau Chief's desk in Peru. I guess they thought he'd put a collar around their necks down there."

"Good for Dick," Matt said.

"He turned them down. I ran into him and Renee in one of those red-leathered Italian restaurants where you pay forty bucks for spaghetti and two meatballs. Dick said he's thinking about opening a bikers bar and laundromat in Pensacola."

"You're kidding," Paloma said.

"maybe he was kidding, but Renee seemed to take him seriously. He invited her to go down with him and check it out."

"That's nice. Maybe they'll open a casino." Matt handed Paloma his drink "I've got to get back to the foundry. Time to check the molds."

"Matt, are you finished with the sculpture?" Paloma asked.

"I hope so. I've got a good feeling, but we won't know until we crack the molds."

"How wonderful. I'd love to watch if that's okay." Paloma touched his arm.

"Not yet, but I'll let you know. You too, Bob. It's kind of like having a baby. The proud father isn't ready to pass out the cigars yet."

"What is it?" Bob asked.

"Twins, I hope. Take care." He walked down the path to the studio.

"Bob, you shouldn't have told him about Renee and Radcliffe."

"Why not? The man needs a kick in the butt."

"He's kicking himself. He doesn't need any help."

"If you say so." Bob hugged Paloma again. "How close were they?"

"Closer than we are."

"I don't like the sound of that."

"Radcliffe didn't seem to mind."

Paloma pushed away. "We need to talk, Bob."

"About us or them?"

"About us, them, and everybody."

"Does that include JR?"

"Yes, it does."

"Why don't we just have a town meeting and invite everybody?"

"Funny. I was just going to suggest that. JR called and said that you need to move your plane ASAP."

"Are you coming?"

"No. I've got too much to do here." She picked up the glasses and paused on the way to the kitchen.

"I'll see you after I move the plane. We can talk then," Bob suggested.

"Sure, why not?"

"Adios, Paloma."

"Good bye, Bob."

Matt went into the studio, opened the refrigerator door, and studied the contents. He settled for a piece of cheese, some grapes and a bottle of mineral water. He carried them over to the coffee table where a worn hardback copy of *The Odyssey* was lying open. Next to it, a thin tattered paperback edition of *The Tempest* had a leather book mark inside. Leafing through it, he noticed that several passages had been highlighted with a yellow marker.

Suddenly, Digger ran through the door and jumped up beside him. "Here, have some cheese." Digger swallowed a chunk in one gulp and looked at Matt hopefully. "You're supposed to savor it. That's all for you." Digger circled the cushion, found a good spot, and settled in.

Matt opened *The Tempest*. "Why not?" he thought and began reading. It was after midnight when he finished and walked over to the window. "Paloma must think I'm a blend of these characters, an Ariel with an oar." He looked down at the puppy. "I've got enough oars to fill an oarhouse," he said to Digger, who raised his head, looked inquiringly at Matt, laid his head on his paws, and went back to sleep. "Well, at least *you* know what you're doing."

CHAPTER TWENTY-FIVE

Sitting in a straight chair and wearing a traditional fringed dress, Betty clutched a beaded purse while her moccasined feet barely touched the floor. Her moon-faced head was framed by braids and coils of black hair. She smiled warmly at Matt, who was seated on a bench by the window in Dan's office.

"What are you feeling?" she asked.

"Anxious, a little excited, strangely even, sad. It's always like this when I finish a piece, when everything comes to an end.

"There are no endings, Matt, and no beginnings, only the sacred circle. We are all on the path."

"Have you seen the sculptures?"

"I have."

"What do you think?"

"I think the Creator has given you many gifts. But I'm more interested in your vision."

He looked out the window at the people circulating around the gallery floor, remembering the Queen Bee's words: "Stinking Springs is a wisdom place. It is below the house that stood over the Eagleman's Cave. Wisdom places help us find our way in the scheme of things. They are filled with mystery and power, a perfect place to find your vision, your identity."

Jay and the Young Hawks had taken him to Stinking Springs. They had piled firewood on a ledge beneath the empty hole that had once been a cliff house. Jay had handed Matt a bottle of water and a box of matches. "Spirit water, non-alcoholic, no magic mushrooms," Jay laughed, "But it has power. It comes from the springs. We'll wait for you at the end of the canyon. Sweet dreams, brother." And the men began walking up the trail.

Matt remembered finding a perch on an outcrop where he sat cross-legged, watching the clouds soaring tier after tier while,

below, each rock, mesa, and spire raged with scarlet-tipped flames.
A pair of eagles rose in languid circles, their shadows sliding
across the ridge. One eagle called, and the sound wafted down the
canyon like an echoing lament. The dying sun slipped over the
mesa, like a wound, and stained the rim crimson. The red rocks
dimmed as the purple shrouds of night spread westward.

Venus was rising in the crescent of the moon which crept
sinuously across the flats and inched over the Black Hills. The tips
of the shadowy cottonwood trees glowed, contrasting with the
sulfur-yellow moon. An owl had hooted as he kindled the fire.
The dry mesquite pods crackled amidst the roaring dark gases,
unfurling serpent tails skyward.

Matt inhaled the vapors rising from the spring water he had
dripped onto the coals. As the sound drifted down the canyon,
echoing faintly off the cliff walls, he listened to the hypnotic
drumbeats and the chants of the drummers. An owl flew out in the
moon-speckled darkness, catching beams on his beating wings as it
banked and landed softly on the top of a bush. No moonlight hit it
directly, though enough sieved through the leaves to make it
appear more silver-blue than black – a blue owl.

The fire collapsed on itself, sending a burst of glowing
sparks into the air. The rock face seemed alive; ripples of orange
and yellow flamed over the coals in luminous waves. Leaning
closer, he poked the fire with a stick causing more sparks to fly,
lighting up his brow and most of his face except for his deep-set
eyes. The effect made him look more like a boldly carved marble
statue than a man of flesh. Tossing the stick into the fire, he drew
his knees into his chest, rested his back against the cliff wall, and
watched the smoke rising from the smoldering fire. Matt's vision
clouded and dimmed.

A silver-and-brown striped eagle feather drifted down from
the sunlit skies. It spun and slipped, carried by the currents of the
wind. Each time it fell, another current carried it aloft. Then it
began to change swiftly. It grew larger, swelling in length and
breadth until it was no longer a feather, but an entire wing, partly

cloud and partly sky. Another wing appeared and then, slowly a body began to emerge between the two wings. My body, Matt remembered. I beat my wings and I rode the air. A gale wind suddenly blew me high into the clouds. Everywhere the world screamed and the clouds were ripped apart. The wind blew in my face, making my eyes water, but I didn't care. I felt wholly alive, and I fell helplessly down and down until I was thrown to the ground.

A woman was sitting in front of me. She sat alone, her bare feet in the water. As the water lapped her toes, she smiled. The water bubbled over the rocks. Black birds warbled and whistled as their wings hummed through the reeds. She spoke: "They are my only real companions in times of solitude. A bird's wings are far more than feathered arms. They are a mystery and a miracle. You are free. You always were and you always will be."

Matt became aware that he had been describing his vision to Betty. He turned his chair to face her. "I woke up at dawn with a clear head, as clear as it will ever be. A hummingbird was circling my head and then fluttered towards me. It watched me closely, flashed away, and disappeared up the canyon. At my feet, I found a pair of wings, the eagle wings."

"And what else did you see?"

"A withered looking crone, a witch. She had a staff and turquoise rings on her fingers. She was standing in a circle of stones with some bones scattered around her feet, and a human skull, I think. What does it mean, Betty?"

"It means that you are an Eagleman with a good heart and great integrity. Your vision told you what you didn't know about yourself. The eagle bones probably fell from Arnold's workshop. He was a taxidermist, and I also know that there's a bit of the trickster in you, Matt. You scattered their records like coyote scattered the stars. Why?"

"Several reasons, really. The syndicate was going to help the Peruvians get the land for a cement plant. Their drug operation was producing amphetamines, the drug of choice for truckers, Indians and school kids. Salvatori had corrupted the Tribal

Council, the Federal, state and local officials. There was no end to it. But Jen, the Gourd Girls, Jay, and the young Hawks had a better vision. I had to help them end the corruption and show them they were right."

"You did the right thing. I let the Governor know that sovereignty is our only protection against white men who want whatever is next door. The tribe has agreed to pay a percentage of our earnings, but only if they honor a covenant which allows us to survive. Our people will no longer be funneled from the Rez to the ghetto. I told her there will be a day when we provide leaders and candidates, not *just* political funding and, thanks to you, Matt, we will."

"Who is the woman by the pool in my vision?"

"The woman of your dreams. She wants you, but doesn't want to possess you. Visions aren't clear; there is always a hitch. You won't find her by looking. If you are patient, she will find you. Just be sure you're ready. Lady eagles like their freedom, too." Betty peeked through the Venetian blinds. "The people are getting restless. We better get going."

The drummers stopped when Betty walked behind the podium. The brown-faced little gourd girls, radiant in yellow and blue dresses, smiled widely, found their seats, and struggled to keep from laughing.

"Blessing to you all," Betty said, blowing a palmful of pollen dust into the air. "Blessings to our honored guests. Blessings to our people and to our newly elected officials. May they always act wisely." She turned to the council members, which included two of the young Hawks. "We have turned a new page in our history. May we all serve wisely and honorably." The crowd began to cheer and the drummers banged their drums loudly. Betty raised a hand. "We are here today for an unveiling. Is that right?"

"Yes, Betty, that's correct," Dan answered.

"Before we proceed, I have announcements. First, I am pleased to tell you that Jay Cook has agreed to return to his post as audio-visual director and will also lead our drug rehabilitation program."

"He sure has experience, Betty," someone yelled, and the crowd laughed.

"And a successful outcome," Betty added, and the crowd cheered.

"We shall call him Jay Two Hats. And if I can find something else for him to do, maybe Jay Three Hats.

"Why not?" someone shouted, "His head's big enough."

Betty left the podium, walked back to the heckler, and dusted him with pollen. "There, maybe your head will grow." The crowd roared. The drummers began chanting, "Queen Bee, Queen Bee," as she returned to the podium. She raised her hand, silencing them.

"Jen Cook has been selected by the council to direct the Cultural Center. There is no one, including myself, who knows our songs, dances, stories, and traditions better. She has been our children's teacher for many years. Our choice must be ratified by you according to our laws. Would you stand up, Jen?"

Jen rose. She was wearing her yellow Corn Maiden dress. Her face reddened as the Gourd Girls squealed their delight and the crowd clapped loudly. There were cheers and whistles as she sat down.

"Who said Indians are a quiet people?" Betty asked, and the crowd laughed.

"It must have been a white man," the heckler yelled, and everyone laughed again.

"My last announcement, would you please stand, Sam? Sam Cook rose from his seat on the side of the gallery. "Our friend. Our father. Our leader. The man who fought our battles for 55 years through all of the bad times. He will be given an honorary doctorate degree from the Arizona Board of Regents. And he will receive a master's degree in literature when he completes his thesis on the modern history of our tribe from NAU. That history will include his memoirs, I'm told.

"I'm still working on those. I'm not dead yet," Sam said.

"Speech! Speech!" The crowd shouted.

"Some other day," Sam said. "You've heard them all anyway."

"I like the story of when Sam led our people to the Verde River, waved an arrow, the river parted, and we escaped from the cavalry."

"That was a drought year, Betty. We waded across," Sam said and started to sit down.

"Don't sit down yet, Sam, the Governor has an announcement to make."

The Governor was sitting in the front row. Facing the audience, she ran her fingers through her silver-streaked hair, adjusted her glasses, and read from a piece of paper. "I am pleased to tell you that I have appointed Sam Cook Executive Director of the Arizona Commission of Indian Affairs. As such, he will see that the needs of Arizona's 22 tribes are addressed. He will work with the executive branch, the judicial branch, and the legislators on tribal concerns, including gaming, revenue sharing, taxes, education, ecology, mining, grazing, and water rights. He will host legislative days, town meetings, and summits where tribes can express their concerns about discrimination and Indian sovereignty. Did I get it right, Sam?"

"Did I agree to do all that?"

"You did, and I'm honored to serve with you."

The crowd rose, clapped their hands, and began stomping their feet to increasing louder drumbeats. Sam waved his arms over his head and waited until the crown quieted. "I thank you," he said. "I never dreamed there would be a day such as this, not in my lifetime. I will do my best, the very best I can. I promise you."

"We couldn't ask for more, Sam. We know you will honor us as you always have," Betty said. "Now, as you know, we are here today for the unveiling of the sculpture created for us by Matt Dillon. I should say *sculptures*, because there are two. I have asked Matt to speak, but he has declined. He believes the sculptures should speak for themselves. Are you ready?"

"Ready," Dan said, pulling the shroud off a sculpture. The audience gasped. A ten-foot circle. A roulette wheel ringed with red and black squares surrounded a bald eagle with outstretched wings. Its body was a shield of enamel with a horizontal blue band with thirteen vertical red and white stripes beneath it. One talon grasped an olive branch while the other held a quiver of arrows. In relief above the eagle's head, an Indian brave stretched his arms skyward. Kneeling beside him, an Indian woman held a child up. The eagle held a scroll in its beak, inscribed with the words *freedom, unity,* and *peace.*

The crowd began murmuring. "Matt has told me that there is no cynicism implied in the sculpture. Rather, a caution: there is danger and opportunity in all of our endeavors associated with gaming. It is my wish to place this sculpture in our meeting hall as a reminder to us all that every time we prepare ourselves to make a decision, we must be responsible. I will do this with your approval."

Someone began clapping and then the crowd rose to its feet. "Thank you, Matt for pointing out to us that the images on our American Seal and the images of our Eagleman have much in common."

Matt bowed his head and asked Dan to pull the shroud from the second sculpture. At first, there was total silence. Then a young girl gasped loudly and the crowd gave a collective sigh. Two enormous bald eagles were tumbling earthward in a magical dance, talons locked, one with outspread wings and one facing upward with sweptback wings. The yellow talons on the upper bird were tinged purple.

"Matt says the sculpture is entitled 'Aguilar and Friend.' With your approval, we will put this sculpture on exhibit in the Cultural Center for six weeks. After that, it will be moved to the atrium."

Jen ran to Matt and embraced him. "Matt, you are I'itoi. The Green River people will never forget you."

"And I will never forget them either, Jen." He returned her embrace. "Never," he said, as several people brushed by in their haste to get a closer view of the sculptures.

"All's well that end's well," Chester Vance said as he patted Matt's shoulder.

"Matt, I just had a thought," the Governor said. "Would you be interested in doing a piece for the foyer of the Capital building? Not a political statement, of course." She grinned widely and shook his hand softly.

The drummers began pounding their drums, the Gourd Girls joined hands, and began circling around the eagles. They started singing the Corn Maiden song as Matt slipped away.

He stopped beside Dan and they shook hands. "Your sculptures are going to be famous, Matt. You did us proud."

"You did the real work, Dan. The firing and casting went beyond the realm."

"It's a new dimension for us. You showed the way. We all learned something. I wish you'd stay, but you're leaving, I take it?"

"Yes."

"When?"

"I'm on my way tonight after I've said my good-byes."

"You know the old saying 'You can run, but you can't hide'?"

"I'm not running, but I'd like to be invisible for awhile."

"Where are you going?"

"California or Montana or maybe back to New Mexico. I'll send you a postcard."

Matt parked his van beside Wally's shack. Wally came out, wiping his new boots on his new levis, wiping his oversized turquoise-laden silver belt buckle with a sleeve of his new dark blue shirt, and adjusting his new Stetson proudly.

"Wow! You're dressed like you struck it rich."

"Maybe I did and maybe I didn't." Wally winked. "After you and that posse pulled out, I saw all that money falling from the

330

sky. I found a bagful of money on top of the ridge. What wasn't burned, I kept. Finders keepers, as they say. If anyone asks, I'm telling them that I sold my nuggets to an Easterner. I'm opening a shop in Cornville with Arnold's stuff, my skulls, some rocks, and minerals. Plus some Mormon tea for the customers. Here, take this jug with you. It'll cool your throat and put out that fire in your belly. I'm taking Jen in as my partner. She's going to make that pretty jewelry of hers. We'll put some of Jay's stuff in there, too. When I'm gone, they can have the business, and if you got any of those sculptures of yours lying around, we could put them in the window."

Matt went to the van and handed Wally a pair of heavy bronze figures -- two Indian women merged into a set of drums. "My first pieces. You can have them."

"Thank you. I think I'll hold onto them for awhile because you just might become famous. Can't tell what they might be worth someday." Wally spat in the dirt. "Matt, if you live as long as I have, there's nothing new under the sun and most everything reminds you of something you'd rather forget. That's why the old timers get forgetful. It's a blessing really. But I won't forget you, and I won't forget the day you kicked Carbahol off his horse. Here, take the jug before I cry. So long, Matt."

"Good bye. Take care of yourself, and Jen, and Jay."

Wally turned and went back inside his yard. A burro brayed. "Shut up, Jen. I'm coming."

Matt picked up a sandwich, a piece of pie and some coffee at Ruth's, said a hurried goodbye, crossed the porch, and got into his Kombi. A solitary figure on a horse rode out from under the casino billboard. He raised his Stetson. "So Long, Matt," Carbahol shouted. "Be good."

"I will be, Jake," Matt shouted. "You take care."

"You too."

Matt edged the van onto the I-17. "C'mon, gal. Let's get where we ain't." The VW gained momentum when he floor boarded it to climb the long hill on the far end of the valley.

CHAPTER TWENTY-SIX

White-capped thunder clouds towered over the red rock country as lower, dark ominous clouds pushed southward towards the Black Mesa. "Spooky-looking things, aren't they?" JR asked Paloma when lightning lit up the cloud's interior. "Late or not, I'm glad the monsoons are finally here. Pass me some more of that jello, please."

"Better late than never, JR." She handed him a bowl of red jello filled with fresh strawberries and cherries. "You want some more, Renee?"

"Just a little. Thank you." Renee spooned a helping onto her plate. They listened to the staccato tap of a wood pecker and watched as it flew across the river. A refreshing breeze rustled through the cottonwoods and the sycamore leaves twisted and danced playfully.

"Well, why don't you give us the lowdown, Renee? All we get here is the stuff in the papers. What are the wheelers and dealers hiding behind that smokescreen?"

"Give her a break. She just got here," Paloma said.

Renee crossed her arms on the table. "I thought you'd never ask." She smiled at Paloma. "You want the nitty gritty, JR, or the power point presentation?"

"I want all the nitty gritty you've got, darlin.' Don't leave anything out."

"Well, I'll tell you what I know, but I don't have all the inside poop, as you say. But starting at the top, the President wasn't happy with the senators or the congressmen. There will be an ethics hearing."

"Hmm. A lot of good that will do," JR said.

"Let her talk," Paloma said.

"The Senator made a trade-off. He's staying on as the chair of Indian Affairs, but he's co-sponsoring a bill to curtail the tribes' political contributions. Therefore, less soft money."

"That's a start," JR interrupted again.

"The Secretary of the Interior resigned. Kessler pressured Kincaid into turning state's evidence for a reduced sentence. Actually, he already had the Marshals' testimony and they're under protective custody, but..."

"But what?" JR asked.

"But, Kincaid will do time, three-to-five years, and the syndicate is finished."

"Where did they disappear to?"

"Peru, but the President flexed some muscle, or the Secretary of State did, so they'll be extradited if they're still there. And the Peruvians won't be able to develop a mine in the Upper Verde. In fact, the big news is that the land swap is off, and the President used the public outrage to instigate -- I should say coerce -- Congress into declaring the Upper Verde a wilderness area."

JR tipped his hat. "Well, I'm beginning to like this man."

"The Senator's establishing a Verde Valley Watershed Commission. The Governor will serve on it, of course, but there'll be a moratorium on mining water and SRP can't exercise its water rights because it doesn't have a storage dam for the run-off. So, for the time being, they are out of the picture. I had a chance to bend the President's ear and, thanks to what I learned from you all, I shared some worthwhile information. The new Secretary of the Interior, well, that's confidential, but she's a real dynamo, an eco-psychologist from Billings, Montana. She's considering declaring an 80-mile stretch along the Verde River a critical habitat for the Southwestern Willow Catcher, Paloma."

"Oh, my God! That's great!" Paloma exclaimed.

Renee searched her billfold. "Here's her card. She's expecting a call from you."

"Really? Oh my God! I'm going to cry."

"Pass me some more of that jello, Paloma," JR asked, ignoring her outburst.

"Oh, my God! Here, JR, finish it." Paloma tossed her red hair and hugged Renee, tears streaming down her face.

"What's the rest of the story?" JR prodded.

"Well, let's see, where do I start?"

"Start at the beginning, and don't leave anything out," JR pleaded.

"When Matt kicked the can, they all started to run. York and Radcliffe went after the robbery money that they had stashed at Arnold's. They flew out in the ultra-light and Radcliffe headed for the cement factory. We're guessing that when York came back, he shot Cooper to cover himself, but we'll never know. Arnold and Cooper...well, there's nothing left to identify."

"Who killed Arnold?" JR asked.

"York says Cooper did and that he tried to shoot Bob, and then Bob shot Cooper in self-defense. Again, we'll never know we only have York's story. Just before the explosion, Cooper warned Matt to watch his back and mumbled something about the ATF. Matt got Jen and Jay out just before the whole place up blew up. York used a GPS satellite, that pink phone that he called his office to set off the charges and blow up the adobe. Personally, I don't think he planned to kill Cooper. But he remembered to leave enough bills to tie Cooper to the casino robbery, although most of it was blown sky high."

"When York came back to get his money from the plane, Bucky arrested him," JR said.

"Matt tipped Bucky," Renee said.

"How did Matt figure it out?" Paloma asked.

"He knew Cooper didn't blow himself up. Matt had left him lying on the floor. York told Matt that Cooper had been shot in the neck. York wasn't able to talk to Radcliffe in the hospital, so he flew to Washington and tried to square things for both of them."

"And Matt realized the only one that could know that Cooper had been shot was the guy who shot him," JR exclaimed. "Bob asked me to move the plane. When we towed it to the barn, Matt found the cash that York had hid in the locker."

"You're right on, JR. Matt had asked his controller, Chester Vance, to check out everyone – Kessler, Kincaid, Radcliffe and Farley. He didn't know about York, but he used Vance's information and my database to connect them to Cooper, Panama, and the Gnome had recorded the serial numbers of the money. Simple, isn't it?" Renee smiled. "After Matt sent me an email, I arrested Radcliffe and Bucky nailed York. Anyway, it all came down when Matt mailed the National Land Conservancy data to the water company owners. Strickland panicked and urged Fallon to pull the plug. He thought Cooper was losing it. According to Matt, Cooper goes all the way back to Casey, Reagan, North, and the Iran-Contra fiasco. Cooper resigned from the CIA. He believed that, later, Casey was poisoned. At least, that's what he was pushing to true believers in his conspiracy magazines. I've read some of his stuff, and frankly, he may have been right. Cooper was a has-been, but he knew where the bodies where buried. They pensioned him off, and funded his training camp for special operatives. Kessler was told to keep an eye on him. No one knew where Cooper might have hidden some very damaging records. By this time, Cooper was paranoid, if he already wasn't, so he recruited a paramilitary group and he wanted Arnold's mountain for a refuge camp. He apparently believed that one day soon there was going to be a political, racial, or economical catastrophe, so his paramilitary goof balls planned to blow up the highways and take over the Verde Valley. Then Fallon went to Bucky O'Neal and made a deal to set up Salvatori and Cooper. I think Bucky contacted Kessler, and they both pressured Kincaid."

"Can you believe this, JR?"

"Yes, I can, Paloma. You could see it in his eyes. So the four of them robbed the casino?"

"But, why? Why Bob and Dick?" Paloma asked.

"Money, greed, bitterness, frustration. I'm repeating myself, but Matt filled in the pieces. That morning, York and Radcliffe took most of the cash from Arnold's. York landed his plane on the mesa and stuffed his share in the cabin locker and flew back to Cottonwood to pick up Matt. When they flew over the mesa, Cooper shot at the plane with an AK 47. He thought that York and Radcliffe had double-crossed him. Meanwhile, Radcliffe took his share and went to the cement factory to close the drug deal. Radcliffe was trying to pull it off when Bucky showed up. After the plane crash, York called Radcliffe; then he called for the ATF bomb squad. Bucky raided the cement plant and followed the money trail to the casino…"

"And everyone started arresting everyone!" Paloma clapped her hands.

"Why did York blow up Arnold's adobe?"

"He was desperate. He wanted to put the blame on Arnold and Cooper. Radcliffe went looking for Farley – well, Radcliffe said that Farley panicked. Farley must have thought he'd been double-crossed by all of them. I don't know whether I believe Radcliffe's story or not. A jury will have to figure it out."

"What's going to happen to them?" Paloma asked.

"Federal prison for sure. Twenty years to life. Who knows?"

"Oh, God. This is sick. Why did they do it? Why did they go along with it all? Bob wasn't one of those people." Paloma wondered.

"According to Matt, he was, Paloma. They all worked for Cooper at one time or another. Bob York flew drugs out of Panama and brought in covert operators and arms. Dick Radcliffe peddled the contraband to the Miami drug lords. A lot of money changed hands. A lot of killing and torture went on. Families disappeared and coup leaders were assassinated. The policy was a mish-mash. Our leaders were constantly waffling. When I arrested Radcliffe, I asked him why. 'Why not?' he said. He said he was just pissed at everyone. Anyway, Cooper contacted him and York, pulled some strings, and set them up here. Radcliffe was on a one-man vendetta to take out drug dealers and discredit the DEA. York, well, he wanted peace and quiet, and a chance to get some cash. He wanted to buy into the balloon business."

"How about Farley?" JR asked.

"He was an MP, an interrogator at Cooper's compound, an order taker and Cooper's personal body guard. Anyway, Matt dug up the dirt, turned over the rocks," Renee laughed, "and he upset Kessler's apple cart. It takes an honest man, Kessler told me, to do an honest job."

"What about Kessler?" JR asked

"Well, the word is out that he's getting a promotion, possibly to the Assistant Director of Homeland Security."

"Is he honest, Renee?"

"I don't know what *honest* means anymore. Matt doesn't trust him. He says Kessler's been in the background since Iran-Contra. He thinks he's part of a shadow government."

"If Matt believes that, you better get the hell out of Washington. Get away from that guy. To hell with those people. I don't know what's worse, a bad good guy or a good bad guy. Sounds like Kessler's both."

"I am thinking about leaving, JR."

"Don't think, just walk away."

"What's going to happen to the tribe and the casino?" Paloma asked.

"The Governor and the tribes are going to have a pow-wow on taxing the casinos. If the tribe elects new leaders and takes responsibility for the operation, they might hang onto it. They'll have to agree to audits at the very least and, thanks to Kessler, Enterprise is on the ropes. The fat cats are running for cover."

"They'll be back; greed is greed. Somebody will pass a law making something illegal, and they'll be back in business the next day."

"Not if Kessler's on the job. He's a real watchdog and he's got guts. He knows Arizona and this Valley."

"Do I hear a tone of admiration there?" Paloma asked.

"He's my boss. He was my controller even if I didn't know it, but I liked his style. I still do."

"Will you stay on with the Federal Gaming Commission?" Paloma asked.

"Good question. I'm on leave for 30 days. Kessler gave me some time off. Right now, I just don't know."

"You don't need these people, Renee. Get out while you can," JR growled. "Have you seen this? It's a clipping of that piece Joe Biddles wrote for *The Village Voice*." JR handed the article to Renee.

"A thunderous explosion sent an enormous white cloud soaring over Black Mesa yesterday afternoon alarming local residents. The cloud spread over the Verde Valley, a cloud of greed, corruption, and bigotry. The thunderclap was followed by a flurry of helicopters, police cars, and members of the Sheriff's posse racing northward to the scene. Several members of a paramilitary group were arrested in a show of force that involved the FBI, drug enforcement officers, the Arizona Department of Public Safety, and the Yavapai County Sheriff's department. "It was pandemonium," said one member of the Sheriff's posse.

In simultaneous raids the Sheriff's department seized a cache of drugs at the Verde River gravel plan and arrested several employees at the Black Hills Casino, including the general manager Vince Salvatori. Sheriff Bucky O'Neil called the operation one of the most significant drug busts in Arizona history. 'International drug traffickers operating in our own backyard, right under our noses, were confiscated millions of dollars and more millions of dollars of drugs.' Sheriff O'Neill declined to comment on the nature of the operation saying only that the investigation is ongoing and further arrests will be coming.

According to our sources, the property owned by a local man, Monty Arnold, was honeycombed with caves lined with enough explosives to flow up a small city. Apparently Arnold and possibly another person died in the explosion and a DEA agent was wounded. Sheriff O'Neill acknowledged that Camp Verde Marshall Robert Farley was killed by a gun shot during the raid but he declined to comment saying the incident was under investigation and the area is closed until further notice.

338

Dear readers, the thunderclap was a wake-up call warning us that everything we love about our community is endangered by these events and by the actions of our leaders. We have no one to blame but ourselves for letting this happen. Arson, bombings, murder, water disputes, illegal land swaps, meth labs, money laundering, pollution, corrupted officials. We needn't ask our neighbors 'for whom the bells tolls?' I hope you'll join with me to put an end to this misery and chaos."

Renee looked toward the trees where the wind was gently blowing. "There's more." JR handed her additional clippings. "He seems to have the facts pretty clear."

"He should. He found my tapes. Everything was there and Matt, of course, sent it out over the net."

"Well, Joe came out okay. Knight Ridder offered him a job and they're nominating him for a Pulitzer. Kinda ironic, isn't it, seeing as you did most of the work?"

"That's history. I wish him luck."

"Have you seen Matt's sculpture of the eagles?" Paloma asked.

"Yes. I stopped by at the Ironworks. Dan let me in."

"Do you like it?"

Renee reflected for a moment. In her mind's eye, she saw two eagles dancing in the air, clouds for wings, claws intertwined, falling through space past the gold tip of a mountain peak.

"How would you describe it, Renee?"

"He's telling us the story of the universe. Fire, water, earth, and air are music to him. You can hear the primal screams of the eagles." Her eyes clouded as a gust of wind roared down the river, swaying the tree tops. "Do you know where he is, Paloma?"

"Let's take a walk. JR, you clear up the table." Paloma lead Renee down the trail to the river's edge.

"I wasn't going to tell you, because Matt made me promise. But, you're in love with him and I'm sure he's in love with you, even though he doesn't get it. He's also in love with creating. That's for sure. And he was angry."

"At me?"

"Sure. You aren't easy to love, Renee, and Matt isn't either. You'll have to work that out between you. But he left his anger on the floor of the foundry."

"Where is he now?"

"He talked about California and Montana. He did say that if you wanted to find him, you'd know where to look. Renee, his days of being an urban Indian are over. You might want to think about that."

"Do you love him, Paloma?"

"Yes, I do, but I love this place and JR more. Besides, can you see me raising a tribe of red-headed Indians?" They hugged each other tightly.

"I'm scared," Renee admitted.

"A leap of faith doesn't require courage, Renee. It requires faith, an act of love."

"I hope I don't fall on my face."

"Don't worry. You'll land on your feet." They linked arms as they walked back to the picnic area.

When Renee was ready to leave, they stood beside the Mustang. Paloma lifted Digger, put him in the passenger seat, and handed Renee a bowl, a bag of kibbles, and a jug of water.

"What's this?" Renee looked at the puppy.

"A peace offering. Don't go empty-handed. Matt loves this pup and Digger sure misses him. Get going, girl!"

Renee turned the car around. "Good bye, you all. Thanks for everything!"

EPILOGUE

It began raining softly. Renee stopped on the wooden bridge to put the top up. She picked up her cell phone, hesitated, and then threw it over the railing.

"Let's go paint. Let's go where we ain't." She rubbed Digger's head.

She parked the Mustang in a No Parking zone in front of the Wild West Wear shop. Inside, the elderly clerk was dusting the shelves. She opened her wallet, peeled off a dozen $100 bills, and handed them to the startled clerk. "I'm taking The Sidewinder. Keep the change."

"You must be in love, lady. Lucky man," the clerk said with a smile.

Renee went next door to the wine shop and came out with a bottle of Chablis and a pair of goblets, real crystal ones, not the plastic flutes. The leaves in the sycamore tress whispered 'Sedona' as she got in the Mustang and pulled out of the parking lot. She passed the Coffee Pot Dome, made a U-turn, and went back to the restaurant.

A few minutes later, she came out of the Coffee Pot, opened the car door and put the carry-out on the floor -- chipolata, strawberries, kiwi, and a three-cheese special for Digger. "Last stop," Renee said, turning onto a dirt road that led to Cathedral Rock where the ancient Indian couple sat frozen in time back to back in the pouring monsoon rain.

THE END

LEGEND OF THE BLUE OWL
By Wayne Parrish

PROLOGUE

Night came and with it a cold wind. I'itoi sat in the entrance of the cave and warmed his gnarled hands over a small bed of glowing mesquite coals. Earlier he had smoked the strong tobacco that made him listless. He watched the bright warriors and the winter moon move across the sky. All the signs and omens told him that the bad times had come again.

I'itoi held up a fiery ember and stared owlishly at the figures the cave guardians had drawn over the millennia on the smoke-blackened walls. A horny toad, beads of water pecked on its back, marked the departure of the Old People. They left after the Great River had run too low to feed their canals and the lakes had turned into salt marshes.

Pale half-men, half-animals, carrying sticks that belched fire and thunder had appeared in the south searching for yellow stones and slaves. These fearsome monster-men had put their marks over those of the Wanderers and the Old People who were there before them on the sacred boulder that stood beside the marshy lake. A spotted lizard symbolized the plague that had struck down the Wanderers. Their young had died clutching their groins, fire arrows protruded from their bellies. The carved faces expressed shock and horror.

The rock drawings told I'itoi many things: of a man struck by lightning; of a child killed by a rattlesnake; of eclipses, floods, droughts, earthquakes, and meteor showers. In the moon following the meteor shower, the Yumans had attacked and stolen the harvest. In the spring, the floods came and destroyed the fields.

Much later, the brown-robes had ventured as far north as the earth dwelling of the powerful shaman-chieftain, Morning Blue, which sat some distance from the wide bend of the river. They begged for food and the people had given them baskets of corn, pumpkins, mesquite beans and the agave fruit. The brown-robes had gone away, but they left behind a coughing sickness that killed young and old alike. Even Curing Woman's skills could not prevent the deaths.

Morning Blue blamed the disaster on HA-AK, the evil giant girl-child of his unmarried daughter, Woman-Who-Makes-Sleeping-Mats. Morning Blue told I'itoi to inscribe these tragic events so that the rocks would speak of them forever.

I'itoi prepared for the arduous work by fasting and smoking strong tobacco. He had let his heart tell his hands what to do. First he selected large rocks in the right shapes from the holy mountain on the east end of the vast valley and had them carried to his cave on the lone butte that overlooked the marshy lake.

Using a hammer and an awl made from the sacred stone that fell from the sky, he inscribed a different figure on each rock. He scraped the soft metal from the yellow cross and the other foreign objects that the brown-robes had left in the pit they had dug near I'itoi's home in the earth. He hammered the filings into the eye sockets of the blue owl that he had inscribed so carefully.

After finishing this task, I'itoi had prayed to the Earth Mother and the Sky Father for a vision, and the Earth Mother had blessed him. Once again, he would be a savior to his people. According to his vision, the people must break up into clans and scatter in the directions of the four winds. He told the people they must collect their shields, leave their houses, and each clan should separate. One to the east; another to the west; the third to the north; and I'itoi's clan to the south.

The Earth Mother told I'itoi that the clans should not return to this place, the center of everything sacred, until she sent them a sign. They must leave behind the objects that once belonged to the Old People. All the rag-dolls and kick-balls must be placed in the cave along with the glass beads and bells the brown-robes had given them.

All this I'itoi devotedly inscribed on the chosen rocks and boulders inside the cave. Only in this way will the clans be forgiven for burning HA-AK. The Earth Mother had told I'itoi that he must remain there forever and guard the rocks that speak.

The sun came up sluggishly. The first rays cast a reddish glow on the lone butte, dispersing a false gray dawn, changing into paler hues of bluish-gray. A velvety shadow at the cave entrance contrasted with the brilliant incandescent light as the sun climbed higher.

Overhead an eagle soared across the cobalt sky, creating a dark shadow that sliced across the yellow ochre earth below. A green-gold eyed lizard slithered inside, and after a brief halt, sped swiftly past I'itoi into the darkened interior and perched beside a small pool of water that had seeped down from a crevice above its head.

Outside the cave a drum began to beat. A singer's song lifted in the air:

"Hear I'itoi our prayer, purify the land, water, and air. Protect us on our journeys to the four directions. Spare us from enemies, sickness, and witches."

At the beat of the drum, the men smartly raised their shields and pounded the ground. The dancers had wood coverings on their heads, woven bands on their arms, and rabbit fur bodices and kit-foxtails on their rumps. The deer bones on their ankles jangled as they imitated the movements of the deer and other creatures. Their bare arms and breasts were painted with red ochre from the canyon walls, with black mud from shale, with white made from pale clay, with brown from the sandstone, and with yellow and violet made from cactus flowers.

I'itoi tasted the sacred pollen made from the blue corn flowers and blew a handful into the air. He tossed his prayer bundle made from owl feathers onto the fire. The blue smoke drifted upward through the spirit chimney as he began his song:

"Tcutcunoni ko'kovoli sis'vunuka-a

Apu tuvavki wunanita.

Apu tuvavki wunanita.

The Blue Owl is bright

And happy when we leave her home alone.

And happy when we leave her home alone."

The first baskets full of stones that would forever separate I'itoi from his world tumbled down and blocked the cave entrance. Morning Blue's voice rang out and echoed in the chamber: "Farewell I'itoi. You are no more, but you will be remembered… forever.

CHAPTER 1

A cloud of caliche dust floated behind the 1936 Ford pick-up, obscuring the overpass where Ocotillo Road crossed over Interstate 10. Jack Reed centered the truck on the washboard road and tried to avoid the deeper ruts. He dodged a pothole and the back axle shuddered as the rear wheels scrambled for a grip on the shale surface.

A cattle pen, with a stack of dog-eared straw bales, cow piles and human detritus bordered the left side of the track. On the right, a ragged curtain fluttered out of a paneless window of a demolished Airstream trailer. Rusted bedsprings and a rotted mattress rested under a palo verde tree. Dashing out from under a tractor tire, half buried in the sandy wash, a roadrunner outpaced the truck and veered into the brush.

The road dropped down into a gully, crossed a cow-guard and climbed straight up the face of a second ridge. A twelve-foot wide, brightly painted white gate blocked the road. The truck skidded to a halt in front of a large sign that was riddled with bullet holes:

Ocotillo Ranch
> No Trespassing
> No Hunting
> No Shooters
> No Motorcycles
> No Off-Road Vehicles

"Someone doesn't believe in signs," Jack said. He reached out the window, pulled a bar and swung the gate open. He drove through the wide gap and stopped the truck. The door creaked when he pushed it open with his shoulder. As Jack stepped out, a puff of powdery silt covered his boots. He put a foot on the bottom rail and rode the gate while it swung backwards and slammed into the support post.

"Damn," Jack said, rubbing his shinbone and focusing his eyes on the crude drawings etched on a huge half-domed boulder that sat at the base of the ridge. A pair of incised eyes stared owlishly back at him. An arrow pointed to a double spiral higher up the face of the rock. A stick-figure man, drawn by some ancient hand, had been blasted by shotgun pellets. Bullet scars also marred the other figures on the rock. "Jerks, mindless macho jerks. Hurray for the NRA!" Jack shouted. He reached into the truck, grabbed a bottle of spring water, and swallowed deeply, clearing the dust from his throat.

Jack crossed a narrow gully and climbed to the top of the ridge. The desert flattened to the south, forming a basin that lowered gradually to the well house and beyond to Mollie Gentry's dairy farm where a laborer was tossing bales of hay off the top of a massive haystack to the cattle milling below.

Beyond the dairy, white-topped cotton fields stretched for another five miles before the land turned brown and barren, marking the beginning of the Indian Reservation. The San Tans stretched in a long line eastward towards the Superstitions; all but the tips were lost in a cloud of dust and brown haze. On the other side of the freeway, an endless sea of pink tiled roofs marched westward. "The Californians are coming," Jack said. The South Mountain range ran from east to west for twenty miles, cutting off any view of Phoenix.

A dust devil swirled across the alkali sand in the lakebed where the ancient HoHoKam canals ended their journey. To the west, broken glass glazed purple by the searing desert sun glittered in the graveled shards. Two gigantic eucalyptus trees towered over the adobe ranch house, stable, tool shed, ramada, and orchard. Terraced cactus gardens surrounded the buildings, the verdant blue-green contrasting vividly with the whitewashed adobe walls and rock buildings. A bent figure of a man was raking the gravel yard.

"Old Ruiz!" Jack almost shouted. The roadrunner approached the top of the ridge, eyed Jack warily with one eye, and turned the other towards a blue-green lizard with golden eyes. "What will I tell the old man?" Jack asked the roadrunner. "This place is mine now, Ruiz. The entire 160 acres. Mine to live in, mine to sell, and mine to pay the taxes. Why did they build here? They might as well have built a ramada on the rim of Popocatepetl."

The roadrunner rushed the lizard and dashed off into the brush holding a quivering blue-green tail proudly in its mouth. The tailless lizard scrambled under a rock. "Everybody's a winner," Jack said. "God, how I hate this place!"

Paco, Ruiz's dog, part-Aussie and part-coyote, raced out of the yard barking furiously. Jack parked the truck under a rustic ramada. Aged ironwood posts supported a roof of ocotillo branches, covered with long palm fronds that offered some protection from the blistering summer sun. Sunbeams filtered through and danced across a perfectly stacked cord of wood. Jack stepped out of the truck and dropped one knee to the ground,

"Come here, boy." Paco hesitated for a moment and then rushed forward, nearly bowling him over. Jack wrapped his arms around the dog and hugged him as Paco affectionately licked his face.

Ruiz was waiting for him, his straw cowboy hat crossed over his chest. "Buenos dias, Jefe," he said solemnly, his eyes twinkling.

"Buenos dias, Ruiz," Jack replied and the two men hugged each other.

"It has been too long, Jack."

"Nearly three years this time."

"You have filled out even more," Ruiz said stepping back and sizing him up. "You are a jefe now, but there is still a little jefito in you. Only a jefito would swing on a gate. I used to tell you that often when you were a boy, but you were so like your grandfather, El Jefe. He was stubborn. He was muy hombre. Your grandmother was even more stubborn. We called you Jefito – Little Boss."

Jack laughed. "How do you know I swung on the front gate?"

"Some things never change, Jefe, but I heard the gate slam shut. Then I heard the truck. I knew you would be coming soon."

"I saw the sign at the gate when I drove in. Looks like we've had visitors."

"That is not all, Jefe. Last week someone shot some milk cows the Gentrys were drying out in the pen by the big haystack. They set fire to it and tore down a mile of fence."

"Who would do that?"

Ruiz hesitated, "Someone who wants to make life hard for you and Mollie. Making it easier for you to sell your land. Are you going to sell the ranch, Jefe?" Ruiz asked softly.

The question floated in the air. "I may have to, Ruiz. My mother left a warehouse full of antiques to my stepsister. She gave me the ranch but no cash, so I'm up to my ears in taxes and debts. I may have to sell, unless I find water, a lot of water, Ruiz. Even then I need financing to develop the ranch. You see, I've left the university, and I don't know what an oceanologist can do in the middle of the desert."

"When the time comes, you will know what to do. It is good that you are here. Someone wrecked the pump house, Jefe, and they shot up the water tank."

"The water tank? When?"

"Sunday, Jefe. Maria and I went to mass in Guadalupe. I was not here. I could not fix it. Too much damage," he said shaking his head sadly. "But I cleared out the old tank and started the pump in the orchard. There is enough water for the trees and the house if you are careful."

"Let's take a look," Jack followed Ruiz down an irrigation ditch on the backside of the citrus grove.

"Careful, Jefe, that old grandfather rattler still lives under the tool shed. Someday I'll catch him."

"You've been saying that for ten years," Jack said as he made a wide circle around the shed. "I saw him once, Ruiz. He was sunning himself on that flat rock. I went after a shotgun, but when I came back he was gone. He must have been five feet long."

"Maybe seven feet now, Jefe. I caught him one day. I grabbed him by the tail and pulled him out from under the shed. The devil turned on me and chased me all the way to the stables. Your grandfather thought that was very funny. Every year he would ask me 'Have you caught any snakes by the tail lately?' and he would laugh. It wasn't funny. I can tell you that much."

The two men entered the clearing where a large steel water tank lay on its side. The supports had been chopped through with an ax, and several large holes perforated the sides.

"Someone used a howitzer on that tank. From the size of the holes maybe a .458 Winchester or a 45-70," Jack said. Ruiz nodded.

"They smashed the batteries and poured acid on the generator. It will cost a lot to fix."

"We won't fix it, at least not soon. We'll use the back up. I can carry in bottled drinking water. I'll survive." Jack listened to the pump on the back up tank; it ran smoothly. "You've done a good job, Ruiz."

Ruiz smiled. "Gracias, Jefe."

"If we drill for water, I think we should try somewhere else."

"Where will you look, Jefe?"

"I think there might be an aquifer under the old lakebed. There should be a lot of water trapped there."

"I think you're right, Jefe. I dug the first well here behind the stable. We found water at twenty-five feet and this well was only eighty feet down. When it dried up, your mother brought in a rig. They had to go to 600 feet. I told them not to drill there, but no one listened. That is the way to go," Ruiz finished and pointed at the dry lake. "No need to pump uphill from there either."

"I'll get some hydrographic maps; maybe they can tell us where to look."

"A willow wand is better," Ruiz said, but Jack didn't reply. "I really hate to see you sell this place, Jefe. Your mother wanted you to have it someday. So did your grandmother." Ruiz made the sign of the cross. "They were good women. Sometimes a little loco." Ruiz grinned at Jack. "Your grandmother made me plant the orchard and the bushes and those eucalyptus trees. Then your mother brought this cactus. It comes from all over the world, from Africa and Baja, California, even some from Asia. 'Ruiz,' she would say, 'I'm going to have the best damn cactus garden in the world.'"

"It must have been a lot of work."

"A lot of work, Jefe. It's been the work of my whole life. But it is done, and it is the best damn cactus garden in Arizona, if not the world," he said proudly. "It will be here when both of us are gone."

"You're right, Ruiz. If I do sell the ranch, we'll save this piece. Make it into a public park. Whoever buys the ranch won't

351

miss a few acres. Tell you what, we'll call it the Vargas Cactus Gardens or Ruiz's Arboretum."

"Thank you, Jefe," Ruiz said quietly and put on his hat. Jack could see the old man was moved by his spur-of-the-moment gesture. "I will tell Maria. She will be happy to know this thing. Adios."

"Adios, Ruiz." Jack carried the groceries into the house through the back door and waited while his eyes adjusted to the darkened interior. After popping open a can of beer and swallowing deeply, he turned on the oven and opened the door. The oven coughed, and he opened a side oven door, hoping to find a plate or a pan to heat a burrito. He bent over and looked inside.

"Keerist," he yelled and jumped backwards, his can of beer sailed upward dousing the ceiling. A spotted skunk was staring directly at him and sitting in the middle of a round copper bowl surrounded by her litter of black-and-white kits. Jack kicked the door shut, but it was too late!

Jack retreated into the dining room and put the burrito on the table. He raced back into the kitchen and opened the dutch door and windows. The skunk odor quickly permeated the entire house, forcing him outside.

The evening star followed a blazing sunset as the sky turned pink, purple, blue, and then black. Jack lay in a hammock swung between the two heavy posts at the end of the front porch, taking advantage of a slight westerly breeze. It was a warm July night, too hot to sleep outside, but inside, the cool adobe still reeked of skunk. He watched Altair, followed by Vega, and then the Pleiades, as they marched across the sky.

REVIEWS for *Legend of the Blue Owl*

"Readers will find no dull moments in *Blue Owl*. Parrish's entry into the fiction field is filled with action and credible characters. More importantly, it's based on original plot ideas"

--- *Tony Hillerman*

"From the prologue where the vision of the shaman I'itoi leads him to be voluntarily sealed in a cave as the perpetual guardian of its secrets, *Blue Owl* draws the reader inexorably into the story, all the while teaching those same secrets to a society as far removed from I'itoi's as the stars...Parrish's plot, based on a Native American legend, is stretched across its framework as tightly as the skin of a tribal drum."   --- *New Times*

"Anyone with the remotest passion for the Southwest will enjoy the *Blue Owl*. In his novel, Parrish has masterfully composed a story that blends authentic desert history with engaging fiction. He weaves a tale of suspense and intrigue involving ancient storytelling combined with archeological and scientific knowledge."   ---- *The Arizona News*

"Parrish gets across his point about environmentalism without beating the reader over the head. He doesn't preach, instead he gives you something to think about. The book is lyrically written, almost musically. You will love the personable characters, get a feel for their lives and they will have a lasting affect on yours. A very good read."   --- *San Diego/La Jolla Light*

"Storytellers are the voice of the past, present, and future. Visionaries walk a long, difficult and often lonely road, but their road is the high ground. Parrish is a natural storyteller."

--- *The Columbus Dispatch*

Sons of the Tropics is also available from Morro Press

Sons of the Tropics, another novel by Wayne Parrish, is set in the 1930s in the unexplored territory of the island of New Guinea, the last unknown in a world that had almost run out of mystery. The exploration of the "Roof of the World" remained the last great challenge. During the economic decline following World War I, the Australians perceived Papua New Guinea as their Pax Africa; a place to step into the international arena. The Canberra government made a decision to pacify the region. The primary task was to civilize hostile tribes and prepare them to live and survive in the modern world. The chief instrument was the creation of a cadre of patrol officers to explore the territory, map the terrain, determine potential economic resources, and prepare the local tribes for the inevitable exploitation of the region by white men. The successful patrol officers became justifiably renowned as "Outside Men."

Patrol Officer Jack Reed is secunded to explore the unknown territory by his mentor Judge Murray. Jack is a rarity, the son of an expatriate Australian couple, reared in Port Moresby where he met the adventurers, the shopkeepers, the missionaries, the colonial officials, the village fishermen, and the nearby hillmen. In this environment, Jack develops a taste for adventure and exploration. He enjoys the companionship of people, but is wary of social institutions. Nature – the forest is his domain.

Jack is chosen over more senior officers to command the expedition to discover an inland route up the Fly River, cross the highlands, and come down the Purari River to the coast; a journey into the "Never Never," the unknown territory. When pressed to explain his choice, Judge Murray replies that Jack possesses the qualities of perseverance and restraint and that he will bring the men home. Furthermore, he won't shoot first and create another

30-year war with the natives. But most of all, it is because the constabulary men trust Jack and are loyal to him.

The second in command is P.O. Tim O'Rourke, a giant good-natured Irishman from Queensland who is well versed in bushcraft and long in patience. Sgt. Manu, a veteran of a hundred patrols, is the NCO in charge of the native constabulary. Somatu, the colorful and complex orderly, is often a thorn in everyone's side, an irrepressible mischief-maker, a morale-lifter, part-conscience, and often the glue that holds the party together.

The carriers, constabulary and supplies are assembled in Port Moresby and the expedition sets out for the Daru peninsula at the mouth of the Fly, the jumping off spot into the lush and foreboding interior. Along the way, they encounter majestic forest, the flora, the fauna, and the mystery of the enchanting river. They trade with tribes, are ambushed by headhunters, are cursed by sorcerers, and discover the Happy Valley, a paradise inhabited by peaceful warriors. Jack has a mystical encounter with the Great Mother, who guides him in the quest to discover the meaning and purpose of his life.

Patrol Officer Jack Reed and his men are marked by their heroic quest and the future courses of their lives are altered forever. Each man, in his own way, becomes a true son of the tropics.